Connected

Aralot's Keepers Book Two

Amanda Heit

Copyright © 2020 by Amanda Heit

Storyline was based off the original book "Keeper Part Two and Three."

Heit, Amanda.

Connected / by Amanda Heit.

1st edition.

Paperback   978-1-949858-12-9

eBook   978-1-949858-13-6

Printed in the United States of America

October 2020

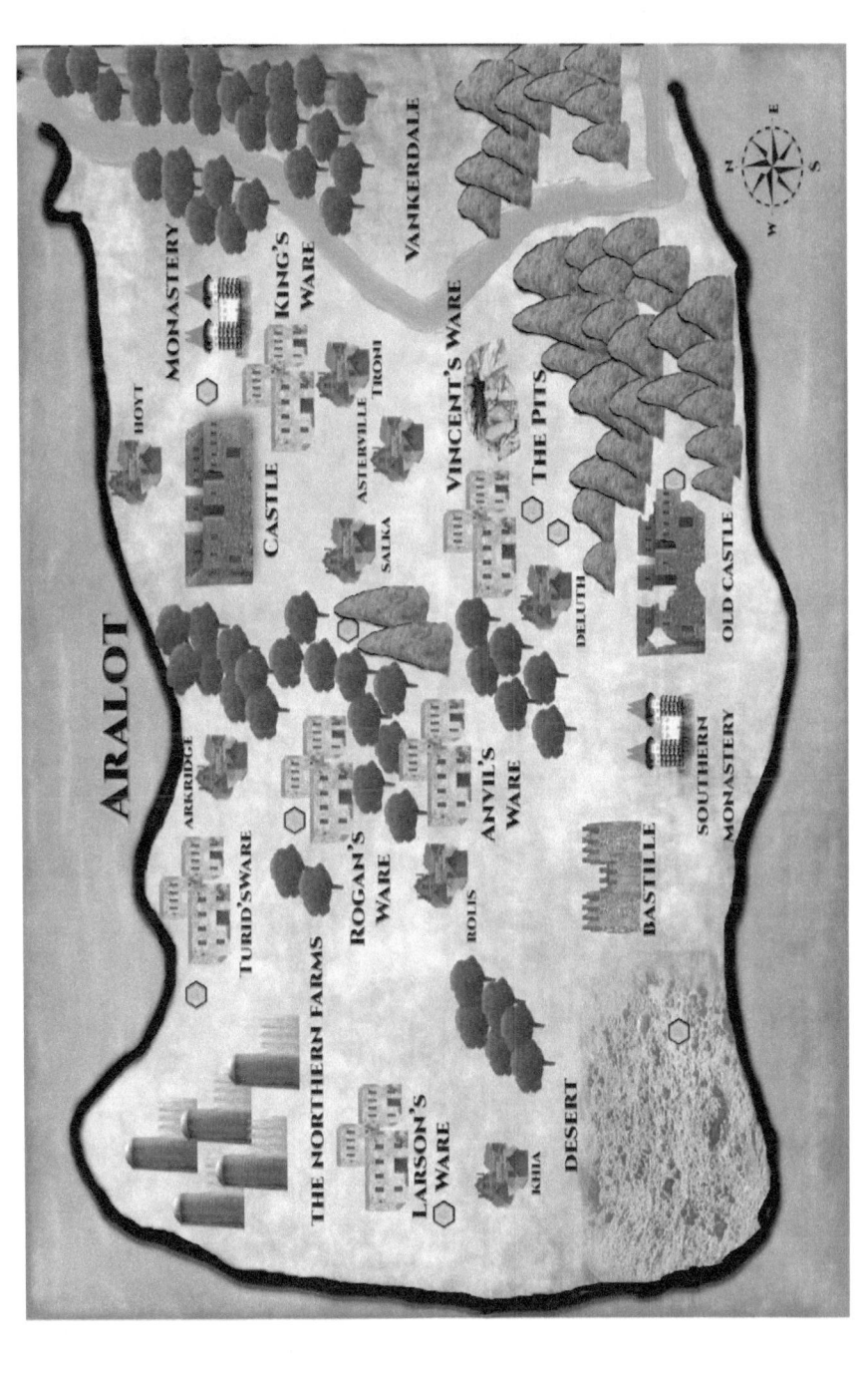

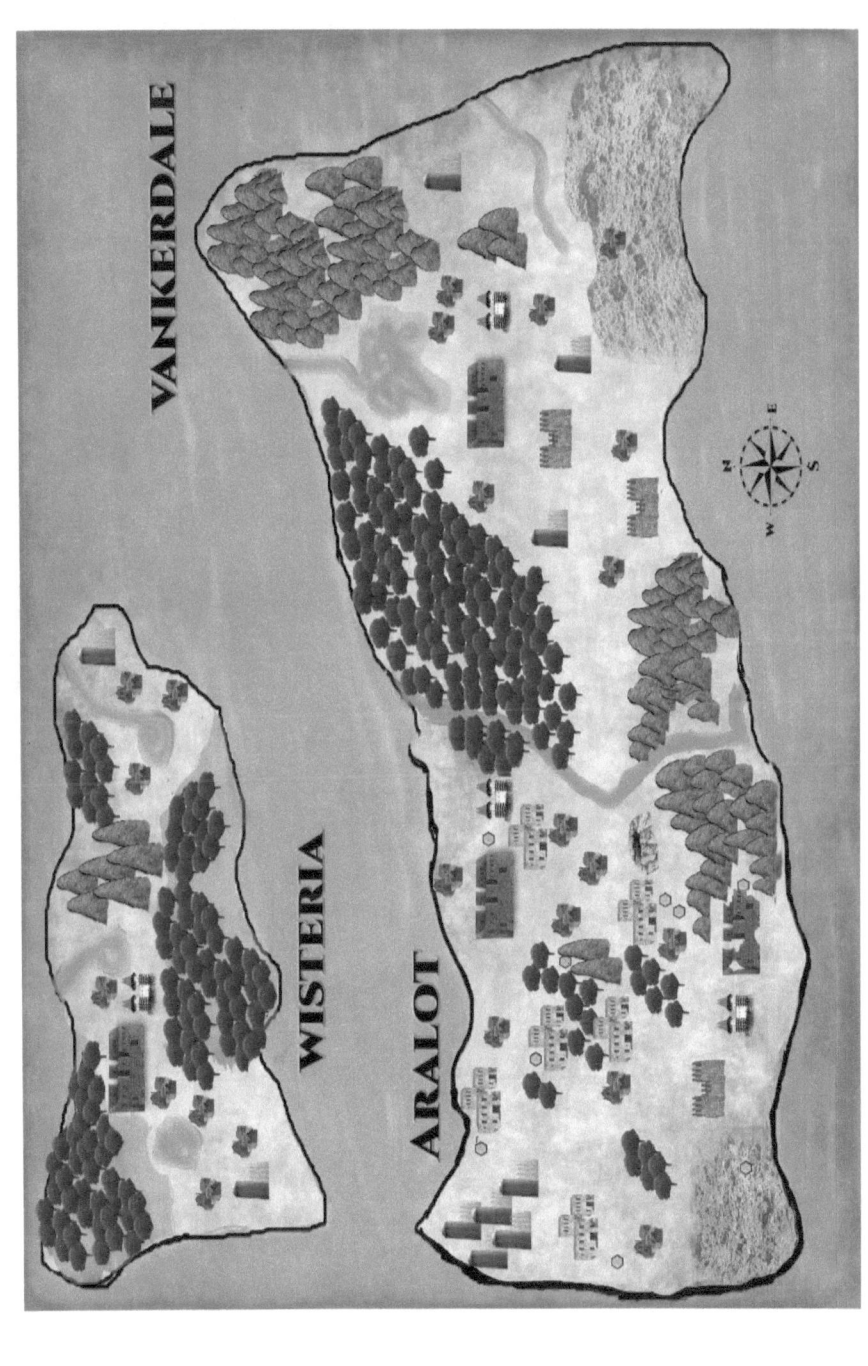

Chapters

Birthday

Kayla

Kayla kicked off her shoes really hard. They went sliding across the room, knocking over her mother's newest music composition that had been on a stand. The stand toppled over with a bang that echoed the slam of the front door. Just great. Now Kayla had created yet *another* disaster to her day. If only she never had a birthday, half of her problems would have fallen to some other day. She was all about splitting up the pain.

Kayla rubbed the side of her face. Her dragon, the blue-gray Valiant, had told her that she no longer showed the fingerprints from the slap. She could still feel it. Even worse, the slap could have been avoided if she had been able to sort through her own nightmares last night. She hadn't gotten over the feeling that they could be real, especially since she had woken up to find that she had mysteriously drawn way too many pictures of Sparkle looking adorable.

Those she had tossed in the fireplace as fast as she could, watching them burn with satisfaction as she destroyed the evidence that she couldn't stop sleepwalking. Or was sleep drawing the correct term? Anyway, she was usually good at picking out what her dreams were trying to tell her, but last night's dream had not been one of her normal nightmares. She had learned that the hard way when she got that slap. She had watched Ritz die, and there was no way he was dead because he had slapped her when she finally saw him.

"Mind over the body, Kayla," Ritz's voice had spoken to her in her dream. He was an ageless man with blond hair and stunning blue eyes. Devious eyes. Harsh, unyielding, traitorous eyes. The man led a group of rebels known as the Colts, and he was known to be brutal, but he'd never extended that same harsh backhand to her before. She wasn't a Colt! He had reminded her of that very well.

In the dream, she had been crumbled to the ground inside Uncle Anvil's dragon training ware. It was one of her favorite places to be, not because of the dragons, but because of Uncle Anvil. He was her uncle by association rather than blood, but he was also one of her best friends. She told him practically everything. He was going to hear all about how bad her date had just gone, but even he never got the details of how her dreams made her sweat.

Currently, Ritz was her accomplice bravely facing his enemies since riders and Colts never got along well. He was trying to coach her through this plague that her body had since she had a broken dragon bond and looking at any other dragon apart from Valiant made her physically overcome with sadness so deep it brought her to her knees.

Valiant refused to fix their broken bond due to some promise he had made, so her condition remained. It would have been nice if they had never been broken, but King Peyton of Vankerdale had forced Valiant to bond her as a baby and then stolen Valiant away. Kayla had just gotten her dragon back, having never known that he even existed until a few days ago. King Peyton had planned on using Valiant to trap Kayla so he could then use her to capture Aralot's magical ice dragons. It was complicated and hadn't worked.

Valiant had been set free by his friend Tyler Valeron, who worked in the Vankerdale castle for Prince Evan. In any event, Ritz had died in her dream. The demon ultra-dragon king with his hardened black scales and fire so hot it was almost blue, swooped into the ware and chomped him. The dragon destroyed buildings and crops and everything he fancied. Kayla called him Reaper. Other people called him Demon and a lot of other nasty things. The dragon had been bred by her grandfather Herb's dragons after the man had died. Reaper scared her.

Kayla had screamed so loud that she woke herself up and brought her parents into her bedroom. She normally saw nightmares about past events in her parents or long-dead relatives lives. She had to admit that she had never dreamed of Ritz before, and most people stayed clear of him and his devilish ways, but Kayla had a particular fondness for the man, so to see him die had her scared.

That was how her bad day had started. It kept going south after that. Happy birthday indeed.

Kayla had done nothing but fret over Ritz being dead all day until she saw him. She had been sick with worry. She needed him! He was going to help her figure out what to do about Vankerdale always trying to start wars with Aralot. He was going to help her find a way to earn her parent's love instead of feeling like they used her as a political pawn against King Klavian, his wife Aria, and his son Tristan. Ritz was going to teach her how to withstand the pressure of her own mind, distancing herself from her emotions. He was the best master of his Colt practices after all. He could fool anyone to think anything. He could help her fool herself to overcome her limitations. He couldn't die!

So when Kayla had seen spotted him on her date, she had run at him and found her mouth talking away the fears she had been holding all day.

"You have to help me escape my own head!" Kayla had shouted.

"I don't owe you anything, Kayla. You are not a Colt."

And she never would be one, because her mother refused to let Kayla take the Colt tests that would earn her a wild stallion tattoo. The tests were often brutal and extremely hard.

"It doesn't matter. You're supposed to help me! You're the only one that cares—"

Kayla's whine had been cut off with a sharp slap across her face. Her date for the evening hadn't done anything to help. Raised as a Colt himself, Tristan had simply stood there refusing to engage with his leader.

"Don't you ever say that lie around me again. This feeling of not being loved is designed to push you out into the world in search of something that could love you, but let me tell you something. You are not to go searching. You have all the love you already need. You just need to open your eyes and see it. Stop hiding. You can change your fate. If you don't, you're going to lose it. Anything from Vankerdale? It still has something you need."

Kayla had to take a step back and think about that for a moment. She already had Valiant out of Vankerdale, but Ritz knew that Conner was there with a broken bonded dragon. He shouldn't know that Conner was a keeper, but he had expressed interest in getting Conner out of there before. Kayla had assumed that Ritz was talking about him now instead of her. And since she was on that date thing, she had walked off on Ritz without answering him.

"How was it?"

Tia Brixton asked, surveying the damage of the music sheets spread across the floor and the shoes that had caused the pages to get jumbled. Kayla's mother was standing beside her brown-haired husband Jack, who wore his leather dragon-riding pants and a plain white shirt.

His starburst brown eyes ignored the thrown shoes to stare at his daughter. Tia's blue eyes flicked away from the pages. She smoothed over her blond bun and tried out a sympathetic smile.

Kayla's parents were not asking Kayla about her nightmares. They wanted to know how her date with Prince Tristan had gone. He was called the prince, but he wasn't really the prince. His father was the steward of the kingdom of Aralot, and the steward handled the affairs like he was the king so he was called King Klavian. Kayla was called the princess. Both of their fathers had been crowned with the same fake crown since Aralot's real crown was cursed. Kayla's father was considered the real king, only he went by his first name of Jack.

Anyway, it wasn't until a few days ago that Kayla had learned she was the princess because she had been cursed previously to never hear of it before. Now to make their parents happy with the friendly feud they had between them and the Clusters, she was to date Prince Tristan. Yuck.

"The date was horrible," Kayla answered.

Both her parents stood there waiting for more. They had sent her out with high hopes. She had left in a bad mood and come back in a worse one. Tristan had been prying at her the whole time.

"Whether you have fun is up to your own attitude, but please don't ruin this whole thing for me. I didn't want to come either. You're the last person I would ever want to date, Kayla, so try to not say anything to ruin my dinner."

If that wasn't charming his "nice dress," comment had nearly made her smack him. He was the last person in the universe that she wanted to dress up for, but she had put a dress on and stepped out the castle door not looking forward to her current reality.

They had run into Ritz before dinner, and the leader of the Colts had slapped her! Slapped! He had never hit her before in his life. Usually Kayla found Ritz to be pleasant to talk with because he was cursed too. He had been alive for a really long time. At least since before her father was born, and he was really smart. The last time Kayla had seen Ritz, he had mentioned her nightmares, making Kayla think that he might know the solution to ending them. It was because of that that she had rambled away to him when she saw him and he'd hit her!

"You keep coming back to that," her dragon, Valiant, sighed into her thoughts. "No one can trust Ritz. Everyone says so."

But she wanted to trust him. Grr! She wanted his help. The only excuse for his behavior she came up with was that he was trying to keep up his vile image in front of Tristan. She had no idea how Ritz acted when around Tristan, but he was usually hard on the renegades he trained. They were the group that took down evil kings. The last evil king had been taken by her father, King Jack, and he had been a Colt at the time. Jack was still a Colt even though he was now also the first Colt that turned into a dragon rider, and became the king, so that he could marry the beautiful Tia Felding. Yeah. He had everything. All Kayla had was a headache. She still had to suffer through three more dates with Tristan.

"You won't give us any other hint of what you did?" Tia asked.

"Why pester her? You'll get it all out of Anvil later," Jack said rolling his eyes.

"Jack!" Tia cried, spinning to face him to prove that she wasn't secretly in love with Anvil while he was still in love with her even after he had married Annaliese and had a few kids.

"What? You will. Kayla will tell Anvil who will tell you. You'll tell your dragon, Sparkle, who will tell my dragon, Pyro. Pyro will tell me, and we will all know how lousy a date it was in the end. I think Kayla wants to be alone to mope for a few minutes."

"We are her parents. She should tell us personally," Tia explained.

"Why? We're the ones responsible for her going on the bad date."

"I simply want to know."

"She didn't spy on you," Jack told Kayla as Kayla pulled her hair down and flicked the hair tie across the room next. Kayla hardly ever got a moment's peace because her keeper mother used her horde of connected wild dragons to follow Kayla wherever she went. Kayla had been spied on her entire life. It was nice to know that her mother had given her a bit of privacy, even if it had come at a bad time.

"When are you going to see Anvil?" Tia asked as Kayla silently made her way toward her parents. They were blocking the stairs and therefore her room.

"Right after I change?" Kayla asked.

"Sounds good to me," Tia answered.

Kayla shook her head at her mother and pushed between her parents, taking the stairs three at a time. She slammed her bedroom door too. In all honesty, dinner had not been that bad. In the minds of King Klavian, the steward, and his wife Queen Aria, the date would be called a success. Kayla had eaten stuffed cheesy chicken with roasted vegetables in the fanciest restaurant inside of the castle town, known as Troni. Candles hung from the ceiling like twinkling stars. The padded red velvet seats had been most comfortable. But then there was the white table cloth that soaked up stains every time she tried harder to be careful. Tristan didn't need to say anything to let her know that he found her disgraceful.

It wasn't her fault! She had no idea that she was a princess until now! She'd not trained in curtsies and eating habits. Her parents were dragon riders. They taught her how to survive in the middle of the woods with nothing. Her father was the kingdom's spellcaster. He taught her how to defend herself against magical threats. Nowhere did her homework say what to do when on a date with a prince.

She had used the wrong fork, spread too much butter, wiggled too much, breathed too loud, and put her napkin in the wrong spot several times. She had probably sat wrong, crossed her legs wrong, and looked completely uncivilized in that fancy room. Her conversations were all forced. They talked about the food and the weather. Please.

"I know you probably don't want to hear this, but Tristan dates riders too. He can't be judging you as hard as you are judging yourself."

Kayla let out a loud sigh and looked at herself in the mirror. She had put on a deep purple dress that matched her skin tone and her red-brown hair. Her blue eyes may have sparkled if she wasn't so tired. She had put her hair half up instead of in a ponytail that she usually kept tucked away beneath her favorite gray sweater that she wore everywhere. She had made an effort to look nice. She had also done a great job looking foolish.

Kayla pulled off the dress and tossed it under the bed. Then she put on her pants and shirt, letting out another sigh when her feet slipped into her boots. This was much better. So much more her. As her finishing touch, she pulled on the gray sweater and gave herself the riding hand signal for "looking good."

"See ya!" Kayla called to her parents as she ran for the door.

They were still talking about her and not hiding the conversation. It hit her ears as she tried to escape.

"I don't see why she hasn't rebonded Valiant yet," Jack told his wife.

"It's all my fault. I injured our baby, Jack. I hurt her and she'll never recover. It's all my fault."

Kayla couldn't open the door fast enough.

"Our daughter is very resilient," Jack assured.

"You call turning into a pincushion around dragon's resilient?" Tia asked.

Nice. She could feel the love in this room very well. This concerned parent thing was working out great. Kayla wasn't privy to all the details of Valiant's promise he had to keep before bonding her again, but he had been defending her her entire life so she had to trust him on this. Crying wasn't the worst that could happen to her. She had to cry.

On that note, she scrambled up Valiant's back and they raced to the magical portal that would take her to Anvil's Ware. Going through portals for most people turned them so sick that they felt like dying. Kayla had never experienced that sensation that she could recall, because she had gotten the antidote rather early in the form of ice dragon venom. Ice dragons were the ones that made and destroyed portals.

Well, the magical ice dragons could make portals. Sparkle wasn't born with magic for a number of reasons. Her mother, Misty, had been too young to have a baby when she had her. Sparkle was also said to have been cursed by Herb Felding too. She could put out ice and venom and bond multiple people, but Sparkle couldn't create magic or portals. The one dragon that could control such things was called Mr. Grumpy. His real name was Bantin.

Kayla had heard the news about him getting old and seen the unstated fear from her father that Aralot would run out of magic soon without Bantin providing it. If their magic vanished, Vankerdale was going to attack. Magic was the only thing keeping Vankerdale on the other side of the river, but Vankerdale had a magic eating dragon too, known as SilverWings, who was King Peyton's spellbinding dragon. Pyro was concerned that SilverWings was sucking up the magic at the border to destroy the spell keeping them out.

Kayla and Valiant passed through the portal as if they had done this a hundred times together. It was really only their third time through a portal like this, and they had never gone to Anvil's Ware together. Each portal was a large stone slab activated by a hexagonal brick in the left corner. Portals glowed purple and blue and dragons loved them. When taking the portal to Anvil's Ware, scouts would converge around the exiting person, blocking off the entrance to the ware if they didn't know the visitor. Kayla had only ever gone through here on foot before. The guards never bothered her, but today they shrieked about Valiant until they spotted her on his back. Then they shrieked at her to explain herself.

"I'm going to see Anvil. He's already met Valiant. I promise."

Kayla kept her eyes on the shape of Valiant's neck scales so she wouldn't see the other dragons surrounding her. She heard them with her ears—the things that she relied on for everything since her eyes made her paralyzed. The closer they got to the ware, the louder the cries became as more riders and dragons sprang up from the field to block the spellbinding dragon. Kayla held them back with hand signals while she closed her eyes. She counted Valiant's landing gait and stride so that she wouldn't hit her face into him when they landed. She gave him the briefest hug to wish him luck with all the curious dragons and took off running to find Anvil.

Her mother must have informed her keeper connected dragons that Kayla was coming, because Kayla heard her mother's dragons fend off the curious crowd around Valiant. A few of them hooted to Kayla that Anvil was in his office. She ran there as fast as she could to avoid running into any pictures. Pictures were her unexplainable curse. Not only did she draw them in her sleep, but there was one guy at Anvil's Ware that drew her all the time. Kayla used to draw for fun until she started scaring herself. Now she avoided the topic of pictures and all the ones drawn for her. It was weird that there wasn't a single image posted anywhere today. Not even a non-descript "Happy Birthday" sign like the last five years in a row.

"No pictures today?" Kayla asked as she burst into the ware leader's office without knocking. Anvil was standing, reviewing a chart on the wall that featured rider names who were ready to take a vacation. Since he was up, Kayla slumped into his chair at his desk and got herself comfortable. This room felt like a second home to her. She could imagine the filing cabinets, the bookshelves, the pictures, the charts, and the desk at any time of the day.

Most of the time she would be excited to skip pictures made for her, but today the sign would have been pleasant. Given the day she had already had with nightmares in the morning, standing around for a birthday lunch in the castle with boring adults, and destroying a table cloth in front of Tristan, she expected Caleb Andrade to have drawn a ton of pictures of her face and posted them on the walls, trying to get her attention on her birthday. It usually irritated her.

"Caleb is busy with an assignment," Anvil answered, watching her reaction closely.

She gave him a shrug to not show how disappointed she actually felt. The one day she would have talked to him was the one day he wasn't around. Kayla had kept one of his last pictures, and she found herself pulling it out occasionally to read the words that were there asking her to be Caleb's friend. He had been trying to be her friend since she was a baby. Despite her ignoring him, he hadn't given up on her yet. She wasn't giving up on him even if he did get himself into trouble by punching

Pg. 11

everyone that made fun of her. Her sixteenth birthday was still devoid of anything cheerful.

"On that note of developing new friendships, Midnight is going to take a nap. I think I'll join him," Valiant told her.

Midnight was her Uncle Clark's night dragon. He had completed his ware training, so he should be waking up now that it was late, not going to sleep. For him to be tired must mean that he had spent the day training on some fancy formation with his day dragon group. How was Valiant making a new friend if both the dragons were sleeping?

"You only sleep next to dragons you trust. That's how," Valiant replied.

It was remarkable how fast Valiant trusted all of her mother's keeper dragons. He had been quick to talk with Pyro, and now he was fast friends with Midnight. Valiant had told her once that since Kayla had thought of these dragons her whole life, they felt like siblings to him. Still though, they were adopting him back rather fast.

"What do we know about spellbinding dragons?" Kayla asked Anvil.

Now when her mother came poking around to ask Anvil what she had talked to him about, he wouldn't tell anyone how the date had gone because he wouldn't know. If Tia wanted more information, she was going to have to ask Klavian and Aria, who would get the information from Tristan. Maybe Tristan would leave out the part with Ritz.

Valiant sure spent a lot of time being lazy and curling up into a rock during the day. If he kept that up, she was going to start thinking that he was more of a night dragon than anything. Day dragons didn't want to sleep this early in the day even if it was to make new friends.

"Are they night dragons or is Valiant just lazy?"

"Blue dragons do tend to be night creatures unless they are water dragons. I'm not sure about the spellbinding ones. Your mother was trying to find information about it and couldn't. King Klavian can't either. They think the answer to spellbinding nature will be found in Wisteria, but it will be very hard to get any answers from them."

Wisteria was the island kingdom to the north. Kayla had never been there, and similar to Vankerdale, hadn't really studied the geography. She asked Anvil for maps of the two other places now that it looked like she was supposed to know these things. Knowing the landscape of Vankerdale when she was running away from Prince Evan, who had kidnapped her, would have been most helpful. She had no idea if she would ever end up in Wisteria, but it was best to be prepared. They were on a tricky balance beam with those guys. Wisteria was still upset that Kayla's great-grandfather Gladius had cursed the ocean so that trade was impossible. Trade had been opened up again, but the inhabitants refused to let Aralot sailors get off their ships to rest in port.

Kayla skimmed over Vankerdale's map first. The river that separated their two kingdoms was very familiar. It was said to have grown larger when her father freed Aralot's crown from the trapped spellcaster that had it. When Kayla first heard that story, she had assumed that her father had given the item to King Klavian to be made the king, because her father worked directly for him. Now she was thinking that her parents had phrased the story very carefully, trying to hint at her that they were the king and queen without being able to tell her due to her previous curse.

"Those curses were back on you again this morning," Valiant told her, even though he was supposed to be asleep. *"I sucked them off you yet again, so I think this will become a daily thing until you can find out how to end those."*

Not being able to hear anything relating to the crown and ruling of the kingdom was one of her worst curses. Before meeting Valiant, if anyone mentioned anything about it all, sound would buzz out in her ears. Her eyes would blur if she tried to read it on a paper or read the sentence from someone's moving mouth.

Since she hadn't known what she was missing out on before, she had not been able to guess who might be cursing her. She had blamed her parents, but it wasn't them. Now that she understood the nature of the attack, she was fairly certain that her problem had come from Prince Tristan. It wasn't his parents not wanting her to take the place of princess. It was the son who didn't want to date her, and didn't want her in the way of his life.

"I think Tristan has it out for me," Kayla sighed. She wasn't going to bring up Tristan, but now that she had, she hoped Anvil wouldn't pry into details of the date. She was going to keep it vague. Kayla set aside the map of Vankerdale to study Wisteria next. It was larger than she remembered and had a lot of forests. If she remembered correctly, the forests were so dense it was rather tropical and warm over there.

"I think the two of you are holding onto childish grudges and need to set those aside," Anvil replied. "From the way you talked the last time I saw you, your bickering and snide comments over your parents won't help make the future easier."

Yeah, Kayla remembered exactly what Tristan had said to her last. Her remarks to him were pretty good. She grinned thinking about it; although, now that she was on the topic, she had insulted him first because he had asked her to keep the date really short, and she had told him that if he tried to get out of it his mom would get on his case. Tristan had told her that she had to wear a dress or her mother would get upset with *her*. Maybe they could have started out better if they hadn't thrown shade over their moms.

"Eh. It's a general dislike on both our parts. He's eight years older than me, Anvil!"

"You're basing your reaction only off his age?"

"He's never liked me," Kayla told him. Anvil should be aware of that. She'd complained about Tristan to him plenty of times in the past.

"You have the power to change that relationship, Kayla. Your father used to hate me. Now we're friends on most days. Tristan is a powerful person in a powerful position and you're giving him fuel to hurt you. Don't add to his fire. I'm still furious about the last thing he's done."

"What did he do?" Kayla asked, looking away from the map to Anvil. She hadn't heard about Tristan doing anything, but Anvil sounded upset, and seeing his face full of hurt made her get the chills.

"When I was at the castle with your mom and Aunt Rosa after you'd been kidnapped by your dragon into Vankerdale, Tristan came here. He searched every inch of the ware and stole an ancient artifact that had once belonged to the ware leader Vladimir. A day later, he was arrested at Vincent's Ware for digging up Vladimir's grave. He was searched and nothing was found on him that was suspicious, but we all think he's taken what he set out to find. It was a coin of some sort with a bear print on it. Octavian was the only one to see it, and he didn't really know what it did, but Tristan sure knows. Then as if stealing wasn't enough, he got his father to sign a document stating that my ware is too large. I can't breed any new dragons next year or accept any new riders until his ban is lifted."

"What?!" Kayla jumped to her feet, horror-struck. Anvil had to be able to accept riders. Niles, Rogan's and the Desert Ware fed into his. If he couldn't take any graduated riders everyone would have to go to Vincent's Ware because the King's Ware was hard to get into and Turid's

Ware only accepted married riders.

Anvil nodded. "I think it's because of what Vermelo did. He was asking Rosa and Clark to take over the throne, because your father isn't noble by blood and that messes up some magical rule or whatever. Clark was born a noble."

"I didn't hear about this," Kayla remarked.

She knew her Uncle Clark was a Cluster, but no one had told her that Vermelo asked him to be the king. What would her father do if Clark said yes? For that matter she liked Vermelo! He was the Captain of the Guard and had always been nice to her. Why was it that everyone she liked was punching her in the face?

"Well," Anvil shrugged, "your parents are used to not telling you anything about the castle because you couldn't hear it before. In any case, right now is a very bad time to get on Tristan's bad side. He's trying to cut off Clark and Rosa by sizing down our numbers. I could handle it fine if it wasn't for the fact that I can't accept you as a rider. You've finally got a dragon. I've been waiting so long… I can't think about it without wanting to hit something. Maybe I'll turn into Jack. Go throw some knives."

Oh boy. Her birthday really was the worst. She should have stayed fifteen forever. Kayla had never questioned once what ware she would train Valiant at because she already spent so much time here. Now she had to leave Anvil, lose her best friend, to spend five years or more training a dragon around people who wouldn't understand her. Tristan had stolen away her future! He'd taken the one part of becoming a dragon rider that she didn't mind and strangled it to death on the signature of King Klavian.

"Can my dad revoke that?" Kayla asked.

Anvil sadly shook his head. "Klavian got all his councilors to sign the document. If your father went against this, he'd have to kick Klavian right out of the castle, and he won't because Klavian holds Aralot together with all those papers he goes over in a day. It would be a battle for the throne again. We have way too many of those going on right now."

Her dad versus Klavian. Rosa and Clark against her parents and Klavian. Tristan against everyone. Yup. That sounded like a bowl of tangled noodles. Where did she fit into that? Was she a knot at the end, or squished into the middle? Once again, she was the person taking the blows due to her parent's political lifestyle. Her mother was still refusing a war with Vankerdale too, even though King Peyton had kidnapped her. Kayla had to rescue herself because her mother didn't want to send dragons which would have broken their bonds.

"I'm going to bed," Kayla declared.

She was with Valiant on this. An early bedtime sounded fabulous. Maybe the nightmares would stay away. Plus, she wasn't going to be allowed to sleep in Anvil's Ware ever again. She had half of her stuff here inside a bunkroom for all the times she stayed late and slept over. She pulled her hood up over her head trying to block the unpleasant news from reaching her eyes before she could start crying over losing Anvil.

"Hey," Anvil gave her a hug. "For wherever you end up. Happy birthday. I love you, Kayla. If you don't write to me, I'm going to cry."

She was already crying. She brushed away a few tears and took the package that Anvil held out to her. She could tell what it was just by the size of the box, but she opened it to be sure. Prongs. They were a dragon rider's most trusted tool and these ones had engraved handles with her name on them. Each one was a metal fork with three fishhook tips. They helped riders snag dragon scales so they wouldn't fall off.

Kayla closed up the box, gave Anvil one last hug, and ran for her bunkroom. She ignored the dragons overhead still asking her about Valiant.

The first thing she did was open her trunk to decide what to take away from here. The act brought out even more tears. Her items were moved around in the box. It looked like her trunk had been subject to the last surprise room check. At least she hadn't lost anything, not even the half-eaten chocolate bar that she finished devouring. She hadn't the heart to remove anything else, so she jumped on the top bunk that was hers glad that the other seven girls in this room had not come to bed yet. She'd sort out her things in the morning.

What was she supposed to do about everything else?? Her entire life had just morphed away from her. She couldn't live at home because she had a dragon to train. She couldn't train at Anvil's Ware. Her available options for starting out were Niles Ware in the west or Rogan's Ware in the center. She refused to even contemplate the Desert Ware where Tristan might show up all the time. Her mother had trained at Rogan's Ware and so had her father, so that would be the next most logical place to go. Rogan would accept her without a hitch.

However, Kayla knew that Rogan was one to keep his riders from hearing castle gossip so they could focus on training and not be distracted. He censored the news quite a bit over there. If Kayla went there, she wouldn't hear what other things Tristan was doing against her family. She had to be where she could keep an eye on him, but not end up directly in his clutches, which gave her only one option. The King's Ware. Only riders who were at a level five and above could transfer to that ware. Tristan had been a level two when he was accepted though, because he lived in the castle right beside it. Maybe she could get in along the same lines. It was going to be hard, and she'd have to accept that she was going to be the worst rider in any class she joined.

"What do you think, Valiant?" Kayla asked him.

"I think it's time for bed," Valiant answered. *"But I will go anywhere you pick as long as I'm with you."*

King's Ware it was. She had to give it a try, because her life wasn't her own anymore. It belonged to the kingdom of Aralot, and she had no idea what the kingdom wanted from her.

Transferred

Caleb

It was a shame. He had been kicked out of Anvil's ware for being nice and asking a lonely girl to be his friend. No one else got transferred away because they were trying to be friendly. In his case, the word "friend" hadn't made it onto his rider report. It was the word "fight" that got on there. He was outcasted from his family and friends for getting into fights over one person in particular. It wasn't his fault that no one else could see Kayla Brixton in the same way he could. That was what he had tried to explain to the ware leader Charles when he had arrived at the King's Ware with his transfer notice in his hand, and his heart breaking.

It was going to be so much harder to see Kayla now. Not impossible mind, but much harder. She was allowed to go everywhere, and she did. She took portals and skipped from one location to the next. She could touch down in every part of the kingdom in a single day, and since Anvil's family lived up near the castle, Kayla was often this direction visiting with his kids. Caleb wasn't privy to the exact location of the house Kayla visited, so it was going to take ages before he ever spotted Kayla in the town. He hoped that his brown dragon, Warner, would keep his eyes open in that direction so they at least had a chance to spot Kayla for a brief ten seconds.

"I'll keep my eyes open and ask around," Warner had promised on

the long flight over.

Caleb felt lost. He had left behind the only home he had ever known to come here. He had accepted the assignment only because there was nothing left he could use to get out of it. Being transferred had been threatened on him multiple times. Breaking Aiden's nose had broken Anvil's goodwill toward him, even if it was Caleb helping Aiden reach the doctor after he was done fighting him.

It didn't matter. The crime spoke for itself. Anvil had transferred him that same day as if he'd been waiting for an excuse to give Caleb the news of his current banishment. Maybe it would have happened regardless. Caleb had thought himself safe after the incident until Anvil pulled him into his office and told him that he'd been working behind the scenes to find a place Caleb would be better suited for. Caleb didn't feel better suited. Even worse, Caleb wasn't repentant. He would break that nose over again after what Aiden had said.

"She's never going to look at you and your ugly face! You're wasting paper on all this drivel of childish fantasies. Grow up!"

It was everyone else that needed to grow up. They wasted time casting hate at a girl that ignored it all, just like her mother, Queen Tia, had ignored the harsh comments when she was young. Caleb saw no point in continuing the cycle of rider mistrust when clearly Tia and Jack and Rosa had solved the problem to keeper poison long ago. No one was going to be poisoned into insanity to attack the very dragons they loved.

"You've got to move on, dude. The Brixton's want nothing to do with you."

Aiden! Could he amend that? Kayla had never shown any interest in him, but her parents had talked to him plenty of times. All the riders in Tia's keeper bond had words to give him over the years. Most of the time it was them telling him to leave Kayla alone, but she was always alone, and Caleb couldn't stand to see her shrinking away, not only from dragon love but human care as well. It was hard for her to know who she could trust with all her relatives being nefarious evildoers on her mother's side and renegade Colts on her father's side. Caleb was going to let her know that he was there for her no matter how long it took for her to realize the same thing.

"It's people like you that drive the Brixton's into hiding. Jack's probably gone because he got tired of your pictures getting all over the place like the disease they are," Aiden had said.

That comment was really uncalled for. Caleb had almost punched Aiden in the gut right then. King Jack had been missing for months, not because of anything that Caleb did. He was trapped inside of Vankerdale, a victim of his wife's spells when he crossed the border, and Jack had lost his bond to his dragon. Jack couldn't think to the animal to help him escape, and he had to rely on Kayla's kidnapping and subsequent escape to help him get back into his own kingdom.

"You're the reason Kayla hides from us all. If you stopped, she might take that hood down. You turn her into a wraith—"

That was the last thing that Aiden had said before Caleb had broken his nose. They could say anything they wanted to about him, but no one was going to call Kayla a wraith. She wasn't a demon of darkness. She was a ray of light, concealed behind hoods because the rest of the world wasn't ready for her sunshine yet.

She didn't dwindle the life from others or even wish them ill. In fact, Caleb had caught her helping the very people that talked bad about her. She worked discreetly, sending them help in the form of others, returning lost homework, replacing broken belt buckles, and sharpening tools when she thought no one was watching. She would shovel dragon dung without feeling like it was a punishment. She would patch mortar in the stone buildings without being asked. She was not a wraith, and Caleb would never ever destroy her.

Oh, what was he doing here? He was so lost! Anvil's Ware he could understand. It had four sections divided by the lines of the compass with the mess hall and ware leader office in the middle. The King's Ware didn't have the same thing. Caleb had felt like an idiot for asking where he could find Charles, the ware leader, so he could deliver his transfer notice. He still felt like an idiot because Charles had taken the notice and dismissed him as if Caleb could figure everything out on his own. He wasn't incapable, but he had come here to be a section leader to people who knew more about the ware than he did. It was going to be hard to lead people that he didn't know.

He'd better get started on learning who everyone was, especially that guy who was currently staring at him. This rider was seasoned with metal victory pins glistening on the cuffs of his rider uniform. He had a section of dyed hair in the color of blue that made him look like the craziest rebel Caleb had ever seen. Every rider at Charles Ware was required to have passed level five training before they moved here. The one exception to that had been Prince Tristan who got special privileges because of his father. Everyone else worked really really hard to reach this place. Caleb wished that his work hadn't brought him here, but he knew he had to make the best of it or he'd make himself miserable instead.

"What section are you in?" Caleb asked the rebel rider with a warm smile to start things off right.

"Yours," was the retort, and it wasn't a happy one at that. It looked like Charles had told everyone to expect a new section leader hailing from Anvil's Ware, because Caleb surely hadn't said anything.

"Perhaps you'd care to enlighten me on how this position opened," Caleb asked.

Pg. 24

He still had no idea how Anvil had gotten him here. Anvil said it was better for him, that people in the King's Ware were not as strict with fistfights, and that his temper would be better over here. Caleb didn't get into fights unless it was over Kayla; at least not fights where he really wanted to hurt anybody. It was possible that Caleb was taking this position from the man in front of him, and the news of his displacement had created an automatic resentment that Caleb would never take away.

"Stanford overdosed on his medication because he'd forgotten that he had already taken it. Then he died."

Well, this was sounding like Caleb wouldn't have to worry about resentment of job-stealing. He still had to worry about the people not wanting him in charge when he was an outsider to their ways.

"That's a shame about Stanford. I'm sorry. I'm sure he was a great section leader."

"I hated him. I'm going to hate you too."

Lovely. His first interaction was already looking like a fight. Might as well escalate it into one so he could get it over with.

"Cool. Come hate me a little bit closer. Your attitude is condescending and your hair is rebellious. Are your muscles just as weak?"

"How dare you?!" the rider screamed.

Caleb waved him forward again. "Come on. Let's get this going so I can move on. Come at me. I haven't all day to take your hate so you'd better bring it forward right now."

And so it came. The man came charging in at him with frustration all over his face. Caleb was well aware that other riders had stopped to watch him, curious to see how everything would play out. Caleb was still in his light tan leather from Anvil's Ware, making him stand apart from the red-dressed men around him. He would need to change his uniform, but he had no idea where the tanner was located, or where his room was, or where his section started and ended.

The one thing he was aware of was the way that his opponent wasn't shielding his left arm. Caleb swiveled around the guy's first punch, grabbed the arm, and pinned the man down in under a few seconds. He heard the anger over the defeat, felt the struggle to rise, the uncertainty of what Caleb might do to him for attacking the new section leader.

"Do you release if one cries uncle?" the man asked.

"Nope," Caleb replied. "Because I came here to teach you what I know, and learn what you know. I'm going to tell you how to get out of this."

Caleb did so, even if this was basic defense that the rider would know. The rider was wary enough to not attack his section leader further without permission, which was nice. Caleb talked the man into griping at his own hand to prevent anything Caleb might further do like break the rider's arm off. He had the man crush down on his foot, punch him in the face, nearly make him pass out from pinching the right vein in his neck. When Caleb was ready to cry uncle, he backed away, congratulating the rider on a task well completed. The man's attitude had changed, which was the point. It was hard to hate someone that encouraged you.

"You're alright, you know that," Caleb said, reaching his hand out to shake the guy's hand. It was accepted without the distrust and anger this time. "I'm Caleb."

"Pence."

"It's your lucky day, Pence. You've just been granted a section leader's task to show me around and help me figure out where everything is. They drop guys into here clueless. I'm going to need smart brains like yours to get out of this one." Caleb pulled on his collar like he was getting hot just thinking about how uncomfortable he was to be here. It made Pence smile.

"Your section runs from half of that field to the laundry room there, past those bunkrooms toward the mess hall. It cuts out the nest which is part of Mulligan's section, but it includes the first storehouse. It zigzags around and excludes the blacksmith shop, includes the water station, and the flag pole, and ends with the glorious opening to the view of the castle."

Caleb followed the pointing finger wishing that his domain was more of a straight line, but he'd take it any way it was offered.

"Forgive the noobie question, but I need to coordinate castle stare-downs with the other section leaders, right?" It was part of the job description that came with living beside the castle. The King's riders were the first to launch into battle to defend the king. They had to be exceptional to make it into this ware. "I have to get scouts blankly staring at the castle walls to defend it. Has anyone ever wanted to go over there and paint a smiling face on the castle to give the scouts something new to look at?"

Pence laughed at the question. "I wish you would. If you can manage it, you'll go down in ware prank history."

"I don't think anyone can beat Tristan's ware prank history," a man with a previously half-charred right arm stepped into the conversation with his hand extended in a welcome. His arm still showed the stretched skin of the burn. Caleb shook the hand offering a brief introduction and name again.

"I'm Notley," the man replied. "I'm the section leader over level seven and any level three's if we ever had any of those. I was the first to get Tristan's grievances. We're happy to have you, Caleb. I'll show you around. Pence is late for his class."

With that, Caleb thanked Pence for his time and followed Notley out toward the field to learn his assigned duties. There were lots of riders that looked as young as he did, but he didn't think he would find any of them in such high leadership positions as he had stepped into. Notley was at least double his age. His section leader job was the one thing keeping Caleb from being mad at Anvil forever. Anvil treated him like he was responsible and capable. If it wasn't for that, Caleb may have set fire to a few places of Anvil's Ware before he left. That's how mad he was.

"You'll be in charge of the level six riders, and yes have castle duties," Notley spoke. Caleb gave the man a sidewise glance wondering if he was secretly not excited about defending the castle.

"You are also in charge of any level two riders by default. We don't have any of them. Malone gets level five, the new kids, and one. Russel has the deleted class of level four, but mostly he makes sure that the married rider's underage kids are entertained and out of the way. When they get old enough to bond, if they want to find a dragon of their own and can't find one here, he transfers them to a new ware. Mulligan takes on the level eight riders and handles everyone who has completed courses."

Caleb nodded as he looked around the field of mature dragons. He couldn't help but notice that Warner was on the field with his head on the ground, his tail curled up, and his eyes in tears.

"You okay, buddy?" Caleb called to his distraught brown dragon.

"I don't feel like making new friends as fast as you do. I want to see Lore, and Gimmick, and Jewel. Especially Jewel."

Caleb couldn't say anything back to that. It was his fault that Warner was banished. Warner hadn't done anything bad to deserve this. He was paying for a crime he didn't commit and it wasn't fair at all.

"He's missing a girlfriend," Caleb said back to Notley's concerned glance.

"And how about you? You missing a girlfriend?" Notley questioned.

"Oh always. That's not a new emotion for me. The girl I fancy hardly recognizes that I exist."

"Kayla kept that picture," Warner pointed out, raising his head off the ground to catch a glimpse of his rider.

"I know, Warner," Caleb answered.

It only made it worse. He had finally made it through her defenses, finally found an image that Kayla would keep, the both of them on a ship playing pirate, and he had lost her. Oh, that hurt bad.

"You can always write letters. It's worked for lots of people to build up a relationship through letters and convince that girl you fancy to transfer." Notley took a few more steps before he came to an abrupt halt, either because he remembered this himself or because his dragon had just pointed it out to him.

"Unless that girl is Kayla Brixton," Notley shrugged in apology with an understanding of who Caleb dreamed about. "Your pictures of her have made it all over Aralot. I've seen a few of them myself. You draw really well, Caleb."

"You've seen my drawings?" Caleb asked, trying to sort out how this was possible. His images were always pulled down, and he thought they were either confiscated and kept by Anvil to go inside the man's personal scrapbook or else destroyed.

"All the time. You should be more careful where you leave them. There's an underground market for your work. It sells fast."

"No one should be selling my pictures of Kayla!" He was turning defensive again. She wasn't an image to be sold around to the highest bidder. His drawings had been done for himself and for her, not for anybody else. "Who's selling them?"

"Riders, Colts, townsfolk, everybody." Notley shrugged. "You won't stop it, and if you stop drawing, the prices on your existing pieces will only go up. There's this one you did of Kayla at the top of a flag pole. She's holding on with her legs reaching upward while a night dragon coos at her. That one is my personal favorite. That night dragon is a cutey. I think Charles confiscated that one because the price on it got too high."

Caleb shook his head as he remembered the particular drawing. It was from two years ago. Kayla wasn't reaching up to the sky because she wanted to. She was reaching because Midnight had stolen her backpack and was dangling it in the air, encouraging her to reach it. She refused to look at him as she tried to find a way to get high enough. Midnight wasn't the dragon in the drawing though. It was Moondust. She was a blue dragon, and yes, she was adorable. Moondust had wanted Kayla's attention so she had retrieved the bag for Kayla and given it back. She was disappointed when Kayla didn't say anything to her, but Midnight had made up for it by flirting with Moondust. Caleb had gotten in trouble for not being in bed.

"I guess I have a reputation already," Caleb remarked, trying to spot the invisible split in the field to know where his section rested.

"In a good way, Caleb. Your pictures are fantastic, despite them being a pathetic cry for attention."

"Hey, I got her attention once!"

Out on the field, Warner shook the water from his eyes and snorted. Notley took that to mean that Warner was calling his bluff. Caleb had to explain further to get around the sound from his dragon.

"I did. Kayla was given the task of sharpening knives so I slipped mine into her pile when she went off to lunch. She gave everyone back their knives in person. Except for me," he admitted. "She left my knife on my bed. I still haven't decided if that was a good thing since it was a more personal location, or a bad thing because she didn't want to see me."

Notley laughed at him, and then to save him from wondering about the interaction all over again, he gave Caleb a more precise and personal tour of the King's Ware. It wasn't so bad when he could walk the grounds. He made sure he knew the exact invisible line in the field between his side and Mulligan's side, but Notley said it didn't really matter. It would matter when they got into flame running. Caleb needed to be on his side. He didn't leave Notley's company until the man dismissed him for lunch. He now had a long list of things to get done during the upcoming week in one hand, and a list of his riders in the other.

He felt unsure of himself when he stepped into the mess hall. Every ware was different with how they approached the seating arrangements. Some wares had riders sitting by assigned bunkrooms even if those riders did not train in the same level. Other wares divided out by sections or last name or had an open seating policy. Caleb cast his eyes around for Pence, hoping to get a general idea of where he should be.

At Anvil's Ware, there was a long table at the front for section leaders and the ware leader. This ware didn't have that. It reflected the way the entire King's Ware worked. It was run by Charles who was the oldest, most seasoned rider here. At any time, day or night, the king was allowed to step into the ware and take control. That person would be Jack if he ever cared to have the job, but he left it to Charles. Since the ware didn't have a firm ware leader due to this rule, there wasn't the table around to set him apart.

Caleb couldn't make out Pence right away, so he got in line to grab some food and kept scanning the room.

"Is it an open seat policy?" Caleb asked the rider behind him giving up on guessing.

"Section leaders usually sit near the door beside their section, but it's not a hard rule," the rider replied, turning up his nose at the leather that Caleb wore. It looked like Caleb wasn't the only one that had a grudge against Anvil, and from this reaction he hoped this guy wasn't in his section. He slid into an open seat near the doorway and fiddled with his fork.

He couldn't take the pressure any longer. It was nearly a week-long flight from Anvil's Ware to here. In that time, he hadn't drawn a single picture of Kayla. Even worse he had missed her birthday by a whooping six days. She was now sixteen, the age at which her parents had declared appropriate for her to start dating. He wasn't going to be there to keep those boys in line. It wasn't going to take them long to realize that Kayla was drop-dead gorgeous, particularly not since they had all seen the way Caleb saw her through his sketches.

He couldn't help it. He pushed his food to the side to take charcoal to a blank page. The first thing emerging from his fingers was Kayla throwing a piece of birthday cake at Aiden while she smiled at Caleb. Caleb ran a finger along his newest sketch of melancholy.

"*Too aggressive?*" he asked his bonded dragon, Warner.

"*Aggressive? You've never gotten her verbal attention once.*"

"She ignores me like I didn't exist except for that picture…"

"You have a dragon. She treats dragons like they don't exist as well."

And that was the problem wasn't it? Not that he would ever trade Warner for a five-minute conversation with the girl he had a crush on, but it would help if she would at least look at him. Caleb stuffed his sketchbook back into his backpack before anyone could think of taking this to sell. To add to his torture, his mind turned back to one out of many times that Anvil had told him off for chasing after a girl that wanted nothing to do with him.

"Stop trying to talk to Kayla." Anvil's voice had filled his heart with despair. *"She's too young for you, Caleb."*

"Sir, our age difference is hardly anything."

"Her maturity level—"

"Women mature faster than men," Caleb had cut off his ware leader. Anvil always got him good when he cut him off.

"Detention for the next three days. I'll give you the specifics in my office after lunch."

Yeah, it was that detention thing again, only this time it was going to last forever. Caleb rubbed at his eyes trying to get away from his current mood. He really shouldn't be whining about Kayla. He had been born inside of Anvil's Ware, as both his parents were riders. He should be missing his family more than that girl.

"I heard you were approachable," a rider with an empty tray said as she slid onto the bench beside him. She looked approachable. She had braided black hair and sparkly green eyes.

"And you have made the approach. What dirt and grime will I be getting into?" Caleb smiled, trying to decide if this girl was in his section or not. Maybe she'd give him some task to take his mind off Kayla.

"Can you draw me with my dragon? I love the way your work is always so mysterious and shadowed and heartfelt."

He had another unknown fan. It was touching, but... "Maybe I shouldn't make myself so approachable. I'm not in the business of selling my work and I don't work for free."

"Do you trade?"

He shook his head.

"Take bribes? Lose drawings to bets or card games?"

"Covering your bases, aren't you?" He had to take care of this right now before everyone came around to pester him for pictures. "My work is personal. If I ever find one of my drawings, I'm taking it back regardless of the price anyone paid for it. If they have a problem with that, they can imprint a picture of my knuckles on their hide. How's that for approachable?"

"Jerk," the rider retorted, displeased with his answer.

"They're my stolen drawings. Every last one of them. What are you doing tonight?" Caleb asked before she stormed off on him. He was setting himself up over here. If anyone wanted his stuff, they would have to steal it from him. He was going to be looking at picture theft soon. Best to keep his drawings locked up. He wasn't drawing random riders and their pals.

"There is one not commissioned work that I'm willing to do."

"What?" the girl asked him, now suspicious of his motives.

"I'm going to sneak beneath the castle guards and draw on the wall. That will give everyone something new to look at." And charging right at them would take his mind off everything else.

"You can't get past them!" the rider claimed.

"Sure I can. You'll be my distraction." She shook her head again, and Caleb looked around the room trying to pick out his next partner in crime. There had to be someone else game enough to try. "Who would?"

"Russel probably."

She conveniently pointed out the man who was in charge of keeping all the rider's kids out of the way. Russel looked like one of those fun, happy men, with his wide smile and short light-brown hair. He had wide ears that he could probably wiggle, and at first glance, Caleb was already amused.

A fellow section leader. He liked it. He thanked her for the information and slipped away from her before she could do the same to him.

"Hey, Russel," Caleb said, scooting his lunch tray in beside the man. "You me and redesigning the castle wall with art?"

"Hi, Caleb," Russel said, already knowing who he was. "You were transferred because you're hard to work with, weren't you?"

"Me? Nope. I was transferred because I'm too good." Russel laughed at him. "I need something to keep my mind off everything else," Caleb admitted.

"I've just the thing for you. I've been handling your section since Stanford passed. Everyone's due to run lines after lunch. You can learn the names of the riders as they glare at you for the work."

Hm. Making running lines fun. He could do that. He'd have everyone singing out their names while he ran right beside them. He needed the work. He was going to go stir crazy if he let his mind sit for too long.

"Lines it is," Caleb agreed.

"And when you find a good way to distract the castle guards, I'll help you paint that castle wall," Russel grinned, revealing that he did enjoy a good challenge. "There's no way Prince Tristan can beat that sort of prank. He's known for them around here. Is it possible for you to put his face up there?"

"Best not make him directly mad at me," Caleb answered. He'd never talked to the prince, but he'd heard all about him, and he didn't want Prince Tristan doing anything in revenge. The guy used magic a lot, so the rumors said. He didn't use it only for training or emergencies like the Brixton's had Kayla doing.

"Besides, the painting will have to be something I can do fast like the outline of some nondescript dragon."

"They'll know it was us and not the Colts if it's a dragon. What about a snowy mountain?"

"Or Aralot's flag large and proud. I can do that quickly." It was mostly straight lines. There was a yellow border around a white flag and a mythical blue flower in the center. That picture could be done by anybody Colt or rider. Russel gave a nod of approval and motioned for him to finish his lunch. Caleb ate lightly because he was running lines after this.

Enrolled

Kayla

She couldn't waltz up to the King's Ware to gain an invitation to train there so she was doing the next best thing and waltzing into the castle. After talking with Anvil, Kayla had returned home to complain to her parents about the new rules, and then she had packed her bag very carefully later that night. One day later, and she was ready to take on the castle. She had never paid attention to the way that people bowed to her when she was here. The guards had been doing it her entire life, so she figured that they were simply polite. Knowing that she was the princess because her mother was rightfully the queen by blood, and her father magically the king, made the bowing feel suddenly uncomfortable.

When she was little, she used to bow back to the soldiers and they would play this game of who could bow last before she was summoned away by her parents. Today she froze before the first bowing guard. He came back up asking her if she was alright. She hadn't even made it inside the castle yet. She was still in the courtyard and already questioning herself. There was no way she could train this close to the castle.

No, she had to do this. If she wasn't here, she was losing knowledge. Every other ware was too far away, protecting the outskirts of the land. She would get great training, if she could manage to train with her eyes shut, but she would lose to Tristan. She wasn't even sure she wanted to win against Tristan in the first place, but she had to be here because she couldn't change her mind about her ware later. Ware leaders would not transfer keepers if they could avoid it. They hogged them because keepers were excellent at taking care of large groups of dragons. Kayla was still learning how to take care of herself.

"Do you happen to know where I can find Vermelo and avoid Tristan?"

She didn't want to meet Vermelo in the customary conference room. Tristan had his bedroom right beside that place on purpose so he could spy on everyone. If she managed to get into the King's Ware, he was sure to know soon enough. Uncle Anvil was right. In the event that she failed this, she didn't need Tristan gaining insight into a defeat that he could use to poke her with.

"Tristan left with his dragon this morning. Vermelo is in his room," the guard answered, looking at the armored man beside him to verify this.

Kayla felt the relief rush over her. She didn't have to go into the castle at all! She could also avoid King Klavian and Queen Aria. Vermelo's room was located in the eastern tower on the wall. He only went there when he was asleep, so she knew that she'd be waking him up. She felt slightly bad about it as she ran to the tower. She had to wait for several guards to escort her up, princess or not, and then wait as they woke him up. Once he was up though, she was allowed direct access to his room.

She had been here before, and similar to how Uncle Anvil bolted shut his magical study, Vermelo hardly let anyone into his room. Kayla was privileged to enter both locations. She gave the gray-haired man a hug as she sat down on his small bed beside him, regardless of the trouble he was stirring up with Rosa and Clark. She needed Vermelo on her good side so she let her hug linger before she pulled back and cast a brief look across his things.

Vermelo didn't keep anything particularly fancy in here. He had a few pictures of his wife and kids that lived in town, a box of clothes, and another locked box that he kept out of sight beneath the bed. He currently had a broken horse harness in a corner of his floor. He bred posh champion horses and was known far and wide for them. When he got the chance, he slept at home.

"To what do I owe this visit?" Vermelo asked her, rubbing at his blurry green eyes.

"Sorry to wake you, but I need ideas on how to join the King's Ware."

"That would make you work directly for the king," Vermelo pointed out.

"And since that's my dad and he already tells me what to do, is there a difference?" Kayla shrugged. "Anvil can't take me. I considered Rogan's but then I'd never hear anything that happens at the castle. The same thing would apply at any other ware, and since I've spent so much time not being around, I should probably start being around."

"Are you going to encourage your parents to mount forces for a war with Vankerdale? Kayla, the King's Ware is not a safe place for you. Any day now that magical wall could fall and this will be the first place they attack. It should be the last place you want to be."

Ugh. He wasn't going to help her. She would have to think up something else. Who might agree that keeping her in sight was a better fit than keeping her away? Tristan was completely out. King Klavian was a pushover when it came to dragons and decisions like this, but only if he was talking to a ware leader and standing in the presence of the man's dragon. The only other person that might write her a letter of recommendation was Aria. Aria it was.

"Thanks for that reminder. Sorry to wake you again." Kayla gave Vermelo another short hug and took the four steps to reach the door in the small room.

"Kayla," Vermelo sighed wearily behind her. "Find something that will make you incredibly happy. You're going to need it."

She looked back at him to take in his sincere worry over her safety and personal happiness. See, this was why she liked Vermelo, even if she didn't understand what he was doing trying to push Rosa and Clark to usurp her parents. Vermelo cared about her, the same way that she felt Ritz usually cared about her. Thinking of the two of them at the same time brought her back to a conversation that she'd had with her mom. Tia had once told her that Vermelo asked if Tia had any strange dreams as if they meant something. Maybe Vermelo had additional insights into her nightmares. He had access to tons of secret information that he kept King Klavian out of.

"Do you know anything about how to end nightmares?" Kayla asked him.

Vermelo gave her a sad smile like he was about to cry. Maybe she shouldn't have woken him up.

"Find a joy that you can't lose or you're going to lose," Vermelo answered.

Was that a real answer? She was finally able to hear what everyone was talking about, but she still couldn't understand anyone. She gave him a shrug and stepped from the room trying to piece it all together. Ritz had said the exact opposite. She was to not go looking for additional things that would make her feel loved and happy. This was making the whole thing more complicated over who to believe. Maybe no one really knew what was wrong with her. It wasn't like she could always feel one way or the other. Feelings came and went and she didn't control what she felt when she was asleep.

She was still thinking about it when she entered the castle and asked to be taken to Aria. Aria was attending some sort of social gathering with several other women, but she stepped into the hallway when Kayla asked to talk to her, looking every part of her queenly role with a flowing dress and intricately braided brown hair. Aria excused herself politely from the circle. She wasn't as polite when she addressed Kayla.

"What do you want?" she asked, not using any of the flowery words she had just used to excuse herself. Kayla wasn't offended by the changing nature. Aria was used to talking to the Brixton's like this because Kayla's mother hated the extra fluff and wanted clear precise answers. Kayla took in a deep breath schooling her mind to think like a Colt. Trick Aria. She had to get Aria to give her what she wanted without making it look like she was really after the King's Ware.

"Well?" Aria asked her. Kayla felt nervous under her scrutiny, but she kept her face straight and her training up. She was going to do this. Aria wasn't going to know what came at her.

"I want you to teach me how to act like a noble," Kayla requested. "I'm miserable at it. I have no idea what fork to use or how to hold a napkin or a fan. I ruined the table cloth on the date with Tristan. I don't know what he told you, but it felt like a disaster, and I still have three more of them that I have to go through."

Aria crossed her arms and frowned. Kayla rushed in with the rest of her excuse.

"I can tell you what plants to eat if lost in the woods, but I can't tell you how to spread butter."

"You don't spread the butter," Aria remarked, with a shake of her head.

Kayla gave her a shrug. This was working out great already. Aria was going to see her as helpless and agree to take on her flaws. Hopefully. Aria was a teacher by trade. She was also a Colt who took joy in watching students progress, which was why Kayla was offering herself up.

"Don't offer too much of yourself. I still want you too," Valiant mumbled at her.

"I have a plan, Valiant," Kayla replied.

"I need to know how to talk to people like you just did. I really don't want to get stuck talking to a noble and have no idea how they think. What if I end up like my dad and get tricked into signing things with Vankerdale?"

He had done that the first time he had gone over there, and had to get bailed out through her mother's keeper connection to help him know what to say.

"In the current atmosphere, it could be me ruining all the years of hard work everyone else has put into Aralot. I never realized until now that I could destroy your life. Please help me not to do that. I would like you to teach me."

Aria turned quiet. Kayla wondered what part of her words was working the most on the woman. The part of the teacher and student where Aria could tell Kayla anything she wanted and have Kayla believe her, or the part where Kayla admitted that she could destroy Aria's current existence. Aria would do anything to keep her husband in the castle, because he had once given her up for the title of the king. Laws had been changed so that they could get married. Kayla had never been able to hear who changed the law for that to happen, but it was probably her parents.

"What are you planning to do with Tristan?"

Bummer. Aria was trying to pick apart every threat that Kayla could bring. Kayla managed to keep a straight face. She was proud of herself for the accomplishment.

"Date him, I guess. He won't like someone who can't walk the same world he does. As I said, I totally ruined that first date. I don't want to be in opposition to all of you."

Which was a true statement. She didn't like being where she was, but she knew that if anything came up to make her take a stand, she would very well stand against the Clusters, Uncle Clark and all. As Vermelo pointed out, she worked for the king, and that was her dad, and she was going to see that he kept his job.

"Take your hood off and stop slouching," Aria told her. Kayla did as directed as her hope flared. She'd done it! Aria was going to tell her what to do! "You're going to need a lot of work. What do you have coming up that will get in the way?"

If that wasn't a perfect line to get in her real desires, Kayla didn't know what was. She barely held in the smile.

"I need to train Valiant. Anvil can't take me so I was going to ask Rogan to let me join there. That will take up most of my time I'm afraid, but you can take a portal to give me lessons."

Aria frowned at her. She wasn't immune to portals and Kayla was purposely telling her that she wouldn't be able to leave a dragon training ware in order to see the fake queen. If she trained with Rogan that was exactly what would happen. Kayla would remain the untrained threat that Aria had before her, and she would be far out of the woman's reach.

"Would you consider training at Charles's Ware? It's much closer."

"Um…" Kayla trailed off as she had never considered it before. In reality, she wanted to scream in delight. She'd done it! Charles would have to accept her if she came at him with a note from Aria! Her Colt skills were amazing!

"Stop slouching," Aria told her again, because Kayla had lost her posture as she pretended to think. Kayla grinned back embarrassed. "You'd like Charles," Aria tried to convince her. "If you go there, you wouldn't have to transfer later. Rogan's Ware is still a training ware. He can't keep people for too long."

"Okay," Kayla agreed. "If you teach me to be a noble, I'll train at Charles's Ware. Will you tell him to let me in?"

"Kayla," Vermelo admonished, stepping into the hallway. She had been too busy thinking about nightmares to pay attention to the fact that he had followed her after she left him. "That puts you right where Aria can watch you." He gave her a glare because he knew her real goal, and she had just won it despite him telling her not to put herself here.

"Exactly, Vermelo," Kayla answered, barely keeping the victory off her face. "Aria can tell me if I'm doing well enough to pass as a rider and a noble. That's the goal. Pass and not look stupid doing it."

"I'll have Charles put noble lessons on your rider schedule," Aria told her. "Just give me a second and I'll send you right over."

"You're making me worry about you, kid," Vermelo expressed.

"That's Princess Kayla," Aria reminded him. "She won't learn how to not disgrace us all if she's talked to like a street urchin."

With that Aria skipped off to write the note. Kayla finally let that grin crest her face.

"I just totally took on Aria!" She whispered, so that the woman wouldn't hear the cheer echoing down the hallway. "I think that's a joy that will last for a while."

Vermelo didn't say anything back to her. He shook his head and told the guard closest to him that he was going to bed in the closest empty room he could find.

Since the King's Ware was super close to the castle, Kayla didn't fly Valiant out of the courtyard to go there when Aria handed her the letter. She ran, still giddy that she had gotten a woman as smart as Aria to do what she wanted. Valiant flew over her head hooting nervously. He growled at a few dragons that got close to him, but it looked like everyone at the King's Ware had been told that Kayla had a spellbinding dragon, so they let Valiant land. With him taking up all the attention, Kayla felt blissfully free to search for Charles without dragons sending her love messages.

Kayla ran up to the ware leader's office, knocked once, and tried the handle. As she stepped inside, she found six men in the room with Charles. All the men looked slightly surprised to see her. After all, she never set foot in this ware. From the stature of these men, and the time of day, this had to be a section leader meeting. One man had short brown hair and large ears. Another had a burn on his right arm. There was a section leader who had half of his blond hair shaved while the top part was left long and pulled up into a bun. The next man had curly dark brown hair, bushy eyebrows, and warm eyes.

The last man she looked at confused. He was the youngest in the room, and his entire face lit up as she stepped inside. He was the kind of person that stood tall and confident in his own skin. He was being serious at the moment, but something about his personality cued Kayla in that he was more fun than a stickler for routine. He had the strong arms and chest that every dragon rider had, and wore the red leather of Charles

Ware with dignity. His dark-brown hair was tamed and his brown eyes beamed like he was proud of her for stepping into the room. It was strange. He had one of those faces that might make her blush if she looked too long, so she looked away.

To contrast the various ages of everyone at the meeting, there was Charles. Kayla had met Charles before inside the castle during one of those yearly celebrations she had to attend. He had white billowy hair, and sagging skin, but he had kept his strong voice as he aged.

Kayla handed him the note and waited impatiently for him to open it. She never thought that she would be so excited to join a ware that was so distant from everything she had come to know. Charles pulled open the seal, skimmed the letter, and looked up at her surprised.

"Do you know how many transfer notices I have seen in my lifetime?" he asked her in his strong voice. He shook the letter and laughed. "This one tops them all. I shouldn't be so surprised. You are your father's daughter after all."

"She did what?" the man with the burn on his arm asked as he grabbed for the note and read it too.

Since Kayla didn't have to keep a straight face for Aria, the satisfaction was bursting through so much so that she was jittery and bouncing on her toes. "That letters got a great story. Aria didn't see it coming, and she thinks it was all her own idea. You have no idea how hard it was."

It had been hard not to laugh. Kayla never had things like this go so smoothly for her. Then again, she'd never tried to trick the Clusters with anything before. Maybe she was naturally gifted at it. She knew what fears would drive the hardest at Aria and she had played into those.

"Unfortunately, Kayla, we don't have a class available that matches your skill level," Charles told her. "We also don't have a teacher that can handle a dragon like yours. Shouldn't your father take this on? He can handle a dragon that dishes out spells."

Kayla tried to hold onto the thrill of accomplishment as it started to leave her. Charles was saying no! He couldn't do that!

"My dad doesn't have time to train a dragon. He's hardly ever home," Kayla fought back. "He's always off watching ships come in from Wisteria, or trying to repair the damages that the devil ultra-dragon king leaves in his wake. If he's not doing that, he's attending to some other kingdom-wide affair on his super long list of things to do. Have you ever seen his list? I once wrote on it trying to get him to play with me, and by the time he got around to it four months later, I had completely forgotten."

"You've grown up between three different wares, Kayla. You can pick any of them," Charles tried again. Kayla almost corrected him to say four. Her house was practically a ware by itself, but yes, she had been to Turid's, and Rogan's, and Anvil's wares.

"I thought all ware leaders liked keepers," Kayla said, before she remembered that she shouldn't use that word with Charles. His dragon had been linked to the evil king Gladius's younger brother Maslon, and Charles may have helped to kill the guy. It was never talked about, but she had seen Maslon's house burning down in her nightmares. Charles thought that all keepers turned into infections which sought to destroy the very dragon they were bonded to. She couldn't do that if she wasn't bonded, and her mother had discovered the cure ages ago.

"I'm not going to go crazy," Kayla promised. "I thought everyone understood by now that keepers only turn into infections if they eat a certain poison. I know the exact composition of that poison—"

"Don't go spouting ware leader secrets!" Charles reproached.

"I'm not infected!"

"Charles, I'll take her," a familiar voice offered to the room. "Every day. Any time of the day. No matter what the problem is. I've spent my whole life watching the adaptation of training techniques on rare dragons. I can train the dragon."

"Well someone had better, before Kayla goes blabbering her advanced knowledge to everyone. You keep her mouth shut tight."

Kayla's inhale was so loud that everyone heard it.

Caleb!

She could pick his voice out from anywhere. Anvil said that he was on an assignment, not that Caleb had transferred! Kayla had never once looked at him directly in all her years of hearing him stand up for her. Now he was doing it again, right in the moment that she started to lose her grip. He'd always had excellent timing, although his quick fists had caused so many fights, that she'd spent a lot of time feeling guilty that she caused Caleb to get in trouble. He was the person jumping in the way of anyone who might call her slinky, shadow, wraith, or ghost for wearing a hood all the time. He was the only one who even tried to understand her at Anvil's Ware anymore. That was probably why he'd been transferred away. It was a good thing Anvil hadn't told her that on her birthday. She would have felt like she had lost all her friends on the same day.

Why had she never looked at this guy before?! An arrow of terror sliced through her gut. Like the horrible friend she would always be, she had no idea that Caleb had been on a transfer list, what skill level he was at, who his parents were, who his actual friends were, or anything else. He was a section leader!

Kayla looked sharply at him trying to read his surprisingly charming face to see if he was going to start in on his friend question. She was going to say yes to him. Now she had no idea what to say.

Caleb gave her a short smile, not the one she was expecting for a guy who had tried to talk to her since before she could walk. Then again, she had ignored him forever, so perhaps his short smile had a point. They didn't know each other. Maybe he stood up for all the underdogs that came his way. Maybe he was just that kind of person. But those pictures... He'd drawn so many pictures...

"I like his pictures. Don't like him," Valiant declared.

"I think he's nice. Probably." Kayla looked in the direction of Valiant and gave him a short smile when she could see him as close as he could physically get to the office window. Charles had the curtain pulled open in case anyone went looking for a section leader so they could see them all in a meeting. Valiant was sitting on his tail like a scared dog while he scanned across every other dragon around. Three feet was all the space he would give her. Her look made the section leaders peek over at Valiant too. He turned rigid.

"These dragons don't fang strangers like they try to do in Vankerdale," Kayla assured her dragon. *"And the people are not mean."*

"These dragons and people coordinate their attacks so they're worse," Valiant replied.

"What did you name your spellbinding dragon?" Charles asked her.

"He was named Valiant by—" Kayla cut herself off. She should have been the person naming the dragon. As a keeper, she *could* be like her mother where one look at a dragon told her the dragon's name. Rosa couldn't look at a dragon to instantly know their name. Kayla's missing Uncle Conner couldn't either. Kayla had never looked at dragons long enough to decide if she could, but still. Naming her dragon was supposed to be her responsibility. Instead, Tyler had named her dragon as if he had a better connection with him. Maybe he did.

Outside Valiant whimpered on her thoughts. Caleb came to her rescue because that's just what he did.

"—by the magic that dwells inside all dragons near and far. Each dragon is given a special calling with his name. The name Valiant is mighty powerful. I think we can expect fantastic feats from a dragon with a name like that. I like it. If that's all, I think I'm good to go. I'll give you the tour, Kayla. Class starts right after breakfast each morning. You get two free hours after lunch before the second half of the day."

"Caleb." Charles's voice asked him to wait, but Caleb simply shrugged at the ware leader and opened the door. "Keep your head in the training," Charles advised.

"I'll get back to you on that paperwork," Caleb answered as he waved her out the door. Kayla stepped outside right into Valiant's face. He hummed at her. She shoved his head out of the way unsure if she had been accepted by the ware leader or not. It looked like Caleb was bold enough to make the decision for him.

"You're behind on paperwork?" Kayla asked. "But you love paper."

"No, I don't," Caleb answered. "I appreciate the lines that can be created on paper. I enjoy taking the images that I see in my mind and shaping them into sketches so that everyone else can see the beauty that I see."

Valiant swiveled his head around to growl at Caleb as they started past him. Kayla blushed. The only thing she had ever seen Caleb draw was her. He thought she was beautiful. Due to the unwelcoming sound, Caleb kept himself on the far side of Kayla, away from Valiant's jaws. The dragon plucked himself off the ground to follow after her as close as physically possible. Kayla wanted to push Valiant back a bit for breathing down her neck, but she let him be. She was talking with Caleb! He must have thought the same thing because he glanced at her briefly with a rather large grin before looking away, trying to wipe it off his face.

"I know you don't know him that well, but do you think Charles said yes?"

"That was a yes," Caleb answered. "If he didn't really want to say yes, he would have firmly said no the instant you posed your question. His pause was no doubt his thoughts on how to break the news to Anvil."

"Uncle Anvil can't do anything. Tristan had his dad and all the counselors sign a paper preventing him from breeding dragons and taking on new riders. I'm not allowed at Anvil's Ware anymore."

"Ohh..." Caleb trailed off. "I can see a lot of people getting mad about that."

"You're handling the news way better than I did," Kayla admitted, as she looked at him again. Gee this guy was hot. Kayla had to look away again before she let him know. She had run off to cry because of Tristan's actions. Then she had gotten herself into here to keep her eyes on him. Not on Caleb. She shouldn't look at her section leader like that.

"This is probably better for you anyway," Caleb decided. "The dragons over here don't have a past history with you. Just listen to the lack of hooting voices. Much better, right? If you stayed at Anvil's Ware the dragons would get in your way, and you'd still be under the constant watch of your mother."

Caleb glanced into the air as if trying to spot Tia's wild dragon guard of the day. He paused on a figure in the air, so Kayla was sure he had found it. His sidewise glance at her and subsequent sly smile was all the answer she needed. She had not escaped her mother.

"The dragons over here are much more mature. They don't hoot at riders that already have their own dragon. Your bunkroom will probably be that one over there," Caleb was quick to switch topics as if he feared he was talking about dragons too long and he didn't want to scare her off.

"I'll need a good hour to figure out how to coordinate an appropriate class. Warner is asking around right now…" Caleb trailed off again as he leaned toward her, trying to see beneath her hood to see how she was doing with the dragon topic. She had avoided Caleb for a long time because she just knew he would bring up his dragon. Warner was a brown-scaled animal that did his share of trying to get her attention. It wasn't until Caleb had stopped drawing dragons in his pictures for her that she had changed her mind about him.

"I have already accepted that everyone will be way better than me," Kayla said.

"You know what? Let's go through the written tests first," Caleb pointed her toward the mess hall, talking to her about the different sections of the ware as if she didn't know them. She had never been inside the ware physically, but she had flown over it a hundred times in her dreams, and she had the sections and layout down better than he did. Valiant whined when he realized that he couldn't stay with her as they walked among the buildings. That was when the dragon voices decided to start up as if they had decided that Valiant wasn't going to charge at them if they hooted at her.

"Hey, cutie! You put one dragon in a spell. You can put me in one too. I'll follow behind you."

"Do you like kittens because you're making me purr."

Those two dragons, whoever they were, were followed by the cries of about twenty others, all talking over each other. Valiant growled at them. Kayla told Caleb to bring all the tests he wanted and ran for the mess hall. Taking written tests would take hours. That would get her away from the other dragons for a time. It would also be interesting to see how she scored. She'd read through all the training manuals, but she'd never been quizzed over them.

Keepers
Tyler

Tyler finished walking down the last of the steps so he could slide into the now empty dragon prison. This was the room that Valiant had been held inside when he was captured. It was the room that Tyler had always come to when he needed to think. Now the room felt lonely without the dragon and customary guard, but Tyler put his back to the wall and pulled out his information sheet.

He was trying to write down everything he could about keepers. They could hear multiple dragons in their heads. They couldn't control which dragon entered their thoughts unless they bonded and had a gatekeeper dragon block out voices. Whatever dragon bonded the keeper first was the gatekeeper dragon until death severed the bond. Not being bonded and hearing tons of voices was supposed to turn a keeper crazy. Eating a certain poison turned a keeper crazy. Having a broken bond to the gatekeeper left the keeper feeling crazy. Keepers could sightshare with more than just their venom linked gatekeeper if they had a rather strong mind according to Kayla Brixton. And since the dragon in Tyler's head had talked to him from another kingdom, and was a powerful ultra-dragon king, Tyler knew that he and this dragon had strong minds.

What he hadn't realized was that he had the ability to be a keeper in his blood at all. The Valeron's used to rule Vankerdale before the Peyton's, but no one ever talked about that anymore. All the Valeron's were known for these days was being indentured servants to the Peytons. Tyler was forced to give Prince Evan answers to all his questions.

It was Tyler finding the way to kidnap Kayla out of Aralot by using her dragon against her. It was him researching all of Aralot's old rules looking for loopholes. Prince Evan had claimed that he wouldn't release Tyler of his service unless he brought him Kayla Brixton. He had done that, but Kayla had gotten away, and Tyler had gone with her, trying to turn himself into her friend so that she would trust him and stop the curse upon the land that prevented their dragons from bonding. Any dragon that entered Vankerdale lost its bond if it had one. Any rider that entered Vankerdale lost his bond too, even if the dragon wasn't there.

It had King Peyton in a rage. He had been angry about it for years, but it was his own fault. Queen Tia had found the cure to the curse and used it to save everyone. Then King Peyton had stolen her daughter's dragon so she put the curse back on. Now King Peyton was pacing the border between Aralot and Vankerdale encouraging his dragon SilverWings to bust through the spells that kept everyone out so he could carry out his next crazy plan. Sadly, Tyler thought it was going to work, mostly because he had given King Peyton the idea of how to get Kayla for a second time.

Since the unbonded dragons by the border were being outfitted for war, Tyler had already heard a host of complaints. It was hard to get dragons to fly anyone, even people they fancied, around here. Being told they needed to fly at Aralot to fight had dragons chucking off riders and fanging them all over the place trying to create a connection. If King Peyton didn't break that magical wall down soon, everyone else was going to break first.

"I was terrifying today," came the thought of his unbonded dragon

into Tyler's thoughts. Hearing this beast was relatively new. The sounds had started up shortly after meeting Kayla.

"It's a shame because I'm no longer close to the border where I wanted to be. I could see SilverWings pacing on the other side of the river, sucking up magic into his stomach and spitting it out into fireworks. Now I'm nowhere close."

The black-scaled ultra-dragon king was a night dragon so Tyler had purposefully gone where he could be alone to reply to the dragon when his new friend woke up. Since the two of them had never met, they had no idea what each other really looked like, and Tyler couldn't decide what the dragon's name should be.

If the night terror thought he had done something scary, he probably had. He had admitted that he was being possessed from a lost dragon scale of his. He destroyed villages and towns and wares and people and dragons inside of Aralot. That's what had Tyler shaking. Whoever possessed the night terror might realize that the dragon could think to Tyler, and if they moved the dragon's brain into Tyler's body when the beast was being possessed, Tyler could be possessed through the sightsharing.

"I've been giving that a lot of thought because I know it scares you. I don't think it's possible. When possessed, my mental existence is completely suppressed and only my body is moved. I don't think that the person responsible for controlling me can hear my thoughts to know that you exist. Don't be scared, Tyler. You're perfectly safe. At least until King Peyton succeeds in his war."

"It won't be much of a war," Tyler sighed out loud. "He's only trying to get Kayla. He's going to do everything he can to get her apart. Knowing that she falls to the ground and trembles when around large masses of dragons makes her an easy target."

"I'll protect her," the night terror vowed, even if they both knew

that Kayla was scared of the demon dragon and would run away from him. Plus, the animal couldn't even protect himself. It might not matter what anyone did. Vankerdale's dragons wanted to bond again, and they would desperately do anything King Peyton and SilverWings ordered to secure those mental links.

Tyler pushed up the sleeve on his left arm to look at the bumpy blue line that Pyro had scratched into him. It was Pyro and his dragon king brain that had understood an ancient monolith and turned Tyler into a keeper in the first place. Now he was hearing this dragon that lived far far away. At the time, Pyro had been unbonded to Jack so he couldn't tell his rider what he had done. King Jack was sure to know of it now. Tyler had no idea what the king thought of him.

He ran his fingers over the magical, blue, four-inch long cut. It had only hurt for a moment, but right now his whole arm was sore from fencing practice. Tyler had gone at it for a long time, wanting to do something to protect the kingdom while knowing that his fencing skills were useless against a dragon.

He pressed his hand over the magical bumpy line to hide it. Since it was there and Tyler didn't want to explain what it was to anyone else, especially Prince Evan and King Peyton, he was now wearing half sleeves in the heat of summer, while he told himself to appreciate the heat, because his parents had lived inside a curse of eternal winter for most of their lives. Tyler had lived through it some too, but he was a baby and didn't remember much. King Peyton took the credit for ending that curse. Tyler gave the credit to Jack Brixton who was the only magical man that could have done such a thing.

"At the time perhaps, and I happen to know for a fact that Jack did stop Vankerdale's curse of winter, but there are way too many magic users around Aralot now. I've tried to find them all again. Magic has a distinct smell and I've been everywhere. However, I still can't decide who is using me. All the ware

leaders have magical protection. They all cast little spells on occasion except for Anvil who casts large ones. I've ruled Anvil out so many times it's not even funny. It's not Tia possessing me because she could never kill a dragon as I've done. Jack loves his kingdom too much to send me to destroy the cities and wares. Kayla can hardly look at dragons let alone be one. I've tried to blame Prince Tristan a hundred times. He's come against me to kill me over and over and I've left his dragon practically destroyed a few times, but I did that when I was awake in self-defense. The problem with linking anyone to the attacks is that it's done during the day when I would normally be sleeping. Most people are accounted for all day long. I can't find who is sneaking off to control me."

"You must have missed someone," Tyler sighed.

"I know. It was the same way when Jack was trying to stop Herb Felding from killing everyone. He killed off Herb and the magical attacks continued. Turned out that Herb was using a spellcaster, so Jack had to stop that person too. No one will say who that person was so I have no idea if the person behind my possession could be similarly related."

"You've checked all the Feldings?" Tyler asked just to be sure.

"Yes. All of them, even the ones that are adopted and not real Feldings. I think I've checked everyone, Tyler. When are you coming to help me?"

Tyler covered his eyes with his hands. He didn't know. He had no way past the border without Valiant sucking up the spells in the way to let him through. Valiant had gone to Aralot leaving him behind because Jack and Kayla had both refused to let him come. Kayla had promised to write to him though, and she hadn't done that yet.

"She said you could send the letter with Conner. He's a merchant by trade and capable of walking through the border spells. You should go see him again, Tyler. I seriously believe that Kayla will be the only one able to save me. If only she would look at me."

Yup, that was the plight of the dragon around Kayla Brixton. They screamed simply to be looked at, not knowing that it hurt her to look.

"You know, maybe she's better now," Tyler mused. "Valiant could have bonded her again since they're both in Aralot."

He got quiet when he heard footsteps in the hallway. It was probably a guard that would pass him by thinking that he was reading out loud some boring book like he used to read to Valiant. This was the room for it. The footsteps, however, got closer to the door and the handle started to turn. Tyler jumped to his feet in case it was one of the ruling household looking for him to give him some assignment.

It was a ruler that stepped into the room, but not one he had anticipated. Tyler's mouth dropped open as he looked upon the brown-haired king with starburst eyes. King Jack! For him to be here, he would have broken his bond again to his dragon. This had to be horribly important for Jack to submit himself to the torture.

"How did you get in here?" Tyler questioned as he jumped forward to pull the king of Aralot into the room and shut the door before he could be spotted. Tyler gave him a muddled bow at the same time.

"I spent three months being locked up around here," Jack reminded him. "It's not hard to get inside once I discovered how to get out."

Tyler blinked his eyes. Seeing Jack walking around the Vankerdale castle was making him jumpy. What was the man doing here?!

"Did you see King Peyton?" Tyler asked. He wasn't a fan of King Peyton or Prince Evan, but what if Jack had slaughtered them? He'd taken down evil kings and spellcasters before.

"I thought your king was at the border," Jack reminded. "So is Prince Evan. It's nice that they left their castle unattended, isn't it? I came here to find you. I passed this room twice already." Jack laughed at himself. "Are you hearing dragons?"

Oh. Jack had broken the bond with his own dragon to ask Tyler what had become of him after Pyro had cut his arm. Jack's eyes moved to the appropriate arm that had the magical cut as if he could see through Tyler's sleeves. Tyler glanced again at the door. He had always respected Jack, and Jack showing up to find out if he was doing alright only made him like him more, but the sneaking through the castle part had him unnerved.

"You didn't see any guards?" Tyler asked, causing Jack to laugh at him. "Really how did you get here? Do you have Valiant with you? King Peyton has the borderline completely blocked off!"

There had to be some magical method that Jack had used to sneak in. If only he would tell Tyler what it was, then Tyler could use the same thing to get out. Come to think of it, Kayla and Jack had both used some sort of magical means to leave the kingdom in the first place, because they had not been seen by the border at all when they escaped. Reports had them traveling north and there were a few dead dragons found there that must have gotten in their way. Tyler would need to search the area to discover the secrets. Jack was still waiting for his reply so Tyler found himself wailing.

"Pyro's the one who did it. I couldn't understand a thing he said and now I can't get this dragon out of my head. I don't even know what the dragon is named because we've never met—"

"Don't tell Jack where I am!" The night terror screamed at him, causing Tyler's senses to play tricks on him. He got so dizzy that he wobbled backward on his feet. It was Jack reaching for his arm to steady

him. Reaching and then pushing up the sleeve to see that cut.

"If he's the one who is possessing me, he could kill you right now for knowing. Don't say anything, Tyler. Don't, don't, don't. I don't want to lose you!"

"Woah, there. I've experienced that before. Is the dragon startled that I'm talking to you? Screaming can knock you over."

"Something like that."

Tyler got his arm back making sure that the sleeve was covering him again. He was only getting a little bit better at holding two conversations at a time, but he wasn't very good at it yet. It was hard to talk to other people when he had a dragon demanding words instead. He had to concentrate rather hard to not think half his sentences and speak the other half. Riders called it splitting sentences and it was a very large clue that a person had been bonded. Tyler had not been bonded. That was part of his issue with being scared he was going to go mad.

"I thought you already discovered that Jack wasn't the one after you," Tyler told the night terror.

"Maybe. But you're all alone with him and undefended. He's got magic and you don't. He's got years of fighting moves that would leave you blinking like an idiot. Don't tell him!"

Jack laughed at him and took a step back. "Dragon just insult you?" he asked as if he could read through Tyler's every expression. "That's always fun. You have my permission to insult the beast back. Anyway, Tyler, I was just stopping by to check if the magic Pyro used worked. I think it did. He was very certain that you'd be a good person to test it out on because you looked like you enjoyed dragons and you were being ever so nice protecting Kayla."

Jack might change his mind if he ever learned that it was Tyler kidnapping her in the first place. And what did he mean by "test it out on?" He wasn't going to use the same thing on himself, was he? What did he need to be a keeper for? So he wouldn't ever have broken thoughts with Pyro? He'd still experience unpleasant side effects if the bond broke.

"I need your help saving Kayla again."

Tyler shook his head. As much as he wanted to tell King Jack what the plan was to capture his daughter, he was selfishly holding back, and would lie directly to his face if he had to. He didn't like the part of the plan where Kayla got hurt, but Tyler did like the idea of her being back in Vankerdale where he could talk her into saving his dragon from being possessed. That part of the plan was very appealing. Try as Jack might, Tyler was all for the second round of kidnapping.

"Pyro found out that you have access to King Peyton's library. I've searched through everything in Aralot as best I could, and I can't find anything to help with Kayla's nightmares. You know how bad they can get. She screams all the time and can hardly sleep. It's a magical pressure that hits her specifically. I can't seem to find the right condition to stop it. Valiant can't either. He's been swallowing her curses that get reapplied to her daily. He's take off things like the curse that makes her seasick, and the curse that prevents her from leaving Aralot, and the one where she can't hear that she's the princess, but even he can't touch this sleeping curse. She still screams in her sleep. It can't be the same thing as the others so I would like you to look into it."

Well, this was somewhat good news. Jack wasn't thinking about the border issues at all. He was thinking about dreams. Tyler wouldn't have to lie to him.

"What's in it for me?" Tyler questioned.

This was sounding like a lot of grunt work, searching through random books that might deal with sleeping issues. He had problems of his own that he needed to work through. He needed to get Prince Evan to release him from the castle. He wanted to go see his family and all the childhood friends he had lost contact with. He wanted to see his older brother Narl who had managed to get released.

"I will let you stay a keeper," Jack said holding up his hand where a new magical ring sat on his finger. Tyler's insides turned cold. Jack wasn't going to kill him. No, he was going to crush his brain and submit Tyler to torture if he refused. If he thought that hearing a dragon while being unbonded would turn him crazy, he most definitely would go loopy if his brain stopped being a keeper. It wasn't supposed to be possible to change the condition, but since Pyro had found the way to create the keeper connection, he would have also learned how to take it away. This was dark indeed. No one knew what mental unbalances would come from breaking a keeper spell.

Jack's hand was still in the air with the new ring. He had lost his wedding ring to SilverWings when he had been captured the first time. Seeing the king without it reminded Tyler of that. King Peyton had buried Jack's ring someplace in the castle after stealing all the magic from it. Tyler should probably find it and give it back, but only after he took care of this threat that was causing the dragon in his head uncensored terror.

"Don't let him take you away from me Tyler! Please! You can't be that heartless and cast me aside, breaking my brain apart even more than it already is. I'll come find you if you do this. I'll tear you apart! I know where you live. I know where your family lives. I know what you most care about."

"Be quiet," Tyler demanded, rubbing at his temples. His head was starting to throb from all the shouting. There was a benefit to kicking the dragon out. It wouldn't be so loud.

"I will whisper then. I'm crying so hard right now I can hardly stand up. Don't leave me, Tyler. Please! You're my only friend!"

Pg. 64

Gee, his dragon was being a super needy and the animal's desperate desires were starting to get to him. Tyler was feeling like crying too, even though he was trying to hold it all back. It was still really hard to hold multiple conversations. What did he need to say to Jack?

"That you will look for the source of Kayla's nightmares," the night terror whispered to him.

"That's really mean," Tyler said instead. It wasn't anything he would ever say to King Peyton's face, but Jack went by his first name and hadn't come off as so cruel before.

"Sorry," Jack shrugged at him. "I didn't come prepared with anything to trade you in return so you got what you got. Come on, Tyler. I need your help. Do you want to trade services? What do you want?"

Tyler got his breath back. Jack wasn't really going to blow his brain apart. Knowing that made standing before him less frightening, although still plenty scary because now Tyler knew what he could do. What Tyler really wanted to ask Jack for he didn't think the dragon would let him say. He had Jack right in front of him. He could ask him how to locate stolen possessed dragon scales. He could ask him to search for the person who was doing this to his dragon. The dragon decided to flood Tyler's thoughts with Tyler's name repeatedly to distract him from the direction his mind was taking.

"I can't concentrate right now. Can I put your question on hold? I'll get back to you on the trade."

"And in the meantime, you'll search for a magical pressure that avoids removal by spellbinding dragons. It's got to be something ancient if I can't find the answer in Aralot. All of our stuff came from Vankerdale from way back before the two kingdoms split. The answer could be here. Thanks for looking, Tyler."

"Sure," Tyler mumbled. Jack put his ear to the door before he stepped out and disappeared.

"I love you," the dragon hummed into his head. Tyler looked down at the list in his hand that talked about keepers and tore it in half. They were brilliant, but they sure came with a ton of problems.

Opponent

Tristan

"You're late," Queen Aria scolded her son briefly, glancing at his brown hair and brown sideburns. The queen's own brown hair was braided today into a side knot. It was simple yet so elegant that she looked beautiful. Tristan smiled back at her tersely. He knew how late he was. It was inevitable, but his mother wouldn't see it that way. Tristan had been battling Vankerdale dragons, not anything that he would ever tell his parents, because he had to make sure that Kayla had not tampered with his magical spells while she had been captured there.

It had been a rough decision to go over the border thereby breaking his bond to Riven. Even if he had performed the spell to fix that broken bond as soon as they got back into Aralot, Tristan had still agonized over the decision to cross over. It was not easy to have his head pound at him, but he thought it was necessary to see if Kayla had destroyed his spells and was turning on him before he realized she was. Tristan had a few particular cursed items that he kept close to one of Vankerdale's portals.

There was that rock that kept Kayla from hearing that she could come to overtake the throne, the dragon carving that prevented Rosa and Tia and Kayla from being able to have any children. There was the piece of sea glass that made Kayla sick if she got more than ankle deep in the ocean. She had never learned how to swim because of it, but she also couldn't escape Tristan by going overseas into Wisteria to group an army against him.

Anything she was going to throw at him would have to be done on the home front and in his face. At least that's how it was supposed to go. Instead, all his spells had failed at the same time. Kayla had been taken into Vankerdale last week. She had heard that she was the princess and therefore would inherit the throne. She had crossed over a river. She was too young to worry about having any kids and she had never dated anyone else but him, so there was that.

The conditional objects were kept inside of Vankerdale so that Jack couldn't find the items to take the spells off his daughter. Tristan had taken the first available opportunity to check on his spells to make sure that Kayla had not found them when she was there. She hadn't. Everything was intact in Vankerdale except for Riven who had suffered some rather nasty rips in his wings breaking through those guard dragons that had been in the way of Tristan looking around. Tristan had healed his dragon before returning so no one knew what he had been getting into. Then he had healed their broken bond ever so grateful that Jack had looked up the spell for this ages ago so that Tristan could use it now. It was most aggravating that Kayla hadn't found his spells when they weren't working on her and he had broken his head to verify that. It really had to be that dragon of hers that was getting in the way.

"Sorry for the tardiness," Tristan replied to his mother as he sat down at the table. He made a quick note that his fork was missing and his mother never let him eat with his hands. He looked back up at Aria wondering what her reason was for taking his fork.

The last time he had anything more than a bag of nuts to eat had been on his date with Kayla so he was starving. The date went pretty much how he expected except for running into Ritz. Ritz had been following him around lately, holding knives to his head, suggesting that Tristan was stupid and needed the Brixtons to save him. Then there was that thing he said to Kayla right after he slapped her. She was not to go searching for love because she had all the love she needed.

Yeah, Tristan knew what Ritz was getting at. He was telling Kayla to slough him off, shove him under and bury him in the war with Vankerdale before she lost her grip on the throne. Vankerdale had something she needed, he'd said. Well, of course it did! It had given her a spellbinding dragon which was plenty powerful on its own. It was now giving her an excuse to turn against her parents as everyone else had been doing lately so they could fight King Peyton for his offenses. The neighboring king had held their king hostage for three months and not sent a single message about it. He'd kidnapped Kayla and the message about that had arrived rather late. It demanded that Vankerdale be released from their curse or Kayla would never be released alive. Oh, and they wanted an ice dragon.

Tristan shook his head on the thought. That was the one type of dragon Vankerdale had never been able to steal. Aralot was still struggling to produce an ice dragon too after Vladimir had suddenly died taking his knowledge of how to produce a magical dragon to the grave with him. That man had been incredible. It was a shame that SilverWings killed him.

"You are paying no attention. We have an important topic to discuss tonight." Aria cut back into Tristan's thoughts. He glanced over at his dad who looked just as impatient to eat as Tristan felt.

"Sorry, Mom," Tristan answered.

"You finished reading the changes to the trade laws in Wisteria?" King Klavian asked hopefully. He rolled his strong shoulders and straightened his sturdy spine. Then he grabbed for the fork by his side and twirled it with an even greater hopeful expression.

"No. Kayla asked me to train her to be a noble."

Tristan wiped at his eyes and avoided looking at Vermelo, who was conveniently standing off to the side of the room as if he wanted to hear everything that they said tonight. Vermelo had been leaving Tristan death threats in the form of notes and actual physical traps in his room that could kill him. He had been trying to dethrone the king and queen, so King Klavian had given Tristan a spell to cast on the man that made him loyal to them. They were probably safe to talk about Kayla when he was around now, but it still felt uncomfortable. Tristan felt the Captain of the Guard's presence larger than normal whenever discussing Kayla. Tristan looked at King Klavian who gave him a brief glance before urging Aria to continue by putting his fork down.

"Her reasoning was sound. She doesn't want to ruin Aralot with stupidity now that she knows what she is. She didn't want King Peyton using her."

"No one likes the idea of King Peyton using her. I think it's a good idea," Klavian expressed. "Did you agree?"

"Yes. I also talked her into training Valiant at Charles's Ware. She will be right under our noses all day long. She was way too hidden before."

"They don't allow gray sweaters on the training field," Tristan agreed. It had been really strange seeing her in a dress on the date away from the sweater. She had been rather clumsy without it, and he bet that she had plowed back inside her comfort the first chance she got to hide her face. Aria looked at Tristan to catch his expression. Visible was right where he liked Kayla to be too. He wanted to know where she was so any threat toward them would be spotted before it took off.

"Do I detect conspiracy?" Klavian asked his family. "Kayla is not an overly ambitious child. She's not mounting an army against us."

He was getting right to the heart of it in front of Vermelo. She might not have an army yet, but she could start one. It was still very unclear what she aspired toward with her life. She was lacking in goals, and Tristan didn't need her picking up the one that called her to kill all the Clusters. Tristan gave his mother a small smile. She had a better brain when it came to the Brixton family. She at least considered that threats could spring up at any time. It was best to not leave the kingdom exposed by failing to prepare.

"You're to be nice to her, Tristan," Aria pointedly told him. She told him this too much. He wasn't exactly horrible to her. It wasn't like he slapped her in the face as Ritz did.

"I am nice to her. All the time."

"You insult her the first chance you get. Shall we recap? You told her that she had a nice dress more of a way to pick on her for wearing one than anything else. You commented on the sauce hinting that she was dry and boring and not saucy."

"Well, she is!" Tristan cried out, wishing that everyone else was out of the room. Where had his mother been during his date? Where? She had been spying on him!

"The sky was looking gray like her favorite color."

"That is her favorite color, Mom."

"You told her not to disturb you while you ate."

"I was hungry."

"Just like you are hungry right now. Apparently, you can't hold a conversation while you eat."

Ah. He understood the reason for his missing fork now. This was to punish him for not enchanting Kayla to fall in love with him on their first date.

"You guys are so unfair. You got to marry who you loved."

"Only after securing the kingdom first," Aria reminded.

"So you're the only one that ever gets a happy ending around here?"

"We worked at it, Tristan," Aria snapped back. Tristan looked at his dad who was remaining suspiciously silent as if he had things to say but didn't want to add to the building contention in the room.

"You didn't even try," his mother continued. "Tia told me that Kayla came home and threw things at the walls, calling the whole thing a disaster. You had better try next time. While you're at it, find out why Kayla thinks Ritz cares about her."

"Because he does, and she's not stupid so she's noticed," Tristan answered.

Great. Now they were talking about Ritz. He had hoped that his mother hadn't seen that part. She'd better not have a comment for him demanding that he stand up to Ritz for Kayla. No one stood up to Ritz and lived for long, not even people who had magic.

"Why? What does he want to use her for?"

Tristan shrugged at his mother. Ritz wanted her for something, probably to control some part of the kingdom that he couldn't reach. Maybe he wanted a good word with the girl so the Colts would stay safe during her reign, since she couldn't become a Colt to be under his thumb, unlike the rest of the current ruling household where Aria, Tristan, and Jack all claimed to be Colts.

"Well, find out. Kayla is your responsibility."

Tristan crossed his arms and that's when he felt it. The gem that warned him that there was an intruder inside his spell room here in the castle was growing warm. Instead of wearing a ring of power like Jack did, or a keychain like Kayla, or a broach, pen, and shoe clip like his dad, Tristan kept his magic in gems sown into little pockets all over his clothes. His seamstress wasn't a fan when he asked for new shirts, but they paid her, so what could she do? The gem that was activating right now was located on the back of his left shoulder.

Who was getting into his room? The doorway had four different spells that blocked entry. A soft warmth indicated that someone was trying to open the door. He was already past that. Someone had already taken down spell number one. Or four. It wasn't clear which one the person was tampering with. It couldn't be his dad entering the place because he was at the dinner table. It wasn't Vermelo, who always claimed to not use magic even though he did, and it wasn't his mother, who claimed the same thing. The servants were not allowed to enter, and they couldn't get inside anyway. Jack had gone into the room a time or two so it could be him. It could be Tia, but usually, the king and queen entering the building were announced because they never showed up without an agenda to discuss with Klavian or Vermelo. Someone was in his room.

"Sorry to eat and run," Tristan griped at his mother for messing up his dinner and then ran from the room down the hallway. He kept his spell room on the west side so that it was farther away from where Vermelo ventured. The downside to that was it was also farther away from him when he needed to reach it really really fast. The gem on his shoulder got warmer. Another spell down. He had to hurry up! Whoever was trying to break in knew exactly how to do so.

He skid down the hallway crashing into a few guards that were changing their posts. Change time. That was a perfect moment for anyone to find an empty slot to slip between everyone. Normally the people who tried to sneak around during a moment like this were Colts. Tristan didn't apologize at all as he shoved away from the guards and tried to pick up his pace.

"You forgot a possibility in your thoughts. Don't sprain yourself," Riven said.

"Don't make me guess," Tristan complained. He normally loved to figure things out on his own even if his dragon could tell him the answer that he was missing, but when a person was breaking and entering into a sensitive room, he didn't want mistakes.

"After picking a bunch of random herbs, Kayla snuck out of the ware half an hour ago. She went toward the castle."

Horrible. How did Kayla even know where his spell room was? She was never here. She came to the castle once a year as far as he knew, and she spent the time standing around looking bored as she had on her birthday. At least that's what he thought. Vermelo could have hidden her stopping by at other times. Blast that guy!

Tristan tried to speed up only he was already going as fast as he could go and he tripped over his own feet, stumbling a few steps as he caught his balance again. The gem on his arm got warmer again. Three down. One more spell to go. Kayla was tearing through his spells like they were nothing!

This wasn't fair. He had never watched her use magic because she used it inside the safety of her house where no magical spying device could see. Vermelo kept the magical spying mirror in the game room, but if anyone tried to see inside the Brixton home with the mirror it told them to mind their own business. Kayla didn't use magic otherwise. She typically reserved it for emergencies. At least she had before. She kept revealing that she was indeed going to be a tough opponent, and she was only going to get worse once she got that noble training from his mother. His mother would do a fantastic job. She would train Kayla to be a queen. Pretty soon Kayla would be spouting lines around him and driving him in circles.

Tristan reached the room, noticed the closed door, and flung it open since he knew all his spells were already down. There was no one in sight, but that didn't fool him. He also knew of a spell that would conceal a person from view assuming they could keep moving, even if it was slight movement. Tristan shut the door behind him and raised up his hand to sweep the room with immobilization. He didn't get much time to cast a spell because one was already coming at him, and he had to laugh despite himself, when it was the same spell he was just about to use on Kayla. He had all those protection spells set up to keep him safe from Vermelo and others, and he had still stumbled into a fix.

Tristan was pushed to the wall of the room where he couldn't move at all. Kayla casting her spell caused her to stop moving for a second so she flashed into view before she winked out again. He wanted to scream at his opponent. It was alarming how quickly she had gotten him. He should have guessed that she was antsy already from breaking in and been faster than her. Now he had to figure out how to get out of his own room. What if Kayla left him like this? It would be days before anyone came around to check for him.

"Don't be silly," Riven told him. "I'd send someone to tell your dad that you're stuck so he can free you. However, I doubt Kayla will leave you like that."

He didn't want his father to come free him. The embarrassment! And it came at the hands of Kayla no less. Tristan wasn't going to explain this to his dad. He'd get out of this himself. He would figure out what Kayla was really up to, and why she felt the desire to be in here with these particular plants. She couldn't have changed too much in the one week she was in Vankerdale. She claimed a dragon, sure, but it was ingrained in her to only use magic as a last resort. What was her desperate desire? It probably was not him.

"Don't make me fight you," Kayla whined as she slowly moved around the room. "I had to immobilize Prince Evan before, and this is bringing back unpleasant memories. I need to borrow an emerald bowl. Yours was the closest one I could think of if only I could find it."

Now that Tristan didn't have anything to do apart from use his eyes, which could oddly still move, he glanced to the table where he saw that pile of herbs Riven had mentioned. Kayla had found his silver knife and put that beside a chopping board. She gave out a dramatic sigh and took down her invisible spell. Her hands were covered in gloves as if she was trying to hide her fingerprints from Tristan's detection. He frowned at her and then realized that she hadn't forced him to be as trapped as he had expected. He couldn't call up any magic to free himself when he tried it, but his entire head could still move, which meant that his mouth could too.

"Get out, Kayla."

He didn't care what is mom had just told him. Being nice to this girl didn't mean that she messed up his spells or got into his spell room. Had it even been hard for her to break in, or had she found the whole thing to be fun and amusing? From the look on her face (she was never good at hiding her expressions without a hood pulled over), she was struggling with what to say to him.

"Tristan, this is important. I'm starving."

"Me too," he told her. "You interrupted my dinner."

She shrugged at him like that wasn't important and kept talking over him as she rummaged through the room looking for that emerald bowl. She was touching everything with her little prying fingers.

"I joined a ware. Why I didn't think of this before I joined a ware, I'll never know."

"Think of what?" Tristan asked, trying to keep his voice level so that she'd spill her secrets. He knew he was hoping too much when she found what she wanted and didn't answer him.

Kayla dumped out a set of beetles that he had collected. He'd put those inside what looked like a wooden bowl to conceal what was inside the cover. Once the bugs were out, anyone could see that the wood hid the real emerald bowl inside. Emerald was the only mineral that didn't absorb any magic. This was the exact bowl he always used, and it bothered him that Kayla was touching it.

"What are you doing?" he demanded to know, failing to keep his annoyance in check.

"I need to cast a spell. The long-lasting sort. I'm going to have to make it up. I can't cast my spell in the ware, and I don't have the time to fly all the way home. I'm so hungry! I didn't eat lunch or dinner."

"I guess you'd fail if you ever tried to diet."

Kayla gave him a glare for that and started chopping up the plants. She was very careful to not let any of them touch each other, and each time she moved to a new plant, she used a spell to clean her gloves. Really, what was she doing? As frustrated as he was, this was going to be interesting. Watching her cast a spell would tell him a lot. He would better be able to defeat his foe if he knew how she operated long before she ever came against him.

"I'm nervous over your curiosity," Riven admitted. *"This could be a spell to put on you."*

"I don't think so," Tristan replied.

Kayla was into hiding her emotions, and she didn't have her hood up right now. She couldn't be here to do anything that made her feel like cowering. Harming him would make the rulers of Aralot angry at her, so Tristan was completely out. What she was up to was making her feel bold enough to experiment with magic.

"Who are you putting this spell on?" Tristan asked, surprised that she even let him keep talking. Maybe it was because she was feeling nervous excitement, or perhaps she was too mentally distracted to care, but Tristan had to admit that Kayla was being surprisingly easy on him. If he broke into her room to use her stuff and she showed up, she'd already be knocked unconscious.

"Myself," Kayla answered." What do you know about Charles? Can I have a gem please?"

He felt his arm free up. Ah. That was the reason why she wanted him conscious. She was going to use him. He yanked his arm away from the wall and tried to bring magic up to his hand partly surprised that he could. He held a spell that would knock her out on his hand, but ended up not using it. She was putting the spell on herself. It was a protection spell of some sort then, and he couldn't hurt her for that. He tossed a gem at her.

"A good gem, Tristan." Kayla rolled her eyes at him as she looked at the one he had selected. "And I need it small. Small and dark. Something that can hold a made-up spell. If you don't give me something good, I'll go ask Vermelo for one, and he might think you did something to aggravate to me to deserve being stuck to the wall."

Tristan's teeth ground together along with his eyes. She knew how to get right at him, didn't she? He hated Vermelo getting close to this room, and he didn't need anyone knowing that she had gotten the upper hand in this, especially not Vermelo even if he was under that loyalty spell.

"Small. Dark in color. Charles," Kayla prompted when he offered no words except to glare at her.

"Charles is old," Tristan answered.

Kayla shook her head at him. "He brought me lunch today because I was testing. I nearly ate it...." Kayla trailed off. "So I can't eat until I've gotten this right. I still need a gem."

This was aggravating. How did Charles bringing her food make Kayla want to cast a spell on herself? Charles wasn't anything special at all. He had gotten the job of ware leader by default for being so old. He had outlived his wife and one of his sons. He had two more sons and one daughter. They lived two cities over in Salka. Charles really liked meatloaf. He wasn't that complicated.

Tristan glanced at the pile of plants Kayla was still chopping up. It was a collection of things that grew all over the place close to the castle. Something about this exact combination was important. Tristan blinked in surprise as the answer came to him.

Keeper poison! Kayla's mother had been poisoned by a new ware leader bringing her food. Kayla was scared of the same thing happening to her. Tristan knew that keeper poison was a collection of plants, but no one had told him which ones. That was a guarded secret known only to Vermelo, Anvil, Rogan, Tia, and Jack. Of course, Kayla knew it too. Kayla had just made keeper poison right in front of him. She had only broken into his room to prevent herself from becoming infected, which was indeed an emergency situation. If she ever ate these plants, the mental links in her brain would start to deteriorate her bond to her dragon. She would fight with Valiant until she killed him off, slashing down against half of her own soul. Tristan could sympathize with that. Everything about infected keepers was terrifying. He would never be able to bounce back on his feet if he ever killed off Riven. It had to hurt. Hurt and rip. It would be the deepest mental, physical, and spiritual torture that anyone could ever inflict.

"Here."

He dug around in his clothes to select a better gem. It was moments like this that he appreciated how he horded gems around his body so he was never without quick magic or perfectly cut gems. Despite being pinned to the wall, he would always have the upper hand over Kayla. Her magical keychain would run out of power eventually, and he would still have some.

"Thanks." Kayla picked up the gem without meeting his eyes and then looked back at the plants. "I think if I experiment a little and make it so that I can't eat this...."

That confirmed his guess, alright. She got to work. She cast a few spells, brought a spoonful up toward her mouth and shivered away from it to cast more spells when it nearly touched her lips. More spells, more experimentation until the spoon vibrated on her hand warning her not to eat the poison. She kept going. She mixed the poison into a cup and nearly drank it, panicking when the moisture must have brushed her lips.

To be on the safe side, she yanked out a different composition of herbs and rubbed that on her mouth next. It was probably the antidote. Funny how Tristan knew the curse but not the cure now. He didn't ask for it though. He kept watching until Kayla got her spells the way she wanted them to be. The spoon shook long before it got close to going into her mouth. The cup glowed a bright orange before she could drink it. She pulled some bread out of her rider's bag that she must have previously packed and shoved the poison in that next to test. She didn't finish until there was no possible way she could get keeper poison into her mouth.

She attached the gem with the spell to an anklet, and shoved the whole thing down inside her right boot where she wouldn't ever lose it.

"You are making me so hungry," Tristan admitted.

"Here," Kayla pulled out a package from her bag that her mother must have made and gave him the whole thing. "It's scones. A little old, but still tasty."

Tristan took the scones and found himself giving Kayla a genuine smile. She wasn't so bad. She'd swap back insults at him, even start him off, but she'd still give him everything she had. In that regard, she was like her dad. Jack would turn against his own feelings to save everyone around him in a heartbeat. Tristan had never seen that before about Kayla.

"Are you still stuck to the wall?" Riven wanted to know.

"Yes," Tristan replied.

"I'm going to growl at her."

Kayla didn't let him off the wall until she had finished cleaning up everything. She even put his beetles back in the bowl although she used a spell and stood well out of the way as if she found them more disgusting than the poison she had been next to all night. Tristan didn't say anything to her when she let him out her spell. The reason for that was because he was conflicted. He didn't think that Kayla would do anything to harm him as long as she had no reason to. He wasn't sure where her line was that would tip her into casting things at him that would actually hurt. Her spell knowledge was vast enough to hurt him, even strong enough to make up something horrible. Kayla was scary.

"What are the odds?" Kayla asked him with a smile as she reached for the door and opened it up. She peeked out the door and shook her head at the sight of a few guards standing around that would no doubt tell Vermelo that both of them had been inside the magic room and snuck past them to get there.

"Only six of you?" Kayla asked the soldiers. "And I was in a room alone with Tristan. Imagine that. Got to keep an eye on him. He's got sideburns. Totally criminal."

"You probably have warts someplace," Tristan glared at her for insulting him right when he'd dropped his guard around her. See!? She did it first all the time!

Kayla glanced over her shoulder to laugh at him, and she kept laughing as she walked serenely out of the castle. Tristan followed her so he could get away from all the prying eyes. They reached the courtyard where Riven growled at her.

Kayla didn't give Riven any recognition. She walked past him as if he wasn't there, which made him growl more and howl for her to come back so he could complain to her. It was rather laughable, because Kayla was always like that. Tristan kept waiting for her to pull up her hood. Her having it down irked him. She could not be feeling bold still. If she was bold, she was capable of anything. Kayla didn't touch the gray hood until she had exited the castle grounds. Only then did she yank the hood up and run. Tristan jumped on Riven unable to let her go that easily.

"Did you see that? What are we going to do with her?" Tristan asked his dragon.

"*Congratulate her for stopping herself from killing dragons?*" Riven asked back.

"That bold streak, Riven. She can be unpredictable."

"*In a rather predictable way,*" Riven laughed at him. "*You'll stay ahead of her.*"

To prove his point, Riven landed Tristan inside the ware right where they could see Valiant long before Kayla reached him. She had to sneak around the night scouts to break out and get back in. Tristan didn't have to worry about that. He had graduated and then decided that the ware didn't have time limits placed on him anymore. Charles couldn't force him back to ware. Kayla, however, was supposed to be in bed. For that matter, she was supposed to be wearing leather and not her hood. How was he going to know when she wanted to hide if she couldn't pull that hood?

"What do you think? It could be worse right?" Kayla asked when she reached Valiant. Tristan couldn't see her at all since she has adopted the invisible spell again to sneak around. He could hear her only because Riven was close enough.

"Do you think Charles has gotten over his old fears of keepers? I'm probably overreacting."

Tristan would do no different if he was her. He'd have overreacted to the threat of keeper poison long before now, even if he didn't have a dragon. Knowing there was something that could turn him into a demon that destroyed everything he himself most loved would have him burning all those plants Kayla had pulled from the ground tonight.

Valiant hummed at her as his reaction. Tristan examined Valiant closer. Moonlight looked good on the dragon. The silver on his wingtips glowed even if his wings were tucked down. His gray coloring suddenly looked a deeper blue tonight. Kayla might not be too bad, but her dragon was horrible news. He was going to know all the spells that Kayla knew, and he wouldn't share her restraint in casting them. They didn't know too much about spellbinding dragons. Every spy they sent into Wisteria lately hadn't come back. It was starting to scare his parents, but it hadn't stopped his mom from sending more people over.

"Spy on that dragon," Tristan ordered Riven.

The dragon was already responsible for blocking Tristan's spells that used to work on Kayla. Tristan's spells had been intact until Valiant showed up. If anything was going to come at them from an unknown location, it was going to be because of this beast.

Valiant blew at Kayla taking away her invisibility and her hood. It blew backward revealing her red-brown hair tied up in a ponytail. Yes, he did know spells. He was far more frightening than Kayla. She shoved the hood back over her head.

"No! It's going to be horrible not being able to wear this! I have to wear red leather. Do you know how bright that is? It's the brightest ware color possible. I've not worn red since... I was not ten. I didn't wear red at... that doesn't count."

Valiant blew the hood off again and Kayla lunged at him, wrapping her arms around his face trying to cover his mouth so he couldn't mess up her hood. He bowed his head so she slipped off and she giggled at him before lunging again. She pulled the hood back up right as Valiant used his tail to shove her over. He misted her with a spell and Kayla burst into more giggles. She tried to pull the hood off but Valiant had made it stuck on her. Tristan did his best not to blink. Valiant had already frozen the entire town around them once. He knew advanced spells and that wouldn't make finding a weakness in him easy.

"I'll get in trouble if it can't come off," Kayla laughed, tugging on her hood. She started to climb all over Valiant pretending to tickle him while he hummed at her and knocked her over with his tail like he was swatting away an eager puppy. Tristan munched on an old scone and found himself laughing when Kayla made Valiant's tail get stuck to the ground. She wouldn't let it move until he let her hood move again.

"I think this is the first night that Kayla has ever amused you," Riven

informed him.

"She'll still be a shadow no matter what she wears. She will be even more dangerous after this."

"Not if you get her to like you. She will give up her control just like Tia did for Klavian. Prove to her that you can do what she can't."

Showing her up would only make her say mean things to him. Besides, Tia hadn't always liked Klavian. Tristan asked her about it once. Tia gave up control because she wanted to be with her dragons and not live in the castle. Kayla wasn't like that. She could ignore wounded dragons. As far as Tristan knew, he'd never heard Kayla say anything about not liking the castle.

She wasn't going to follow after her mother. There wasn't another dragon that she responded to except for Valiant. Watching her play with him was fascinating, similar to the way watching Tia play with her dragons could hold people captive for hours. Tia always gave others new ways to engage. Due to that, the night scouts of the dragons were not screaming at Kayla to go to bed yet. None of them had watched a person play with magic like this before.

Valiant blew Kayla into the air. She turned his air into a rock and scaled back down. He changed her clothes to be all green. She turned his scales into a rainbow. Valiant's dragon voice suddenly became a full orchestra. Kayla stole his voice and started singing the song for him until he rolled over laughing. Then she set everything right, gave him a hug goodnight, and left him with a challenge to fix the moon. She laughed herself all the way to her bunkroom. Tristan looked up to the moon to see why. Somehow the moon had the image of a sheep on it. A challenge indeed. Was the image something that could only be seen from inside the ware? Did it last for only a certain amount of time? Did Valiant see something different?

Valiant was staring upward with his head tilted to the side trying to puzzle out what Kayla might have cast as if he didn't know either when he could hear her thoughts in his head. She must not have thought too hard about it. It was probably harmless. Kayla came off that way, but then again, her mother had started that way too. Tristan couldn't lower his guard for an instant. His mother was right. His father had spent every waking hour for a few weeks straight around Tia and Jack sorting through their reactions so he could push them where he wanted them. Tristan would have to do the same. He needed to know Kayla and Valiant way better than he did.

Breakfast

Caleb

What had started out as a reason to hate his life, had suddenly turned into the largest unforeseen blessing. He never would have imagined this. Watching Kayla step into the ware leader office and then *look at him* had felt like someone had taken one of those large frozen magic orbs, plopped it in his hands, and told him he could make any wish he wanted in the entire world. This was magic. Beautiful magic.

It only got better. She had talked to him, which made Caleb want to kick himself. She had no problem with talking to people. He could have broken through her defenses long before now. If only he had sat down beside her at lunch away from all the dragons (who cared if he was eating at the wrong table), and asked her how her day was going, she may have looked at him ten years ago. He felt so stupid for never trying it out.

Her hood was still up in the office, but not pulled down, and she had been laughing about influencing Queen Aria. That was an expression that Caleb had drawn over and over again last night before going to bed. It must have been gratifying growing up around all those rulers and realizing that she was just as brilliant as they were.

The one thing she hadn't been so exuberant over was the reason she had come to the ware. Kayla had a dragon. He hadn't heard the news before Kayla mentioned it herself, but it nearly had him grabbing at her and holding her in close to protect her from the one thing she had never been able to face. He might have done just that if she hadn't been so calm about it.

Warner had told him about Valiant when he spotted the animal. Spellbinding dragon. Shy, nervous, looked easily spooked. The other dragons were being as careful as they could be around him since the older ones had seen how deadly SilverWings could be. Still, it hadn't stopped a few of the older dragons from calling out to Kayla anyway. Caleb wasn't surprised. He thought she was incredible too; although, he still wasn't sure about the dragon.

What was it about a spellbinding dragon that had finally gotten Kayla's attention? He hoped it wasn't a spell because she was cursed with too many of those as it was. It was in her blood to attract the exquisitely rare animal. Her mother had an ice dragon, and her aunt had a water dragon. Her father had a dragon king. Valiant felt scarier than all of them.

Caleb had been itching to hear Kayla's story about Valiant, but he had decided not to ask her directly. He'd asked one of the other section leaders if they knew. Apparently, they had all seen Valiant before. He'd frozen the nearby city of Troni in time, kidnapped Kayla into Vankerdale, and then brought her back along with her father who had been missing. This was the sort of thing that Anvil would have announced to the entire ware over breakfast. The king was back safe and sound. Caleb had missed it all because he had been flying over here thinking his life was punished.

Now he was loving his life, although still wary of that dragon. He was her section leader which was one step above teacher and a few steps above riders, but he had found a way to bypass the feeling of unreachable. He was going to teach her class himself because he had no idea who to promote to the level of teacher, and he didn't want to put anyone else there anyway. Caleb was looking at hours and hours of getting Kayla's attention. Nothing could be better. He still didn't know very many people around him, but having Kayla nearby took away all that loneliness. He didn't feel lost. He didn't dread waking up. He felt like a large chip on his shoulder had been taken off. He could just fly right now into the clouds straight up.

"You took Kayla," Charles said, stepping up behind Caleb as he left his bunkroom the next day to head to breakfast. Caleb had wondered when he would get a visit like this. He'd been section leader for only a day and was already undermining his ware leader's decisions to take on a rider. However, he didn't care. He was going to fight for this. If Charles was Anvil, his words would be a rebuke. Actually, Anvil would never have let Caleb take her in the first place. Caleb had told Kayla that it was better over here for her where she could get a fresh start, and he was thinking it was better for him too. Kayla was listed on his rider profile over and over again and not in a good way. He had to convince Charles to let him have his way.

"It won't be a problem, sir. I swear that I'll put my personal—"

"No need, Caleb. I didn't come to sensor you. I want to thank you for volunteering to take her. As you know, Anvil has this theory that there have to be five keepers alive to satisfy some ancient magical law. While Tia was the first female keeper, her sister Rosa is one too. With their father, Herb, gone, the magic was unsatisfied and Kayla was born in the very month she was conceived. No one was ready for her birth. It nearly killed her mother. Magic pushes on keepers harder than anything else. Given the circumstances of Kayla's birth, everyone believes her to be a keeper born to keep some balance with the law. Anvil is certain that there are two hiding keepers still among us.

Pg. 89

"Anyway, the magic is still unstable despite the wonderful things Jack has done to restore balance after King Gladius. You be careful with that girl and her magical dragon. When keepers take dragons, it means something big is coming. It takes brave people like you to handle it. Not many would have done so."

"Thank you, sir."

This was by far easier taking on Kayla at the King's Ware than at Anvil's. Charles had decided to not fight him at all. If Caleb had tried this at Anvil's, he'd be in so many fights Anvil might decide to unbond him from his dragon and cast him from the kingdom. Caleb had heard the reasoning behind Kayla being a keeper, but not the reasoning for why she was born early. Anvil made a point of holding a yearly meeting to remind everyone about the history of keepers. He'd never said that Kayla needed to fulfill magical rules.

He had also never mentioned to the entire ware that there needed to be five keepers, or that they didn't take on dragons until some large event was going to take place. Knowing that, Caleb could picture all the ware leaders preparing their riders with a renewed vigor. They needed to be ready for anything because Kayla had a dragon, even if she didn't look fully ready to take one on. Caleb had heard it mentioned that magic worked on keepers differently than normal people. There was a large shoving pressure of magic attacking Kayla, and Caleb felt it his job to get her ready to handle whatever it was that she needed to do. He wasn't going to let her down.

"Mulligan and I approved your class list," Charles mentioned. "That's a good group, especially for a dragon like Valiant who doesn't have any manners."

"Thanks," Caleb said again, not sure exactly who was on the class list. He had let Warner pick all the names that he submitted and he didn't connect the names to faces yet. Warner was the one who should get credit for putting Kayla in an appropriate class. It looked like Caleb would need to talk with his dragon to find out what had been going on while he had been lost in fantasies drawing Kayla's face all night.

"The comment about manners needs your attention right now. I've tried everything but he's growling at me. Valiant is stealing food. The red dragon he's taking it from is ready to flame Valiant's wings," Warner told him.

"See you later, Charles," Caleb said, and without waiting for the ware leader to dismiss him, he ran toward the field where he picked up on the commotion right away.

Valiant was standing on top of a dead animal that must have been the catch of the red dragon over his head because the dragon was indeed gearing up to flame him for stealing his food. The only thing holding him back was the mandate to not flame inside the ware. It probably wouldn't stop the beast for long because the reason for that rule was so that dragons didn't accidentally flame other people's riders. The riders had cleared the field, but there were a few of them screaming about the theft too. Warner was trying to get Valiant to back away from the food probably telling him that stealing wasn't what they did in Aralot.

Caleb looked over Valiant now that the dragon wasn't slinking behind him. He was particularly interested in his stomach. Caleb could tell when an ice dragon was churning up ice and when a water dragon was gearing up to shoot a geyser by the shape of the lower part of their stomach. That part looked full, so Valiant probably had magic to shoot if he was anything like other magical dragons. However, his belly above the magic was rather slim. He was undoubtedly hungry.

"What have you tried so far?" Caleb asked Warner as he continued to run toward the scene with the intent of getting in the way so that the red dragon overhead didn't let his flame out. It was risky, especially since he had no idea who the red dragon was or how patient the creature could

be, but Caleb's job was to make sure that Valiant didn't start casting spells, and that would only happen if the dragon didn't get attacked. He also had to get Valiant away from that food without him eating any of it.

Move a starving spellbinding dragon. There was no training anywhere that told him how to do this. This wasn't something he would ever try against Sparkle or Pewter or Pyro. When rare dragons claimed things, they really claimed things. They didn't let them go.

"I didn't try getting Kayla to tell him off," Warner replied.

"No," Caleb said out loud as he was joined by a rider that burst from the crowd to follow him close. The rider running with him had dark hair and a crease of worry on his face, but he looked congenial at first glance. Caleb had no idea who the rider was, but he didn't shoo the guy away.

"We are not involving Kayla. Her actions are not the same as her dragons. We need her accepting her friend not being mad at him. I think I have an idea."

"Good, because he's stealing from Cuprite," the rider beside him answered the words Caleb had said to his dragon.

"That's a type of rock isn't it?" Caleb asked, as he glanced at the rider at his side and made the connection that the guy was linked to the mad red dragon overhead. Caleb had never been one to collect rocks, but he knew that Kayla did, so he'd studied out rocks in the event that he ever got her to talk about them. The rider beside him shrugged and Caleb held him back as they got within spitting distance of Valiant. The dragon hadn't looked down to acknowledge them yet. He was too busy flashing his tail to tell Warner to go away and growling back at the dragon whose food he had stolen. That didn't mean that he wasn't paying attention though.

Stories indicated that spellbinding dragons bowed to people they accepted as friends. SilverWings had bowed to Tia before, although that never stopped him from trying to hurt her or kidnap her. Caleb tested out his skills as he bowed to Valiant. He winced when the dragon shot a spell at Cuprite that froze him in the air. He hissed at Warner and looked at Caleb with a snarl, apparently only wanting to keep two mobile enemies around him at a time.

"Morning," Caleb said. He had the dragon's attention so he bowed again trying to pass along the information that they were friends. "You look hungry. Can I help you with that? We don't steal from each other in Aralot. If you need someone to show you where the hunting grounds are, Warner can take you. You don't have to fight for food, Valiant."

"He doesn't know where to find food?" the rider beside him asked. At least he wasn't screaming. It sounded like the guy was trying to problem solve the situation too, which was a great start to Caleb's day. Rational riders. He liked the rational sort.

"No. He's from Vankerdale. What's your name?"

"Sherman. You're my new teacher."

Caleb nodded as if he knew this, but he really had no idea who Sherman was apart from the fact that he would be a level six rider. He still needed to get his class in order and figure out how he would juggle teaching with section leader duties. All the same, this meant that Valiant had strategically picked Cuprite to steal from because he had no doubt heard that they were going to be in the same class. This was sort of like picking on a sibling or other members of his new herd that might eventually forgive him. Caleb glanced upward at the still frozen dragon in the air and then back at Sherman. He was holding his whip, probably wanting to snap it to make Valiant back away, but the man was indeed very calm about all this otherwise. Sherman met Caleb's gaze and Caleb gave him a smile.

"You're doing great," Caleb let him know. "Valiant would you like Warner to show you where you can hunt or would you like Cuprite to do so?" Caleb tried again.

Valiant talked back to him, but he didn't know what he said. Whatever it was, it had Sherman lowering his hand on the whip as his dragon translated for him. Warner hadn't translated yet because he was busy responding to Valiant shoving the dragon's tail away from him with his own tail.

"That's dragon dung," Sherman muttered.

"Valiant says that King Peyton had him locked up and he doesn't know how to hunt," Warner told Caleb. *"I've offered to teach him. Thanks for the assistance. I can handle it from here."*

"Oh anytime. Try bowing," Caleb shrugged at his dragon as the brown-scaled animal gently pushed Valiant off the food he had tried to take. Warner and Valiant were both in the air before Cuprite was released from the spell. He landed on his food and tore through it before Valiant could come back to try to take it again.

"I thought it was instinctual that a dragon learns to hunt," Sherman said from beside him.

"Yes, but dragons like that will hunt differently..." Caleb trailed off and then sent Warner with the instructions to try out a few different methods of hunting. Ice dragons fell down on their prey and stabbed them with their strong tails. Water dragons either scooped fish into their mouth or else tripped prey with water before chomping down on the fallen animal. Then there were dwarf dragons. King Jack was bosom friends with one although not many had seen him since the animal lived beneath the castle. The waist-high adult dragon was said to spit out tar, so he probably burned his prey. No one in Aralot knew how a spellbinding dragon caught food. Maybe Valiant could shoot it with a freeze spell before he gobbled it up. He had to work with his own inner nature so that was Caleb's first suggestion. Warner told him that Valiant laughed at him when he passed along the hint.

"We've got it," Caleb told Sherman. "It would be really hard to trust his own instincts if he never had to use them before, but Valiant will figure them out. Thanks for being patient, Cuprite. I appreciate it," Caleb told the dragon before he turned and headed back toward the mess hall. He didn't mind watching a dragon eat, but he had an aversion to smelling it sometimes.

"I heard that Kayla doesn't ride dragons," Sherman said, eyeing Caleb as he kept up with him. They were joined by a few other riders that Caleb didn't know, but they walked beside Sherman easily so he guessed they were friends.

"Kayla has problems with other people's dragons," Caleb agreed. "I've not seen her much around her own either. She'll make it work."

"I hear that she's attached to her sweater. That's got to go." Mulligan dropped from the sky right in front of Caleb's face, making him jump backward. Caleb tripped on whatever rider happened to be behind him. The section leader's curly dark-brown hair was looking bouncy this morning and it matched his steps. "You will need to get the sweater off. Here's your list of duties and your time frames," Mulligan passed Caleb a large stack of papers. It felt like Caleb was already in class himself. "And I know that Charles already said, but thanks for taking that ravenous magic shooter. Do you think you would have still taken on a spellbinding dragon if you weren't trying to impress Kayla?"

Caleb rolled his eyes. Everyone thought he was so hopeless because he drew her all the time. He loved every second of her talking to him, but he wasn't a creep or a stalker, or desperate.

"I don't try to impress Kayla." Anvil had knocked that into him a very long time ago. One of the reasons why Caleb was so good at fist-fighting was from sparing with his past ware leader. He'd been trained by the best to stay away from the man's adoptive daughter.

"Everyone gets it wrong. Kayla fights things all day long. Spells, curses, and the status quo. She doesn't have very many people helping her in that fight. My goal is to be her friend to help her. If she happens to look at me along the way, that's an added bonus."

He grinned because he was going to be getting that added bonus a lot today. If it wasn't for Caleb explaining himself over and over again to Anvil, he would have been transferred a long time ago and never seen Kayla look at that last picture. Now he had to explain himself to a new crowd, but at least these guys listened.

"I heard that she's really nice," one of the girls following in his wake said. "One of her extended Colt cousins said it."

"Kayla is fantastic. She does a lot of behind the scenes helping that she never gets credit for. Why are you all following me?"

"This is your class," Mulligan named all the riders around him. Caleb memorized the names feeling fantastic about his class. They already had a positive impression of Kayla. That was going to help. "Charles and I graded Kayla's tests last night. She passed. That girl knows enough to be a ware leader if only she could mount a dragon. So, you need to run her through the physical tests today. You can record her progress on that top sheet there."

Mulligan pointed to the paper at the very top of the pile and then walked off. Caleb knew what the physical tests included already, but he couldn't help but look down at the sheet and feel his spark of joy fade to a whimper as he scanned over the list. Kayla was brilliant, but as far as he knew, she'd not mastered those curses on her that kept her down.

"We've got a rough day ahead of us," Caleb told his class who already felt like accomplices. Together they were going to try to get Kayla Brixton to like a dragon. A daunting feat indeed.

Dirt

Kayla

Kayla was looking through the eyes of Troy Felding's bonded dragon. He was her third great-grandfather, not that anyone had ever told her this. Felding records were all destroyed after her great grandfather the evil King Gladius, but Kayla had picked up enough clues to piece together her ancestry this far. Troy was the oldest keeper she ever saw nightmares from. It was easy to tell when Kayla entered his dreams, because his dragon, Bandit, had gotten weak eyesight when he got old. Kayla's current dragon vision was blurry on the left and even worse on the right.

Troy was one of those keepers that had been bonded to an already aged dragon before he hit the state where his keeper abilities activated. So Troy who was young and fit had to tone himself down to the slowness of his bonded dragon. Kayla focused on the wooded area, the distance of the trees, the sounds in the air, and decided that she had to be in the top northern area of Aralot, butting right up to the ocean that took ships out to Wisteria. In Troy's day, this location was well used since trade with Wisteria was thriving. In Kayla's current time, trade was again open, but there were not very many ships that crossed the ocean in comparison to what she saw four generations ago. Wisteria still had a distrust of Aralot ever since Gladius. Not to mention that Vankerdale still stole Wisterian dragon eggs so they distrusted them too.

In the dream, there were six ships coming in from Wisteria to reach the beach. Bandit was standing on the sand getting it stuck between his large curved nails while Troy tried to get a better look at the dragons flying in with the ships. He gave up and slipped out of his dragon's head, returning Kayla's view to that of a normal twenty-something human male.

"I can't tell. You decide on your own," Troy told Bandit, making Kayla curious to know what it was they were talking about and why she had come into the conversation so late. "I can't see anything better than you can."

Bandit snorted beside Troy because Troy could see better, he just couldn't see farther. Looking out from Troy's eyes, the ships were still specks in the distance, but the clarity was crisper.

"Let's get some backup," Troy decided. "Not enough to make them wary of us, but enough that we have some defenses in case they've decided to be prick's today."

"I'm telling you that it feels wrong," Bandit spoke to his rider's thoughts. "We were only expecting four ships at the most and not this early. We should tell the guards. Wisteria is up to something."

"Go tell them," Troy agreed.

He started pacing the beach while he waited for more information either from Wisteria or the guards who would inform the current Cluster king in Aralot. Kayla always guessed that Troy worked under King Virgil Cluster the second, but she couldn't verify that for certain. Given his age, the king could also be Cluster the first. Kayla had tried to get Troy's father's name before, but he never thought of his dad by the man's first name, and Uncle Anvil didn't happen to know it either. If anyone was to know the past keeper names it would be Anvil. Whoever kept the records during this time frame had done a bad job or not liked the man, because Uncle Anvil had Troy's name but his dads had been passed over.

Troy looked over at Bandit and made a disappointed noise. His thoughts were not loud enough for Kayla to hear them. For some reason, human thought in her dreams was never as clear as dragon thought, but she could guess at Troy's emotion. He wished that Bandit was a bit younger so that he could charge into things and see without the stipulations of old age. Bandit was a green-scaled dragon whose scales couldn't keep a shine anymore, even with wax. He was really old. He had a limp on his right side and a tremor on his front left arm that shook at times without him wanting it to. It was shaking again right now. Despite his physical limitations, the dragon had lived for quite some time after this. Kayla knew that because she had seen him later on when he was much worse and had a tremor in both his front arms.

"Is anybody coming?" Troy asked Bandit. He stopped pacing for a moment to get the answer assuming that Bandit had talked through the power of keeper bonds.

"Yes, but not as fast as that missile," Bandit growled along with his thought causing Troy's head to spin toward the ocean. He screamed. Charging in on double speed were two spellbinding dragons both of which had spells already halfway out of their mouths.

"It's an attack!" Troy hollered. "We're no match for that on our own. We have to go!"

Troy raced up his dragon's side, but Bandit couldn't get into the air with his slower muscles and his leg trembling. There was no way for him to pick up enough speed. Troy glanced again at the incoming spell-shooting dragons while Bandit moaned.

"Go. I'll fend them off," Bandit volunteered.

"We're in this together," Troy replied and didn't abandon the ground stuck beast. He pulled out a prong and sat tall in his seat, waiting for the moment for the dragons and spells to slice through him.

"Run, Troy!" Bandit screamed at his rider twisting over to his left side which caused Troy to slip from his back onto the ground. Troy refused again, scrambled back to his feet, and screamed as the two spellbinding dragons reached him. Right as the two spells headed toward him to blast him apart, Kayla woke up.

"Don't you carry your own magic?!" Kayla heard herself shout as she jumped to her own feet, with a spell on her hands ready to defend the keeper and his dragon. She'd do it. She'd stand with them and hold off Wisteria. Now wide awake, Kayla looked down at her blue glowing hands. These people and dragons were long dead so it was pointless for her to interfere.

Kayla pulled her magic back in and looked around the quiet darkened bunkroom. She didn't remember having very many bad dreams, so hopefully she had not kept her new roommates awake. She'd never had to share a room before, and she was anticipating the complaints because she screamed most nights. The room was empty of people and secretly drawn pictures so she had probably overslept and was late to class. That was a great start to her new life. Late. At least she wasn't hungry and she didn't have to worry about burning any pictures she may have drawn in her sleep. This would be hard as she no longer had the fireplace from her parent's house to use.

"Who would you stand with against Wisteria?" Valiant asked her before she could pull open her trunk to put on her new gear. She now had to wear red-stained leather pants and shirts. Her weapon belt was tan, but it felt clunky around her waist. All the same, she clipped her magical keychain to it and pulled on the rider boots. Boots were not new to her, but these ones were, and they were stiff. Kayla made sure that her red-brown hair was up in a ponytail and then stared at the gray sweater on her bed. She would get in trouble for it, but she still needed that crutch.

"Who would you fight for?" Valiant tried again. "I never see your dreams. I only hear about them afterward when you think of them, and you don't always provide the details like right now."

"I was with Troy and Bandit," Kayla breathed out as she fingered the sweater.

"We're not at war with Wisteria. Maybe one day we could go see that place."

Kayla looked in the direction of the kingdom, skimming over a map in her head that she had seen before. She needed a more detailed map. Maybe if she was suddenly dreaming about spellbinding dragons she would get to see into Wisteria. She had never had this particular dream about Troy and Bandit before. They had been scared by the spells while Kayla hadn't been. Maybe dreaming about attacking dragons was foreshadowing how her day in class was going to go, although she hoped not.

"You have not been casting spells, right?" Kayla asked Valiant.

He didn't answer which was very telling. Dragon's would say nothing at all if they didn't want to say the truth because a bonded dragon was physically and mentally incapable of lying to a bonded rider. They were not bonded, but the sentiment was there. Valiant didn't want to lie, and yes, he had been sending out spells. Lovely. Hopefully, they hadn't caused problems.

"Wisteria?" Valiant asked again.

Kayla shrugged. Valiant's family was from there, so naturally, he would be curious about the kingdom, but she had no way to get into it. Wisteria blocked off visitors, even the sailors who went to trade.

"I only want to see it out of curiosity. I am not sad that I don't know my parents. I've always had you with me, Kayla. Jack and Tia feel like my parents more than anyone. Pyro and Sparkle feel like my siblings. You feel like the other half of my soul."

"That's because I am," Kayla replied.

She put on the sweater, pulled up the hood, and ran for the field as she listened to sounds to tell her how late she was. Drums were not banging out the time. Dragons were practicing on the fields. Scouts were flying overhead. She didn't know very many dragon voices here apart from the ones that had transferred from Anvil's Ware in her lifetime, but she could distinguish one dragon voice that had never trained at Anvil's Ware regardless. Riven. He was Tristan's dragon, and he was laughing at her for being late and telling her that he hoped she had to shovel his dung for it. She had no idea exactly where she was supposed to be, but it didn't matter. She picked out Caleb's voice running some riders through basic skills and headed over. He would tell her where to go.

"When Valiant gets back, the sweater comes off," Caleb told her. He ignored her after that and kept running the other riders through questions and techniques to see where they were at in their training.

"*Where are you?*" Kayla asked Valiant.

"*With Warner. You might not be hungry, but I can only shrink my stomach so far before I have to let the spells go and eat something. I was starving. Warner said he'd show me where to hunt. Caleb told me how to do it.*"

That was nice of him. Kayla risked a glance at Caleb and noticed again how confidently he could stand in red. He was always self-assured, and it made Kayla sigh because she was lacking in that area. She also had slacked in noticing that her dragon needed food. Once again it was Caleb coming to her rescue. Kayla had asked Valiant to have Pyro teach him how to hunt once, but they'd never gotten around to it. The poor dragon hadn't eaten in days, not since Conner's keeper dragons had given him free food. Since she didn't have to do anything but worry about losing her sweater, Kayla went back to Wisteria.

Before King Gladius cursing everyone and their dragons Wisteria was known for breeding two rare dragon types. One was spellbinding dragons and the other breed was dwarf dragons. Valiant wasn't the only one wanting to see Wisteria. Merlock, who lived beneath the castle, would have a curiosity for it too. He had been born in Aralot, but he was the only dwarf dragon here so he had to have guessed that his kind was elsewhere, like Wisteria.

Vankerdale had been known for ultra-dragon kings. Aralot was known for ice dragons and the lesser, but still powerful, dragon king. Now Aralot had everything and the other places hid what they had. Wisteria had to have other spellbinding dragons if they had managed to hatch Valiant, and dwarf dragons lived beneath the ground so those must still exist over there too.

"You are not paying attention to class," Riven said in dragon speech, landing directly behind her. She had been staring at the ground half-listening to the riders around her so she could start memorizing their walking patterns. Caleb hadn't shooed her away, so she assumed that this was her class, and she needed to be able to identify her classmates with her eyes shut.

Riven's bronze hide caused those riders to shift around. Kayla looked over at them, noticing how the people checked their pockets and glanced around as if anticipating someone coming to snitch from them. Tristan. He probably used his dragon as a distraction so he could steal from people. She hadn't heard him yet, but she started to listen for him too. In the meantime, she matched steps to the riders she could now see.

There were five men and three women in her class besides herself and Caleb. She really should have paid more attention to Caleb before, because she didn't even know he was a teacher, but he made a really good one. He'd also said everyone's names so Kayla could piece together things on her own.

Avery was the man with sandy blond hair. He had a slight limp on one leg which was no doubt injured in some dragon related training. Then there was Davis who walked with heavy steps and was bold in returning her glance with his green eyes. He looked to be the kind of person that was usually given the front position in formations since he had that all-in attitude.

Norrin was next. He had a dragon tattoo on the side of his neck and sewn patches on his shirt that were not exactly a uniform infraction but were not favored because in an attack it made him easier to spot. He had smooth movements, and when he smiled back at her, Kayla got the impression that he flew in the back. He was bold on his own, but he didn't mind others going first.

There were Nick and Sherman who both had dark hair and the attitude of caring for everybody else, judging from the comments they had already made about placing people in a formation. Junia was a girl that Kayla already recognized because they shared the bunkroom last night. She had short blond hair and a scattering of freckles. Brea had straight black hair with almond-shaped eyes and had the tendency to skid herself to a stop slowly instead of jolting to a sudden stop like Keran, the frizzy brown-haired girl did.

"Are you going to fly on a dragon?" Riven asked her in dragon speech. "Yours is gone, but I'm available. I am really good at flying."

Riven kept inching closer to her. Kayla rolled her eyes. On his own, Riven might not be too bad, but he was with Tristan, and she didn't want to give Tristan any reasons to get mad at her. She happened to agree with her dad that a person and dragon couldn't be blamed for their bonded partner's actions—at least not all of them. However, she wasn't going to trust that Riven was acting on his own.

"Kayla. Can you get this dirt off my claw?"

Kayla gripped at her magical keychain, which caused Caleb to spin around and signal Riven to get lost as he recognized the use of her dragon name. He wasn't fast enough. It was in her blood to feel the pressing desire to help a dragon that cried out to her like this. She had tried to help animals before and never made it farther than falling to the ground in tears. She shut her eyes tight as the sensation to turn around coursed through her. She couldn't turn around to help the dragon. She couldn't look at Riven, so she sank to her knees, breathing in deeply to hold back the pressure of not being what she was born to be. At least she wasn't crying—yet.

Caleb ordered Riven out of his class again, but it was Valiant that made him leave. He came charging in along with the sounds of his still struggling live prey in his claws and screamed at Riven to back away. That got him to scramble. Valiant dropped the animal he'd caught letting gravity and the ground end the animal's cries before he chomped it up. He was back, which meant that Kayla needed to take off the sweater. She groaned as she pulled it off and stuffed it into her bag, refusing to take her eyes off the ground.

She got back to her feet and did her best to not look at a single dragon. It was hard to do on a training field like this. They were running and flying everywhere. This was going to be the hardest part of her new life—standing. But at least she knew why the problem persisted and could hold onto the thread of hope that one day Valiant would fix their bond so she didn't have to fall over so much. That was going to be her happy thought today. She could cast sunshine at her torn soul by anticipating the future. She hoped it was enough.

"I heard that Valiant was trapped in Vankerdale," Caleb said, now looking directly at her along with the rest of the class. Kayla hated being singled out, but it was unavoidable in a setting like this. She nodded still looking at the dirt.

"Valiant was locked up in a dungeon by King Peyton for sixteen years. He's not used to other dragons," Kayla answered.

"Or people?" Caleb questioned. "Not to worry. This is a really fantastic team. I am super excited about the group that we have here. You know how you see those groups that are so well matched that they make formation changes with silent perfection? That is what I see happening with this group. You're all really attentive and intuitive. You've got the drive and the team-building skills. You guys are going to be dropping jaws.

"As we all know, it's in levels one through five that you run through the lesson manuals on techniques and in levels six through eight that you perfect those skills. All of you have really great knowledge. We need to get your body to be in tune with your brain. For that to happen we need to first see where everyone is starting so I need you to perform a few basic skills for me, Kayla."

Here it came. Kayla nodded, well aware that her classmates were eyeing each other and wondering why she enjoyed staring at the dirt. At least Caleb wasn't making a fuss about it. He was probably impressed that she'd made it this far. She had to push this farther.

"The first thing you need to do is mount a dragon."

It sounded so simple. Even King Klavian could mount a dragon without looking silly. She could do this. In fact, she had done it before in Vankerdale when she flew on Valiant. Kayla waited until he had finished eating and then climbed up while he continued to sit there. Valiant was looking all over the place, and she had no idea what he was thinking, but so far she wasn't doing bad.

"You'll need to prove you can saddle him later, but for now you need to jump off Valiant and onto Warner."

Okay, here came the tricky part for her. Level five students were the ones who had to practice jumping between dragons. They did this in the air with ropes tied to the back of their shoes in case they were to slip and fall. Everyone else around her had a full year of practicing dragon jumps because she'd read on her schedule that she was in a level six class. She'd never jumped once to a dragon, but that didn't mean that she couldn't. It was like jumping to a large unmoving rock.

Kayla shut her eyes and listened to Warner get closer and then sit down to match Valiant's height. They were making this really easy on her. So easy that any child could do this. She judged her distance to cross based off her ears, but when she stood up and attempted to jump, Valiant shrieked and spooked. He jumped to his feet so that she was knocked down onto his back while he hissed at Warner.

"Valiant!" Kayla screamed at him, getting back up with the use of her hands. His hide felt warm and smooth beneath her palms. The width of his scales unusual. She found herself tracing the outline of the scales only because she had never done it before. She had been with her dragon for over a week, but she still felt rather new to everything. The class she should really be in was level one, where her only requirement was to sit around and pamper her dragon like it was a baby who couldn't fly or flame or hunt on its own. She'd missed out on all of that and had to start six years above her own level.

"You chose to come here," Valiant reminded her. *"And I don't like you jumping to Warner. I don't trust him."*

"We can try jumping later," Caleb suggested, before she could get mad at Valiant for tripping her. Valiant had his own struggles to go through and they had to respect that each of them was broken. It would be nice if Valiant was encouraging her to succeed today, but she gave him a hug for getting this far, choosing the love method over the anger method to repair her broken bond. She had tried anger before, and it had worked but not for long.

Caleb picked something that should have been simpler to accomplish but was in fact way harder. "You like rocks, right? This is Cuprite. That's a kind of rock. He's Sherman's friendly red dragon and Valiant met him this morning. All I want you to do, Kayla, is find Cuprite's side with your eyes closed."

Touch a dragon that wasn't her own. It was required to know the dragons on her own team because they trained to fight things together, and if one got wounded, she would need to care for the dragon on her team. Touching a dragon was super easy for every other rider in the world, except for her. She hadn't touched any other dragon apart from Pyro and Valiant, not even when she got brave enough to play around a few of Uncle Conner's keeper dragons.

That had been really fun, but it was her shoes touching the dragon backs she ran across, not her hands. She had also been able to look at them at the time because she had been feeling incredibly happy at finding her lost father, and joy could counteract the sadness that dragged her down. She wasn't feeling that burst of light today, so she anticipated crumbling in front of everyone, making a fool of herself. Gloves. She could use gloves and she'd be just fine. She wouldn't fall to the ground in a bucket of tears.

Kayla plucked her gloves on from her bag and slipped off Valiant trying to judge where Cuprite might be without looking at him. She could do this. All she had to do was reach a nonmoving dragon. It was a shame that her mind was on overdrive as she started to move. Kayla tried to block out all the times she had tried this before. Dragons would call

Pg. 110

out to her asking her to approach and help them. Sometimes she would shove at her brain to comply. Try to force herself to move against the pain as if she could make herself overcome the torment that sliced through her soul for being shattered.

It hadn't worked yet, but she still kept fighting against it. Those other dragons had come to her. This was her going to a dragon. He was a red dragon, Caleb had said, and he had bonded Sherman. Kayla could pick out Sherman's sounds, and she could distinguish dragon scale colors by their vocals most of the time too. Cuprite wasn't talking, but she guessed where he was based on his breathing pattern.

She estimated that she was an inch away when she felt the start of the tears flood her eyes. Valiant screamed, and sucked her back toward him before she could fall over. She was standing, but the trembling rushed through her nerves anyway. She shook like she was terrified. Her body betrayed her real desires and she had to lean backward into Valiant or fall over while the convulsions took over. She would have touched the dragon. She would have faced it. She'd look at all of them if only it didn't hurt her like this. If only she could fight off the reaction of her own body!

"You're forgetting to breathe," Valiant thought to her as he started humming.

Kayla took in a large gasping breath and let the tears slip from her eyes. They were not sad tears. She just felt incredibly embarrassed that she had to do this in front of so many people that she didn't know. She was revealing her darkest and deepest hurt. She couldn't touch dragons. Gee, why had she been so exhilarated to be here when she was going to get kicked out? She couldn't work at a training ware if she couldn't even touch the dragons.

Everything had been going great until now. She had made it into the ware. She had felt that luck was finally on her side instead of only ever with her father. But it wasn't. It had mocked her, teased her into trying to be something she couldn't be. The pressure of her complete failure made her fall to her knees again. The tears picked back up. Valiant tried humming louder.

"You can't flood my emotions to change them," Kayla informed her dragon. He could if they were bonded, but they weren't. He hissed at her in reply, angry that he wasn't able to help her.

"This is the result of a curse, yes?" Caleb asked. "Kayla, what exactly can we do to help? Where is the line between action and inaction?"

The line was everywhere. It was all around her, like a net squeezing into her lungs. Wait. No. That was her forgetting to breathe again. She took another gasping breath and pushed her hands at the ground trying to get herself back upright. She wiped at her eyes in an attempt to stop the water. She looked at her new boots trying to think up something positive about them to give her the courage to stand.

"Oh. That's right. I was going to try giving you happy thoughts. Remember when you tricked your parents that you were sick so that you could run off and spend a full day rock climbing. You found a real gem that day. It's that purple amethyst that you hid beneath your dresser instead of inside of it. Every now and then you would take it out and shine it up."

She remembered that, but she also remembered something else. "I spotted Ritz later. He probably flicked it at me because gems aren't normally found in that area."

He must have guessed that she had been sneaking out of school so he had given her a reason to be cheerful. He'd rewarded her bad behavior, almost like he knew that she needed to be cheered up because she'd had a lot of bad dreams that night. It had been the first night she had ever dreamed about Gladius torturing his own dragons.

"Okay. That memory is not going to work. How about the day you got your magical keychain?"

"It was great until I blasted a hole in the roof and didn't know how to fix it," Kayla reminded him.

"Well, what about the time you crafted your first firework with your Uncle Kyle and he let you launch it out over the river?"

"That was also the day I realized that if I ever tried to swim, I would be blasted away from the water due to a curse. I smacked my head on a rock."

Valiant sighed and bonked his head lightly against her a few times trying to come up with something she couldn't ruin with another bad memory. He was going to fail. She had far more bad things happen than good ones, and she could clearly picture herself being sent away by Charles for being the worst dragon rider in all of history. She would be shamed away from everyone, left to live in isolation where the only one who could witness her weakness was herself and Valiant.

"Your memory is too good," Valiant huffed at her.

"Are we supposed to be doing anything?" Nick hissed as her classmates started to get restless.

"I'm not sure," Caleb answered. "I've personally never been allowed to see her get past this part. They always carry her off the field instead of giving her time to get back up."

"By *they* you mean…?" Junia asked.

"Everybody," Caleb said, and she could picture him shrugging. "Her parents and their friends mostly, but I've seen section leaders do it too, and the random rider that wants her out of the way of his current training path."

She was holding them back. She'd do everyone a favor if she gave up on the idea of living with dragons. Dragons and her didn't mix. She'd do better if she turned into a Colt. Valiant hissed at her thoughts even if it was that very one that suddenly stopped the trembling and allowed her to shove back to her feet.

"No really, it can work," Kayla told Valiant as she gave him a hug for support.

It was what Uncle Conner did. He pretended to be someone else. Someone that wasn't scared of dragons. Someone that didn't have his condition. Kayla would pretend to be her mom. Her mother would never fall down like this. Kayla pulled her hair into a bun, turned it blond with magic to make the disguise more certain, and started to think like her mom. Reach a dragon and touch it. Super easy. The thing wasn't moving. Kayla took confident steps forward and reached out again. Her hand brushed the side of a dragon, it wasn't Cuprite, but she didn't care. She was trying to psyche herself out...

Gr! Her knees gave out and it felt like a giant hand shoved her over, pressing her hard into the ground. She couldn't even curl up this time. Her face was smashed into the dirt while everything inside screamed at her.

No! Where had it gone wrong? She wasn't being herself. Had she messed it all up by telling herself that she was trying to not be herself? She'd thought about herself and broken the one thing she was trying to do.

"I think that the characters that your Uncle Conner pretends to be are not other dragon-related people. He avoids dragons except for his keeper ones."

"That time it totally looked like a spell got her," the voice of Keran mentioned. "It's not going to get us, right?"

Kayla's lungs were burning. Her head was pounding. She couldn't make out what Caleb said in reply but it was probably that no one else suffered through this but her. She wasn't contagious. She was split in half and her soul refused to interact with dragons when it couldn't have the one dragon it wanted.

"You are forgetting to breathe!" Valiant hissed out behind her. She felt his tail land against her side and shove her over so her face was out of the dirt. She couldn't breathe. She had touched a dragon that wasn't her own, and it was the first dragon she had touched since she had managed to put one finger on her Aunt Rosa's dragon nearly twelve years ago.

"Breathe!" Valiant screamed at her. She couldn't so she blacked out.

The dragon birthing song filled her head. It was a sweet melody but it was ruined by this one dream. Kayla had seen this before. This was one of the dreams that she did her best to not think about when she woke up. It was one of the ones that Valiant didn't know of completely. This dream had Shane Felding who was Troy's son. Shane was her great-great-grandfather. She was already breathing hard as the dream started up. That made her smile. She'd found a way to breathe! If only she could skip the dream so she could return to herself and fight everything while she was awake.

"It's time!" Shane cried out happily. Kayla always pictured him being in his teens at this time but it was all a guess. He could have been younger, which only made this dream even more of a bad one. She was in Shane's eyes the whole time, never going into the head of his dragon named Tang. Since she never heard the dragon at all, she guessed that Tang wasn't born yet and Shane not bonded.

Shane ran from his bunkroom at the King's Ware tugging, on his red leather and black boots as he raced to the nest where the dragon eggs were kept. If Kayla could have shut her eyes she would have. This was the year that Shane was allowed to watch the hatching from the inside of the nest instead of wait on the outside like everyone else had to do. He pulled open the door and Kayla's pulse picked up even more. She tried to wake herself up. Tried and failed.

"Shut the door!" Troy screamed at his son. The first time Kayla had heard that she knew that something was wrong. Shane still hadn't picked up on the clue yet as he closed the door and skipped toward his dad in his excitement. Troy Felding was blocking off the first cracked open egg. No, no, no!

Troy raised up the dragon. It was all brown, but it had two heads, two tails, five feet, and three wings. "I'm very sorry you have to see this, Shane," Troy told his son, "but it can't survive like this. It can't run or fly like this. It won't be able to hunt. Terribly sorry. Twins hardly ever make it." With that Troy snapped both baby dragon necks and tossed the malformed baby into a corner to clean up later. Shane couldn't move, but Kayla could. She snapped back awake screaming like it was her own neck that had been snapped.

"*I don't like that dream,*" Valiant said with distaste. "*Whatever it is, you hate that one.*"

Kayla quite agreed. It was one of the dreams that made her glad she wasn't a ware leader. She didn't have to make hard decisions like that. She didn't have to put dragon life and death into her hands on such a continuous basis. She respected ware leaders rather well. They not only had their own dragon to care for but everyone's dragons. They had so much to worry about that the job could break a man down. Uncle Anvil got heavy-hearted at times, but he was always able to bounce out of it. She, on the other hand, couldn't even get herself comfortable around a small group of dragons.

"I am never going to be a ware leader," Kayla declared. "Not ever."

"Turid is the only female ware leader we've ever had, so the odds are stacked that you're right," Caleb said. "You okay? You passed out. Mulligan told me to get you out of the sweater, but if you need it to get through this, I'm going to let you wear it."

She had permission to disregard the dress code! What rider wouldn't jump at that? Kayla flipped off her back so she could pull the sweater back on from her rider's backpack. She pulled down the hood, replaced her hair color, and enjoyed taking in the crisp air that smelled like dragon hide.

"Is it possible for you to verbally tell me what it is that you can't do?" Caleb asked.

She took a while before answering because she was hugging her sweater while Valiant hummed at her. The sweater wasn't a cure, but it did help her navigate around better when she could block out dragons overhead. She had tried to explain the sensations of falling down to her parents before, but hadn't been able to describe it because she had no idea at the time that she had a broken bond to a dragon. She still didn't think she could explain that to Caleb. He would suggest that Valiant bond her again and then she'd have to explain that Valiant made some weird promise not to, which wouldn't be anything that a bonded rider could ever understand. There had to be something else that she could use to trick her eyes.

"What about shadows?" Valiant asked. He misted her with a spell. *"They are not real. Try to look at a dragon."*

It was worth the effort if it worked out. Kayla looked upward ever so slightly to find that every dragon through her eyes turned into a shadow image. It was like she had stepped into a world of dreams with the way dragon shapes had become black and see-through. The dragon she had touched was a green dragon named Fisher.

Hey, wait! She was like her mother and could pick out dragon names just by looking at the dragon! Uncle Conner and Aunt Rosa couldn't do that. Kayla had never looked at a dragon long enough to tell if she could. Kayla spun around to view the rest of her class while she had the chance. With her, it was all about taking advantage of every second. Besides Warner, there was Summit, Mordred, Flint, Cuprite, Forge, and Sulphur. The names were the last thing she remembered before she was out again.

"Can you hear my name?" the thought pounded into her brain. The voice was distinctly dragon. It was sweet but it had Kayla screaming. She didn't recognize the voice, and being unbonded meant that if Valiant didn't block out other dragon voices, she could start adding to her brain an innumerable amount of unbonded dragons that would drive her crazy. Her fear radiated through Valiant who woke her up by screaming at the air to back away.

"It was probably nothing," Kayla tried to console as she jumped back up and hugged his neck. "Just another new dream that I've not had before."

"It was probably that demon ultra-dragon king!" Valiant spat, jumping away from her arms to continue to look upward and snarl.

"It was female," Kayla assured. *"And I've not heard from Reaper in weeks."*

"That doesn't mean that he's stopped trying," Valiant replied.

Caleb had stopped trying for the day. He tossed a piece of paper down at her feet and told her that if she got any new ideas on how to pass her required tests to let him know. He turned to the rest of the class leaving her standing there in the hood, looking down at the words that demanded she interact with dragons. It was the first time that Caleb had ever stepped away from her that she knew about. He'd wanted to be her friend for so long, but now he hadn't the time for her. He had a class to teach which made her feel like a strain. Kayla sat down beside the list and tried to come up with a new life plan.

Encircled

Tyler

Tyler did his best to tread lightly, but that didn't stop the sleeping bronze dragon from waking up. It shined its luminescent yellow eye on him and then without growling at all, shut her eyes and went back to sleep as if Tyler wasn't knowingly breaking into a circle of the most formidable dragon team in all of Vankerdale. Last month he would have rather smashed his toe with a hammer than walk into the huddle of Conner's mind-linked keeper dragons, but since being around them, he had learned that they were really not as horrible as they made themselves out to be.

After talking with King Jack, Tyler had run into a bunch of problems in keeping his end of the deal to remain a keeper. He was hoping that he could fix at least one of those issues tonight by reaching the sleeping man that was in the middle of the dragon circle. Conner didn't live out in the woods normally. He lived in a house with his wife, Esmay, and their three children Sashi, Ruth, and Tova. However, Conner liked to make himself a pest at the castle, so when Tyler had spotted his dragons tossing fertilizer at King Peyton's normally clean windows, and heard reports that the annoying merchant was trying to break into the castle again, Tyler had set himself down in front of a window.

It had been rather interesting to watch all the ways Conner tried to break into the castle. He had even launched himself into the air, but each and every time no matter where he started from, he was magically transported a good three miles away. This had to be SilverWings doing, and Tyler was fairly certain that the spell was directed at Conner specifically, because King Jack had no problem at all in breaking into the castle when the rulers were gone.

Most of the dragons in the circle that were protecting Conner after he had exhausted himself all day stayed asleep. If Tyler had never met Kayla these same dragons would have already roasted him. The only dragon that had decided to wake up was Conner's large green one named Tempest. That was the dragon that Conner used to be bonded to until Conner came to Vankerdale and lost that bond.

"He's not really asleep, is he?" Tyler asked Tempest, stopping a good distance away from the shaggy headed blond man. It was strange how Tyler now trusted the dragons that could crush him more than he trusted the man in the middle who could strangle him. "He was born a Colt. He's got to be awake with me stepping around."

"Go away, Tyler," Conner answered as he covered his head and tried to stay asleep.

Well, that answered that question. He was awake, he just didn't want to admit it.

"You know, I never would have expected to find myself coming to ask you for help, but Kayla mentioned that you used to be a mail runner—"

"I am not delivering your letters. Going into Aralot turns me into a puddle as it does to Kayla. I doubt she's been able to recreate her dragon playing episode. Magic seeps into everything over there, and it's particularly strong against keepers. I am not as strong as she is to push against it all the time."

Tyler hadn't forgotten that Kayla promised to write him and

hadn't done so yet, but sending her a reminder letter wasn't the reason why he had left the safety of the castle to ask a man who should be his enemy to help him.

"You said that you'd do anything to King Peyton. I remember you saying it." Conner snapped upright at that sentence with his blond hair dusty from the ground and his eyes so alert that Tyler took another step back toward the dragons.

"This isn't exactly against King Peyton personally, but it does defy his wishes. What I need is someone that can copy handwriting. I need to access a room that I can't get into otherwise. So can you please write out a note allowing me access? My attempts at copying handwriting are horrible."

"Tyler, you think too small. I have it all planned out. It's not a room that you need to reach, it's everything. Hand over the handwriting sample of King Peyton, and I will turn you into the king. I can change up his statements to designate you to be in charge of the kingdom in his absence. Lots of people already recognize you as the kingdom's spokesperson for all the work you do anyway. I can't see anyone complaining about it for long. The only hitch is to get King Peyton away from SilverWings so we can kill him. Then everyone will be free of him. It won't be too hard to take down Prince Evan after those two are gone. Tia will finally take back the bonding curse and everything will be beautiful. Boom."

Tyler crossed his arms trying not to panic. Conner was trying to make him the *king*. King Jack was making him research his daughter's curses, and the dragon in his head was making him crazy.

"I beg your pardon. I stay quiet most of the time."

Yes, the dragon was being quiet tonight, but that was only because Tyler had told him rudely to pipe down. He had to find at least

Pg. 123

one thing about Kayla Brixton to prove to her father that he had searched. He had spent hours looking already without getting any new information. What he needed was to see inside the king's personal study, and he couldn't get into that without authorization.

"There are far more Peyton's than Valeron's. You can't declare me the king and get your way," Tyler pointed out.

"I will. I'm going to get into that castle and end the Peyton's reign of terror. I'm going to make you the king, Tyler."

Tyler took another step back. From the look on Conner's face he meant every word. Conner was very very tired of being broken, and he blamed King Peyton for his problems because it really was the man's fault. It was a good thing that Conner couldn't get into the castle and that King Peyton didn't leave without his dragon being nearby. The combination had been stopping Conner for sixteen years, but after all this time, he was bound to find a way to break inside eventually. When that happened, Tyler had to be ready. As if he didn't have enough to worry about, he now had to look into who should be made the king after King Peyton and Prince Evan were murdered. It was a rather unsettling thought.

"You don't want to be king?" the dragon asked him. *"I thought that your family name used to rule Vankerdale."*

"Well, yes, but my brother Narl is older than me. He should have first say."

"Age doesn't make him better. Does Narl have a connection with Aralot? Has he ever talked to King Jack or Princess Kayla? Would he know what to do if Aralot lost all its magic because King Peyton's plan succeeded? Would he be able to stand around with Queen Tia and be her friend instead of her next enemy? I think it should be you."

Tyler rubbed at his neck, annoyed with how quickly the dragon was agreeing with Conner's plans of treason.

"This is not treason. This is liberation. What has King Peyton done for the people and dragons that has helped them? All he's done is cheat and steal. His every breath destroys the chances of hundreds of people from bonding again."

"Be quiet!" Tyler yapped. This was taking too long. He couldn't stand around looking off into the distance while a dragon talked to him. It was going to give him away!

"Conner, all I need you to do is write a note in Prince Evan's handwriting telling the guards that I am allowed to enter the royal study. That's it. Before you ask, no, I don't have any of the king's letters for you to copy. It's the prince that gives me instructions all the time and no one would believe it if it came from the king. Are you going to help me or make everything more difficult?"

He had left the king's handwriting behind on purpose actually. Tyler didn't want a man like Conner getting ahold of it and changing things up all over the kingdom to his pleasing.

"Me? Tyler what I am really really good at is spotting out and crowning kings."

So he was. He had helped to put Jack on the throne, but he had also tried to run off with the man's crown so there was that. Conner could be planning another similar trick, only this time he wanted to take over the Vankerdale crown. Tyler had to keep him from it. A blaze of rage filled his chest simply thinking about Conner getting into the castle to steal it. Maybe SilverWings felt the same way.

Conner stood up from the middle of his circle and Tyler took another step backward, aware suddenly that the dragons that used to be asleep were all awake and blocking him off from leaving. It felt like he had stepped into a trap. It looked that way too. Conner hadn't been attacking the castle to pester King Peyton. He had been trying to lure out Tyler all day long. Look who fell right into the trap.

"You, Tyler, have been trying to hide something from everybody. Kayla may have been too distracted to figure out what your problem was, but I wasn't. You've somehow become a keeper. I know exactly what that's like. One moment you're living life on your own, and the next there's a voice in your head distracting you all the time, begging to meet, asking to be bonded, filling you with ideas that you would have never dreamed of reaching for. But you try to hide it. Oh yes, you try and try because to have everyone else realize what you've become would be the absolute death of you."

"This is Vankerdale!" Tyler cried. "We don't kill keepers as people did in Aralot."

"Really? Then where are they?" Conner asked with a shrug. "Do you think that king Peyton will let you live if he finds out? Have you ever wondered why the king keeps your family as servants? It's so he can poison you off if you ever start showing signs of rebellion. He might not even need real probable cause to end your life early. You might be safe momentarily, Tyler, but once those Peyton's get back in the castle, they're going to kill you. You are everything they can never be. It's you or them. With those choices, I've already voiced my opinion of who I want to see alive."

Tyler could not back up anymore. He was pressed up against the face of a dragon that belonged to the intelligent man in the middle. See, this was why he wanted that dragon to not talk to him so much! Conner had figured him out, and Conner was going to use it against him the same as King Jack was. Why was he letting these bullies pick on him?!

"I think he's right." The dragon spoke into his head. *"If they suspect you, they will kill you, and then I won't ever be able to hear you anymore. Don't*

die, Tyler!"

"Then stop being so loud!" Tyler screamed back, wincing when he realized that he hadn't left the comment inside his head. This was too scary. He had never planned to overthrow a kingdom before the king and prince came back home to kill him. Sure, it looked like Conner had the details worked out, sort of, but no matter what he thought he had planned, it was going to be Tyler in the end scrambling to hold it all together. He already had enough pressing onto his mind as it was.

"I need a letter from Prince Evan allowing me into the study," Tyler said again.

"And I need King Peyton to die," Conner claimed, with a face that suggested he would never bow to Tyler's wishes until they made such a horrible trade. Tyler moaned and shook his head. He couldn't do it. He could not kill off the king that he worked for even though he hated the guy too.

"I see," Conner stepped in closer, causing Tyler to consider jumping over the dragon that blocked him. He wouldn't make it far, but it would spare him a few minutes of Conner's intense eyes. Actually, maybe it was better if he forgot this whole thing. He didn't need to research why Kayla had nightmares. He could make something up to tell Jack. He could tell him that there wasn't any information available. Only the thought of lying to Jack made him whimper. It wasn't so much as Jack, but Kayla who would continue to suffer if he did nothing. He didn't know Kayla too well, but there was just that… that…

"Oh, what is it?" Tyler complained. "Jack asked me to look up something for Kayla and I can't let it go for the life of me!"

Conner laughed at him. Really laughed at him. He didn't ask Tyler when he had seen Jack or even what Jack was after, he snickered until his eyes started to water and he had to wipe them away. It was very

very unsettling.

"Kayla is the queen of keepers! What troubles her, troubles us all. You better be glad that she doesn't believe her role yet. Once she starts telling us what to do, you're going to feel it in your very soul to do it. You won't be able to escape the pressure, Tyler. You'd break your own bond for that girl. You'd throw your whole life away for her."

"You want to make me the king when I have to listen to Kayla?" Tyler wailed.

Throwing his life away was exactly what Conner had already done for her. No wonder keepers didn't write down these qualities about themselves. There were so many strange things that were just hard to describe, and how could he have his own actions if he had to do Kayla's for her? Come to think of it, he had already been trying to do that while she was here. He'd talked to the dragons that had them surrounded, trying to defend her. He'd tried to help her get up off the ground when she fell over sobbing. Great. His life was stolen, and if he didn't do a better job of hiding it, it was going to end soon against King Peyton.

"You're a keeper. She'll listen to you and accept your refusal. She's very reasonable. At least I think she is. You spent more time with her than I did. Anyway, hand it over. What did you need me to write to help Kayla?"

Ah. Tyler couldn't help the short chuckle that came out of his mouth at how easily Conner would agree to his wishes if he knew it was all for Kayla. That girl had a magical name. All Tyler had to do was use it, and he could get Conner on his side. Perfect, as long as Kayla didn't find out about it all and came to tell him to stop using her name.

Tyler pulled the handwriting sample out of his pocket along with his attempt at writing the authorization himself. He had done a bad job. Even he could tell that he had tried to forge this. He really hoped that

Conner could do this justice, since the guy would have spent years comparing handwriting as a mail runner. Conner took the papers, looked them over, and started to write.

"Do you think that Kayla's nightmares have anything to do with her role? She was dreaming about Gladius. He was a keeper. A crazy poisoned one, but he still was one. Does she dream about other keepers? Do all queen keepers have dreams like this? What is the purpose of the dreams? How do you know that Kayla is this keeper queen person?"

"Because I want to save her," Conner replied without glancing away from his work. "I used to have these feelings for Tia until Kayla was born. Rosa was insistent on saving Tia too. So was her insane father Herb, which was why he used a spellcaster against his daughter instead of coming at her himself. He couldn't hurt her. It's a weird magical thing, Tyler. I don't know what's to come, but I do know that when keepers start revealing themselves in greater numbers like this, it's because all of us are needed to save something. Usually, that something turns out to be dragons. Kayla is needed alive to do something for a dragon that no one else can do. Until she can figure out what that is, it's our job to hold her up from behind."

Tyler sighed. He didn't like the sound of this at all. His brain was highly against it. Here he was, once again, consulting with the enemy, respecting them above Vankerdale's rulers, so that they could do some mysterious thing that no one knew anything about. It all sounded crazy. Too bad it felt right.

"Do you happen to know what the ultra-dragon king in Aralot looks like?" Tyler asked. He wished he could take the question back when Conner looked away from his precise pen strokes to study him. Even without saying anything more about it, Tyler was certain that Conner knew why he was asking. That was the dragon in his head. The one he couldn't see or reach.

Pg. 129

"That dragon was born after I left, but yes," Conner nodded. "Give me a second and I'll sketch him out for you." Conner went back to his work, grinning as if he was scheming the most ingenious plan of all time. He shared it with Tyler before Tyler wanted to hear it. "That thing is a beast. I know what you're needed for Tyler. You bring that dragon over here and SilverWings won't stand a chance."

"He doesn't kill things," Tyler pouted. Not on purpose anyway.

"He's the answer to SilverWings," Conner said again. "Yup. I knew I would have a good day today once you showed up. Ultra-dragon kings have strange magic. Have you asked him about it yet? He's got to be using it in Aralot."

"Are you using…" Tyler didn't want to ask him, because he was still scared to face all the answers.

"I won't disappoint you. I have no idea how to use my magic. I know that I should have some, but since no one can tell me what it should do, I have no idea what to try out. Pyro had it easy. He learned what he was from his mother. I'm pretty sure that I killed my mother."

Oh. That was rather tragic.

"Yup. I thought you were going to look up what an ultra-dragon king can do so you can tell me."

He didn't need more things to do to keep him up in the middle of the night. Tyler shook his head and then told the dragon what the animal could do having already looked into this many years ago. Ultra-dragon kings were responsible for creating magical artifacts. They made unbreakable human treasures that were currently all hidden inside of Aralot. Ice dragons loved hunting for them.

"I create artifacts?"

"Not the artifacts themselves. The spells that go on them like the mace of might, and sword of strength, and the shield of protection. That sort of thing. You make people stronger."

Darn. He was talking out loud again! Even worse, it wasn't going to take Conner very long to figure out who he was talking with. Conner kept his comments to himself as he finished writing up the letter that would make it look like Prince Evan was ordering Tyler to find a specific note about Aralot in the king's study. That would get him into there.

"And I'll start on a rough sketch of that dragon. I'm not as good as some people, but I've seen a drawing of him once. If you really want an amazing likeness of dragons the person you need to watch out for is Caleb Andrade. All his images have Kayla in them, so there's something weird going on there, but he's fantastic. I just got this one the other day. What do you think?"

Conner took out a folded paper from his pocket and passed it over. On it was Kayla, looking about four years old, running after bubbles inside a dragon ware. Tyler had to sit down as he looked. They didn't have dragon wares in Vankerdale and seeing one like this was almost like he was there. Each dragon was perfect. The picture wasn't in color, but the shading told him everything he needed to know. He could make out Sparkle, the ice dragon that he had never seen before. She was adorable. He could tell which dragons were in Sparkle's keeper bond by the way they grouped behind her, watching Kayla. He could see riders in gear and buildings in stone. He wanted something just like that. Aralot had no idea how lucky they were.

"I think that I like this guy," Tyler decided. "Can I keep—"

He didn't finish his sentence before Conner had pried away the image and shoved it back into his pocket. "Not for sale. Caleb's stuff costs a lot and I never resell it after I get it. If you want, you can come over and see my collection someday, but you're not getting any of Caleb's drawings from me."

Alright then. Conner had found a way to spy on the girl he had given his life up for. Tyler didn't want to get in the way of his one doorway that connected him to his heart. He waited for that picture of his own dragon because he was still curious to see it.

"Not me. What if he makes me look stupid?"

Tyler grinned at the dragon's misfortune, although he didn't have much to worry about. Conner wasn't half bad. It was nothing as detailed as Caleb's work, a name that Tyler had already decided to memorize since it happened to be important to a fellow keeper, but Conner did the black dragon justice. It was good enough that when Tyler had the image in his hand, he felt as though he was meeting his dragon for the first time. His skin prickled and his eyes stung as if he had suddenly turned into Kayla, broken and unable to be with the dragon in her soul. There was a good side to it too though. He knew the dragon's name.

"Is it a good name? What is it, Tyler? Please tell me that my name is not Devil, or Night Terror, or Demon."

"Coal," Tyler spoke. "His name is Coal."

"Nice to meet you, Coal," Conner spoke looking directly at Tyler. Coal hummed into Tyler's head.

"He's not talking to you," Tyler complained. Coal was his dragon, and didn't need to hum at Conner.

"You haven't tried sightsharing yet? Bonded or not that's not stopped Valiant from walking Kayla around in her sleep."

On that creepy note, Tyler grabbed the fake letter from Prince Evan and climbed over the dragon that he was still smashed up against to get away. He had seen Valiant moving Kayla around, and no, he wasn't going to try out sightsharing to let Coal move him.

"I already explained that it would not be possession, but I still agree with you. The first session of sightsharing is supposed to leave you with a pounding headache. Not only that, but it's hard for a dragon to learn how to control something so small, so we do all sorts of weird things when moving riders around. It's quite funny to watch, but I won't do that to you, Tyler. It would give you away."

Speaking of being given away, he really hoped that the guards believed Conner's forged handwriting because he was going to get into that study first thing in the morning and start searching. He had no idea how long King Peyton and Prince Evan would both stay at the border. He hadn't been scared for them to come back before. Now he was terrified. He had to learn everything he could before they came to kill him. Outsmarting them was the only way he was going to survive this.

Cloth Scales

Tristan

Tristan snuck into the mess hall because that was the best place to spy on Kayla Brixton. She didn't have her hood up while she ate inside walls that protected her against dragon stares. He had thought that she wouldn't be allowed to hide anymore once she joined the King's Ware, but he was wrong, because guess who her teacher was? Caleb Andrade. Caleb had never tried to hide his fascination over Kayla so of course he was going to let her wear her gray sweater over the top of her riding gear.

Tristan spotted Kayla's ponytail of red-brown hair easily as she sat down beside another rider at the bench. She looked a little hesitant to sit down, but the other rider was rather warm to her, giving her a short hug to accept her right away. Tristan glared at that sweater. Kayla's mother still wore chainmail beneath her riding gear wherever she went. Kayla wore a flimsy sweater, but the thought process was the same he realized. It was an added protection against dragons. Did all keepers do something like that? They all needed an extra physical layer to make them brave enough to handle their own brains?

"Is this you finding something likable about Kayla?" Riven asked into Tristan's head.

"No. I'm simply trying to look at that sweater from all sides like a Colt

would do."

"Fancy. Colts often talk themselves into lots of things." Riven laughed as he said this and Tristan shook his head for all the times he had talked himself into doing something that he shouldn't. Riven was probably right. He shouldn't be finding anything positive about the sweater, but it did have an interesting meaning associated with it.

It was a tough hide and that was suddenly something that Kayla needed. She brought her spoon up to her mouth and it started shaking. Kayla put the spoon down, pulled up the hood, and sat there for a few minutes. Keeper poison already? That was just too weird. Something must have prompted Kayla to create that spell on herself as if she knew that someone was coming after her.

Then again, she might not have any concrete evidence at all. Keepers were known for doing things oddly in advance if their actions would help save a dragon in the future. Kayla in retrospect was slow. Her mother showed up two to three days in advance when dragon issues were coming. Kayla had only headed this thing off by a single night.

"This makes me shake to my talons," Riven declared. *"No one should know how to create keeper poison to give to Kayla."*

Somebody had to know because there it was, and there Kayla sat, not eating. She glanced around the room miraculously avoiding making eye contact with Caleb who was staring at her, as she tried to pick out who may have slipped the poison onto her food. Was it the rider beside her that had just given her a hug? Was it one of the cooks? She glanced that way too. Then she saw Tristan and stopped looking around.

Tristan frowned at her, wondering if she had given up because she expected him to solve the problem for her. It was a really good mystery and something that he would enjoy doing. He scanned the room again paying attention to Charles since Kayla had mentioned him earlier.

Charles was not anywhere near her, and he hadn't been when she entered the mess hall or when she moved through the line or when she sat down.

Tristan knew that in the past it was people who were scared of keepers that poisoned them and made them into the very things that they feared, but why continue to do something like this when everyone knew that without the poison, keepers were not out to harm riders or dragons?

Someone was looking to create mass chaos. It might not be directly related to Kayla, just a random rider who wanted a scare so he could get away with something else. On that thought, Tristan started to pace through the room trying to pick out anyone who looked suspicious. Since he was moving, suddenly everyone looked back at him like they were in trouble. Riders. They were horrible at hiding their thoughts and they often followed the crowd where emotions were concerned. It came from training so much to act as one team instead of a sloppy group of running mice.

Tristan made his way to the counter where he scanned over the food. He plopped an apple on Kayla's tray wondering if she would eat it, but she said nothing to him at all and refused to take another bite. Well, he had tried. He would have to try again later because the scout on clock duty was calling out the five-minute warning to bedtime. Everyone who hadn't left yet scrambled to finish their food and clean up their trays.

Without any suspects in the zone of interaction, it was going to be hard to pick out who had placed the poison. All the same, Tristan got himself ready to sneak through the ware so he could decide if the poison was an attempt to stage some other prank or dare. This was going to be an interesting puzzle indeed.

Calling
Kayla

"And what is on the young keeper's mind tonight?" The voice behind Kayla was a dragon, asking with confidence, clearly recognizing that she could understand everything he said to her. Kayla pulled her hood down to her chin so she wouldn't be tempted to turn around and view the unfamiliar voice. Everyone else was leaving her alone, even Valiant. He had taken off without saying goodbye sometime while she ate a new dinner that she had made for herself in the kitchen. She had claimed that she had strict dietary needs so she could avoid the keeper poison. She had expected her teammates to ignore her after all the stress she caused them all today, but they didn't. Maybe it was something that Caleb had said to them, or perhaps just who they were, but they had sat with her at dinner and remarkably not talked about dragons.

Kayla had stubbornly returned to the field on her own rather than hide away in her bunkroom, because she was a glutton for misery it seemed. Actually, she just wanted to find a way to conquer herself, if such a thing was even possible. The talking dragon was giving her a new idea for taking baby steps toward her ultimate goal. She could interact with dragons by talking to them. As far as she knew, she'd never fallen on her face from a conversation.

"I was contemplating keeper nightmares. All everyone ever talks about is the bad things that older keepers did or the bad things that happened to them. I don't like it. What about all the good things that they've done? The saving people, and the caring for dragons. Those always seem to be mentioned in brief glimpses or talked about so quickly that no one gets a sense for the real struggle of the save. Take Herb for example. He would run away from Vladimir's Ware to collect cures to stomach aches. Shilo said so once. Why is that stuff never talked about?"

The dragon shifted on his feet uncomfortably, but he had been the one asking so she had answered. She hardly heard anyone talk about the past keepers who had fallen in favorable terms. Colts though, they could fall and still get tales of their bravery before their defeat. Why not keepers? She had to be prepared for everyone talking about her falling to the ground all the time, and really, that's not what she wanted to be known for. One negative trait was all it took to ruin all the positives.

"Let me ask Charles," the dragon replied.

"You're Charles's dragon?" Kayla asked, trying to decide on the scale color of the older animal. She was guessing green.

"I'm Clipshire," the dragon replied.

"Pleasure to meet you. I appreciate the normal talking instead of rolling on the ground trying to get my attention with really bad pickup lines."

That brought a laugh and hum from Clipshire. "I'm too old for pickup lines, but never too old to pick you up."

"Oh sure," Kayla rolled her eyes. "That was not a good one."

The dragon laughed at her again and Kayla smiled. She was doing it! She was holding a conversation with a dragon and not falling over. Even better, since this was the ware leader's best friend, the other dragons hadn't decided to barge in to be seen.

Pg. 140

"Charles would know keepers," Kayla added, more to herself than Clipshire. "He was really young at the time, but he knew Gladius. He's seen the lives of four or five keepers so far. There were Gladius and Herb and my mother. He could have known Maslon and Arvid. Now he's watching me. You'd think that in all that time he's heard something positive about us. Not all of us got poisoned. Troy and Shane never did."

Yet she only saw their nightmares too, instead of their triumphs.

"Who?" Clipshire chirped.

"They were keepers. Shane was Gladius's father and Troy was Gladius's grandfather. Gladius knew them. Their deepest struggles were battles against Wisteria and then later Vankerdale."

"How do you know that?" This time the voice was Charles himself, stepping out from his office. The office wasn't all that close, but Kayla looked toward Charles and gave him a shrug. She had never explained the keeper names to her mother when Tia asked. Kayla wasn't going to explain the dreams to Charles. She still had no idea where they came from.

"What kind of keeper do you want to be, Kayla?" Charles asked her. "I'm yet to see you patch up dragons or go find them cures. You hardly look at them, hardly talk to them. Do you detest being a keeper?"

"No. It's not like that," Kayla assured, but she couldn't quite explain herself fully. She had tried to explain her own reactions to herself so many times in the past that it had caused her great anguish. She finally had the words, but not the actions. "Broken bonds on keepers look different from other riders."

"And now that you are bonded?" Charles pried. He started to walk over to her, causing Kayla to shift about on her feet. She wasn't bonded. It sounded like he expected her to be when her problems were clearly the same as they had always been. "You still don't look at the dragons."

"Yeah well, not all wounds are healed right away. Some take a lot of time."

"Time will not always be on your side. I think you don't like being a keeper. Even as a baby you looked away from dragons and didn't accept their attempts to stop your crying. There was another keeper like you."

"Really?" Kayla asked, focusing on Charles. He wouldn't have seen every time she ignored a dragon, but Kayla had spent a lot of time with her parents at the castle town of Troni and in the castle courtyard where Charles could spy on her growing up. "Who?"

"You already named him. Shane Felding."

"He didn't ignore dragons!" Kayla cried out. "At least not all the time. Maybe he did for a time after he watched that conjoined twin dragon die. That got to him, but after that, he bonded Tang and spent his time trying to save riders that had gotten lost or injured in battle."

"He did," Charles agreed, looking impressed with her knowledge. "However, Shane refused to live inside a dragon ware. He ran from them, ignoring ware dragons and ware practices, only poking around when he was bringing back dead riders from battle. He didn't like ware teachings and couldn't understand why his son Gladius wanted to join them."

Oh. Kayla hadn't known that. She could see how Shane may have disagreed with ware practices enough to leave it all behind him and go rogue. It had turned his son Gladius into the man he was, wanting to take over the wares and kingdom to change up the practices. Perhaps Gladius's first quest to take over the kingdom hadn't been an evil one, but one that was to reform what his father found to be broken.

"What are you going to be like, Kayla? Will you turn against the wares too?"

Aha. That was the reason why Charles had stepped out of his office to talk to her. At least he was blunt about it, asking her if she would turn on him outright. She knew where he stood now, and why he normally ignored keepers. He saw them as too controlling and meddlesome. There were other ware leaders of Charles's time that had shared those views.

"I like dragon wares. They're good places that help riders understand their bonded friends."

"So if you have decided to not ignore your calling as a keeper, when are you going to start acting like one?"

On that pushy note, Charles turned and started to walk away from her. She so badly wanted to blame him for the keeper poison on her food, but it didn't feel right that Charles had given it her, especially not with what he had just said. He wanted her to act like a keeper because it would benefit his ware.

What it really came down to was that Charles wanted Kayla to be a dragon doctor. That's what keepers really were. It required long hours and endless service. It also didn't sound much fun to have her arms covered in dragon blood and diseases all the time. It didn't seem fair that she couldn't choose what she wanted to do with her own life. It was already sentenced for her the instant she was born.

Kayla sighed and oddly enough it was words from her mother's training that came into Kayla's head. She needed to be more aware of her surroundings. Tia got in trouble for not paying enough attention a lot. Kayla didn't usually, but she was in trouble for it now. She'd not seen who put the poison on her food.

"Maslon was a shoemaker!" Kayla called after Charles. "No one says he ignored his calling."

"Maslon was murdered for betraying the trust of the riders in his bond," Charles called back to her.

"Yeah, and you could have helped kill him," Kayla mumbled. Charles's dragon sent her a growl, having heard what she said. It was true though. Charles could have been involved because his dragon was said to have been connected to Maslon's bonds. Among the riders who turned traitor to the shoemaker were two other ware leaders named Hilton and Vladimir, although, they had since died.

"No one understands," Kayla wailed. "They never wanted to be evil. Never. Not once. It hurt them to be the way they were. They fought themselves every day. If you've never had to fight against yourself that much, you can never understand how hard it can get. Gladius was trying to save the wares and make his father proud of him for fixing the problems that Shane ran from. Troy was simply trying to survive against Wisteria attacking them with spellbinding dragons. Herb was trying to stop the Clusters from killing off all the keepers. He succeeded mind, but he never gets credit for *that*. My mother wants harmony between both ware and wild dragons. I have no idea where I'm going yet, but I know that I don't want to be remembered for doing something horrible when everything inside me tells me to do what's right. Whatever that is," Kayla shrugged.

Charles had stopped walking away to listen to her. He had his back to her and it reminded her too much of herself. This was what it felt like to be talking to a person who never looked at you. It was a bit annoying.

"All keepers mess up Aralot in some way or other. Hopefully, I will be long gone before I see what you do with it," Charles replied.

Pg. 144

"They try to fix it," Kayla contradicted. "Rosa has never done anything to mess up anybody." On that note, neither had Conner. And if Anvil was to be believed that there were always five keepers around at a time, then there had to be more keepers living in the time of Troy and Shane that got no recognition at all. Kayla didn't know their names, but they had existed, served, and vanished. She really didn't want to end up being the vanishing sort.

"Rosa is not the chief keeper," Clipshire replied, backing away from her as Charles jogged back to his office to put walls and doors between them.

"So everyone else just vanishes from existence like they never lived when they fought just as hard as the rest of the keepers. It's not fair. Maybe some of them didn't need the recognition, but to not acknowledge that they lived at all is cruel. Rosa is amazing. If it wasn't for her my mom wouldn't be alive."

"You are changing the subject." Charles's dragon blew her with a puff of warm air. Normally that meant that the dragon liked her and it was considered a dragon "kiss," but this blast wasn't anything of the sort. It was designed to chastise her.

"You're the first and only keeper so far in your generation. You are the lead keeper. Therefore, you will be making changes to Aralot."

"That doesn't mean that I'll destroy something," Kayla retorted.

Conner was the first keeper in his generation and he hadn't broken anything. She was the oldest, but not the only keeper. However, she would die before she ever gave away the secret of Conner's kids. Maybe that was her role in this life: to protect those young girls from people like Charles who would never see the beauty in what they were.

Tia and Rosa couldn't have children. They shared the pain of all their miscarriages, and it was a dark evil curse that her father couldn't destroy. The desire to defend Sashi, Ruth, and Tova moved through Kayla so strongly that even without the feeling turning to anger, Kayla knew it was strong enough to combat the feeling of tears. Any emotion that could fight the soul-splitting loneliness was one she took advantage of. Kayla spun around to look at Charles's dragon. Clipshire by name; he was indeed green with a wide nose, but a slim head. He screamed at her for looking at him and ran off.

"I think I know what I need to do, Valiant," Kayla said, even if he wasn't around and she had no idea if he was really listening. She was going to defend all the other keepers. All the ones that fell without recognition and all the ones that shined with glory. She was going to defend all the ones that could never be born and all the ones that were waiting to be. She needed to save those keepers who could lift up the dragons around them when she couldn't personally help the dragons at all.

That meant that she had to figure out why Rosa and Tia couldn't have kids. It was a curse. She knew that much. But had the curse come from her grandmother Alice Felding, or did it come from someplace else? Digging into Alice's collection of spells that she had written down would tell her. Her father had found and buried that spellbook, but Kayla knew exactly where it was. Merlock the rare dwarf dragon had it with him deep beneath the castle. She had never gone to see him, but the idea of a visit didn't frighten her anymore. He lived in the dark. She wouldn't have to pull her hood down to avoid him, and she had proved that she could hold a conversation just fine.

Kayla headed toward the edge of the ware with sure footsteps, disregarding the night scouts that hollered at her that she wasn't allowed to leave. The only thing they could do was report her to Caleb, and he'd give her some chore to carry out. Saving her cousins was worth every second of physical labor. Valiant finally decided to say something.

"Merlock rubs on everyone. He's going to touch you."

She had forgotten that part. The dragon was very affectionate with her dad. If she couldn't keep him off then she would be in trouble and no one would think to come find her for hours on end... Wait. She had a dragon! Valiant could go get her dad or her mom, or even regrettably Tristan, to come pull her out of the tunnels. There were three options of rescue so that left her no reason to not head down.

Entering the dark tunnels was done by first getting into the castle. She walked inside, was followed, and then the guard stayed outside the door of the armory room when she stepped inside it. They had to know that there was a secret passage in this location, but the guards didn't venture near. Kayla reached behind the suit of armor near the wall, pulled the lever, and watched as the floor slid open revealing an infinitely inky hole.

The smell of stale tar burned at her lungs the instant she stepped down, but it wasn't enough to stop her. She had seen dreams of her father walking these tunnels so much, that her direction felt like second nature. The curious dragon sound that came at her when Merlock heard the door open and close was a familiar tone.

"Kayla Brixton," Kayla said into the dark, while she navigated the paths that used to confuse her dad. They were all odd angles and sharp turns even if the tunnels themselves were square and long. "I need to see my grandmother's writing. I don't know how you feel about that, but I have to do this. Also, my dad has probably mentioned before that I'm cursed. Don't touch me okay?"

Merlock had never met her, even when she was a baby as far as she knew. He wasn't trapped beneath the castle anymore, but he stayed because it was his home and the brown dragon loved the dark. That and treasure. He had piles and piles of treasure down here. He guarded it along with magical ice orbs that he was stingy on giving up. Kayla heard the dragon claws scramble against the sticky ground as he raced after her. He was very good at following people inside his tunnels. He was also good at blocking them off if he didn't want then touching his things. As a dwarf dragon, Merlock had a rather special tail that coiled like a snake. He could open door handles he was that talented. He could also strangle her to death. There wasn't another dragon alive that could do that. Merlock gave her another chirp, not a full word, but more of a sound indicating hello.

"I understand all dragon speech, so if you want to talk, feel free," Kayla invited. She turned another corner not bothering to use her keychain to light her way as her father did. The steps were familiar even if her feet had never been here. She'd not crashed into a wall yet.

"I was just talking with Charles about past keepers in fact. He is under the impression that we all destroy things. I don't think that's the case at all. Gladius was a maniac, but even he had good days now and then. Or at least good moments."

"I pretend he never existed," Merlock voiced, managing to catch up to her. He sniffed at her, taking in her scent. Kayla heard his tail start to sneak closer to her and she reminded him not to touch her again as she kept calmly walking along. She didn't expect much resistance. She was heading away from his most treasured rooms into a corner that Merlock himself hardly ever visited. Being small for an adult dragon, Merlock's head reached a little above her waist like he was still a hatchling, but his mind was full of secrets both from Gladius and Jack.

"I've been trying to picture what Gladius was like before he went mad, back when he was nice," Kayla replied. Merlock shivered behind her. He had been tortured at Gladius's hand, and he had some memories that he probably would never share.

"Sorry. Change in topic." Kayla jumped as she heard Merlock try to reach for her again with that wandering tail of his. She kept her ears trained on him while her legs made another correct turn.

"You smell strange. Do you know any other dwarf dragons?" Merlock asked her.

"No. I assume that they're all inside Wisteria still. I don't smell like cinnamon and flame like my dad and mom?"

She had always assumed that she did. Pyro put his dragon king protection on every keeper that he wanted to keep safe.

"You know the dragon word for dwarf dragons?" Merlock hummed at her, and tried to jump in close to rub his head on her legs as a cat might. She rolled out of the way into a side tunnel and reminded him to not touch her. If he touched her, she would fall down unable to budge, but since Merlock didn't like goodbye's, she simply told him it would force her to leave. He wouldn't touch her if he thought it would make her stay longer. To test out her lie, she walked right toward him, listening to him back up while she avoided the glow of his eyes.

"You smell like a different kind of magic," Merlock decided.

"That will be from Valiant. He's a spellbinding dragon. He bonded me when I was a baby. Speaking of which, could it be possible that the curse on my mom and Rosa came from a spellbinding dragon? That could be why my dad can't take it off."

The question had her stop walking. All this time they could be looking for answers in the wrong place. Valiant could be the one to save them all.

"I can take off the curse while I'm around your mom," Valiant told her, *"but the curses go back on when I leave. It's the same with a few of yours that I digest daily."*

"They're conditional curses then," Kayla spoke. They couldn't be broken unless one first discovered or guessed the right condition. To do that, she needed to find out who had placed them. Then she had to get inside that person's head to figure out what they might use as a condition. Then find the condition, fulfill it, and end it. It was a lot of steps.

Kayla found the correct corner and pulled out a prong from her rider's belt, shaking her head as she realized that she'd not once used her birthday prongs yet. She scraped at the putty that her dad had put in the way and Merlock sat down to watch her. She put her back to him when she pulled out the writing of her grandmother and turned on her keychain to create light. Merlock hummed.

"Why have you never come to see me before?" he asked. "You have a pretty voice."

"Thanks," Kayla said, rather than answer the question. If she answered that, she might not get out of here. Merlock would know how to trap her.

Reading over Alice's collection of handwritten spells was interesting because Kayla realized that she knew most of the spells already. They were things that her dad had taught her, or at least warned her against. There were a few comments where Kayla could get a sense of her grandmother's fears, but apart from taking away that Alice was scared that all Felding's were already doomed, Kayla found nothing to indicate that she had cursed her daughters to not have kids. It didn't look like she had thought that far ahead. She wasn't planning out weddings for them. She was trying to stop them from having any desires to be around dragons. She had failed in that. Then there was the glaringly obvious fact that Valiant had just brought up. The spells kept coming back. The magic should have gone away after he ate it, but it didn't. So someone or something had to keep shooting out the same spells over and over again.

It couldn't be SilverWings, although he was easy to blame due to his magical nature. He was the one responsible for causing Kayla to be born in the first place. So he would want keepers to be born to give King Peyton more people to target.

"It would be someone who wants to stop King Peyton from getting in. Political," Kayla said out loud. Merlock hummed at her simply for talking. He was an easy dragon to please. "Someone who would benefit from a lack of more keepers," Kayla added. "Old enough to have cast this spell before I was born, and with magic at the time. That takes out most ware leaders because they got magical protection after my dad sealed off the border. It's not my parents or Anvil. King Klavian is the easiest person to blame, especially with how he handles thoughts of keeping Tristan on the throne."

He had made that rule that she had to date him. Kayla squirmed. What if the condition for ending the curse on her mom and aunt was to marry Tristan? There were so many unsettling things about that.

"Then again, my dad would have already thought of that years ago," Kayla decided. He had spent years trying to stop this because it hurt him every time Tia sat around for several months crying. He would cry too.

"Okay, it's someone who can turn a blind eye to another person's pain. Someone who is really good at separating out emotions and locking them away. Colt?" Kayla guessed. "That leaves me with two options, Merlock. Queen Aria and Tristan. Both were alive at the time of the spell, and both could have taken Klav's magic without him noticing. I'm in a position to spy on them. I'm going to narrow this down. I'll find out who keeps doing this."

"What spell are you looking for?" Merlock asked her.

"The one that prevents other keepers from being born in Aralot," Kayla told him. She put back her grandmother's spell collection and turned out her light before she started to walk back through the tunnels.

"That is an evil spell," Merlock agreed. "Spells that tamper with life leave a mark on the spellcaster."

"Really? What kind of mark?" Kayla asked.

"It leaves a mark on their soul."

She was going to prolong Aria's lessons and Tristan's dates for as long as it took her to end this curse. She'd figure out the condition of the spell eventually.

Distractions

Caleb

"Hey!" Caleb gave RJ a high-five as the man came to sit beside him at breakfast. RJ had transferred out of Anvil's Ware three years ago, and he was a welcome sight to behold. Caleb needed a friendly face after the defeat had threatened to take him yesterday. He had no idea what to do to help either Kayla or Valiant. Both appeared to be helping the other one and yet holding each other back at the same time. It was highly confusing. After he had given Kayla the clipboard list of accomplishments she needed to reach, it had taken a good half hour before she decided to return to class. If return was the right word. Valiant would encourage Kayla to get close and then pull her back to him. Kayla had encouraged Valiant to join in with the other dragons while she stood there alone, but then she would whimper when he started to move away from her so that he came back. Since Caleb couldn't hear anything of their mental conversation, the give and yank was spinning him in circles.

It had been particularly hard on Sherman, as if he couldn't stand to see someone who was supposed to be a legendary rider fall to her belly so much. Caleb had tried to include Kayla, but figuring out how was difficult so he had let her join when she was ready. Two hours in and Sherman had been wailing.

"Oh Gosh! She's crying again. We have to do something."

Sherman's desperate voice could still make Caleb feel the same way. He had heard the crying, but pushing Kayla forward hadn't helped. He was waiting for it to pass. It was one of those hard cries, the kind that usually ended with one of Kayla's relatives picking her up and taking her off the field. Her family wasn't here to do that anymore. Caleb had really wanted to see Kayla beat this.

"Stay in line," Caleb had barked directing Warner to get between Sherman and Kayla. He had obediently moved in place having done this many times before at Anvil's ware to stop dragons from adding to Kayla's chaos. Sherman had called him a dung pattie, and Caleb had wanted to crack down on him the way that Anvil always came at Caleb for showing his own overprotective sensor.

Anvil claimed that Caleb had the makings to be an inspirational leader for everyone except for Kayla. A lot of the time Caleb suspected that Anvil simply wanted to keep the girl all to himself, since he hoarded keepers like it was nobody's business. He had them all, especially Kayla who regularly flung her arms around the ware leader.

Warner had to get aggressive with Sherman and his dragon Cuprite blocking them off several times from swooping to Kayla's rescue, but then the others in the team had flown down while he was busy, and Caleb didn't know what to do. He'd offered to help Kayla so many times over the years. Leaving her alone when she started crying was hard on him too, but it was what he'd been told to do. Now he was looking at a team full of people like himself, all at a loss of how to help Kayla Brixton.

He was forced to let Sherman down by being outvoted, and he had asked Valiant to take Kayla's curse off her, but the dragon had growled at him and Kayla had kept crying for another half hour before she had stopped. This was hard. He hadn't even started on figuring out how to train a spellbinding dragon who spent most of the day curled up. He had been stuck on saving Kayla like everyone else.

"You know how Anvil used to say that if you didn't see what Tia did firsthand that you were missing out?" RJ asked. Caleb nodded. "Well, you missed out. You should have seen Kayla last night."

"What did she do?" Caleb asked, craning his head around the mess hall trying to spot her. She would show up really early on the field at Anvil's Ware, but he was yet to spot her at breakfast since she got here. She kept sleeping in.

"She was talking with Clipshire and it was amazing! They rambled off a conversation like it was nothing. She understood every single sound that dragon made like talking to dragons was second nature. I know she's not been able to touch them, but that girl has dragon speech down better than anyone I've ever heard of before."

"What did they talk about?" Caleb questioned. This was new. Kayla had never shown before that she talked dragon.

"Ancient keepers. Maggie wrote down Kayla's half of the conversation so you'll want to hook up with her to read it. It's worth it. Then Charles came out and I swear Kayla let him have it. He was telling Kayla that she made a lousy keeper and she was like, 'I know far more about keepers than you, dude, and you are so wrong.' That girl was fire. I've never seen Kayla say anything like that before. Then she turned around and looked at Clipshire, and he ran like her eyes were burning."

"Wait, what?" Caleb grabbed at RJ's arm bummed that he had missed this. "Kayla found a way to look at a dragon? How did she do it? Who is Maggie and who is Clipshire?"

Caleb hated being the new person around here sometimes. He knew everyone who was important at Anvil's Ware, and if he didn't, he could often guess. He still hardly knew his own section, but he was working on it. He'd been memorizing names last night but he couldn't recall a Maggie. Clipshire turned out to be Charles's dragon, and Maggie was a chatting girl wearing a red headband. Caleb didn't waste any time before he headed over.

"Maggie, Maggie, Maggie," Caleb said as he slid into the seat across from her. He had to scoot a few people out of the way to do so. "You've got some notes that I want to read."

"You can trade a picture for them. I'm not letting anyone read them until I get a picture from you." Maggie yawned and covered her mouth, cluing Caleb in to the fact that she was a night scout. She should be in bed, but she was up spreading the word around about her notes because she had found a way to get from him what everyone wanted. Blast these people and their underground selling of his work! He needed those notes. He had to have them to see what made Kayla look at a dragon! He knew he said that he'd never trade, but he was already crumbling. It was one picture against Kayla's future. He had no choice. He didn't want to start off on the wrong foot here and become the bully section leader that ordered people to give him what he wanted only based on his title. He wanted to earn the respect.

"What do you want?" Caleb asked feeling set up by RJ suddenly. He would know exactly what to say to him to get Caleb coming to see Maggie. This was rotten.

"I want a good picture of Kayla with Valiant," Maggie decided.

Caleb yanked out paper and his drawing utensils with a grunt. He'd never dawn Valiant yet. His first picture of him was going to be lost into the void of rich collectors. Caleb spun his pencil between his fingers while he thought. Valiant was a hard dragon to get right. When he wasn't curled into a ball, he was very expressive, gazing at Kayla like he'd hum at her or sing to her at any moment. Then there was that expression he sent out when he was mad and his eyes got a bit stormy. He was unlike any other dragon that Caleb had ever encountered. Valiant was either looking asleep or ready to charge.

Pg. 156

How should he draw him as knowing that some other person would take his picture and judge the dragon and rider from what Caleb had seen? He really wanted to put down the expression of the fight, those keen eyes of ember that Kayla could look into, but he chose another image. He picked the one where Kayla had lit up at the news that she could have her sweater back. She was hugging it as it enclosed her off from the rest of the world. Valiant was humming at her back looking fortified in his decision that he was going to be the dragon that could take on the cursed rider.

Despite the cloth wall, Kayla kept passing out and Valiant kept hyperventilating while he had hissed into the air like it was the sky that made Kayla stop breathing. Caleb wasn't going to draw any of that, just the happy part.

"If you take this, I'm keeping your notes of that conversation," Caleb told Maggie, holding out his sketch of Valiant. He'd left Kayla as the top half of her sweater, not really wanting to share her with everyone else. Maggie hesitated, which had to mean that the notes were rather good if she considered changing her mind. However, she nodded and they made the trade. No sooner had Maggie tucked Valiant into her bag then the whispers started up, raising the price on his image. The number kept climbing which had Caleb amazed at how secretly famous he was. These people were crazy.

Caleb skimmed over the nighttime conversation he had missed as he started to walk away toward the door, only to sit himself down on a random open bench to read them again. Whoever he'd sat next to started to read over his shoulder, but he was too enthralled to care.

Fire indeed. Caleb had never heard of Troy and Shane Felding. He'd never thought about Gladius having a dad or a grandfather. His legs gave out over the suggestion that Herb and Gladius were not the evilest people to have ever lived. How did Kayla see these people so differently? It was eye opening. She hardly ever looked at anyone, and yet she saw them like this—looked straight down to their hearts regardless of their actions.

"Warner she is so beautiful," Caleb expressed.

He jerked his head toward the door when he heard her voice finally. She wasn't standing there alone. Holding open the door with a mocking bow was Prince Tristan. He wasn't dressed in his rider gear, but had chosen to look nice with a dark blue shirt and gray pants. Caleb wished for a moment that he was out of the red leather himself. Kayla, beside him, had her sweater over her red gear which did soften the blow of the vibrant color some.

"I don't see why you don't want to also have lunch with me even if we just ate breakfast together. That can count as another date you know," he said.

"Still trying to get it all out of the way? I like to prolong your misery," Kayla answered.

Caleb sucked in his breath. He wasn't the only one. Riders here always hoped that Tristan wouldn't stick around to play pranks on them. For Caleb, he was stuck on the word "date." They were dating? He was doing his best to keep his personal feelings away, but his eyes were turning moist.

Why were they dating? No one had said anything about this to him. He felt incredibly stupid to have never thought of it at all. Tristan was the prince and Kayla the princess. Caleb had nothing royal or noble about him at all. That had never stopped Jack and Tia, but Tia hadn't dated Klavian.

Caleb wanted to jump the tables, pull Kayla to himself, and tell Tristan to go steal something else. Caleb had been waiting for ages for Kayla simply to look at him, and here was Tristan with a hand around her heart.

"Oh, Warner," Caleb sniffled. *"What am I going to do?"*

"Be patient," Warner replied.

"You know you are very good at prolonging misery," Tristan agreed. "It's one of the reasons you'll never be a Colt. You can't step away from your emotions."

Caleb was on his feet so fast that he didn't have time to contemplate that Tristan could blast him over with magic in addition to his fists. Too bad the person he had sat beside was Russel, who was another section leader with the job of keeping everyone else in line. The guy had probably been told why Caleb had been banished here. As such, he was holding Caleb's arm in a tight grip to prevent him from flying at the prince. Caleb hated people picking on Kayla. She fought her emotions harder than anyone as she had just said last night.

"If only you could hide from your emotions, I wouldn't have learned the secret to you giving up gems," she shot back.

"Oh, shut up. You always start this. You act like the angel, but you're a criminal."

"Like a Colt." Kayla smiled at Tristan as if he'd dished out a compliment. "Thank you. I knew I could fool everyone with those emotions."

"I am not fooled. Have lunch with me, Kayla."

"I'm eating with your mother. I'll be in a dress if you must know, and you're not invited."

"Well good. She'll reform your uncivilized tongue."

"Too bad her teaching didn't work on you," Kayla quipped.

Pg. 159

Tristan glared at her and Caleb yanked at his arm to break free of Russel's grip. Tristan could do anything to Kayla for a comeback like that. Caleb was ready to put himself in the way, but Kayla already had her next words coming, as if she didn't need him to stand up for her. It left him feeling lost again. Who was he if he wasn't Kayla's defender?

"Sorry. I shouldn't have said that. That's the sort of thing my dad would say to his best friend Joss. They always bash each other and you were talking about Colts. I was thinking about them."

"I have never seen you argue with Joss," Tristan declared.

"I save it all for you," Kayla replied, still sassy, and then she started laughing while Tristan shook his head at her.

"You do. You really do. You —"

Tristan trailed off as they both looked over their shoulders back out the door. Tristan looked into the air. Kayla looked at the ground, but it meant the same thing. They were getting information about a dragon.

"Pyro is here with Jack," Warner informed him.

On that note, Kayla took a few steps away from Tristan into the mess hall. She pulled off her sweater, shoved it into her bag, and redid her ponytail like she was preparing for a lecture.

"Angel face." Tristan couldn't help but jab at her one last time.

"Devil brain," she spat back and then she gave the doorway a smile as her father walked in. Since this was the King's Ware all the riders stood to their feet to give Jack a bow. Caleb cast his eyes around for Charles. The guy was hiding something in his pocket like he shouldn't have it. Kayla didn't bow. She ran at her father and gave him a hug.

"What did you do?!" she hissed at him next. She pulled back, scanning him over from head to toe. Caleb couldn't see anything different about him.

"Think your mother will notice?" Jack asked.

"When your vibes suddenly feel like that, yes…" Kayla trailed off taking more and more steps away. She stopped when the answer to what she wanted to know came to her and she had to cover her mouth so she wouldn't scream.

"Kayla it's not bad. A little weird, and Pyro complains that his head is now odd, but—"

"Dad you can't!" Kayla let her emotions out again. "That's supposed to be impossible! I was wondering what happened to Tyler but I didn't think it was you! Pyro actually. It was Pyro. What is he doing? If I could look at him right now, I'd scream at his face!"

Caleb sighed. Not because Kayla was disagreeing with her dad over something that he was clueless about, but because she didn't think she could look at another dragon. He fingered the paper in his hand and put it carefully back into his backpack, trying to sort out why she was able to look at Charles's dragon last night and the reason why the dragon had run in fear.

Fear. Kayla had never agreed with Charles that her bond was fixed. She had turned angry, and anger was an emotion that overcame broken bonds. Clipshire had run like her eyes were burning, and they were, because Kayla had been mad. The reason why Kayla still had so much trouble was because she wasn't bonded!

"You are very clever," Warner replied. "I can see that now. Riders with broken bonds usually have trouble being around their old dragon, but in Kayla's case, it's as she said. She's a keeper, so for her, being with Valiant isn't the harder struggle. It's being with everyone else."

"Why haven't they fixed their bond?" Caleb asked his dragon.

Pg. 161

"I don't know. What if he can't. What if he has to wait until the right season for his bonding venom to come back in?"

If that was the case, they were looking at nearly a full year of Kayla training where she fell to the ground and passed out. She knew it, and yet she was throwing herself at it all anyway. She had a will of iron.

"Where's Charles?" Jack asked. "And you, miss, are in trouble with your mother. I'm gone for a few days and you're sporting red. Couldn't stay away from Caleb, could you? Anvil told me you asked about him."

"But Uncle Anvil didn't tell me where Caleb was. Gosh, dad. Why are you picking on Tyler?! He can't... He's got to be... I'm going to write to him. I promised I would and I still haven't."

Who was Tyler? Did anyone else know, who they were talking about? Caleb looked at Tristan because if there was a guy that would understand this part of the verbal battle it would be him. He looked just as puzzled as everyone else, and Kayla was changing the subject on purpose. She had been rather sly about it too. Kayla was keeping the conversation away from her asking about Caleb. He had to grin a little. She had noticed that he was missing.

"Still friends with the guy?" her father asked, spotting Charles and giving him a nod like they needed to talk. "That's got to be a record for you." Jack shut his mouth after saying it and spun around with an apology for his rather mean comment. Kayla didn't let him suffer for it. She gave him a sad smile and nodded.

"Yup. If you need my help, Dad, just let me know. I will be here. You won't make me transfer no matter what you, Mom, Vermelo, or Charles say."

"You raised her rightly stubborn," Tristan mumbled to himself, but it was so quiet that everyone heard him anyway. Kayla ran out the

Pg. 162

door.

Jack turned his attention onto Tristan, making the guy straighten as if he feared a spell coming at him.

"Took her on a date this morning? She likes omelets, sandwiches, and stew. Stay clear of pasta."

Jack turned to move toward Charles, and Caleb sat back down in his seat, feeling like his heart had been stabbed. Jack was telling Tristan how to date his daughter. From what Caleb had just seen, the two of them were not best buds, unless that's how Kayla acted when she liked someone. He thought he knew her. He thought he could see through her pain into what really mattered, but maybe he had been lying to himself his whole life, because Kayla had Tristan and this Tyler guy.

As if Caleb was everyone's cue to stop respecting the king, the other riders slowly slid down to their seats too. Charles was the only one that remained standing. Tristan slipped in beside Notley and started whispering to him, probably trying to get information he shouldn't have.

"Do you know anything about Tristan and Kayla?" Caleb asked Russel.

"Recent rumor claims that they're supposed to get married and Tristan is mad about it because his girlfriend dumped him."

Caleb felt his spirits drop even lower. Anvil had forbidden Caleb from asking Kayla on a date unless certain circumstances were met. This had to be why. The girl was betrothed and wouldn't get to make her own choice in who to marry, just like every other queen that sat on the throne, except for Aria and Tia.

Caleb had always thought that once he got Kayla to be his friend there would be a magic moment where she would look at him and smile. Their hearts would beat at the same time, and their minds would think the same thought. I love you would pass between them, and then Caleb would be able to stay with her forever. Anvil was right to hold him back. He was never going to get the girl of his dreams. It made him want to cry, except he was in the mess hall in front of everybody. Crying wasn't allowed.

He slipped out of the mess hall trying to redefine himself. He might not get to live with her, but that didn't mean that Kayla didn't still need him. Just because Kayla couldn't marry him one day, didn't mean that he couldn't become a secret lover under the guise of being a really close friend. Anvil made it work.

Caleb ground his teeth together as hard as he could, not wanting to end up like that man. However, if Kayla was going to be forced to marry Tristan, she was going to need that one good friend that would listen to her when Tristan got her down.

Caleb had already made his promise to be her friend no matter what. He couldn't leave her to handle this hard life on her own. He found her right beside Valiant as she hastily wrote out a message and stuffed it into an envelope that she stuck to Valiant's scales with a spell. Valiant launched into the air, so Caleb suspected that the dragon wasn't going to be around for class. He couldn't help but ask Kayla about the one thing on his mind.

"Are we still friends?"

Kayla turned around to look at him. She had to open her eyes, making Caleb wonder if she had shut them before or after she had written her short sentence to the mysterious Tyler. Caleb really needed to get to know her better. She had so much going on beneath the surface that no one ever got to witness. Now that she was away from her parent's constant supervision, Caleb hoped that there would be more conversations like the one she had last night. More instances where she revealed her hidden thoughts.

"I was going to answer your question about being friends right after you wrote it and then you weren't around anymore. Uncle Anvil said you were off on an assignment. I'm so sorry that I kept getting you in trouble. I do want to be your friend, Caleb. You always show up instead of leave me behind. You might be the only one."

She said that part with a slight tremble, and Caleb glanced around to identify which dragons were watching her right now. Her dragon had just left her. She was feeling the abandonment kick back in. The creatures were not talking to her, but they were all watching. Kayla shivered again.

"Hood," Caleb directed.

She shook her head. "Not until my parents are gone."

He looked around to find Pyro sitting nearby but that was it. The other dragons that had their eyes and ears on her were flying. She only had one parent here, but she was a better judge of when they would show than he was. Her mother had to be coming too.

"Do you really regard evil keepers differently from everyone else?" he asked, trying to distract her away from thoughts of the missing dragon. It worked.

"There are a lot of people in this world that become unsung heroes. You get all those stories where the hero starts to falter, and the best friend or some random stranger comes up and says that they believe in the hero. The friend says that the hero was born to do this, and they have everything they need to succeed already. Then the hero completes the ridiculously hard task and is praised forever. What you never hear being sung about are all those friends who gave that one final ounce of encouragement. Without them, heroes would doubt themselves and might fail the final task, missing that fortification in their soul that they can do this. That's what keepers used to be. They were the fortifying friend lifting up all the extraordinary people and dragons. Everyone's forgotten that."

"Maybe that's because we see keepers as the heroes instead of pushed into the background," Caleb replied.

Kayla shook her head. "Not everybody sees that. There are records about only a handful of keepers even in the ware leader books. There are hundreds of them that have gone missing. Most keepers never got any recognition at all. I've been thinking about them a lot lately. There were so many of them that fell without a friend to pick them up. They were desperate, lonely, broken, and shattered. Someone needs to save all those hidden broken keepers…"

Kayla trailed off as her trembling picked back up. Caleb felt her words flow through his entire being. She was sharing part of her inner soul with him. He wished the moment would never end because this was precious. Friends had suddenly turned into soul-sharing friends in a single instant.

Charles had said Kayla was being called to do something. It sounded like she might have already figured out what. She wasn't here for the dragons. She was here for all the forgotten people. Everyone who ever felt lost. That was a large undertaking, because even the most prominent man had felt lost before. With the way that Caleb was currently feeling, he felt like Kayla had been magically sent to this ware for him. His blessing. His one spark of hope to hang on to before he lost her to Tristan. She had agreed to be his friend.

Kayla shut her eyes and Caleb contemplated telling her to get her sweater out again. He didn't because a white blur descended behind her with a thud. Sparkle. Riding on the dragon was Tia and she didn't look particularly pleased.

"Where did your dragon go?" Tia asked, while Sparkle cooed

sweetly at Kayla, trying to get her to turn around and play with her.

"He's flying. Dad's in the mess hall losing to Charles," she answered. "Charles might not like keepers, but I've never known a ware leader to give one up. Can you tell Pyro for me that he's being dumb?"

"Pyro you are being..." Tia trailed off, jumped off Sparkle and ran for the mess hall, nearly tripping over her own feet. Caleb had never seen Tia more uncoordinated. He wondered what had them all so jumpy. At the same time, he found himself smiling at Kayla. She'd done it again! She had distracted her other parent away from thoughts of getting her in trouble. From the sound of things, Kayla hadn't told her parents that she was joining the King's Ware.

Pyro snorted at Kayla and Sparkle hummed at her. Then without warning Sparkle's tail slashed toward the girl. Kayla jumped it. Caleb barely scrambled backward in time. Since Kayla always refused to play with Sparkle, she was forcing the attention by attacking. The white dragon came in again, this time with a ball of ice.

Caleb grabbed his section leader whistle and was about to blow it to tell Sparkle to cut it out when he remembered that ice dragons only listened to a handful of people in their lifetime, and he wasn't one of those. If he told Sparkle what to do, she'd turn him into an ice sculpture. He'd seen it happen before. Kayla dodged the ice, which had Sparkle humming at her. Caleb couldn't handle the dragon on his own, but there was one thing that could do make her back away.

"Warner, get my class out here."

Not half a minute after the request, Kayla's eight teammates abandoned the rest of their breakfast to join him on their dragons. Caleb gave them the signal to form an advanced blocking formation and they eagerly took to the task of facing an ice dragon. She was a formidable foe, but she respected dragons, even if she didn't listen to their riders.

They held Sparkle back from picking on Kayla while Kayla tried to grab air into her lungs, and Sparkle started sending ice flakes out. It was cold! But Caleb stayed on Warner's back regardless, not rubbing at his arms until Sparkle abruptly stopped and lowered down to the ground on the harsh thoughts of her rider. Tia was still inside the mess hall with Jack, but Pyro walked behind the defenses to nudge Sparkle with his head before he too groaned and lowered down, a sure sign that indicated they both had very angry riders.

Caleb had never watched Tia and Jack fight with each other, but they both pushed out of the mess hall with Charles behind them. All three leaders noticed Caleb's blockade. Kayla was on her knees closer to the mess hall than not. She didn't bother to look at any of them.

"It's best for Kayla," Jack said.

"She would have never—" Tia started to scream back, then switched the words to her head instead. Caleb looked down at Kayla wishing that she could explain the commotion, but knowing that she wouldn't.

He climbed off Warner when Jack signaled him to come over. Caleb approached feeling uneasy. Both Jack and Tia had told him to stay away from their daughter before. He refused to lose the friendship he had just gained, but he wasn't sure he had what it took to stand up to the king and queen of Aralot. Normally he nodded back to them without mouthing off. He let his mouth run around Anvil instead. He could lose this whole thing right now, see Kayla leave the King's Ware and leave him in the dust, if he couldn't figure out how to navigate around her parents in two seconds.

"She's doing great. You'd be really proud of her," Caleb said, feeling a desperate need to prove that Kayla was best suited for being here instead of at Rogan's or Niles's Ware, which was where she should be, given her training level, age, and residence. Caleb had nothing to show for his current teaching, but there was one thing that would give him a small edge. Those notes from Maggie. It was the perfect solution. That was how Kayla handled her parents in any case. She distracted them away from the problem and got them thinking of something else. If she could do it, he could too.

"She interprets dragon speech. Did you know? And you've got to see what she said about keepers."

Caleb pulled out the notes and both Jack and Tia lunged for it. It looked like a hot topic. They both read the words over a few times until Jack pointed to a particular spot.

"She's mentioned those men before. I think she dreams about them, Jack."

"Her nightmares are about dead keepers?" Jack questioned. "That's really creepy. We're going to figure this out, Tia. We've got extra resources on our side now. I'm going to go look at something."

"Me too," Tia agreed.

Caleb felt chilled at the very thought that Kayla had nightmares of dead people. Tia snatched the notes from Jack's hand and took them with her as she mounted Sparkle. Sparkle launched into the air without getting a running start. Ice dragons could do that. No matter how many times Sparkle did this, there were still some dragons that cooed over the sight every time. They hummed as Jack left next, wordless to his daughter and Charles. Charles rolled his eyes. Caleb turned his attention back to Kayla.

Her words made so much sense. How many times had this happened to her where her parents rushed off to solve some complicated question and left Kayla alone on the ground? She felt like the forgotten keeper, the one that never had anyone there to raise her up. Although this time, she wanted it to be that way.

"That was a fantastic formation," Caleb praised his class. "Since we're all here we're going to start class early. In the woods." He pointed out of the ware where Kayla could escape the dragons now that Valiant was gone. "It's going to be all of you guys against me. I'm the invading army and you can't let me get through to reach the ware. I'll give you a head start."

Charles gave him a wink as his indication that he approved of Caleb's chosen activity. Caleb watched his class head for the forest while he looked at Kayla still on her knees. He felt like he wasn't getting everything right here. He had guessed at what really dropped Kayla to the ground, but he hadn't done much of anything to figure out Valiant who had his own unregistered troubles.

"Since you're right here, do you know anything about spellbinding dragons that I don't?" Caleb asked Charles.

"They shoot spells. It is currently impossible to get any information about them from Vankerdale."

That was because the Vankerdale border was closed off. Caleb didn't know why. It had been opened right after King Klavian took the throne and then closed off nearly just as fast. The only other spellbinding dragon they knew of lived in Vankerdale and was King Peyton's dragon. Was it too much to wish that people had asked questions about the creature before they had bad relations again?

"I can tell you this," Charles decided to say. "Valiant's behavior is not normal for *any* dragon. When SilverWings makes his way into our territory he is alert, savvy, and flies everywhere. The beast hardly lands. Valiant hardly stands up. I've been making inquiries, and Valiant came from Vankerdale after being born in Wisteria. Kayla was captured there and brought him back. You remember when the town froze beside us?"

Pg. 170

Caleb nodded, even if he hadn't been aware of this at all.

"Well, what froze the town was Valiant. Then he kidnapped Kayla until she talked sense into his head and brought him back."

Caleb pinched his eyes together in thought so that Charles dropped off, silent, waiting and patient. Perhaps "back" wasn't the right word. Valiant could be milling around because he was homesick. He might not like living here. It was either that or maybe his closed nature was because he was scared of all the new sights around him.

Caleb sighed and stretched out his arms while he thought. Terror. That was the emotion Kayla typically wore when around dragons that were not her own. How often had Caleb seen her trembling, trying not to cry? He used to think it was because the girl had been told not to talk to dragons that belonged to her mother and aunt. They had their own keeper thing going on. Rosa had taken over the north and west sides of Anvil's Ware and Tia got east and south. That didn't leave Kayla with anything once she revealed her dragon prowess.

But maybe he was wrong. Kayla didn't cry because she was told not to look at dragons. She cried because she had a dragon that cried. He was looking at everything wrong. It wasn't only Kayla that he needed to fix in order to get her off the ground. It was Valiant too. Both of them fed on each other's fears. So perhaps the better question wasn't what made Kayla scared of dragons. It was what made Valiant scared of everything?

"Valiant is scared of Kayla getting hurt," Warner answered.

"But that would mean that he has reason to believe that she'll get hurt. What could hurt her? She's had an entire kingdom protecting her her whole life."

It wasn't like she had abusive parents who would threaten her in secret. Her parents were amazing. It wasn't like she had Colts that were out to get her. Caleb knew that she often talked with her father's old gang, but no one would hurt Jack's child when he was the real king of the land and everything that he did was to save them all regardless of how mean others could be to him and his wife. It wasn't like Kayla needed to be scared of dragons hurting her either. They all loved her despite her cold shoulder.

"That's what he's scared of," Warner insisted. *"He's scared of losing Kayla. That's every dragon's worst fear to lose their rider."*

That wasn't the same thing as getting hurt. There were lots of other ways to lose a person.

"Oh."

Caleb rubbed at his chin as he watched Kayla conquer herself yet again. She got off her knees, and with hood tucked down rather far, started for the woods. Charles gave Caleb a nod as if he had faith that Caleb could pull everything together and returned to the mess hall. Caleb heard the door close behind him.

Valiant's struggle was a variation of Kayla's. It wasn't only about getting hurt. This was about losing Kayla completely. The girl hadn't had very many friends growing up. She didn't join in games with the rider children. She mostly played with Colts far away from dragons, or with Anvil's kids in the nearby town behind walls, away from dragons.

Kayla never had a boyfriend, that he was very certain about. And the reason for that? A love relation could make Valiant feel like he was losing his rider. A friend relation could be close to the same thing. What Valiant really lacked was the same thing that all other dragons hooted for when Kayla walked by. Turn around and see me. Come love me. Bonding. Valiant was horrified that he didn't have Kayla's keeper bond. He acted like he might somehow lose her keeper bond, or her trust, or her love. He pulled her to him because he didn't want her looking at anyone else.

Valiant was always sitting as still as death. Why did the dragon feel like he had no love? Kayla wasn't incapable of loving dragons. He'd seen that about her. She might not look at them, but she cared for them. There were so many times that she'd helped them discreetly. Caleb turned back time to his favorite example.

Kayla, fourteen, hood over her head, running through the west dragon field trying to escape the warm greetings all around her as the dragons and riders said hello. She ran faster past a dragon that was crying. Caleb had just barely bonded Warner and Warner's words on the matter were rather fascinating.

"She smells delicious. I know why those dragons like her so much. She smells like flame and cinnamon, sheep and deer. She smells like hope and glory, like life and love."

"Who?" Caleb had asked.

At Warner's answer to who he was spying on Caleb had dropped his breakfast all over the ground and left it there to run for the field. He finally knew what dragons saw in Kayla, and he had to see her for himself. He had no idea who had cleaned up for him, but some kind soul had done so without asking for anything in return. Warner mentioned the crying dragon and where Kayla was headed. Caleb caught up to her when she skid to a halt behind the hospital wing. She had found a crying person, Joal, the rider to the crying dragon. Kayla glanced at him briefly and then she continued running through the ware. Caleb followed her, noticing her fast breathing and hearing her words.

"I heard a strange noise behind the doctors." Kayla had stopped before Tiana as she pointed. Caleb couldn't help but grin and pull out his paper and pencil to record this moment. Kayla wasn't interacting with the dragons that were not hers, but she still helped them by sending their riders the help they needed. Tiana was sweet on Joal. It was the perfect person to send to him when he had a hard day. Kayla didn't linger as Caleb drew, but he knew where she would turn out so when he was done, he put his paper down on the ground before Anvil's office and waited.

Kayla froze at the sight of the drawing. The shadow dragon crying, the shadow person crying, and Kayla pointing the way for help. He'd captioned it "unseen hero." She looked at the drawing for about half a minute. It was still Caleb's longest time to date at getting Kayla Brixton looking at something he made for her. Then she was off again.

Anvil came out of the office next, found the paper, smiled at it, and stuffed it into his bag. Caleb never saw that drawing again, but he had it imprinted on his mind. He liked to think that Kayla had enjoyed it, a small piece of recognition that she was as beautiful as all the dragons saw her to be. As beautiful as he saw her to be.

Valiant usually refused to see anything. Charles was right. That wasn't normal. Valiant had come from Vankerdale so something over there had made him this way. Something over there made him feel like love wasn't something he could attain, even if he longed for it. What had happened to Valiant? Caleb wasn't sure if he had what it took to fix him, but he was going to try. This was going to be a long job. Good thing he had learned how to be patient where Kayla was concerned years ago.

The mess hall door opened up again and people started to pour out. Caleb was surrounded by his fellow section leaders who were grinning at him. He wasn't sure why. It wasn't like he had left everyone in this ware free pictures posted on the walls hoping that Kayla would look at them.

"Charles has declared that all of us are invading and defending the woods today," Mulligan told him. "Great idea, Caleb. Really practical. See you out there. I'm going to catch you and tie you up."

Pg. 174

Caleb laughed and then bit his lower lip as he watched people stream toward the woods. His class was the only one unaware of the additional forces. It looked like they would learn really quickly, and Kayla had a full day where she could perfect her hiding.

Letter

Tyler

Tyler shut the door to his room with a soft click and lit the candle, careful to not burn the paper in his hands. He didn't want to open his window to let in the afternoon light when he was trying to hide from everyone after he had managed to break into the king's things. Tyler kicked off his shoes and turned. His heart jumped. His legs jumped. His arms grabbed for the sword at his side as his paper that he'd kept without a wrinkle fluttered down to the ground. Perhaps that was for the best because the person whose dark image he had seen and reacted to was Prince Evan sitting on his bed in the dark.

What if he knew!? Had some guard run to the border to verify Tyler's permission into the study? Did Prince Evan have spies that watched everything he did, and they had guessed that he had a dragon in his head? Now Prince Evan was here to kill him?

"You are aiming a sword at me," Prince Evan remarked in his usual annoyed half-angry voice.

"You're in my room! In the dark!" Tyler pointed out.

"You don't own the castle. Technically it's my room. I'm in my own room in the dark," Prince Evan answered.

Tyler didn't own the castle, but he knew how to. Best not think about that right now. He had to calm himself down. There could be a much better explanation for why the prince was here. Another dark figure shifted out of a corner and Tyler aimed the sword over there next. King Peyton. His heart was beating faster than SilverWings could fly.

"Put the sword down, Tyler," King Peyton ordered.

He didn't want to. To lower his defense could cost him his life. Then again, if he was pretending that he wasn't doing anything suspicious then he would have lowered his sword. He slowly put it down, but he kept it in his hand. They were both in his room.

"I suggest you keep that up," was Coal's contribution.

"What do you want?" Tyler asked them. That was what he would say if he was being normal, and not overtaken by the fears of Conner telling him that his rulers wanted him dead and the fears of Coal that he needed to fight.

"I want you to tell me the punishment for traitors," Prince Evan told him.

Tyler gripped the sword handle really really hard. Neither of them had a weapon drawn against him, and from what he could see, neither had a weapon attached to their side either. That didn't mean that they weren't planning his doom. They could poison him. He shouldn't eat in the castle. They could have put snakes in his bed. He should sleep in a closet far away from here. That and calm himself down.

"Traitors get a really long holiday," Tyler answered. They died. That's all that happened to them.

"Tyler, fight them off!"

"Shh!" He hissed back. He couldn't look like he was conversing inside his own head. That would only make this whole thing worse!

"What do you want? You're making me nervous."

King Peyton moved closer to where Tyler was and pried the sword from his hand. Tyler wanted to use it, except to stab the king would surely have the son calling for his death right away.

"Prince Evan was frozen in the woods by a spell that Kayla put on him. You avoided a similar spell due to Valiant, and then you followed, not trapped, Kayla into the house of a merchant. You sat around with her making no effort to bring her back to the throne. You have two minutes to defend yourself."

"Did you happen to see those dragons?!" Tyler blurted. "We were completely surrounded. Sure, it was only Valiant at first, but he's Kayla's dragon not..." He barely stopped himself from saying "mine," and he felt his skin start to sweat. "...not the most helpful creature," he said instead. "The team of formidable dragons pinned us in. They shoved Valiant through the air and plopped us down at the merchant's house who was nice enough to give us dinner while the dragons kept us trapped inside. There wasn't anything we could do."

Had it been two minutes yet? He really hoped not.

"Then Pyro showed up and Jack showed up, and they took Kayla and Valiant away and left the rest of us behind, and I came back here while the merchant finally got his house back. I think the dragons were mad at him. He probably owed them some gems or something, so they made it look like he was a traitor too. Anyway, I'm not a traitor. I had a full day to study Kayla. I can tell you anything you want to know about her."

"I want to eat you," Coal growled into his thoughts. Tyler ignored it.

"How much torture does she require before she can get her Mr.

Grumpy over here?" Prince Evan asked.

Tyler squirmed. That was the part of their plan that he didn't like. "Uh… I guess I can't tell you that. I don't know."

King Peyton reached down and picked up one of the pages Tyler had written out today. Tyler held his breath. He had been finding all sorts of things. A lot of it he hadn't written down because he was scared that it would incriminate him for being in the room he shouldn't have been inside, but he had to write down what he found about bad dreams. He had to give it to Jack so he could keep the dragon in his head, although the dragon now wanted to eat him.

King Peyton skimmed over the information and looked up at Tyler, waiting for another two-minute rant. He had it all ready.

"Prince Evan is always asking me to find him odd things about Aralot. I thought that if I could find the answers to his questions ahead of time then I wouldn't be scrambling to find them when he asks."

"And my question would be what?" Prince Evan asked, reaching for the paper in his father's hand as he came over. He tilted his head to the side as he read it.

"What happens to the queens of Aralot," Tyler answered. "Kayla has nightmares. She was screaming all night long when I was with her. I wanted to know why."

"She's used to scary things," Prince Evan remarked sourly. "So she'll be hard to torture."

"Use your brain." King Peyton passed Tyler the paper. "If Kayla dies before we get to use her, we're out of luck again. Did you decide when she's going to die as a sacrifice to her kingdom?" King Peyton asked Tyler.

"Why is Kayla dying?" Coal whispered into his head.

Pg. 180

"No. But as you can see, I've written down the dates of all the other past queens that had this problem. The odd part is that Kayla is not a queen and her father not fully crowned, so I don't know if she will become a sacrifice like the records indicate."

He felt even a larger pull to get Kayla into Vankerdale and out of Aralot now that he had read this information. Kayla could help him take over the kingdom once Conner and Coal killed off King Peyton and Prince Evan. If she could be kept away from the crown or any title of becoming the queen inside of Aralot, she might not actually die.

"Explain the sacrifice, Tyler," Prince Evan demanded. See, this was why he tried to stay a step ahead of him.

"Since Aralot was first founded the queens of Aralot have suffered from bad dreams. Our records don't give us the nature of those dreams, but I do know that the queens all have a similar nightmare right before they die. Their life spans are jumbled all over the place, not indicating how long they have to live. Some of them lived up to the age of ninety. One died at twenty-four. Personally, I think Kayla shouldn't be having nightmares at all given her single status, but I can't tell you the exact nature of the spell cast on these people, so I don't know if there are exceptions or if her nightmares are unrelated."

He was pretty sure they were related or King Jack would have solved this already.

"After the third queen's death, Vankerdale was blamed for it, because the Aralot kings thought it was a curse we had put on them. See the dates? We warred with Aralot during these years." He pointed out all the years that they had trouble. It was more than half the page. That was probably why Jack had asked him to look into the nature of the nightmares because if the nightmare of death was a spell from Vankerdale, Tyler might be able to direct Jack in how to fix it.

Pg. 181

"Every time another queen died, we got hate-filled letters," King Peyton told his son, having already looked into this before it seemed. "And the queen's last words were recorded onto some of them. They all had one thing in common."

"They talked about being a sacrifice for Aralot," Tyler nodded.

"So the kings of Aralot naturally decided that we were to blame," Prince Evan huffed.

"King Gladius blamed the crown," Tyler added. "And King Virgil Cluster IV, Klavian's father, did too. Virgil killed off all the keepers he could find trying to minimize the crown's curses. We all know what Klavian's done."

He had used Tia to get himself into the castle. Now Tia's daughter was having complications.

"Well if Kayla dies over here then Aralot will finally get the blame right," Prince Evan shrugged.

"Perhaps." King Peyton let Tyler's sword drop to the floor as he started for the door. "I have no idea what that curse is. However, I am fairly certain that Gladius knew. See you later, Tyler."

"Bye," Tyler answered, watching as Prince Evan walked out after him asking questions about if Kayla would die on them before he wanted her to. Tyler sheathed his sword, and sighed in relief that he'd gotten away with his infiltrations so far.

"*Is Kayla dying?*" Coal asked.

"*I don't know,*" Tyler finally talked to the dragon. "*She shouldn't be.*"

Tyler paced the room and then decided to step outside to see if he could spot any of Conner's dragons. Maybe he wouldn't have to wait around for Jack to sneak back inside Vankerdale's castle if he could talk Conner into taking this information over.

He walked past the courtyard feeling nervous when he passed the guards who could tell on him or stab him in the back. That had been really scary with the king and prince. If he hadn't had anything good to tell them to defend himself, he might not be walking right now. It was Jack's question that had saved him. Tyler was able to pretend that he was trying to help the Peyton's by researching information about Kayla.

He headed out of the market still with no signs of keeper dragons. He moved to the woods where he had seen Conner before and kept going until the a rather strange sound came across his ears. It sounded like a missile, like something had been launched through the air at an incredible speed and was going to crash into him. Tyler inhaled for good measure as he rushed to the side looking behind him at the castle trying to see what was coming to hit him.

He couldn't see anything from that direction, but the whizzing sound got louder and louder until a disturbing thump landed right beside him. Too close! Whoever was trying to hit him had nearly gotten him killed! Coal was unhelpfully telling him to fly away.

Tyler scrambled behind a few trees, listening hard for more projectiles only to look behind him when an animal hummed in response to his scrambling. Valiant! What was he doing here? He must have been going nearly twenty times his normal speed for him to have created that kind of speed. He appeared riderless which was probably the reason for his rush. He had left Kayla behind and would want to get back to her as soon as he could. Without her on his back, he didn't need to take it slow.

Valiant gave him a bow and Tyler ran at him hugging his face while tears prickled at his eyes. Valiant had spent all his life waiting to reach Kayla, and she might die on him early. He didn't want to tell him.

It was better to live without worrying about that.

"I miss you. I was reading in your old room and it wasn't the same," Tyler said instead. "How's Kayla doing?"

Valiant rambled off an answer that Tyler couldn't understand, but the tone of it wasn't upset so he guessed she was fine. The dragon turned so that Tyler could see a piece of paper that was stuck on his side. Guessing it was for him, Tyler reached for it and pulled it off watching as a puff of blue ran away into the air as the spell on it was released from him getting the letter. It was from Kayla and not very long.

"Tyler, I'm sorry that I didn't realize earlier. What can I help you with?"

Realize what? That she could be dying? That she was going to be kidnapped again because Tyler had told the Peyton's how to do it?

"That you have a dragon," Coal provided.

Oh. That. Kayla had figured it out. That didn't make him feel any better. There were too many people who knew. This was bad timing especially since Kayla was heading for torture and could spill his secret. He had to save her before the torture got too bad. Tyler read the second sentence again. He needed help with everything. Conner could claim that Kayla was going to tell them what to do all he wanted. He didn't really know her. Lead keeper or not, she was defaulting to everyone else, and Tyler had his reply written on that note for Valiant to take back as fast as his fingers could fly.

"Locate and destroy the ultra-dragon king's missing dragon scale."

He paused his writing when the light green dragon that had once chirped at Kayla fluttered down and nudged into Valiant like they were friends. It was strange to see the green beast hanging around as if waiting for Valiant to show himself again. Valiant chirped hello to the animal doing much better at making friends now that he was out of his prison. They talked for a while until the dragon looked toward Wisteria and whined. Valiant surprised Tyler by magically adding to the words on his paper to include: *"Find Lena Sherman for Reed."*

It looked like this dragon was missing his rider someplace and asking Kayla for help. Everything really did need her. She would find Reed's missing rider, and he would be happy. Kayla would save Coal so the dragon would change his mind about eating Tyler.

Tyler moved to put the letter back into the envelope and then put it in his pocket instead. Asking Kayla to do anything was useless if she was captured first. It was a shame that he needed her. Coal needed her. Vankerdale needed her. Aralot needed her. She needed herself. Busy person.

Valiant snorted at him. He couldn't read Tyler's mind, but he could tell that there was something wrong. Tyler couldn't share with him what it was. He was supposed to be some keeper that protected Kayla from everything and he *still* didn't want to stop King Peyton from bringing the girl back into Vankerdale. He was instigating the capture, so really, there was nothing that King Peyton or Prince Evan could get mad at him for—yet.

"How long until the border spells fall?" Tyler asked Valiant.

The dragon answered but Tyler had no idea what he said. Valiant was doing much better being with Kayla. He was talking and wide awake and free to move and live. Already his muscles and wings didn't look as shriveled as they had when he was in captivity. He had a fast turn around.

"I can't send back a letter if you could get caught by King Peyton. This would kill me, Valiant."

It really would. If his taskmasters never guessed that he was distracted from a voice chattering into his head, they would surely see the proof that he was conspiring with Aralot behind their backs through this letter. Valiant barked out a few more words that Tyler had to shrug at. Then the dragon snorted at him, annoyed for not understanding him as Kayla would. Tyler had to resort to yes and no answers. It would be really nice to not have to do that.

"Will SilverWings catch you?" he asked.

"No," Valiant chirped.

"Then how do you keep getting into Aralot past him? How is it done? What sort of trickery or magic...." That wasn't a yes or no question. He would never get the answer like that.

"Do you take an alternate path instead of flying through the border?"

Rather than answer that, Valiant curled up into a ball. Tyler expected him to close his eyes as well and shut him out of everything that would be going on inside the dragon's mental universe, but he didn't. Valiant kept his eyes open. They stared at his pocket. Valiant probably knew a spell that would take the letter out of there. The larger question right now was if Valiant respected him enough to not steal from his pocket. The dragon didn't want to answer about his route, so it had to be a yes. There was some kind of work around. A passageway. Kayla and her father had flown north. They could have gone all the way to the ocean and looped around the border spells to arrive back into Aralot from the ocean.

A dragon laugh snickered through his head. Tyler glanced upward expecting to see Coal right there with how close he sounded.

"Tyler, they took a portal. Everyone in Aralot knows about them. Why don't you?"

Pg. 186

He knew what a portal was only Vankerdale didn't have magic to use on such things so Tyler never thought about them. However, the king and prince may have contemplated their use. They had complained about seeing Tia in a magical library without being able to nab her before. They had complained about not being able to take "the special route" to get into Aralot after Jack's border spells went up. He could have closed them out from using portals. Now that it was brought up, Tyler realized that Coal was right. Aralot used portals way more than they did.

"Want me to search for the right portal?" Coal offered. "It might not be closed off for you. You're not a Peyton."

Tyler knew the general direction to go so it couldn't be that hard to find the portal. It would be hard to make it work though, because he had no idea how to use it. At least not yet. Next on his agenda was looking into hidden information about portals. He pulled out a new piece of paper and changed the wording of his response to Kayla.

"Watch out for possession spells. Also, Reed, that light green dragon, wants to find Lena Sherman who is probably his rider."

"You decided against asking Kayla to help me. Tyler, why?" Coal pressed for the answer.

Valiant uncurled from a ball and nudged Tyler with his nose. Tyler pushed it away. Valiant probably wanted to know who he was talking to.

"She's going to be captured again. She won't have time to help you."

"How long do you expect to keep her? She got away from you last time," Coal asked annoyed.

"She won't this time. We'll keep her until we get Mr. Grumpy," Tyler replied. Given Aralot's timing, that could be looking at years of more waiting.

"Mr. Grumpy is old. There's no point in taking him when no one can breed another magical ice dragon."

"True," Tyler answered. "But that's what Kayla is for. She will bring over Valiant. We have to breed Valiant with Sparkle. Only a spellbinding dragon and an ice dragon can make a magical dragon. Getting Mr. Grumpy is the first step to knowing if we have something good enough that Aralot will bleed for. If they care enough, Tia will send over Sparkle. We can use Mr. Grumpy's magic while we wait for Valiant to dazzle her."

"Vankerdale is twisted," Coal snarled into his head.

It was twisted. Very very twisted, and along with it was Tyler who had secretly devised his own plan for once he got Kayla on this side of the divide again. With her over here, he could finally fix the break between Vankerdale and Aralot. It might even save her life, provided he was faster than King Peyton. This whole thing still left him in knots, especially since Kayla could say no. But if he got his timing right, she could save both kingdoms. He hastily wrote out a new letter simply telling her that he'd reply later.

Souls

Kayla

Playing defend the ware was really hard. So it was nice when Kayla could slip away because she had way too much on her mind. She kept bouncing back and forth between her dad and Tristan and Aria.

Jack had walked into the mess hall and Kayla had that same strange feeling she got that day Tyler started to feel like a respected friend. One day he was Prince Evan's lackey, and the next, Tyler was different, the same way that her keeper cousins had felt only she hadn't realized that the feeling was the same at the time. Feeling it again on her dad had her jumping. Being a keeper was supposed to be inherently related to blood. Sure, there was that old story where an ultra-dragon king gave the "gift" of being a keeper to the first keeper, but since then its properties had never changed. Until now. Pyro could make keepers, and he had made two of them. Tyler and Jack.

Oh, how she had wanted to scream in fear, but she couldn't because of her location, and because she knew that her dad was there to kick her out of the ware. It should have been easy for him. Then her mother had come to do the same thing, and she was in charge of all the dragon wares as her main job. It should have been easy for Tia to kick Kayla out too. Only the most startling of distractions was going to keep Kayla in the ware, and she had used it. Her father could control keepers.

Why then didn't he take it all away from her? He could. Should she ask him to? Ask Pyro to free her?

"Change who you are? Nice dress by the way," Valiant said as Kayla looked at herself in the mirror and half thought about how she didn't like the peach-colored dress. She was leaving the ware to attend lunch with the queen. It was her first lesson on how to behave like a princess. She assumed she had to try to look like one. Valiant couldn't even see her. What did he know?

"I know that you are always adorable," Valiant replied. *"If you stopped being a keeper would that mess with my head?"*

Oh, probably. Breaking bonds hurt. Breaking keeper bonds would probably hurt too. There would be some rather bad side effect and maybe some extra nasty curse and who knew what else. It wouldn't be easy, and the end result wouldn't be worth it, especially if she was carving into Valiant's head.

"Oh good. I thought you were going to ask Pyro to torture me. That would be terrifying."

"It was just the thought of not feeling all this pressure around dragons all the time that is enticing," Kayla replied.

She looked down at her boots, not having anything else. Aria would probably dock her points for wearing them with her dress. Kayla made a mental note to pass the store on her way over to the castle.

Thinking of the castle had her thinking of Tristan. He had turned his back on her during the breakfast date this morning, and she had cast a spell on him. She had never cast a spell on him before so she had thought it out all morning, trying to make sure that it would be something he wouldn't notice and yet have it tell her if he had a stained soul. Merlock had said there would be a way to tell. Since she had never seen a disconnected soul before, except inside nightmares of her mother's soul being stuck to King Klavian, she wasn't sure if she had learned anything at all. Tristan had two shadows for a moment. One was at his side and one was behind him. The one behind him had been split between man and dragon. It was time to test out the spell on Aria, assuming that Kayla could find a way to do so without the queen noticing.

Kayla crossed out of the ware, flashing her class schedule at the scouts. before she crossed over to the shoe store. She glanced in the window not spotting shoes she liked that would match a dress so she pressed on.

"You are late," the guard that let her into the castle told her. "You were supposed to magically arrive an hour early and read this entire rule book." He showed her a really fat book that Kayla stared at. "So I'll sum it up. Don't slurp. Keep the napkin on your lap. Chew with your mouth closed. Fourth room on the third floor on your right. Good luck."

There was no way that the guard could have summed up an entire book on manners in that short amount of time. Kayla took the book from him to read later, tossed it into the bag on her back that she probably should have left behind, and dashed across the courtyard to reach the right room.

What she saw when she opened the door had her freezing. The place was set up for a tea party, not lunch. Queen Aria was reading a book waiting for her to show up at the beautiful round table. Kayla stepped into the room slowly, only to be shoved in deeper from behind by Tristan.

"Love tea parties," he claimed.

He waved his hand to make himself a chair and a plate with magic and sat down with a look at his mother like there was nothing she could do to kick him out. Kayla sat down too, really wishing that Tristan

Pg. 191

hadn't shown up. She might have to hold off on casting the spell on Aria unless she could get in a really good distraction, like spilling all the tea, so Tristan wouldn't notice her magic use. Kayla glanced at the kettle and then down at her plate that already had cookies on it. Tristan noticed his empty plate and grabbed a similar spread so he could match everyone else.

"There is a right way and a wrong way to eat a cookie," Aria told her, deciding not to kick out her son. "Do not bite into it and spill crumbs everywhere. Don't dip it into your tea."

"I like to shove the whole thing into my mouth and chew loudly," Tristan said, picking up a cookie that his mother knocked from his hand.

"Perhaps I should back up a little. When you eat with royalty you are not allowed to start eating until the king or queen does, and when they finish eating, you must be done too, even if you are still starving."

"It helps if your mother gives you utensils so you can eat," Tristan added, and then he laughed at the look his mom gave him. Kayla couldn't see Aria's lap, but she did notice that the woman's napkin was missing, so Kayla placed her napkin across her peach-colored dress as the guard had suggested. That earned a smile from Aria and an eye roll from Tristan as he did the same thing.

"You may have the tea and cookies now," Aria said. "I'll correct any mistakes afterward." She gave a glance at her son who had three cookies in his mouth already and was reaching for a sandwich. Maybe Valiant was right. Tristan couldn't care that she had bad manners if he was this bad. Then again, it looked like he was doing it on purpose to annoy his mother.

Kayla reached for a cookie and brought it to her mouth as she watched Aria so she could get tips on how to eat a cookie. Aria made it sound hard, but it looked rather easy. You bit it and chewed. Kayla was about to take a bite when her hand started to shake and an orange glow revealed that keeper poison had been sprinkled on the top of her item. Tristan reacted faster than she could. He spit his food out all over the table, earning a scolding from his mother, while he knocked the cookie from Kayla's hand.

"How could you?!" he shouted at his mom.

"You're the one throwing up on all our food," Aria said, throwing her napkin down at the table and standing up.

She had stopped eating, so Kayla removed her napkin and looked back and forth between her two foes. It had to be one of them that had put on the keeper poison. Was it Tristan trying to destroy the tea party and blame his mom? He had seen how to make the poison. Was it Aria trying to kill her and Valiant? The poison didn't exactly link either of these two people to the curse on her mom and Rosa. Why was this so hard? Kayla picked up her teacup next and dipped a finger into it watching it glow orange as well.

"That is Kayla's indication that her food is laced with keeper poison," Tristan told his mother.

"That's not allowed in the castle." Aria looked alarmed. She looked at her own plate and clutched at her stomach, asking Tristan if the poison would work on a person who didn't have a dragon. Kayla tried to detect insincerity in her face, but both of them looked rather stricken. No wonder her father had not gotten far in this. They either acted really well or were innocent of this particular crime.

Tristan hadn't poisoned her food on their dates, and he had been the one keeping her safe, but still, he really did know how to make this, and if he wanted to ruin a tea party because she had refused to eat lunch with him, this would really do the trick.

"I will look into this. I'll have the kitchen scrubbed and the cooks questioned. I am really very sorry, Kayla," Aria said. "We are going to get different food."

She headed out of the door so Kayla waited for Tristan to go out first.

"I like your dress," Tristan whispered as he passed her. For once he sounded like he meant it so she shook her head at him. He was so twisted, running himself in circles all the time. Did he ever exhaust himself with putting her down and trying to defend her at the same time?

Kayla took the one moment she had with both their backs turned to use her spell on Aria, careful to keep whatever image came back at her out of Tristan's sight. A shadow appeared on the floor before her feet and then vanished. No sooner was it gone than Vermelo was seen walking down the hallway with his hands casually behind his back as if he was patrolling the floors. He gave them all a worried look when he noticed them not in the room.

"The food got too cold?" he asked Aria.

"It got poisoned." The queen answered. "I will be questioning your guards for this as well."

"Madam they would never do anything like that," Vermelo replied, giving Tristan a glare as if this was his doing.

"It had keeper poison," Tristan provided. "Don't look at me. I wouldn't make Kayla into a dragon killing machine. I don't need her wanting to kill my dragon."

"I'm fine," Kayla quickly mentioned as Vermelo rushed to her and yanked her toward him talking about getting her the cure as soon as possible. "I promise," she added.

He came with her anyway to supervise the new sandwiches that got made for them. They ate them right there in the kitchen, and Aria didn't bother saying anything about how to properly do that. Kayla made sure that she started and stopped when Aria did, and was really glad when she got to skip out on Vermelo and Aria arguing with each other over who would question people first. Kayla took the back exit out of the castle so she could run through the trees and avoid the blockade of riders on her way back into the ware.

She didn't feel safe anywhere. What was she doing here? It couldn't be Charles adding the poison that time. He could have been responsible for getting that poison on her food at the ware, but he couldn't have made his way directly into the castle. For the poison to get there, it would have needed to be added to the food before it reached the castle. Was it a Colt that was out to get her? If that ended up being the case, she was a helpless cause. She'd be starving for years to come because Colts didn't give up, and she would have no idea why one of them would want to hurt her like this.

"I personally think that it's all Charles," Valiant added.

Well, it was hard to blame Aria and Tristan. Searching for stains on Aria's and Tristan's souls hadn't done her much good. Both of them had been shadows with the exception that Tristan's shadow had been split vertically with half man and half dragon, which would have reflected Riven. Since both had been dark in nature, Kayla wasn't sure if that proved that both Aria and Tristan were using curses that touched life, or if neither one was, or if she had gotten the wording and intention of her spell all wrong. She needed a different person with which to compare her findings. She needed to find a person that wouldn't scream in terror if she cast a spell in his or her direction and peeked into the intimate nature of his soul. Caleb would do nicely.

Kayla sighed as she made note of where the current clashing rider forces were in the forest. The sounds were relatively distant, so she took a few more steps wishing that she had all the answers. Arms reached out of the silent placid earth yanking her downward. How had she missed this trap?! She should have been paying more attention to where she was instead of where everyone else seemed to be.

Kayla gave out a shout that was strangled by a set of sweaty arms overtaking her. She scrambled to stop the hand reaching for her keychain that was unclipped from her side as she squirmed. She couldn't lose that! She was horrible at defending herself. First, there was Tyler tying her up like he was special when he kidnapped her into Vankerdale, and now she had lost her magic to a group of sweaty men in a trench! She was not going down!

"Ow!"

All her defenses exploded, and with it the keychain that she was losing. In her head, she heard Valiant scream, although he couldn't reach her since he was still someplace between Aralot and Vankerdale due to that letter to Tyler. She struggled, and the magic blazed red as she willed it to attack the person who knew how to take it from her.

"Kayla, stop," Caleb's voice hissed into her ear. "I can't have you blasting everyone. You've been captured. I'll give this back in a minute. Are you in a dress?"

There was something about the way he asked her that question that led to her turning rigid. Why was she giving in so quickly to his voice? It was stupid to give in when he'd caught her, but his was the voice that usually saved her. On that note, she hadn't canceled her own spell even if it hadn't hit anything. Caleb still had the keychain in his hand, so she had to assume that it was him controlling the magic. With anyone else that would have scared her silly, but from Caleb, she couldn't help but lean back and look into his face.

He had turned her magic off. She had spells on her keychain

keeping other people from using it, and he had used it. It took magical respect from Aralot for magic to bend instantly to another's will like that. Her father had that respect, but Caleb? She didn't think that he'd ever touched magic before. It was illegal. Regardless of that, he didn't look like he realized that he was magically respected, or that it was him that had made the sparking stop. Magic involved understanding how to set the correct intention and conditions, but it also took a lot of mental will power. He had shut down her curse by *wanting* it to go away. He was amazing.

"Dress?" Caleb tried again, flicking at her shoulder. There was a smile attached to the question, and a warm satisfied glow that she turned away from. Caleb Andrade was holding her down in a pit of other captured riders, and he was rather pleased with himself. This was the first time he had ever touched her, and it was making her turn sweaty.

No.

That was the result of all the other stuffed bodies around her. She was making stuff up because she was suddenly bursting with curiosity over why Caleb could use her magic. Yes, that was it. She wasn't blushing from the satisfaction of those eyes or the firmness of those arms. She'd been held by lots of men before. Okay only Uncle Anvil, but still. There was no reason to be thinking about leaning even farther back to completely relax into a pair of strange arms that happened to be attached to a most adorable face. No reason except that it was making her body buzz with excitement, and if she got that emotion high enough, she could climb out of this trench and not be scared if she happened to run across a dragon. Was it worth it? It could be worth it.

"You got bored and went shopping?" Caleb guessed.

"I had to eat lunch with Queen Aria," Kayla replied.

"Oh, right." Caleb chuckled and the movement of his diaphragm brushed against her back, causing her to close her eyes. She was in trouble. There was something about being this close to Caleb that had all her defenses knocked out. It was like she had suddenly stepped out of a dark fog and into a lone patch of sunshine, so bright it could chase away any nightmare. There was a peaceful pulse coming at her again and again that she never ever wanted to step away from. It was either that, or Caleb was accidentally causing the reaction in her because he still had her magic.

"Give me that," Kayla squirmed, reaching for the keychain.

It was one of them creating that brilliant light for sure, and she had to figure out which one. If it was Caleb, then he had just given away that he had a crush on her. Not that she couldn't guess. If it was her, she had to make sure that she didn't reveal the same thing, because she still had to get closer to Tristan. Maybe her overall intentions were talking too loud because she wanted to check the nature of Caleb's soul to compare it to Tristan and Aria's.

Kayla got her magic back and looked around trying to decide if now was a bad time to ask him if she could cast a spell on him. Then again, why ask? She was in a trench with a bunch of other riders who had been captured. This was a perfect place to get a large sample of souls to compare. She cast the spell, watching as glowing images came streaming up overhead from the rider's bodies. They all screamed at her. Caleb tackled her for her magic again.

"What are you doing?! I don't know what that was, but you need to stop."

Kayla couldn't help but laugh at him as he reached the keychain in her hand and made her spell disappear yet again. This was amusing. When she had first started using magic, she had been disastrous and blew things up. Caleb touched it and it practically sang for him. What other spells could she test out to watch him cast away?

Pg. 198

She blinked. The brightness of the images were stained on her irises, and when she looked hard at the afterimage, she could tell that Caleb's glowing soul had been the brightest of all of them. It was him then that had been glowing. He had a rather glorious soul. And if that contrasted with the souls of Aria and her son, it said volumes, because these men glowed while Aria and Tristan were shrouded in darkness. Both of them had been using magic on lives. Kayla didn't think that they were both responsible for the same curses, so what exactly was Tristan casting out and what was Aria casting out? Aria never let on that she used magic!

"Kayla," Caleb hissed at her while Russel told the other captured people to be quiet. "This is no time to play around," he declared. "Being captured is not supposed to be fun."

"I'm finding it really fun," Kayla admitted. Looking at Caleb was like looking at a beacon of potential. He would be really good with a bonded spellbinding dragon.

"*I am not amused,*" Valiant told her, which only made her giggle.

"Shush, Kayla. Your resistance was pathetic. If it was Vankerdale that had gotten you, you wouldn't be looking so cheerful. You failed. This is the pit of the dead so be quiet."

She didn't want to be quiet. She wanted to start telling Caleb all about magic even if she really shouldn't. He wasn't supposed to use it, but he hadn't released her hand, and he was looking at the gem on the keychain like he was finally catching on to why she was smiling at him. He was the one moving the magic.

"It's warm isn't it?" Kayla whispered.

"There are some things that should not be shared with friends," Caleb whispered back.

He dropped her hand and turned away from her before he could be tempted by the tingle that came along with magic harkening to a will. Russel sent her a glare and shoved her away from Caleb farther among the rest of the dead crowd. That wasn't fun, because with the magic no longer distracting her, Caleb had been right. She had failed to escape him. Familiar voice or not, she should have run. Any day now and Vankerdale would be slamming into them for real. She had to do better at this, but she could worry about that later. Right now, she had a great view of Caleb Andrade.

Her view was soon ruined. The whistle of an invasion blew hard and long cutting across everyone's ears that were already playing invader. Kayla looked up at the two section leaders. Was this a trap or not?

"Get out! Everyone back to the ware! This is not a drill. Get up!"

That was Charles screaming. The riders ran from the trench, kicking up the leaves and destroying the trap that had been dug and would need to be filled back in later. Kayla was the slowest because she was still in a dress. This was a horrible day! Everything was turning ugly all at the same time. Caleb kept glancing over his shoulder, but she waved him onward and he nodded as if agreeing that she would be fine for a time.

The closer she got to the ware, the easier it was to see the problem. Fire was spewing out from the direction of the town as the first wave of the attack struck and riders scrambled around to coordinate a resistance. The flames were the real trick, because the attacking force had moved away from the distraction and landed right behind her nestling into the trees. She heard the source of the invasion instead of seeing it. If she had seen it, she would have fainted. It wasn't Vankerdale. Not yet. It was something just as horrible.

"Kayla."

The dragon voice still left her trembling. She gave up on reaching the ware and grabbed for her keychain. So far the only thing they knew about ultra-dragon kings was that they were practically indestructible, but she was going to blast this beast if he tried to touch her. Why was Reaper so close to this place that he could find the perfect way to get her alone? He was not going to sink his fangs into her. She knew what he was after. He'd been after it a long time.

"I will tear your wings off!" Kayla screamed back at him.

"I will trade you for information."

"Go away, Reaper."

"My name is Coal. I can tell you how to breed a magical ice dragon. All I want in return is for you to find my missing scale."

The magic on her hand rolled into a blue ball and sat there. She couldn't blast him. The greed to know this information was too large. If they could make another magical ice dragon, then Aralot wouldn't fall to Vankerdale. They would have magic after Mr. Grumpy died. There was also that part where Coal had said his name. Someone had finally told him.

"Promise that you know?" Kayla asked.

"I promise. Promise to look?" he asked back.

"Why do you want your scale? Lots of dragons lose scales. They grow back. Don't your scales grow back?"

"Just help me, please," the dragon begged and risked taking a step closer. Kayla took a large jump away and he stopped moving.

"Why do you want me to look…" Kayla trailed off listening to the sounds of a team of dragons that happened to know where Coal had landed. They were heading this way grouping up to chase him out. She didn't think he noticed them since he was so eager to talk to her.

"Okay. I will look for your scale," she agreed.

"You have to breed Valiant with Sparkle to get a magical ice dragon. It takes a spellbinding dragon and an ice dragon to get the magic. Good luck, and watch out for Vankerdale. It's full of traitors!"

He screamed the word traitor like he was particularly angry and then ran through the trees until he could launch back into the air to fight off the team of warriors that had found him. Kayla stayed where she was. Valiant with Sparkle? How was that ever going to work?? Ice dragons wouldn't mate with anyone they hadn't known from birth. It was a bit of a stretch to think that Sparkle would consider Valiant a potential mate based on the information that she had known Kayla from birth. It was also a bit of a stretch to assume that seeing Valiant once when he bit Kayla's leg as an infant would suffice against her inner nature. That was all the interaction they ever had.

There was more going on that had to play into everything. Scale. Traitor. Coal knew his name and he was talking about Vankerdale. Tyler! Knowing how to get a magical ice dragon was something that Tyler would know. Coal must have Tyler in his head, which was why the dragon had decided he didn't need to fang Kayla anymore. He still wanted her to look for a scale though. So weird. She had to tell her mother about Valiant and Sparkle getting together. On second thought, maybe she would just tell Valiant.

"Maybe Valiant already knew," the dragon replied.

"Does it scare you?" Kayla asked.

"Does marrying someone to preserve the throne scare you?" Valiant questioned back. Kayla sighed. They lived the same life. It wasn't fair that one of them couldn't escape it.

"I like Sparkle. I think she's beautiful. It won't be as hard for me as this is for you," Valiant told her. "Nice work figuring out Coal."

"He is still terrifying," Kayla answered, as his roar filled through the skies. This was a bad time for him to be here. Everyone was already out ready to defend the ware and castle and town. She heard more teams of dragons head over. Coal was going to get surrounded and beaten up! She knew that he'd escaped such things before since he attacked everything all the time, but it just felt different today. Knowing that he was with Tyler suddenly made Coal not as demonic, even if Coal considered Tyler to be a traitor. That had to be hard on Coal. Tyler worked for Vankerdale, so he had probably thought about helping his kingdom more than Aralot and made Coal mad.

"I have to get him out of here," Kayla thought to Valiant as she heard Coal scream again, this time in pain.

She wasn't supposed to be using weather magic because she wasn't that good at it yet, but she did it anyway. She aimed a wind spell upward toward Coal and let him get shoved out of everyone's way, sending him flailing backward. Then she wrapped her arms around her waist and focused on breathing because Coal thought she was fabulous for blasting him in the face, and left by screaming out her name in a rather happy, satisfied hum.

She was not going to look at him! She wasn't going to turn around! She reacted the same way that her mother did when a dragon screamed her name, especially when it was that loud. Everything inside her told her to turn. A rock hitting her cheek tore the feeling away.

"Hey!" Kayla cried out, turning to see who had lobbed it at her. She couldn't hear anyone and there was one particular person around here that she had trouble hearing. Ritz. She smiled, understanding exactly why Coal had shouted out his thanks. It was a nuisance to be hit in the face, but far better than the alternative.

"See you around," Kayla said, loud enough that Ritz would be able to hear her. Then she ran for the ware so she could get out of this constricting dress. She'd never liked wearing dresses. That was always Rosa's thing.

Images

Caleb

The blue mist rose up like a wave crashing over everything, transforming the blast zone from ashes and flame back into green plants and lush forest. Caleb finished putting on the last stroke of color and leaned back to see what he had made.

"What am I doing?" he asked Warner. "Really what is she doing to me?"

He was drawing magic. The picture didn't even have Kayla in it. Warner didn't answer because he was asleep. Caleb couldn't doze. He was the section leader on night duty tonight, and he was spending his time remembering Kayla's rapid attention when he had taken her keychain. He had drawn through her expressions and gotten the full length of her in a dress already. Now he was coloring in unrealistic images.

Kayla had asked him if magic was warm, but that wasn't a very good description. Touching magic was like running his hands inside a plume of smoke. It felt weightless, yet harmful and safe at the same time. Tipped too hot and it would boil him. Warmed just right and it could save his body.

Caleb stared at his hand, the one that had tickled with the magic inside of it. It was Kayla's face that told him what he had really wanted to know. *He* had stopped her spells. He didn't even know what he was doing, but he had commanded the mists, and she had stared at him the rest of the night like he still had a part of her. It was the same way that Valiant stared at Kayla.

Caleb flipped through his sketchbook to compare his images. There was Valiant admiring Kayla's turned back, and there was Kayla admiring him. Caleb had tried not to notice. Under different circumstances, he would have been dancing that she was giving him this much of her undivided attention, but she was supposed to be dead. She had fallen because Caleb had snatched her. He had no idea what made him do it either. He hadn't heard her walking. She was way too quiet for that. He had just felt an unexplainable urge to reach up and snag something. The person he had pulled in was Kayla. In a dress. A really adorable dress. He flipped back to her in the dress and smiled at it. Then he looked up when he sensed something hovering over his shoulder and jumped.

There were brown dragon eyes staring at his drawings, and there was only one kind of dragon with brown eyes. Valiant had returned, so Caleb was guessing that this Tyler person couldn't be too far away. The dragon had managed to walk behind him, lean over Warner without waking him up, and watch the drawing process for who knew how long.

"I suppose you want to see?" Caleb questioned. "You could ask you know, instead of scaring me like that. I'll show you, but you can't keep them. You don't have pockets for it anyway."

Caleb looked around the field just to make sure that the night riders were still fine with their lessons before he crawled on top of Warner so that Valiant didn't have to put his claws over him. He felt a little nervous to be sharing his drawing with Valiant, but he turned to the start of the sketchbook and started to point out when each picture took place. Most of them were of Kayla. He hoped that this would help Valiant trust him better. The dragon still hadn't bowed or hummed at him. The most Caleb could get was silent attention like this.

Caleb looked up from the book to Valiant and then out at the field again. All the day dragons were down, even the ones that might stay up late to talk. Valiant should be tired too even if Caleb was up and drawing. The only dragons that were wide awake were the nighttime ones. Dragons worked best when they worked with the natural rhythms of their body so... Valiant was a night dragon! That's why he was so lazy during the day. He was tired. He only kept himself awake because Kayla was awake, and he didn't want to miss a single second of being near her. If Caleb had known that, he'd have scheduled Valiant a daily naptime already. He would have to add one in so that the dragon had time to restore his tired body.

"What do you think?" Caleb asked.

He grinned when Valiant offered him a short hum of encouragement. He'd take it. It was the little things like this that would help him draw closer to Kayla and her dragon. Valiant didn't have to be anywhere close to him, and yet here he was. Caleb pointed up into the sky at the night scout's routine and started talking formations while he had this dragon's attention. He'd teach Valiant to trust him.

Sightsharing

Kayla

Kayla usually assumed that everyone was good in nature. Today she was taking the opposite approach to assume that everyone was bad mostly because Tristan was confusing her. Did he want to help her or kill her off? His soul was stained as was his mother's so they had been doing something that was ugly. However, she didn't know if that meant they were still doing something nasty or if it was all in the past. How long did a stain like that sit on a soul? Could it be cleansed off? If so, how? That was probably a question she would have to take to the monks, but she never had time to run off and chat with other people. She was supposed to be in class. She was physically here, but her mind was miles away as Caleb started talking to everyone. She drowned his voice out until it abruptly cut off and then she looked at him to see that Russel, the level four section leader, was dropping out of the air to attack Caleb.

Caleb rolled and his full-blown laugh left Kayla feeling suspicious of what had caused this intrusion into their lesson for the day. Caleb feinted to the left and then charged back at Russel egging him on. Since Kayla had never liked watching Caleb fight, she considered turning away. She normally left Caleb's moves to her ears only, but now that she was watching, she found a large reason for why she should continue turning away. Russel was angry, making his actions harsh and quick.

Caleb flowed through his moves with such an ease that he could have been choreographing a dance.

He rolled, flipped, and jabbed like the expert fighter he was, turning Kayla's face an uncomfortable shade of red as her heart panted. There was not any doubt in her mind that Caleb would win. He was seamless; a breeze of magical air that slipped around his opponent. Her belly churned next and she forced herself to look away. She did not have time to consider how gorgeous her current teacher was. She had to find a way to take down Tristan!

"You know why right?" Nick whispered to Sherman. "Caleb hung Russel's boot up the flag pole this morning."

"No, he didn't. He put Russel's pants in a girl's bunkroom," Sherman replied.

"I'm not saying who but someone cut some holes in Russel's pants," Brea laughed.

Kayla shook her head so she wouldn't start grinning like an idiot. She had heard of lots of pranks before, but some of them were too funny to remain stern about. Maybe she got that attitude from Uncle Anvil. He would often laugh his head off before giving out a punishment for a prank. It made the offender not feel so bad for having to do something rather horrible. It was also funny to watch Uncle Anvil laugh.

"What pranks did Tristan do when he was here?" Kayla asked, sneaking into the opening that her classmates had given her. Caleb congratulated Russel on a move that had pushed Caleb onto his back. Kayla resisted looking over as she focused on her team. Caleb's voice was already plastered into her thoughts. She didn't need his strong image there too.

"Oh man, Kayla," Sherman laughed at her. "Tristan was the worst."

"He rubbed socks in plants that gave riders rashes," Nick told her. "The doctor was not his largest fan."

"He stole everyone's money and left it in the bushes," Junia told her. "There are always people digging for coins when they can't find theirs."

"I heard he stole a few things from Charles and hid it in other rider's packs. Charles was always conducting surprise pack checks to find where his lost items had gone. Sometimes they wouldn't show up for a few weeks," Nick said.

"One time he painted the mess hall blue," Junia added.

"That was not him," Nick replied.

"Was too," Junia declared.

"Everything bad got blamed on Tristan," Sherman noted, "so he got away with all of it because no one could decide if it was him or not. The crime rate went way down when he left."

If the crime rate had gone down here, where did it go up? This wasn't looking good for Tristan. Kayla had not made a habit of paying attention to where he went all the time, but she still knew anyway because she'd heard her parents talk about it before. After the King's Ware, Tristan had started to frequent the Desert Ware. She didn't think he trained there. What did he do? Hang out with his girlfriend?

"Is he considered transferred?" Kayla asked.

"His name is still on the ware roster," Sherman told her. "But it's Prince Tristan," he offered a shrug. "He does whatever he wants. He passed level eight and then stopped showing up for class. He still shows up every now and then, but everyone knows he spends most of his time at the Desert Ware."

"Picking on girls no doubt," Junia told Kayla with a frown. "He likes weird people."

"No he has great taste," Nick contradicted. "He asked out everyone that was super cute and he never stole the girl's stuff."

"He totally stole Sheryl's stuff," Junia told him. "There's a frilly undershirt stuck on the bottom of my bed with a note that says its Sheryl's and it's from Tristan. I tried pulling it off. Magic is keeping it there."

"That's gross." Nick mimicked barfing. "I agree that Sheryl is hot but she's older than him."

"Just another prank," Sherman nudged Nick.

Caleb had pinned Russel down now and was denying messing with his pants. He took credit for the boot though, and told him not to insult Kayla ever again. Kayla sucked in her breath. She was the cause of this. She hadn't heard the insult, but if Russel was saying anything about her lack of dragon skills, he was probably right.

Kayla looked over at Russel and mouthed a "sorry" at him. She thought that everyone already knew to not say mean things about her if Caleb was in earshot. Russel returned her look with a glare.

"Caleb really did put those pants there," Sherman whispered. "I saw him do it."

Russel stormed off and they all stood at attention when Caleb turned around to view his class. He was slightly sweating but other than that he didn't look like he had been fighting with another section leader at all.

"Right then. Sightsharing. It's time for your heads to burst. No one tell me that your dragon is not old enough," Caleb said looking directly at Kayla.

She wasn't going to complain. It was part of the training. She knew it would come up sometime. She just had never done it before, unlike everyone else that would show their superior skills yet again and remind her that she was failing class. Would she ever pass a single level?

"Do you think I'll be bad at it? You'll help me right, Valiant?" she asked him.

"Kayla you are the master of sightsharing," Valiant replied.

Sure, she was. It was going to be really weird to grow to the size of her dragon that quickly and suddenly see things in sharp detail. Sightsharing required that she looked out of her dragon's eyes. In the meantime, her dragon would be seeing out of hers. It gave people headaches. Practice was useful to train the mind to avoid the pounding sensations that came afterward. It wasn't fair that it hurt human heads and not dragon ones.

"I think it's fair," Valiant told her blowing her with warm air and a laugh. Kayla turned around to smile at him. It wasn't fair. He was just lucky.

"Okay. What are you waiting for? Sit down if you need to and get started. I'm timing today." Caleb gave his dragon a nod. Kayla wasn't sure if she needed to sit down or not so she did. She wasn't the only one. Valiant hummed at her, and then she had the briefest of moments where human sounds turned to a higher pitch. She lost the mental words of Valiant and her vision grew larger and wider. Despite having brown eyes, Valiant's dragon vision wasn't any different than that of any other dragon. She would know. She'd had tons of dreams where she was being a dragon.

Oh! That's why Valiant said she was the master at this! Kayla moved his head around to look at some of the other dragons in her class and found a few of them with their eyes still closed, allowing their rider a moment to get used to changing heads. She didn't need a moment. She did this all the time!

"You ever done this before Kayla? Valiant?" Caleb asked them. He was watching them more than anyone else and so was his dragon Warner. Kayla looked at Warner trying to decide if Caleb was sightsharing or not. She flicked her tail hello. Then she bugled her excitement. She was looking at dragons!

She craned Valiant's head up to the sky and then looked downward at herself to see how she was doing. Just fine actually. She wasn't sitting anymore. Her mortal body was standing, regarding the other humans around her. Some of them were laughing. A lot of them were making fun of each other as if they were still dragons, claiming that their scales were dull and their fire wimpy. It was really funny what dragons would say to each other if they had a human mouth to say it, and their tongues did a bad job at creating the dragon sounds so it all came out jumbled and hilarious.

"I can look at dragons like this," Kayla told Valiant pulling off perfect dragon speech on her first try.

Her classmates and the dragons near them all quit their antics to look at her. It took years to achieve that kind of mastery with another creature's vocal cords. In fact, Kayla didn't know of any person that could verbalize so well. The best sightsharers could get their dragons to say yes and no and simple phrases that they could understand. As far as she knew, none of them rambled off dragon sentences. Her team and Caleb gawked at her.

Valiant talked back to her just as easily using her voice. "Yes, you can," he agreed. He pulled off the hood that she always kept up and blatantly looked around at the dragons using her eyes. This was remarkable. Since they both knew dragon speech and human words, communication was a breeze. They couldn't share mental thoughts while they were like this, but they could get around that the same way that Jack and Pyro did. They could invent their own language of signals.

Kayla couldn't help but dance using Valiant's toes. They could trick their broken bond like this! There was no pulling sensation of sadness if she was being the dragon that she was missing. She had nothing to miss! This was the absolute best class ever! She could have Valiant pass her classes for her. They could switch places. He would be her, and she would be him, and no one would know the difference.

"You did switch, right?" Caleb asked, stepping in closer to her mortal form as if she was going to fall over for looking upward at all the dragons.

"Can I fly?" Kayla asked Valiant. She tested out his wings and tail trying to get a feel for them. Flying a sightshared dragon was the next largest step. She had never flown from inside of Valiant's eyes before, and the weight of him was different from other dragons that she had been, but she was fairly certain that she could figure it out without much trouble. She'd jumped into the air and started flying from all over Aralot already in her dreams. She tested the wings out again and jumped.

"Woah Kayla! You are not flying today," Caleb instructed, turning away from her mortal self to her dragon one. "Down puppy."

"Why not?" Kayla asked him, sounding exactly like Valiant. She had to laugh about that. He had a fun voice that he didn't use very much. Kayla tested out his vocal range, running up and down scales.

"Because," Caleb told her after his dragon translated the question, "You might plop over," he indicated her real form. Valiant crossed her arms and made her look smug.

"We are not falling over," Valiant told him. Kayla hummed at her dragon, which had them both looking at each other and grinning.

"Alright out!" Caleb pointed to Nick when he started to wobble. Nick struggled to return to himself so Caleb slapped him. That did the trick. Nick moaned about how loud everything had gotten, which was what normally happened with people when they were still getting used to sightsharing. Their brains buzzed, and they had to keep their eyes shut or they might throw up when they got back inside their own heads. Some people couldn't handle this very well.

"How am I doing?" Kayla asked Valiant.

"Just fine. We could keep this up."

"How long?" Kayla wanted to know. Sightsharing was supposed to last only a few minutes when they got started. She was the youngest here, but while she may fail at everything else, this was the one thing she was surprisingly good at.

"Hours and hours. Your head won't hurt."

Hours. Just the word sounded wonderful. She could go hours without falling on her mortal face. What about her dragon one? She looked up into the endless blue sky and spread the wings again. Warner snarled at her.

"Hey!" Caleb shouted. "Out Kayla! No flying."

"Why?" She asked Warner, and Valiant kicked her out of his head so he could snarl back at Warner to defend her.

"Stop it," Caleb ordered.

He reached out to Kayla when he suspected that she had returned to herself. She wasn't wobbling. Her head really didn't hurt but her blood pressure picked up a notch at the thought of Caleb touching her again.

"*I had a thought,*" Kayla spoke to Valiant as she pulled the hood back over her eyes now that she was herself again.

"I missed it," Valiant replied.

"You could be me in class and I could finally pass the lessons," Kayla told him. Valiant was so quiet that she held her breath. *"You don't think you can?"* she asked. *"You couldn't learn to hold a knife without cutting my arm?"* A lot of dragons couldn't, even after hours of sightsharing sessions. It had been so easy stepping into Valiant's form that she had forgotten that he might not have thought the same thing. She had tons of practice in her dreams, but he hadn't had any practice being human at all.

"I can make you do anything," Valiant declared. *"I just always suspected that you would be angry about it."*

"Why?" Kayla questioned. This was a perfect opportunity to take.

"I don't want to explain. You will get mad at me."

That was just weird. Why would she be mad at him if she could finally make it through class without falling onto the ground? Who cared if it wasn't really her passing? She wouldn't have to feel so weak around dragons. She wouldn't be helpless, immobile, and defenseless. Before she could contemplate what Valiant might mean, she felt Caleb's hand press more into her back.

"I imagine your head is feeling fit to burst after that. That was amazing, Kayla. You and Valiant are inspirational. Your talking had me confused if it was even you or not."

"Act sick," Valiant thought to her, *"or he's going to know that we've switched places the next time you want to pass class."*

Fair point. Kayla spread her feet wider as if she needed to brace herself up. She gave off a fake wobble.

"You sure try to push limits when you face them," Caleb

continued, referring to her talking and trying to fly. He tried to peek beneath her hood so Kayla shut her eyes and let out a soft moan as if he was talking too loud.

"Oh, sorry," he whispered before he looked again at the others in her class. He slowly moved his hand off, making sure she wasn't going to fall over and hurt herself, and then moved on to someone else. Whoever it was, the person started shaking when they returned to themselves and Caleb carried the classmate off the field and right into bed. He came back with Mulligan laughing beside him.

"You are sneaking out," Mulligan accused. "You're not the first person to have thought of knocking out their entire class."

"I have a date with destiny and the castle wall," Caleb returned, which made no sense to Kayla at all. The castle wall was boring and she doubted that he was going to try to break into the castle. Why would he need to get in there? Maybe he had heard about the poison in her food. Was he trying to track it down?

"Only if Russel is not still mad at you," Mulligan said. "He's not going to help you anymore. Did you really cut up his pants?"

"No. I might have moved them a bit. He said that Kayla was a sorcerer of malice because she cast a spell the other day in the woods. I figured if he was going to let his words run away from him, his pants could do the same thing."

Mulligan laughed again. He helped Caleb pick up the next rider who had started moaning to carry the person off the field. Kayla sat down and cradled her head, pretending that it was killing her. In reality, she was still trying to figure out what Caleb was doing.

"Are you scared of magic?" Caleb asked Mulligan. "Kayla's spell lit everyone up. I don't know what it was, but it wasn't malicious. It was beautiful."

"I heard about it," Mulligan replied. "I can't say that I'm scared of magic, but I'm not as comfortable with magic as you it seems. I would never touch a Brixton's source of magic."

"I didn't really plan to," Caleb answered, "but it was awesome."

Kayla grinned, careful to keep her expression beneath the hood because she was supposed to be sick. She knew that Caleb had enjoyed it. It still sounded really fun to walk him through using magic even if it was strictly illegal.

When it was her turn to get carried off the field, she let Caleb scoop her up and she gave up on trying to figure out what he planned to do with the castle wall. If he managed to do anything at all, she was going to hear about it eventually. Caleb tucked her beneath her blankets in her bunkroom and stepped away, still with Mulligan on his trail. Whatever he was up to had the interest of his fellow section leaders.

Kayla listened to the other girls in her bunk moan until they dozed off. Then she sat upright not feeling in the least bit tired. It was the middle of the morning. She hadn't slept the greatest last night, but there was no way she was going back to sleep to invite more scary dreams into her life when there were so many other things she could do. Her class was canceled for the rest of the day. If Caleb was sneaking out, she was going to sneak away too. He couldn't blame her for doing the same thing he was doing.

"Want to check out the Desert Ware?" Kayla posed to Valiant. They could check out what had Tristan there all the time and spy on his old girlfriend. They could take a portal to get to the desert and then Valiant could pull off a speed spell so they wouldn't be too late getting back. Even better, Valiant could let her fly him! Then she would be able to pull off being him when they switched places in class.

"It is not as easy as you make it sound. I will let you launch me into the

air once we reach the desert, but you are not going to be me if I'm casting spells on myself. One thing at a time. You can't learn to fly and cast spells all in the same day."

She probably could if he would let her, but she didn't argue. Instead, she smiled that he was agreeing to sneak out with her and reached into her trunk, looking for the sunscreen. She'd need that. She thought that she had left it on the left side, but it wasn't there. Was this a ware prank? Had someone taken her sunscreen or had it just gotten moved in some surprise bunkroom check that she had not known about?

Kayla searched on the right side and then dumped the contents of her trunk onto her bed. Her gasp had her wobbling way more than the sightsharing had done. She had not stopped her unexplained nightly pictures when she joined the ware! She had been thankful to not find them scattered all over her room now that she had to share a room. They had not been scattered onto a desk; they were being stuffed into her trunk!

There were more pictures of Sparkle looking charming. Why was she obsessing about that dragon? She still never talked to Sparkle. There were pictures of Ritz. That was weird. She'd not drawn him before. She tore those ones up. She had made pictures of herself playing with Valiant, and pictures of both Troy and Shane that were very realistic. She ripped through one and Valiant wailed at her.

"Why do you always destroy them!?"

"You try living with the feeling like you're being possessed even though there is no magic to explain why I keep doing this!" Kayla said, ripping up the picture even more.

"I live with it just fine. I knew you would be mad even if me learning to control your fine motor skills could help you pass class."

Kayla stopped herself as she got another rip into a picture that featured Sparkle. Valiant was doing this? She'd been waking up with these random pictures for years, feeling like she was cursed. A dragon had to be older than one before he could sightshare, and even though Valiant was the same age that she was, she had to be mentally ready enough to handle swapping forms. These pictures had started up when she was rather young. Had she been nine or twelve? Somewhere in there. Gee, her brain was ready for sightsharing when she was that little? No one else's was.

She shook her head and set the ripped picture in her hand down on the bed. Valiant was the reason why she didn't have a splitting headache when she sightshared. He had been training her in her sleep. Kayla tugged at her sweater feeling violated. He was being her every time she closed her eyes.

"Not every time. Are you mad?" he asked again. *"I had no other way to be with you. I tried to tell you that Jack was locked in the Vankerdale castle through a picture once. You burnt it. I tried to communicate that dragons were not as scary as you drew them to be. You burnt those too."*

"You could have said something. All this time, I thought I was crazy."

"I couldn't talk to you! You didn't want me in your head! You'd have been more terrified to know I was alive if I ever said anything and we'd never met."

True. Meeting Valiant had put her into an emotional swing. It could have been worse if she hadn't already been contemplating the connection of the scar on her leg where Valiant had first bonded her.

"Not cursed," Kayla said, sinking onto the bed and locating her sunscreen that Valiant must have misplaced. That was a very relieving feeling, although it still felt odd that Valiant had been her when she was in pajamas so much.

"Oh please. It's not like I taught myself how to roll and flip and cartwheel, use the bathroom, brush your hair, and draw."

The bathroom? There were some things that she didn't really want to think about. Valiant was way too familiar with her body.

"Please, please, please don't be mad."

"A little grossed out, but not mad anymore," Kayla answered. She couldn't be mad at him when she contemplated what she might have done to reach a person that didn't know she existed. Valiant knew that he had bonded her and had to hold it all to himself for sixteen years. That was a long time. She would have gone crazy trying to stay quiet that long.

Kayla tossed her things back into her trunk and then rushed to meet him. Valiant's pictures aside, she had to learn how to fly him, and she was still determined to reach the Desert Ware. He had way more experience being her than she had being him. So it would work out perfectly, actually. Valiant could pass her class, and if she ever found that she couldn't do something, all she had to do was curl up into a ball and refuse to move. That would make her look like Valiant in a heartbeat.

"Cute." Valiant blew her with a blast of affectionate air when she reached him. "While we're on the subject of sharing my secrets, I curl up a lot because I'm tired. It's exhausting being me. I feel more awake at night than I do during the day. I happen to be a night dragon who refuses to sleep because you're awake during the day, and I don't want to miss anything that you're thinking. I do doze off when I have to. When I'm being you, you're letting me sleep when I can't get to sleep because I'm too awake to rest. You don't feel like you get enough rest sometimes, but that's because you sleep for the both of us."

Huh. She had done a lot of sleeping inside of Valiant then. That was crazy to contemplate because she had never once woken up to find herself locked away inside the castle in Vankerdale.

"You are a very deep sleeper," Valiant reminded her.

She didn't want to be. Now that the mystery of her pictures were explained, maybe Valiant would explain her nightmares.

"Sorry. They are not from me. I don't like them any more than you do."

Well, it had been worth a try to ask. Kayla climbed up onto his back and Valiant covered them in spells so that they could sneak past the scouts in the air that hollered at them for breaking away. They knew that they were getting out, but they couldn't chase them all the way to the portal or the Desert Ware when they couldn't see them or smell them. She loved having a spellbinding dragon even if it came along with a few surprises that had scared her before.

Kayla applied the sunscreen as soon as they made it out of the portal on the desert side. Then she nodded to Valiant that she was ready to change places, and she found herself trying to adjust to the strange brightness of the sun that came along with dragon eyes. She could squint, but Valiant's eyelids were different. Squinting wasn't the answer, and she couldn't change the focus of his eyes to make it less bright. She tested out shrugging with him and then looked backward at herself to make sure that Valiant wasn't going to knock her off when she jumped into the air. It was strange to watch herself nod back before she ran and jumped.

Kayla shut Valiant's eyes so she could focus on the sound of the steps only she was on sand so that didn't help. She had to blink out a lot of sand that she was tossing up into her own face and had a few false starts where she flapped the wings and didn't get anywhere because launching off sand was different than the hard ground. She finally made it up into the air and was able to get the dragon in a good place before she gladly sank back into herself.

"Hard?" Valiant asked her, when he took control of the flying from the air.

"A little," she answered.

She made sure that she wasn't going to fall off when Valiant applied the fast-flying spell and then she closed her eyes. All this sun was too warm and bright. It was making her sleepy, and since Valiant was flying, she decided that she would sleep for one of them. Her mind faded out on the thoughts of Valiant calling her lazy with a laugh.

It was Valiant's voice waking her up sometime after he had landed and probably taken a nap too. They were tucked in beside a sand dune from which she could hear dragon ware sounds. Since she couldn't see Valiant as she sat on him, she knew that they were still being invisible. Spells were so lovely. She could walk into the ware without anyone knowing a thing. She did just that.

The people in the Desert Ware were far more prepared to deal with the sand slapping them in the face. They all wore head coverings and loose robes instead of thick leather. Kayla had no idea who Tristan had a crush on as she walked around the buildings. Each building was made of sandstone, blending right into the tan color of everything else around them. Kayla tried to pick out who was who by the sounds of their voices, but the only visible people currently were scouts up in the air. The rest of the human sounds came from the mess hall.

Valiant had picked a good time for her to snoop around. She didn't want to look up into the air and spot any of the rider's dragons so she didn't see anyone at first. She kept her hood as low as she could, wondering if coming here was pointless, while she tried to not leave any footprints. At least the sand was so chopped up already that nothing she left behind was noticeable unless a dragon or person started to watch the sand by her invisible feet.

"Not pointless. You were learning to fly," Valiant provided a positive.

"I have no idea how you squint," she told him.

She wandered among the buildings, debating with herself if she should sneak into the mess hall. However, opening a door and not seeing anyone enter would clearly give her away to all the people inside.

Kayla crossed behind the large building and her eyes stopped on a lone guard. He was standing in front of a door that was leaking blue light from around the edges. There was only one thing that would leak that color. Magical ice spheres. Since when did the Desert Ware have magic? Who was using it? Tristan? No one else was allowed to use it down here. Kayla cast a spell on the guard to put him to sleep and then another on him to make him stiff. She propped him up against the wall near the door and then slipped inside.

Her skin grew goosebumps on what she saw. It wasn't just one single orb that had been put inside the room but about thirty or more of them. She'd never seen this much magic stored in one place before! Not even her dad collected this much. Merlock probably had an accumulation equivalent to this horde, but that was at the castle, and it was much better protected than the one guard that was standing in front of this place. There should be more guards with a stash this large. Anyone could break into here and use up the magic on some horrible spell, especially since Kayla could make out an emerald cauldron in the corner where Tristan could melt the magic spheres to open his fresh supply. Emerald was the only type of material that could hold magic as well as an ice sphere could. Tristan really knew what he was doing.

Did her father know about this? This room felt like a place that was asking for trouble. It wasn't even protected with spells like Tristan's magic room inside the castle was, unless the spell that kept people out was something weird like only people who were familiar with magic already could enter. However, that would be a bad spell, one that invited the very trouble she felt was going to come from this room. Maybe

Tristan had forgotten to replace the spells the last time he left. That was very careless of him. What could have been the reason for his lapse?

Kayla moved around the room, running her hand along the balls of ice that were so cold they pricked her fingers even with the heat around her. She reached the cauldron and picked up a long strip of paper that had been left there. Her breathing started to come out heavy as she read the spell. A loyalty spell. Tristan was stealing the loyalty of someone. She had no idea who, but this was utterly evil! No one should be forced to like him. If he was using this on her, she was very glad to have escaped it so far. This was an advanced spell and hard to pull off. By the looks of it, it required more magic than Kayla was allowed to use at one time.

She pried open the emerald lid noticing only a trickle of magic left inside. Yup. He had been casting this spell the last time he was here. She lowered her keychain into the pot to recharge her magic while she had the chance to do so, and then looked around trying to find the counter Tristan may have used for the loyalty spell.

It required him to cast his evil deed onto another object that would hold the spell and apply it until the item was destroyed. It made her wonder if he often used spells of this nature, because if he did, this was similar to how a possession spell worked. It was dark magic that, yes, messed around with other people's lives, stealing from them aspects of their agency. From this one room, Kayla was leaning toward blaming Tristan for the lack of other keepers inside of Aralot. That spell was reapplied constantly too.

If he had left his counter item for the spell in this room, she was going to destroy it. Anything that was not a frozen ball of ice drew her attention. She picked up a rock in a corner and used a revealing spell on it. Nothing. She searched stains on walls trying to decide how tricky Tristan would be with his casting. She tried a pile of sand, even if that was too easy to destroy with a draft. She searched a knife. An image of Vermelo flashed up wearing chains.

Vermelo! At least the spell wasn't being used on her, but this was still wrong. Even if Vermelo was acting weird and trying to mess around with who should be in charge, Tristan shouldn't be solving his problems by using magic. Magic wasn't to be used to take away anyone's will to act, and no, freezing people for a time didn't count as making her evil. It was spells like this that stole away the ability to make choices that got her angry. No one wanted to be controlled to do things that went against what their heart was telling them. Waking up to find that you had done something you couldn't remember was terrifying. Did Tristan even have a heart?

She glared at the knife. Tristan attacked others that were a threat to him staying in the castle. He had to be the one that put that curse on her mother and Aunt. Given the time frame, he would have been between the ages of eight or nine when he cast it. Where would a child put a spell? What would he put the spell on? How had his father not noticed that Tristan had stolen his magical broach for the day?

This was going to be hard. Children were often more irrational about what they used. He could have hidden the cursed objects anywhere, and even worse, he wouldn't have been used to magic at the time. The exact wording of his spell would be something very very willful. That was why her father hadn't managed to change it.

Kayla took down the spell on the knife, careful to leave the knife intact so that Tristan wouldn't realize that his spell was gone—at least not right away. Kayla made sure that the knife was exactly where she had found it, and scanned around the room again trying to decide what else he might have been doing in all his years of uncensored magic use. Russel had called her a sorcerer, but the term was best applied to Tristan. What other things felt off lately?

Besides everything, there was Coal asking her to locate a lost scale. She couldn't think of why a dragon would want help with a particular missing scale unless the object had some curse on it that he didn't approve of. Coal had to know something that she didn't. It wasn't very surprising. She had spent her life in the middle of Aralot instead of on the eastern or southern sides where Tristan had been terrorizing everybody.

Kayla snuck back out of the magical room, replaced the guard that she had moved, and released him from his slight slumber. She stuck around long enough to make sure that the person yawned and then snapped back to attention, looking around to see if anyone had noticed the short nap. They hadn't. The scouts were still flying around in hazy heat, probably wishing that they could go eat instead of be on guard duty.

Kayla returned to Valiant more nervous about Tristan than before. It could have been Vermelo that poisoned her food in the castle if he was doing things against his own will to save Tristan's position. He could still be interrogating the cooks and servants, but what if he was the one responsible? After all, if she went mad and fought with her dragon, no one would keep her alive for long. She'd be killed off by someone else's hand, either a Colt or her own parents, and that would leave the throne wide open for Tristan to sit on.

"Why do I have to date this guy?" Kayla complained to Valiant as they sped back the way they had come. She wasn't sure what she had expected to really find in the Desert Ware, but it wasn't what she had found. Piles of magic that rivaled the king. Spells designed to stop those who had influence. Tristan would do anything to keep himself where he wanted to be. Dating him was going to start and end as a wrecking ball. He was going to try to confuse her the best he could. That's why he had sounded sincere when he complimented her dress. That's why he looked stricken about the poison…

Pg. 228

Grr. The poison. She had believed him before that it wasn't him that put it there. He wouldn't want to risk holding an infected mind close to his own dragon. The poison couldn't be him. Assuming it wasn't Vermelo, that left her with Aria to blame. Aria had the same sort of dark countenance. She wouldn't know that Kayla had taken preventative measures against eating it.

Tristan already knew this so applying poison would be pointless. He'd get at her some other way like with that dress comment. If he got her to fall in love with him, which would never happen, they'd marry and he would keep the castle. Aria though could have used the poison. She had no dragon to protect. She was already known for doing things to keep her husband on the throne. Why not things to keep her son there as well? Kayla needed to find out what spells that woman had been casting.

Kayla was still unsettled when they reached the King's Ware, although one look at the castle wall changed her attitude right away. Caleb. He had painted the castle wall! It looked like he had gotten permission from the guards and Vermelo because Vermelo was standing outside looking up at the mural instructing some professional painter to copy the image.

"Make sure you get the whole thing before the rain washes it off. I'm going to frame that," Vermelo said with his hands spread out wide just like his smile.

Kayla hadn't seen Caleb use color in his work in a long time. He normally used sketches and charcoal, but he had painted the most beautiful scene and message onto the wall. Above the picture was an inscription that read, "together we rise." Below it was an image that represented everyone inside of Aralot helping each other. Farmers were using dragon fertilizer. Colts were selling to riders. Riders were protecting the farmers. A castle guard was feeding a beggar. There were other smaller hidden images of helping hands too, and behind everything was the shadow of a giant dragon rising upward toward the words as the sun shone down.

There were a lot of ugly things going on right now, but Caleb wasn't one of them. He was too quick to get into fights, and he had this mischievous side to him that Kayla hadn't known about, but for all that, he was absolutely beautiful.

"You be careful where your thoughts are taking you," Valiant advised. *"This is starting to sound like a crush."*

"I have no time for crushes," Kayla answered, but if she did have time for them, Caleb wasn't a poor choice. Below her Valiant snorted.

Taken

Tristan

Tristan lounged against the trunk of his favorite tree at the ware. He had spent many days lingering at the base of it and it felt like a natural place to be. The reason why he liked it so much was because he got a great view of the training yard. Yesterday Kayla hadn't done much after that sightsharing session. Today she was faring better. Caleb hadn't managed to get Kayla up on her dragon flying a formation yet, but he could get her to do things that didn't involve looking at or touching another dragon. Valiant was asleep behind them as Caleb ran Kayla through another defensive position. Kayla hadn't noticed Tristan or Riven spying on her yet. She was too busy falling over on her rear.

"Keep your elbows in!" Caleb told her for the sixteenth time. He rushed at her again trying to teach her how to defend herself, and once again Kayla failed to block him. She wiped her hair out of her face as she got back up and rubbed her elbow.

Malone, the nighttime section leader, dropped off his dragon from a rope right behind Kayla. Tristan covered his laugh. Malone was always pulling pranks like this. People expected him to be asleep at this time because he normally was, but he couldn't help but scare the daylights out of riders on occasion. Kayla was going to get shoved over for the hundredth time.

Malone started to topple her leg, but he had startled Kayla more than he realized. She flipped him over her shoulder and had him down on the ground while she pressed into his windpipe. She jumped off him when she realized who she had just knocked over.

"You're holding back!" Caleb accused her. "You can totally do this. Keep your elbows in and try it again!"

Tristan didn't feel like laughing anymore. She *was* holding back. Maybe she had noticed that he was watching her, and she didn't want him to see how good she was. Kayla sighed and gave off another reason for her lack of focus.

"I know all the defensive moves. It's just that I can't pull them off against people who should be my friend. What if I hurt you?"

"I'm not your friend," Caleb declared, and then he laughed when he realized that the lie wouldn't hold up for long. "Pretend that I'm your worst enemy."

"Do I have one worst enemy?" Kayla asked back. "I thought that I had several of those."

"They are all coming to get you, Kayla," Caleb declared bracing his feet for another attack on her again.

"I know," Kayla replied sadly.

Caleb pulled back up to look at her with a stab of pity over her current predicament. Tristan squirmed beneath the tree, wondering who she included in her worst enemy category. There was King Peyton and Prince Evan. He had no idea what she really thought of him. That was why he was spending all his time bumming around this ware trying to keep an eye on her. Four eyes to be exact. Riven had been watching her too.

"It's hard to judge what she really thinks of you unless you interact with

her directly in a natural setting," Riven thought to him. *"I don't think the dates are going to help much. Kayla comes at those with her guard completely up."*

Tristan did too. Riven was right. If he really wanted to know what Kayla thought, he would need to get through those initial defenses.

Malone gave Caleb a look Tristan knew well. They were going to team up against her. They were going to pull from her every defensive move she had and push her instincts over the edge. It had happened to him lots of times. Sure enough, both of them rushed at her. Kayla shrieked and suddenly pulled off the move she had been failing to complete for the last half hour. She sailed through more defensive moves, climbing higher and higher up the skill level chart until her trainers had her knocked over and panting.

"Great. You can pass those tests," Caleb told her. He picked a clipboard off the ground and tore off the first few pages instead of checking them off to hand to Charles. Malone helped Kayla to her feet while she caught her breath.

Tristan wiggled his fingers against his knee as he tried to step inside Kayla's head. She could defend herself if it was against Malone who she didn't know well, but one-on-one with Caleb Andrade and she was slipping. Why? It could be a mental struggle. Did she think that Caleb should be better than her so she didn't try as hard to defeat him? Could she really not defend herself against anyone she considered to be her friend? If that was the case, best friend status was the very thing that Tristan needed to achieve. She wouldn't come at him if she liked him.

How was he going to be friends with the shadow? Every time he tried to be nice to her, she looked at him like she didn't believe him. Tristan curled his fingers into a fist. He had to stop rising to her comments that put him down. He had to be a source of positive intention like Caleb's latest painting, declaring that everyone could work together.

Tristan glared at Caleb for the painting. It had people being disgustingly nice. Caleb had used a few Colt children to distract the guards while he painted, even if none of the guards were really distracted from what he was doing. They just went along with it because who didn't want to see what Caleb was going to draw? The world was a succor for his art. It made Tristan want to find all his past drawings and burn them, particularly all his images of Kayla that destroyed Tristan's relationships. Dani had used a picture of Kayla on him when they broke up. Caleb had bought all the Colt kids dinner afterward. They kept bringing in more and more kids to help taunt the guards, so he ended up feeding about fifty of them.

Then there was Kayla annoying Tristan before breakfast. She had gone to spy on Russel of all people, and learned of Russel's vision problem. He always had his dragon hover over him when reading and she had noticed.

"Can't read?" she had asked him.

"Yes, I can. The letters just get scrambled sometimes," Russel snapped and tried to send her away. She had cast a spell on him, and the next thing he knew, his dragon was cheering.

"It's not a waste of magic," she had smiled. "Every rider needs sharp eyes."

Then she had skipped off like the goody goody that she was. Trying to get Kayla to see him differently was going to be a challenge. It would be hard, but worth it if it kept her away from turning against him.

He continued to watch as Kayla rushed from the field so she could change her clothes for her next lesson. Tristan had been invited to this one because his mother wanted Kayla to learn how to dance. Tia and Jack were fantastic dancers, but their daughter had always stood in a

Pg. 234

corner and pouted when asked to flit across a room with a coordinated dance partner. Tristan was hoping that Kayla wasn't as bad at dancing as she had always appeared to be, because it would be hard to stay positive about her if she was.

She was meeting his mother, and the last time that happened, poison had destroyed the lesson. Tristan was still trying to figure out how the poison got onto Kayla's food. He'd gone back to check the table with Vermelo while Aria intimidated the cooks afterward, and the only spot that had the poison was where Kayla had sat. Every other plate of cookies was clear, making the attack deliberate. Vermelo was still fuming about it as was his mother.

Tristan rose to his feet looking in the direction of Kayla's bunkroom and then sighed. Watching her was boring, and he had another endless day of it. At least when she had been knocked out by sightsharing he had been able to skip off and play games with the younger kids who didn't have dragons around here. If he was lucky, he could do the same thing again.

Tristan moved toward the ware leader office, picked the familiar lock on the door, and opened up Charles's gaming drawer. Over the years, Charles had moved the location of his lucky dice game, but Tristan always found it again. He pulled out the dice, put them into his pocket for later use, and was standing before the mess hall door where he was supposed to meet Kayla and his mother right as Kayla showed up, this time wearing a light blue dress. It was crumpled from being shoved into her trunk, but at least she was making an effort to be ready for talking with the queen.

"Can I talk to you about people getting pummeled," Kayla whispered to him, "or would that be very unladylike?"

Tristan laughed and nearly made the comment that Kayla never behaved like a lady anyway, but he bit his tongue just in time. He decided to play stupid instead.

"Who's been getting pummeled?" he asked.

"Me mostly. These guys… they come at me from nowhere! They just drop out of the sky at the most random times and start picking fights."

They had been doing that. The section leaders and teachers all got passed a list of people who had "died" during the defend the ware game and Kayla's name was on it. Anyone who had not managed to stay alive during the training was getting extra practice today at defending themselves on the spur of the moment. After about the fourth time of Kayla failing to stop the random attacks on her during class, Caleb had taken her aside to make sure she got the training she needed.

"It's because you died," Tristan explained. "You need to be prepared for anything. You're at the King's Ware and the border is supposed to fall any day now."

Kayla looked in the direction of the river that kept them apart from Vankerdale and shook her head.

"My dad's not replacing the spells?"

"Not that I last heard."

Tristan had been listening to Jack, Tia, and King Klavian agree on a strategy for the war just last night. Vermelo was finally going to be satisfied that he could get his revenge. Tia was hanging around in the castle kitchen baking while her dragon kept trying to draw Merlock into the open so she could play with him. Jack was someplace staring at the border waiting for his spells to fail so they could surround the Vankerdale team from behind. If Tristan got bored enough, he could probably help the border spells fail to speed it all up.

"Your dad is letting King Peyton in so that we can have the fight everyone is itching for on our side of the divide and not risk anyone else breaking bonds by going across the river. Once SilverWings gets that hole made, we're going to be fighting."

"Right, but don't you think it's better for everyone to stay well-rested right before an attack instead of being made to fight each other all day long to wear each other out?" Kayla asked. She tried to soothe out a few wrinkles in the dress and then gave up.

"Don't you have any kind of stamina?" Tristan asked her and then regretted his words when he realized that he was making fun of her again.

"Of course I do, or I wouldn't still be walking around. I expect you to be in top shape with all that rest under the tree you've gotten in. What is your favorite color of sock?" Kayla switched topics all in the same breath, causing him to arch his eyebrows at her. Was that a compliment or an insult that she had just given him?

"Socks?" he asked.

"Your mother is coming. Don't you hear her footsteps? She can't get upset if our topic is socks."

"Oh yes she can," Tristan refuted. "You leave dirty socks around and she'll give you an earful."

"Why not just pick them up?" Kayla shrugged, making him feel like a slob right as Aria stepped around the corner in a gray and black gown fit for dancing.

"What were you two talking about?" Aria asked.

"Socks," Tristan replied, and laughed when his mother looked just as confused as he had.

"She did it again," Riven commented.

"What?"

"Kayla amused you."

"Be quiet," Tristan ordered. She had not either. He wasn't smiling because Kayla had amused him. He wasn't going to enjoy dancing with her. He wasn't really going to like her.

The instant Kayla stepped into the mess hall that had a few tables stacked out of the way to provide them some room, Kayla bowed to his mother. Then she turned and bowed to him and her entire character changed. This was what Tristan feared: Kayla being able to slip into another character on a moment's notice. If she thought that she could pass as a noble, she wouldn't need him to do anything for her. There had to be some way to stop that from happening.

Tristan returned the bow only because his mother was in the room. Then he stood around bored while the two women exchanged information over where they thought Kayla's skill in dancing rested.

"Are you ready, Tristan?" his mother asked him.

"Do you realize that Kayla just got out of defense class?" Tristan asked his mother. "She can't dance after that."

His mother looked at him annoyed, but decided to divulge the details for herself.

"How was the defense class?" Aria asked Kayla. Tristan rolled his eyes when the only thing Kayla told her was that it gave her a good work out.

"She's exhausted, mother." That's what it had sounded like to him. He could stop Kayla from learning how to dance, and she would still need him to be the civilized face around the castle.

Aria sighed and looked at Tristan like he was going to ruin yet another lesson. She didn't fight it though, so he guessed that next time he wouldn't be invited at all. She allowed the lesson to stop before it even got started.

"Very well. You are both dismissed," Aria told them.

Tristan gave Kayla a charming bow and then walked out. He put his hand into his pocket ready to play the dice game against some rider's kid only to find it missing. Why was it missing? He scanned the ground and looked around at the sporadic riders that were close by. None of them had gotten close to him at all. No one should have picked his pockets.

"Did you take the dice?" he asked his mother as she stepped outside after him. He watched Kayla ignore the comment as she made her way to the flagpole and sit down.

"What dice? Tristan, I wish you would see all the good that can come by keeping Kayla from disgracing us."

"Mom," he complained back. "You told me to be nice to her. I am being nice to her. She's tired."

"Fix this," his mother ordered, before she stormed away on him going back to the castle. Tristan watched her, wishing that she wasn't so good at telling him what to do. When he was little, one of her favorite phrases to tell him was, "you'll know what to do." She'd stop saying it now and replaced it with the annoying "fix this." She had a look that she gave him that meant the same thing. He didn't want to go talk to Kayla, but he guessed that was exactly what he needed to do. Maybe she had his dice. She wasn't savvy enough to pick pockets, right?

"You're lounging," Tristan remarked, stretching out his legs as he sat down beside her. Friends. He had to fake this friend thing. For some reason, Kayla was sounding better at it today than him.

"At a dragon ware? I know. It's a rare sight."

"Sorry that you got all dressed up and I canceled your lesson," he lied. He wasn't sorry. Not one bit. Hopefully, Kayla couldn't tell, but even if she did, she chose to focus away from his part in that.

"I've decided to wear the dress as long as possible. That way no one will think I can handle more defense lessons."

Tristan opened his mouth to make a retort, shut it and then said it anyway. He couldn't pretend to be her friend if he couldn't ever say anything to her. "Why didn't I ever think of that? If I wore a dress, I wouldn't have to strain my muscles."

"Nah, you should try wearing Sheryl's undershirt. That would get it out of my bunkroom," she told him.

Completely stunned, Tristan went speechless again. He'd forgotten all about that shirt. He had taken that thing nearly six years ago. Sheryl still hadn't found it? He had cast a spell on it so that she was the only one who could take it off the bottom of the bed.

"Man, Sheryl is slow at finding her stuff," Tristan laughed.

"Straining your muscles isn't a bad thing you know," Kayla continued. "Maybe if Russel had more, he could beat Caleb. I bet you couldn't beat Caleb either."

He was trying not to laugh, but he couldn't help it. Kayla was trying to set him up as a Colt would. She had to be the one that had stolen the dice from his pocket. If that was the case, she would put them back, because Charles's name was written on each one. Tristan could see right through her dare. Kayla wanted a good look at how good, or bad, he was at personal defense. She probably thought it fair that if she had to embarrass herself in front of him, that he had to risk embarrassment before Caleb. Had anyone ever beaten Caleb without the guy letting it happen?

"Tristan's scared of Caleb." She teased him.

"I'm not scared, but I've not seen anyone take down Caleb."

"I'm going to do it one day," Kayla declared.

Where was this coming from? She didn't have more resolve than he did. She hid for a living! Her spunk to do something that he would have avoided had Tristan on his feet ready to take on that dare she had given him. There was no way she could show him up in a fight. He'd been practicing for years. So if he was going to charge at Caleb, he'd better set his mind to win. At the very least he couldn't make himself look stupid.

Tristan reached down to help Kayla to her feet and then strode back toward the field where Caleb was laughing at a rider's explanation of the phrase "tail in smoke." It was usually said by dragons when they were calling another dragon a wimp. This rider was taking it literally.

Tristan saw his opening and leapt in. "With great teaching like that, it's no wonder that there are smoked tails around here."

Caleb turned to look at him, glanced briefly at Kayla standing behind him, and then lunged forward as if Tristan had meant the comment that Kayla was the one lacking. Tristan kept his eyes sharp and his moves precise as he faced off with Caleb. As far as he knew, there were only a few people that could get Caleb out of a fight once he started it up. Those people happened to be his parents and they were not here. For anyone else, Caleb wouldn't stop until he'd hit something. At least Tristan had so many spells that nothing Caleb could swing at him would hurt. However, not being able to get physically injured wasn't an excuse for not being on his best game.

Caleb was always a tough opponent. Tristan did his best to pay attention to everything he threw at him. He dodged the worst punches and avoided all the wrestling moves. He got hit a few times regardless, but Caleb was an adaptive fighter. He recognized that Tristan wouldn't be taken down with a punch and increased his attempts to wrestle him down to the ground where he would be weaker. Tristan slipped out of one hold only to be snagged on the leg that threw him off balance. Right before Caleb got him, Kayla jumped between them and tackled Caleb sending him sprawling. She shoved him down and pressed a knee into her teacher's back.

Tristan's whole face burned with rage that he tried to keep down. He did not need a Brixton taking over his fight and winning it for him! Kayla was oblivious to his sudden anger because she was too busy listening to Caleb laugh while she cheered.

"And I took you down in a dress. I'm the best!"

Caleb rolled back over and grabbed Kayla around the middle to pin her down way faster than she had gotten him.

"You've got no skills," he told her holding her down. "You cheat. That's what you do."

"I enlisted backup."

"Cheater," he laughed at her again. "Your backup was about to get crushed."

He was not. Tristan rushed toward Caleb to finish what he had started only to find that Caleb jumped away from Kayla and swerved away from him.

"Woah, buddy. Once a day is the limit. We can't encourage Kayla to cheat," Caleb deferred.

"It's not cheating! It's strategy!" Kayla protested.

Pg. 242

And it was a good strategy at that. She had effectively used him to get back at her teacher that she couldn't pin down on her own. Why was it that the more time he spent with Kayla that Tristan found that she was far too capable of pulling off stunts that he had not planned on finding? As far as opponents went, she made a good one.

"Sweet moves, Caleb," Tristan told him instead.

Kayla laughed again when Caleb sent her a charming smirk and Tristan straightened his spine as quite another idea came to him. Kayla might not have been using him for the same type of personal gain he was thinking. She didn't need to prove herself better than Caleb. She was flirting with him! Oh, this was just bad. This was the worst. He'd helped her flirt with a guy who was obsessed with her. Yuck. This wasn't fair at all! Not only did he need to become her best friend to stay away from her plots, but he had to prove undying affection.

"You're going to make yourself fall in love with Kayla?" Riven asked him skeptically. *"This will be the strangest thing to watch."*

Tristan was done watching. Kayla was on her own if she was going to start using others to flirt. What he should have done was let that dance lesson play out. Then he would have had a great opportunity to pick Kayla's pockets and get the dice game back.

"You return those dice," he told her as he started to walk away.

"Really? You're ordering me to be respectable?" Kayla questioned as if she couldn't believe those words would have come from him. He glared at her. She kept it up. "Don't forget that you're helping Sheryl with her laundry," she told him.

"Anyone ever tell you that you're insufferable?" he snapped.

"Anyone ever tell you that you forgot to get your hair cut?"

She could grate against him like no other! It was on his to-do list. He'd been too busy trying to get inside her head to have time to focus on his hair. He knew that it was long. He was going to cut it on the day that Valiant had frozen the town and never got back around to it after the barber had been able to move again.

"I am so done with you."

He glared at her as he started to storm away. He had to get his hair in top shape or she was going to pester him about it forever. Why was it that impressing Kayla took so many large drastic steps? She was way too hard! If he didn't have to do this, he'd have dumped her a long time ago! She was always annoying him. She laughed at his back.

"Hey! Thanks for being back to normal. You were getting weird there. You failed in psyching me out. Your nice streak didn't even impress your mother."

"Stop talking to me!" he screamed back, feeling like he was returning to the ungainly age of fourteen where he still wanted to act like a child but was too tall to do so. She brought out the worst in him. That's all there was to it.

Tristan slammed shut the restroom door so he could have a moment to pull himself together. Kayla! The thought of her drove him crazy. The sight of her drove him insane. Being around her made him frustrated no matter what he did. He was losing this battle and she was winning, despite the fact that she had no idea how to behave like a noble at all. She had his mother convinced that she was trying, and he had his mother convinced that he was trying to fail.

Even worse, she could make him shift around her to give her everything she was after. He'd given her a gem. It was a really good gem! He'd given her a free hour where she didn't have to work and could flirt around in a dress. He'd given her a way to achieve that flirting while he had shown off all his hardest moves so that Kayla could know where his strengths and weaknesses lay.

He took back everything he had ever said about her being a horrible Colt. She made a fantastic Colt. She was in his head. She had to be because two sentences from her and he was handing her everything. This was not going to work. He had to get better at sorting out what she was after. So far the only thing he could tell she was after was staying safe from keeper poison. He wasn't even sure what she wanted from Valiant, because apart from the occasional spell playing fling, he'd not caught them doing anything together. She didn't aspire to be the greatest rider in the world, or have a lifelong friend that sheltered her soul, or prove she could defend her kingdom.

"What is it that Kayla most wants?" Tristan asked Riven hoping that he had picked up on something with his larger ears and eyes. The dragon screamed back at him.

"Where is Kayla?!"

"How should I know?" Tristan asked as he stepped out of the restroom concerned. Riven hardly ever shouted. He only did that when he was incredibly worried.

"Because you were right beside her!" Riven screamed out Kayla's name and along with him so did a lot of other dragons. Their sound was immediately followed by the drums beating out the sounds of war.

They were under attack! By Kayla? It wasn't her that had frozen the ware last time. It had been her dragon. Tristan rushed to the top of a crowded rooftop as other riders tried to discover what had everyone turning frantic. He gasped.

There were thousands of realistic-looking images of Kayla walking all over the ware with her hood down. That's what had the dragons screaming out her name. The cause for the ware drums was because the border spells had fallen. Flying in toward them was a mass of unbonded dragons from Vankerdale. In front of their massive formation was SilverWings. He had to be the reason for the Kayla images.

"We have to find her!" Riven screamed into his head.

"We have to stop that!" Tristan declared, running toward the field to meet up with his dragon.

"They are coming to take her again!"

Losing her last time had been bad, but Tristan was more concerned with stopping the flaming angry Vankerdale mob. More dragons screamed out Kayla's name. The images showed Kayla pulling out a prong to fight back. Was she really doing that? Every other time a dragon had shouted her name, Kayla fell to her face and couldn't get up. With so many dragons screaming at her, she was going to be helpless. Anyone could pick her up off the ground and carry her away.

Tristan inhaled. Vankerdale had learned the easiest way to take Kayla Brixton. They might already have her. All they had to do was look for the one Kayla that couldn't move and they could snag her up! Knowing exactly that, the dragons from Vankerdale started to cry out her name too. Several of the images featured her curling into a ball on the ground with her hood up. Which one was her?! There was Kayla running away. Kayla throwing spells that didn't do anything. Kayla was cowering, hiding, and climbing buildings. She was all over the place.

"Okay we have to find the real her," Tristan agreed. She was a pain, but she would be even worse of a prick in his side if she was taken by Vankerdale again. He would be back to trying to take her down from a distance instead of up close. He'd be back to hearing her name spoken along with the rest of Vankerdale's demands for an ice dragon. Kayla would turn into a symbol that all of Aralot had to fight for, and once that started up, she'd sneak her way into more of their little hearts so that by the time she was saved, everyone would love her enough to put her on the throne.

The other riders scrambled into their fighting formations and rose to the air to meet the oncoming crowd. No one else was going to be allowed to find Kayla; although, from Tristan's glance downward, he could make out Caleb abandoning his other duties, frantically punching into every Kayla image he could reach trying to find her. His section rose upward without his direction led by the voice of Caleb's dragon Warner.

Tristan ran at Riven, scrambling up his side and noting how poorly Kayla would be able to run in a dress. She should have taken it off and changed. If she wasn't already snagged, the best thing she could do was toss on pants and ditch the dress on the ground.

He glanced again toward the oncoming dragons wondering how good they were at fighting. Even if they were lousy, the Vankerdale dragons already had flame coming from their mouths and were liable to plow over everyone with sheer size. Vankerdale's dragons were using really large formations, and they rotated out the inside flyers when the outside ones got tired.

Aralot's groups were much smaller, ranging between ten to twenty in each formation, while Vankerdale was running about fifty in each. Most of the ready riders were pushing Vanderdale's dragons up instead of down. Down was easier since fire naturally traveled that direction, but Tristan could guess that no one wanted Vankderale's riders crashing into the ware or town or castle.

What was the attack strategy? Tristan signaled a rider trying to learn it, but the rider didn't respond. If they managed to get Vankerdale in their net were they going to kill them all? Were they going to chase them back over the border? Would they try to force a surrender? Why had nobody told him this? He should have asked. He shouldn't have been putting all that effort into Kayla.

"I see Tia's wild dragons," Riven told him.

Tristan looked around trying to find them too. He spotted a group of dragons hovering in the air watching the scene without moving toward it. Tia would be mentally controlling at least one of them from inside the safety of the castle. She wasn't safe outside the walls herself. Why was it that no one had forced Kayla to run to the castle the instant the ware drums sounded?

That was it! Kayla wasn't an idiot. She would run for safety. He could trace the path that she would take and catch up to her. On that note, so would Valiant. He had been sleeping on the field and Tristan could make out a lump that looked like him still there, but he didn't believe it was really Valiant, because the Kayla on top of him was holding up a whip to the air flashing around rather bad tail speech. He looked into the air next and had to groan. There were hundreds of Valiants just like there were hundreds of Kaylas. Some of the Valiant images were running headlong at Vankerdale to make the display more realistic. However, when the dragons reached them, Valiant vanished from view.

On some invisible cue, dragons took turns screaming out Kayla's dragon name. Tristan turned his face away from the horror to scan the ground again. Kayla had to be here someplace! He didn't get a chance to look farther because Riven veered sharply to the left as a full tree that had been carried from Vankerdale into Aralot came speeding straight toward him. It was drilled into every level one rider that during an attack the worst thing to do was get separated and become a single victim. Since Tristan wasn't part of any formation, he was making that easy target.

They dodged a spell from SilverWings and watched as the dragons clashed in the air, shooting out fire that created puddles of heat beneath them. Trees burst apart. Buildings catapulted into the sky. Dragons screamed. Riders shouted out orders and formations. Shooting in from behind Vankerdale's trap Tristan could make out riders from Vincent's Ware, led not by Vincent but Jack on Pyro. They became invisible and a moment later one of Vankerdale's formations was torn apart by a blast of magic that left behind screaming voices and painful wounds.

Tristan shot out a few spells too. He couldn't just stay here and let everyone be torn apart. He blasted back a group of riders before they could shove down an Aralot formation. He had to dodge another spell from SilverWings for his efforts. Even worse, the spell started to follow them.

"Get rid of that!" Riven screamed at him as he was forced to swerve and veer through the tangled mass of riders in the air. There was something to say about wearing a uniform. Everyone in Aralot expected to see it, and if they didn't, they shot. Why wasn't he wearing his uniform today? Riven was hastily rolling through both friend and foe, trying to escape heat and claw and tail from all sides. It took all of Tristan's effort to stay on while he cast back spells to stop the one that was chasing them. Flame erupted right in their face forcing every nearby dragon to pull back at the risk of charring their rider.

He couldn't do anything about his supply bag catching fire except to throw it off. He couldn't do anything for Riven's wing that was stabbed through by an opposing tail. Riven clawed and flamed his way free while Tristan punched the random Vankerdale rider in the face, knocking him off the dragon so that he fell. Once free, the Vankerdale dragon screamed, trying to rescue the rider. Tristan didn't check to see if the man lived because that spell was still too close!

He was grateful for Riven's training in flying with broken wings, missing scales, snapped claws and the like. Riven kept going,

Pg. 249

disregarding the pain as he adjusted his flight pattern. Tristan finally got the spell chasing them to break apart.

"Just in time too. I think I've found the real Kayla."

"Where?!" Tristan screamed.

"Below us."

Tristan grabbed onto the guide ropes tighter so he could hover over the side and look down. There was still an insufferable number of fake Kaylas and Valiants going around, but there was one that caught his attention right away too. This Kayla had her hood off. She was crying clear to her toes, but she shoved at the ground with each painful angry step running toward one of the Valiants that lay on the ground with a torn wing. She had four to choose from. Tristan felt his own eyes prickle even if he didn't want them too. There wasn't anything that hurt quite like seeing your dragon down and defeated. Somewhere the real Valiant was down and wounded. Kayla wasn't in hiding because she was frantically trying to find her real dragon.

Kayla cast a spell at the fake dragon before her, watching it break apart proving that it wasn't really him. She screamed her frustration as she tried again. That was her. Tristan had to get her out of here. Riven started to head down, but he wasn't the only one to have found her when all of Vankerdale was after the same thing. Three black dragons zoomed in toward her, purposely riderless. Their job would be to grab Kayla no matter what it took. They screamed her name, but she was too mad to fall. She screamed back a dragon phrase that had to be particularly nasty because Riven coughed as if she shouldn't know how to say that.

One of the black dragons was picked off as Tia's dragons flanked it and shoved it about between them. The situation was looking bleak for her wild dragons with three full formations headed right at them. They didn't seem to care yet. They'd do anything to save Kayla too.

Tristan settled back into his seat so he had a better grip and cast magic on Riven's wing to heal it. That would help them get in there. A few of the dragons from the closer formation split from the group, regardless of their rider's stern shouts to do otherwise. They started to charge in toward Kayla and the two remaining black dragons screamed at them. They launched higher to shove their own friends out of the way.

The charging dragons sent down a wall of flame right as Riven swooped through the commotion. Riven was going too fast to stop, and he wouldn't want to put Tristan in the wall of the flame, but all Tristan could think of was how he had a plethora of protection spells on him while Kayla had none. Valiant kept eating all the spells and curses that were around her. He jumped from Riven, landing right beside her, casting up a shield at the same time she did.

"What are you doing?" Kayla asked him jumping away from him. It was her all right. Tristan didn't think that a replica could glare at him so well.

"Saving you," he answered, which only made her look fit to scream at his face. She did. She was full of rage for the wounds on her dragon that she couldn't find.

"You can't save me!" she protested.

"You're welcome."

"You've been trying to kill me my whole life. You can't just switch sides and save me."

"I haven't been trying to kill you!" Tristan denied. He really wasn't. He had given her a few curses, but he had also given her protective spells.

"I know it's you. You would have prevented me from being born! You prevent any other keeper from being born. If you are switching sides, then you really should take your curse off my mom and Rosa. Your curse is wrong, Tristan. Rosa wouldn't send her children to pummel you. Do you have any idea how much you hurt us? Have you ever considered what Aralot would be without keepers? We'd end up like Vankerdale. An uncoordinated mess of bullies that have to use size to overpower everyone. You can't save me now unless you're going stop killing us all!"

Kayla was way too good at shooting through his every protective spell right into his heart to force it to bleed open. Now he felt like screaming back at her even if he finally realized what Kayla's life goal was. She existed to make him miserable. She wanted his spells gone. She wanted him to fall over so she could protect keepers. She didn't even like being a keeper! This girl was wacko.

"You're just like your mother," she continued, with her face a flame of red that didn't stop her tears from falling. "You hide your crimes well."

"My mother does not commit crimes!" Tristan screamed, infuriated.

"You have no idea what your mother does. You're both horrible. Take your curse off and leave us alone!"

"Stay away from me!" Tristan ordered, not wanting to face Kayla when she was like this. She was scary. She had already gotten inside his head in under a week and exposed him for his most hidden crimes. He raised up a spell to defend himself from her and ended up using it on a black dragon that managed to get around Tia's defenses to slash a tail downward.

"I would love to!" Kayla screamed at him while she jumped in the opposite direction. Then she took off running again.

She wasn't kidding about that stamina thing. That girl could run through a field of scorched trees. However, she was still running the wrong direction. Maybe what he needed to do was find Valiant and heal him. Why wasn't Valiant healing himself? What was going on? That had to be the real Kayla that he had just spoken with. No image would have unleashed her real thoughts at him like that.

Valiant should be right beside Kayla, but he wasn't. He was acting like a wild dragon, because a bonded beast wouldn't leave a rider stranded like this. Wild dragons refused to let riders fly them into battle, although Vankerdale was pushing against that to fight them. Tristan refused to believe that Valiant was really hurt as that image had shown. He shot his own spells and he was clever. The dragon had to be faking his wounds, matching an image that was beside him so that he could blend in and hide. Kayla then was furious with him for not being close to her. They weren't bonded!

The realization had Tristan staring after her in shock. Was Valiant even her real dragon if he refused to bond her again? He could be acting this whole thing out so that Kayla would trust him and he could turn her back over to Vankerdale. He could be staying away from her because her real bonded dragon was somewhere nearby, and that beast would be furious with him if he let Kayla ride him into battle. There were so many possible small wars going on inside of Kayla's head that Tristan blinked, afraid that he would never be able to make sense of it. She probably had no idea how to make sense of herself either.

"Are you going to help or stand there thinking about Kayla?!" Riven shouted at him.

Tristan looked around him again. Where was Riven anyway? Tristan might be able to withstand a blast of fire, but Riven needed to rise higher.

"I'm not leaving you!" Riven shouted at him. But he should leave him. He should get someplace above the crash of dragons that were all

Pg. 253

converging right where he was standing.

"That's why I'm not leaving you! Move!"

Right. He needed to run but which way? He wanted to run after Kayla but what if that gave her away again? Maybe he could pull some of the attention away from her. He cast a spell that made a really strong smell spread through the area. That would prevent dragons from finding her. It might also prevent him from breathing. He gagged and took up running the opposite direction that Kayla had gone.

His rouse worked on two of the formations as they thought he was the figure they needed to follow. They didn't flame at him. Instead, they took turns diving toward him, trying to grab him up in their claws. Tristan kept up a shield of blackness around himself so the dragons wouldn't be able to see with their eyes that he was the wrong person.

"Are you out of the way, Riven?"

"I just dove at you and missed," Riven replied.

"Don't dive at me. Get out of the way!"

"If I don't dive at you, I'll get flown through! Have you seen the horde behind us? I clawed off my headgear. I can be taken for a wild dragon."

It was that bad? He had no idea how long he could keep running. He could run a good distance, but dragons could still outfly him. He would get too tired to move eventually.

"If you let yourself get caught, I can get below you when the dragon rises. Then you can use a spell to burst from the claws and drop to me."

Getting caught was a horrible plan, but Riven told him to do it sooner rather than later, before Tristan wore himself out. It wasn't easy running and dodging all the attacks. He stumbled and let one of the dragons catch him. Its claws were really sharp and covered in small bits of woody splinters from tearing up trees. Tristan was glad that sharp things and splinters couldn't hurt him. He dropped his shadow spell hoping that he had provided a good enough distraction for Kayla. Once it was obvious that the dragons had grabbed the wrong person, they still didn't let him go. They shrieked out his disguise, but since he used magic, they assumed he was someone important and didn't let go.

"I'm going to use the medallion," Tristan told Riven. He'd not practiced too much with it, but since finding the linking portal coins at Anvil's Ware and in Vladimir's grave, he knew how it should work and now was a good time to use it. *"Do you think you could find a way to locate this half after it falls? If I stay here, they will continue to attack you when I drop. Get yourself someplace safe."*

Tristan had put the receiving half of the medallion on his bedroom floor, concealed beneath a spell so no one else would spot it. But to shove himself through a coin would leave the thing where he had just been. It was going to fall through the dragon's large claws and get lost in the fire pools below if he wasn't careful. However, his other choice was to kill the dragon that had him in the air or be carried away to Vankerdale.

Riven agreed with the change in plans. Tristan said the spell for the medallion, and it zapped him safely back to his other half. He waited anxiously for Riven to tell him that he was no longer in danger as he ran to the game room that held the magical mirror that could spy on people. It wasn't there and Tristan cursed. Vermelo must have snagged it first so he could watch the battle. Tristan didn't know how he was going to know what was going on without it either.

He raced back out to the castle courtyard hollering for news from whoever might give it to him. The guards ignored his cries, but the sky claimed his gaze. There was a large flash of magic that lit up the air. Tristan strained his eyes to see it. In the middle of the flash was a red dragon wearing a glistening crown on his head. On his back was a rider brandishing a golden scepter. It had to be Jack and Pyro making use of ancient artifacts that Tia hoarded. It looked like they had finally located the lightening scepter, and the celestial crown, the one that gave a dragon extra strength.

Pyro let out the loudest defending roar that Tristan had ever heard. Tristan was glad that he wasn't in Pyro's path of wrath as the dragon king charged at a full formation that was nearing the castle. A few of the braver dragons tried to stand against him. The rest fled. They were the lucky ones. Jack and Pyro zapped the other dragons with bolts of lightning, sending them down to an instant doom. Tristan could only stare at the realization of how deadly Jack and Pyro could be.

What dragons didn't turn around and flee back toward Vanderdale were brought down. Flashes of lightning lit the sky. Every time another burst of lightning showed up, Aralot's riders cheered and Vankerdale's dragons screamed in fear. Tristan didn't move out of the castle courtyard until hours after all the dragons had been pushed back, killed, or returned to Charles's Ware. Interestingly enough it was Vermelo that came to fetch him at the request of his mother.

"Did we keep Kayla?" Tristan asked, still staring upward searching for signs of Kayla's treacherous spellbinding dragon that wasn't going to come.

"No. That's what put Jack in a rage," Vermelo replied. "Come inside, Tristan. There's nothing left to see."

Double bonded

Kayla

Kayla was blocking out the pain by trying to stay asleep. When that didn't work, she let her mind run back to happy thoughts. Well, not exactly happy, but grateful thoughts all the same. She wasn't grateful that Tristan had tried to save her again, but she was grateful that he appeared right when she needed another reason to scream so she could continue to stay on her feet, instead of becoming helpless on the ground. She regretted giving away her thoughts about what spells he had cast, but from the look on his face, she was right. It was him that was killing off keepers. It was him that was tormenting her family, and that rage had lasted long enough to break away after those dragons had screamed her name in unison, commanding her to look at them and come with them.

Valiant refused to shift forms so she could be him and him her. His voice was one loud whimper of refusal. He wouldn't run with her toward the castle. He wouldn't fly into the air. He wouldn't shoot spells back at Vankerdale. He wouldn't give her reasons for why he refused to fight, although Kayla had figured out some of it. He was trying to stop the spell that made her show up all over the place. He was trying to stop other dragons from screaming her name. She knew that from some of his angry comments that made it into her head.

"Stop calling her! Stop looking like her!" He was furious, and his

anger hadn't done him much good when her thoughts reflected her anger at him and her fear of the dragons that kept getting too close.

Then it had gotten worse. She could handle fake Valiants running around on the ground, but he had screamed inside her head at the same time she had seen that wounded version of him. She thought he was hurt, and she had changed course to reach him. Bonded or not, she was like every other rider and would rather die fighting than leave her dragon to an attack all on his own. It hadn't been him, and her despair had hit at her right as those other dragons came in.

Then there was Tristan. She'd skip over that part.

She'd made it away again, but had run out of easy options for escaping. The path to the castle was blocked off. Her next available safe point was getting into the monastery, so she could hide away in the secret tunnels with Merlock. She hadn't made it. Now everything hurt.

No. She wasn't going to think about that. She was going to think about Ritz. He had appeared in the woods right as her anger ran dry again. She had stumbled right into a pyramid of dragon tails that crossed over each other and slammed down around her. The dragons screamed her name and caused her to fall.

Ritz had run at her, even with the devilish dragons in his way. He was remarkable. Kayla had never known him to do anything with dragons, let alone fight them, but the man knew exactly what he was doing. He'd thrown rocks, knives, and metal shards at the dragons, taking one of them down by blinding an eye and injuring another with a shattered wing. There were three of them though. The last dragon used the other two as a shield and snagged her up.

She was still amazed that Ritz had come for her. It wasn't her father or even Uncle Anvil that was there to save her when she most needed it. It wasn't even Uncle Conner who claimed that all he did was seek revenge in her name. No, it was Ritz, the leader of the Colts, running against his own fears of dragons, trying to keep her safe. She absolutely loved him right then and still did. Not many people would ever understand that. Despite how mean he could be, Kayla was going to love him forever.

"Fight hard, Kayla! Be a Colt!" Ritz had screamed at her as she reached downward toward him, knowing the same as he did that their hands were not going to connect.

Ritz. He would send her help. He wouldn't leave her alone.

"I am so spitting mad right now!" a female voice screamed into her thoughts. It wasn't Valiant, and Kayla tried to shut it out because she didn't want any distractions other than the one she was trying to give to herself to avoid the pain. Why wasn't Valiant blocking out voices from reaching her? That was his job. Once again, he wasn't doing his job. She was mad too.

"He'd better not block me out. I had to use all forty of us to knock sense into that stubborn head of his so I could talk to you for once. He is not going to keep me away from you forever! How are you, baby? Your mother is making herself sick with worry. It's either that or morning sickness again."

What? There was only one dragon that refused to let her grow up and that was Sparkle. She would have control of forty dragons to take against Valiant. What was she doing to Valiant!?

"He's fine," the voice assured.

"Give back Valiant," Kayla demanded. *"What are you doing in my head?"*

"Kayla, love, I have always been inside your head. You were simply too young to hear me, and then when you started hearing voices, Valiant blocked me out because he's incredibly jealous that I had your bond and not him. I could

Pg. 259

only reach you through your dreams."

A horrible sinking feeling ran through Kayla's chest that had nothing to do with the exploding pain in her legs. She wasn't so sure how long she was going to hold up against the torture without screaming for it to stop. She didn't want to scream, because she knew that once she did, the demands were going to start up, and they would keep going and going until she gave Vankerdale everything it wanted.

She was bonded to Sparkle. Ice dragons were the only ones that could bond multiple people. That's why Valiant refused to bond her again. It was also why she always felt so sad when she was tried to look at Sparkle. The evil ice dragon had double-bonded her when she was a baby, and it wasn't so much of Valiant's fang mark that her mother had tried to conceal, but the second bite from Tia's own dragon that caused Tia Brixton to crave up her own baby's leg and hold Kayla hostage for three months until it healed.

Oh, her poor dragon! Valiant was linked to a child that couldn't love him back.

"If you don't love him, I love you very much," Sparkle cut off the rest of Kayla's thought process. *"You can stay my rider forever."*

Kayla found that annoying. She liked Valiant. He let her finish her thoughts before talking around them.

"I do love him. Give Valiant back," Kayla insisted again. What she had meant was that he would feel like she wouldn't love him, because she had spent more time being bonded to some other dragon. *"You already have a rider. You can't have me too. Valiant got me first."*

"And lost you."

"You lost me," Kayla redirected. "The first time I was taken into Vankerdale, the bond would have snapped. I am not currently bonded

to any dragon. Valiant can bite me again."

"Don't remind me of that. When you were kidnapped my head was pounding. I thought it was something that Valiant was doing until we learned that you were gone. Valiant insisted that he had you and you were safe. Unlike right now."

Ugh. Sparkle. Kayla wasn't going to think about not being safe. That would spoil her mental distraction. How did Valiant cope with the ice dragon? Was it even possible for one dragon to be mentally linked into two keeper bonds? For that matter, Sparkle was double-linked as well, so anything that affected that bond would affect both of them. If Kayla was ever poisoned would she attack both dragons? No wonder she had so many mental problems. She was bonded to two living dragons. Didn't her mother think that would cause complications?

"Not if Valiant died before you ever met him," Sparkle answered. *"King Peyton had him. We had no idea if he would last, and we couldn't tell what he was up to, or if Valiant was still alive without stealing into your link. We've been talking with Valiant ever since you were born. He didn't tell you?"*

"Can I talk to Valiant yet?" Kayla asked, knowing very well why Valiant hadn't told her anything. To admit that she had lived her whole life being bonded to Sparkle instead of him would make him cry.

Kayla wished that she could control what dragon she talked to since she'd had both their bonds, but she questioned that. As far as she knew, her gatekeeper dragon, the one that currently had her bond, was the one that could prevent her from reaching other dragons. Tia's first ice dragon, Misty, had prevented Tia from hearing other thoughts when she was scared. Maybe this was an ice dragon thing. Sparkle was scared, and wanted to hear Kayla's thoughts. In any case, it was hard to say who her real gatekeeper dragon was; although, Valiant was blocking Sparkle, even if she had been the dragon with the real bond.

"I usually can't focus on your thoughts much unless you are exceptionally emotional and loud. That gets around Valiant blocking me, at least when you're awake. When you are asleep, I tell you lots of things. I send you images of your parents and images of dragons because you never look at me, Kayla."

"I want Valiant!" Kayla screamed, not able to ignore the physical sensation of her legs burning any longer, or the one fear that was exploding inside of her. Everything was wrong. At least when she screamed the torture came to an abrupt stop.

"You're welcome to call him over," King Peyton's voice told her. She didn't want to call the dragon into Vankerdale. It wasn't like he could move right now surrounded by Sparkle's army of bullies.

"If by bully you mean that they are all kissing my face, then you have it right. I think you should tell Sparkle that I don't like dragon kisses."

The tears that leaked from her eyes were more out of relief to hear Valiant's voice than anything else. The dragons were blowing him with warm air. Sparkle wasn't harming her dragon.

"Did you just get possessive and claim I was yours?" Valiant questioned. *"Tell me that you didn't fight Sparkle off. She acts sweet, but I think that she doesn't respect anything fully unless it can fight her. She's weird. It's got to be an ice dragon characteristic. She'll think she's in charge of you if you can't prove otherwise. Then when you prove it, she loves you even more. So, when I told you that you have nothing to worry about if you want to breed a new magical ice dragon, what I really meant was that I have it all worked out already. We're going to fight for who keeps your bond. When I win, she will be super thrilled in a strange, angry, backward sort of way and then love me."*

"You're what?" Kayla cringed. She didn't want to get into the specifics of dragon mating. It did indeed sound completely crazy and backward.

Pg. 262

"Why don't I get to decide?!" She screamed at Valiant. It was her bond that they were trying to take. She should be the one who got to determine who kept it. She was going to pick Valiant. So he'd better not lose.

"You get to decide how long you get to hurt," King Peyton told her.

"You be quiet," she directed at him, not opening her eyes yet to see him. "I'm dealing with something here."

"Valiant, tell me why Sparkle claims that she sends me nightmares. Now that I know about her, I want you to explain it."

"Did you know that when a spellbinding dragon gets incredibly happy that the silver on their wings glows?" Valiant asked her. *"You just made me really happy. You said that you want me. I've been waiting my whole life to hear that. I had no idea that I could light up like this. You'd love it."*

Kayla groaned and opened her eyes. Her current mood wasn't anything positive. She was glad that Valiant was happy, but she wasn't in the best of places here, and she was still upset over those nightmares.

From what she could tell, she was in a round room that was composed of gray stone brick. There was not a window to tell her the time of day or to let her find her location so she had no idea if she was at the Vankerdale castle or someplace else. Blocking the door were six guards decked out in weapons that could probably slice them all up. In front of the guards were King Peyton and Prince Evan. Kayla thought it would be pointless to reach for her keychain, but she did so anyway, and was surprised when her fingers found it. She tried to take the magic out to blast a hole to escape, only to realize that the keychain was completely empty of magic. It was only still with her to add to her torture, to make her upset that she was useless. Well, she wasn't pathetic if she didn't have magic to use. She could still find a way out of this.

Pg. 263

She looked at the door again. It was made of metal without any visible crossbar or key slot. There would be no way to burn it down. The mortar between the stone was thick and firm so she couldn't carve her way out.

"*You're in my cage,*" Valiant decided. "*I couldn't break out of that.*"

"*How often did you try?*" she asked him.

"*Every thirty-nine days.*"

"Well, I'm going to get out," Kayla declared. People had to be able to escape or no one would ever make it out of this room. Maybe it required fingers instead of large dragon talons to push a button hidden in the wall to spring open the door.

"*I will come save you.*"

"*Wait. It's you he wants. Don't sacrifice yourself.*"

"*About those nightmares,*" Valiant finally answered, "*I've seen the ones from Sparkle that show you as a baby or show Jack and Tia's worst fears. However, you don't get all your dreams from Sparkle. The ones about those other keepers I have no idea where they come from. I can't watch them with you, and I can't hear them at all. I believe that you see them though, and that they really did happen in the past.*"

There was still a spell she was missing. There was still some magic that clung to her that she couldn't escape, even with Valiant being her dragon. What was it that could give out dreams of past keepers?

"What do you think?" King Peyton asked his son.

Prince Evan nodded. "Yup. It's the same look."

What was? Kayla looked between the two of them trying to decide what they were talking about. It wasn't her, but they were using her to decide something. The only thing she had been doing was

Pg. 264

communicating with Valiant and Sparkle. They were trying to sort out what a person looked like when they talked with a dragon in their head. The only person she could think of that would have started to do that around these two was Tyler. They were onto him. Great. She couldn't do anything to help him because she was locked up in a pit.

"But we can reach his dragon to warn him," Valiant reminded her. *"I'm going to find Coal."*

"State your demands," Kayla voiced. "I know that you have them. Go ahead and blurt it out so we can all move on with our lives instead of watching all of us rot."

"She's like her mother. Pity she's not more like her dad," Prince Evan commented.

Was that supposed to be an insult? Most people would love to be compared to Tia Brixton, even if Kayla wouldn't. Kayla gave the prince a shrug. It was probably because she was purposefully not giving these two a bow or talking to them like they were special. They were not special. They were mean.

"You will bring us a magical ice dragon," King Peyton ordered.

"Done," Kayla replied. "Anything else?"

The king looked at her like it was too easy. He wasn't going to believe her even if she had every intention to give him exactly what he wanted. By bringing over Bantin and Valiant at the same time, the two dragons could blow King Peyton up.

"You think I'm a liar, don't you?" Kayla asked her captors. "I see no reason to keep fighting this battle when you've already won it. You've got me. Having an ice dragon doesn't mean that it will give you its magic. They are temperamental. I'll bring Mr. Grumpy over and prove that to you. What are your other demands that you think will solve all your problems? Wait. I remember. You want to use my blood to end the curse against you not being able to bond dragons. Prince Evan was after that the first time. Give me magic and I'll break that curse for you."

King Peyton laughed at her and talked to his son instead of her. "She's got a bit of her dad in her, doesn't she? She thinks we'll hand her magic. Imagine that!"

"Remember when Jack told us the same thing? He'd end our curse if we gave him his ring back?"

They both laughed together, causing Kayla to shake her head at them.

"The only thing we need from you is to bring the dragons and give them an incentive to not leave. Once we see those dragons, docile mind, we will feed you."

With that King Peyton turned his back on her and led his son out the door. They left the guards, but Kayla tried to see how they got out. The metal door swung outward so there was that. She eyed the guards who all got nastier looking now that the king and his son had left the room. They would probably attack her if she moved too close, and she wasn't capable of taking on all six of them on her own especially not in a dress.

She glared at the light blue dress and then frowned when dragon laughter came into her head. That wasn't Valiant and it wasn't Sparkle either. She wanted to curse. She wasn't bonded, and her mind could start randomly claiming dragons that she knew. This had happened to her mother before when Tia had added some of her best friend's dragons to her thoughts. Distance was no barrier to stopping certain dragons that just felt "magically" right.

"Your bonded dragons are both distracted right now, aren't they? This is marvelous! You were thinking about me. I get to hear human thought! I love

you, Kayla. I've been waiting for you. I hoped you'd be mine the instant I saw you."

"Don't make me guess," Kayla muttered out loud. Whoever the dragon was, it knew all about her double bonding. One less surprise for this thing to find out. She turned her back on the guards so she could examine the walls in more detail. If she was in the same room that had once been Valiant's jail, she should see signs of that. There would be a stained spot where his dung had ended up. Maybe scratches on the walls or gouges from his tail.

"I have to tell you? You don't know who you were just thinking about?"

Valiant, Sparkle, Bantin, and Coal. Kayla ran through the names of the dragons that had just been in her thoughts. Coal wouldn't be happy to hear from her because he had Tyler. So that left Bantin. She had claimed the only magical ice dragon that anyone knew about. It was surprising that her mother had never thought to him. Then again, she wouldn't want to risk creating a rival with her own dragon. Ice dragons opposed each other from an early age. Thinking with Bantin wouldn't be too bad. Now she wouldn't need to send Valiant to find him so he could charge over with her dragon and blast King Peyton.

"Ah. It is thoughts of war that has brought you here. I appreciate you knowing my name. How many people do you think know my name? I've always wanted to ask Tristan but never have."

"Why would you ask him? For that reason, why do you give Tristan so much magic? Have you any idea what he uses it on?" Kayla asked, spotting a darker soiled area on the floor that had been scrubbed clean. She walked over to it and stared at the stone color. Yup. Valiant could be right. She was locked in the same prison.

"Tristan asks me nicely. I don't think he uses the magic on much. He hordes it like a dragon would because he thinks it's shiny."

"Nope," Kayla sighed. Bantin had no idea what he had been feeding. Tristan was using it to attack keepers, and Vermelo, and anyone else that got in the way of his perfect life.

"What did he do to Vermelo?" Bantin asked before he changed his mind and told her that he didn't want to know. *"Shall I blast him the next time I see him?"* Bantin asked her. *"How many people know my name?"* the dragon persisted.

Tia knew for sure. She took one look at a dragon and the dragon's name came into her thoughts whether she tried to know it or not. Tristan had to know. Kayla knew mostly from her dreams that Sparkle had given her. The only way for Tristan to know would be from reading it someplace. So the information was either in the castle or else at Vincent's Ware, where Bantin had been born. That would make it possible for either Vincent or Vermelo to know the dragon's name as well.

"About five people," Kayla answered. *"Do we have any current plans on taking down Vankerdale that you've heard of?"*

"I am not small enough to fit inside the castle to tell you," Valiant replied. "Shall I shrink and crawl through the doors?"

Kayla rubbed at her eyes. She was horrible at controlling this. She had no idea at what point she had switched away from talking with Bantin to go back to Valiant.

"You did what?" Valiant asked. *"You're not supposed to do that. I cursed you so you couldn't do that."*

Kayla really wished that Valiant could continue blocking that magic, but she knew that right now, she was unreachable to his curses. King Peyton had probably ordered whatever curses he could find on her to come off, just in case they could somehow be turned against him. Kayla picked a random spot on the floor and sat down so she could close her eyes and focus. Maybe focusing would help her get through this. She was in Vankerdale without her dragon. SilverWings would have eaten her curses, even the ones she unknowingly liked.

"He probably cursed you with something nasty," Valiant growled.

"Like extreme hunger," Kayla mumbled. *"They plan to starve me."*

"You'll get worse. Don't give in. Shut your eyes and block them out."

That's what Valiant had done. She didn't know if she would be very good at that. She had never starved before. It would be a sensation that was startling and draining. Starvation usually took a toll on a person's brain, right? How would she keep functioning if she was hungry? Kayla closed her eyes tighter as the sounds of the guards shifting reached her ears. They were getting anxious. Nope. They were growing bored and wanted to ask her annoying questions.

"How does having your bond break feel?" The question came at her in harsh tones. She didn't bother to look over to see the angry guard's face.

"You're asking the wrong person. My bond has been broken my entire life thanks to your king. Why don't you tell me what a nonbroken bond feels like?"

"You said you would save us," another guard piped up.

Kayla opened her eyes to regard them that time. The six men were looking at her with both hope and anger surging beneath their skin. They were having a hard time holding still when all of them wanted answers.

"I will, but I need magic for that."

"You had magic before and you didn't save us," one of the men accused. "All of Aralot is the same. You only help others if it helps yourself."

"I help people without needing it to benefit myself, but you are right that I held off on ending your curse earlier. The reason for that is found with your king. If he bonds SilverWings again, he has an easier time attacking us for magic and our dragons. You heard him. He wants to take our dragons away. Dragon theft is not something I encourage, so I have lived with a broken bond my whole life to prevent him from his theft."

"You told him that you'd give him the dragons."

"A gift is not considered stealing." Kayla shrugged at them. Furthermore, she wouldn't let him keep the magic. The dragons would come over to help her and then they would all return home.

The guards looked at her with disbelieving eyes. She closed hers to block them out, although she could still hear them conversing with each other over what sort of tricks she was planning. They thought that she had let herself get kidnapped so she could get close to King Peyton for revenge. She didn't tell them it was a horrible idea. She never wanted to get close to this guy. What she wanted was a clever way to outsmart him. She needed a person who could figure out how to prevent King Peyton from taking over their entire kingdom by controlling all the magic.

The person she wanted to talk with was Ritz, but that would never happen. What was her mother doing? She should have asked Sparkle for information on what was happening inside the castle. Everyone would be standing around in the conference room running their mouths in circles over what to do about her being gone. Tristan would be in a corner laughing at everyone, and his dragon Riven would be hovering near the window in case Tristan got bored and decided to jump out.

"I don't think jumping out the window is advisable," a new dragon voice came into her head. "You don't have the medallion in your pocket."

"I don't have anything in my pockets," Kayla pouted.

She'd done it again! There was no need to guess what dragon she was talking to this time. She had just cut her foot off by talking to Riven. There was no going back from this. She was always going to have this nagging connection to Tristan, when she would rather they stay on opposite ends of the room from each other at all times. He could stand around and laugh all he wanted to just as long as he would stop staining his soul black by killing off her family. Then again, maybe this wasn't so bad. Riven could tell Tristan to take those curses off.

"Oh..." Riven's voice trailed off. *"You know, Tristan has been looking for a way to get inside your head."*

"Tell him congratulations. You ended up inside the thoughts of an unconnected keeper and now I can't get rid of you."

Kayla started to cry. She was broken and locked away and King Peyton would be back to torment her. Was it too much to hope that he didn't think to cast spells on his own magic to prevent other people from using his magic? Maybe she didn't need to have anything in her drained keychain. If she could get him back in the room, she could take the magic from him before he thought to use it. Why hadn't she thought of that before?!

"I am not thankful that you thought of me," Riven declared. *"Now I get to live being rejected by you physically and mentally. What dragon wants that?"*

This was the worst day of her life! She had Tristan in her head! She had to stop thinking about Riven. That's what she had to do. She would think about something else. If she focused on Valiant really hard, he would come back. He wouldn't make her cry. Or maybe he would because they were broken, and Valiant had left her unbonded until he could get a good look at his opponent, so he could decide how best to win out against her.

"*Valiant has a rival?*" Riven asked. "*Terrifying.*"

Kayla gripped her empty magical keychain in one hand and tried even harder to reach Valiant. Would thinking of him work or did she need to stop trying in order to switch over her mental focus? It wasn't like she had tried to talk to Riven or Bantin.

"*That was nice of you. Bantin has been devoid of a human connection his whole life. I bet he's creating your likeness in ice blocks all over his ice-covered hovel right now. He's made you before, so I think he likes you.*"

He would like her, because he would know what she could provide him with if she happened to end up unbonded like this.

"*Where are you?*" Riven asked her. "*Because you know what happens to unbonded keepers. Any dragon that is remotely close is going to try to reach you to bond you, especially if your previously bonded dragon is not around. Be careful, Kayla. There's going to be a war going on if you make it outside.*"

Maybe not. Wild dragons converged around keepers with broken bonds, but that had only happened when the keepers bonded dragon was also dead. Kayla had never experienced the death of a bonded dragon, so she didn't have to worry about that particular fight. Wild dragons would be fools to even try. She still had two living bonded dragons. They were more than enough.

"*Come again?*" Riven asked.

"*Do not tell Tristan,*" Kayla ordered.

Riven went silent on her. Kayla moaned, but Riven wouldn't be able to tell Tristan what she had just thought because that would be a betrayal of their unwanted connection. Magic prevented his betrayal. Unfortunately, it gave her a lot of unwanted bonds.

Stolen

Tristan

"**I** *need to tell you something,*" Riven said for the fifth time. Tristan was trying to ignore him because he was busy.

Jack and Tia had grouped together into the conference room, so naturally the room was packed with everyone who could fit. The counselors were there along with Charles, Vincent, Klavian, Aria, Vermelo and whatever guards had squeezed inside. Tristan almost didn't make it in. Vermelo was personally shoving people out by the time Tristan got around to coming inside, and the man looked ready to strangle him. It had Tristan questioning that loyalty spell. Vermelo shouldn't be able to give him a look like that if he was being loyal. Tristan had shouldered his way inside, regardless, as he made a mental note to check up on his spell. Kayla could have gotten to it. She was getting into his spells lately, and he kept missing it, even if he had been watching her *the whole time*.

"Pyro is willing to go," Jack voiced into the heated tension of the room.

It was the same argument as always. Jack was tossing a knife into the air, catching the handle over and over while he felt stressed. Tia refused to take down her curse or send in dragons to Vankerdale, which was ridiculous because they had no other choice left. Vankerdale wanted the fight on their side. They were going to get it. Tristan would see to that.

Even if he didn't like Kayla, Tristan didn't want to lose her to Vankerdale. She wasn't that complicated now that she had straight out told him what she wanted. The absence of curses. He could use that to get his own desires. He'd take down the curses if she agreed to let him keep Aralot. It was one swapped desire for another. However, he couldn't get her to agree to his demands if she wasn't here.

"We won't require that anyone break their bond. It will be a volunteer operation," Jack suggested. "Only those willing to fully fight will sign up."

"You're going to get more than you bargained for," the ware leader Vincent told Jack. "People like Kayla. She is a subject of bragging rights. She's not come down to my ware, but I still hear all about it. She talked to this Colt. She ignored this particular dragon. She got a new picture sketched of her face. If you ask people to charge over the border and break their bonds, you'll get most everybody. The people who like to brag will drag in the people who are more reserved. If you want small numbers, I think the ware leaders should decide on what teams go."

Tristan felt his shoulder muscles tightening. He wouldn't get picked to go because he didn't train with any of the teams as often as he should. If it was a volunteer mission then his name would be on the list. Kayla wouldn't give Tristan anything if he couldn't prove himself to her. He had to prove he was her friend so she would believe him, until he hit her with his demands.

"I need to tell you something. It is very important!" Riven tried again.

They shouldn't even be having this discussion in the first place. Tristan had been right beside her. He had her within arms distance, but he had let Kayla's words throw him backward. He should have grabbed her arm and pulled her through the medallion into his room, where she would have been safe. Instead, he had lost her right after she accused him of murder.

Tristan glanced at Vermelo to find that the man hadn't taken his eyes off him. There was something messed up with that loyalty spell. Tristan hadn't been able to find the magical spying mirror earlier. Vermelo probably had it, and if he had been watching Kayla, he would have seen everything that she had said to Tristan. Vermelo probably thought justified in his death threats against Tristan now that Kayla had confirmed his suspicions.

As soon as this council was over, Vermelo would be trying to kill him again. Tristan would need to do something about that. He looked away from the Captain of the Guard's angry face, because he didn't know what to do about Vermelo anymore. He was too valuable for anyone to want him dead. There probably wasn't anything Tristan could do to ever get the man back on his side. Well, Vermelo liked Kayla. So maybe if Tristan proved himself to her, she would pass that along to Vermelo, and the man would change his mind.

"Tristan! Valiant was talking with our ultra-dragon king whose name is Coal. Coal said that Tyler said that they already have an offensive attack planned for Vankerdale. They are going to kill SilverWings and defeat King Peyton and Prince Evan before the king kills off Tyler and Kayla."

Tristan's head jolted toward the window, trying to spot his dragon. Riven didn't disappoint. The bronze animal was hovering in view staring inside the room with a keen focus to break through Tristan's own thoughts. The ultra-dragon king had been named, which meant that he had a rider, which meant that it was going to be that much harder to kill the devil off. Who was his rider?

"Tyler Valeron," Riven answered.

"Who is that?" Tristan asked. *"What are you even talking about?"*

"Plans to save Kayla. Conner, who sounds like a dragon trainer living in Vankerdale, is going to distract King Peyton and Prince Evan with his dragons. Then Coal is going to charge at SilverWings and Tyler is going to set Kayla free. Mr. Grumpy and Valiant are going in together to shoot spells at everyone."

No. That wasn't the answer he was looking for. Tristan staggered backward, wheezing, causing everyone in the room to look at him. Riven couldn't know all of that. He had been hovering in the window this whole time and Valiant had flown away. Riven was getting information directly from the inside of Valiant's head.

Tristan gasped again, causing Jack to raise his magical hand in the event that Tristan was being cursed all the way from Vankerdale or something. Well, he was! He felt stabbed in the chest. Kayla had stolen his dragon! This was the exact sort of thing he didn't like about her being captured again. She could get desperate and do something like this!

"She didn't want me in her thoughts. Her bond is broken and all her curses off so she can't stop herself. She was very clear that she wanted me to stay away from her, but Valiant told me that he doesn't mind I'm here as long as I don't try to tell him what to do. I'll be fine."

Riven might be fine, but Tristan wouldn't!

"What happened to you?" Jack asked. He stopped flipping his knife and let it drop to the floor without trying to reach for it. His action had everyone else reaching for weapons as if Tristan was going to be possessed or something and charge at them all. It was best to put a stop to that idea as soon as possible.

"I don't think that any of us need to go into Vankderdale," Tristan whispered, wishing that he could say this with a much braver voice. His shakiness was getting noticed. There was no way to hide what Kayla had done to him. She was destroying him from the inside out, for all the times he'd wanted to destroy her. Anvil had tried and he failed to hide that he was connected to a keeper. Tristan wasn't even going to start trying. Not on this.

"Riven heard from Kayla and Valiant that Mr. Grumpy, and the demon ultra-dragon king are heading toward Vankerdale in accordance with Tyler Valeron's plan to work with a man named Conner and save Kayla. It sounds like this Tyler guy has it all figured out."

Everyone in the room closed their mouths to stare at him. Yeah, he felt like that too. Kayla had talked to his dragon. She had been upset about it, but there she was destroying everything in his entire life again. She took his girlfriend, his castle, his best friend, and half of his soul. He really hated her right now.

"You need to stop hating keepers," Riven declared. *"The more you hate them, the more of them will come after you. Please stop, Tristan. I don't want to see them kill you. They will come after you and I won't be able to save you."*

"I am very mad right now. Leave me alone," he pled. Actually, he was starting to cry. This was a bad place to cry. He was around everyone who could change his life. The silence in the room was particularly solid. It pressed down against Tristan as his tears tumbled to the ground. He'd lost his dragon. Being with Riven was the one thing that mattered to him most. Now he was gone.

"Nope. Try again. I am still here," Riven claimed. *"You didn't lose anything. You gained new information."*

"You know what?" Tia asked. "I am mad too."

Tristan couldn't look at any of them. He stared at the floor trying to come to terms that the life of his dragon was gone. Riven would no longer be concerned for his safety all the time. He would have this collective hive of dragon thought, and his focus would shift over to Tristan's most disgusting enemy—Kayla Brixton. He might deny it, but Riven was hers now. If she ever wanted Riven to do something, he would do it in opposition to Tristan's own desires. This was shattering. Kayla had taken everything away from him.

"You goof. She doesn't want me. I'm still here. Don't forget that I can't lie to you. I really mean it. The only thing she suggested was that I advise you to drop the curses, but you already know that."

There was the proof. Riven would hackle him until he agreed to Kayla's demands. She was going to be the dictator in his head, forcing obedience.

"Bother. I doubt Kayla is a dictator. She likes to hide away in the background, not take charge. Besides, she's not unjustified. Take the curses down, Tristan. Kayla is giving you a chance for redemption. I suggest you take it before she tells her other keeper friends what you've done and they all come to kill you."

Tristan sank down to his knees. This was too much. He hadn't intended to hurt anyone when he put up that curse. He had been seven! The only thing he had wanted was for the Brixtons to not come against him and kill off his dad. He'd lived without his dad his whole life up until that point. He hadn't known who his father was before. Suddenly the man was there, stepping into his life and offering Tristan a completely new one that he had latched onto and couldn't give up.

He'd put up those curses so that rivals didn't spring up to take from him what he had just gotten. His father wasn't the real king. Jack was, and while he seemed alright, it was always the younger generation springing up tearing down what the older one had just accomplished. Aralot was full of examples of this. Tia's father had killed Tristan's grandfather. The Clusters and Feldings had been fighting for ages. All Tristan had wanted was some peace and a living father.

Pg. 278

"I don't blame you," Riven said kindly, *"But when circumstances change, the spells must be adjusted accordingly. With recent events, the safest thing you can do to protect your family is to protect Kayla's family. You can stop them from turning against the Clusters. You have the power to do that."*

"Don't be mad, Tia," Jack spoke, breaking the silence and pulling Tristan's gaze off the floor to see how everyone else was handling his stolen dragon. They had already stopped thinking about it. Tristan felt offended by that when Jack's words reflected that he had moved on already.

"Tyler is only trying to help."

It sounded like Tristan wasn't the only one who didn't know who that was, because Vermelo asked to know about Tyler. Klavian didn't ask. He looked at his wife as if she would know. Tristan hoped so because he had no idea.

"Tyler Valeron has to be one of the indentured servants to the throne in Vankerdale. The kings demand that that family line serves him for some long-lost deed no one ever talks about," Queen Aria said. "Did you just say Conner?" She asked Tristan. "As in Conner the Colt who helped Jack free the Colts from The Pits all those years ago. That Conner?"

"Yes, that Conner," Jack agreed. "I saw him when I was in Vankerdale. I should have thought to ask for his help too. I guess I was just too emotionally invested to realize where all our allies are. Conner won't let us down, and I assure you that we have Tyler on our side. I saw to that personally. He won't turn on us when he ascends the throne."

"Excuse me," Klavian rounded on Jack. "We agreed to discuss matters from Vankerdale together before making large decisions. You're crowning a new king behind my back?"

"I'm not making Tyler the new king," Jack replied, reaching down to pick up his knife again. He put it away, indicating that he wasn't feeling nervous anymore. "All you need to do is take one look at Tyler's face to see what he's going to do. He opposes King Peyton and Prince Evan. He was getting rather invested in Kayla's issues while she was there. Stepping in trying to solve them for her. Asking her to write to him so he can maintain leverage with Aralot. Cozying up to her dragon.

"He was standing around like he was her defender or something. Conner agreed to keep an eye on him, because Tyler was up to something. With another threat against Kayla, Tyler will step up his plans and solve the issue with Vankerdale for us. I know you probably don't feel like it, but case closed. Do keep us informed on what's going on over there, Tristan," Jack said. "If Tyler needs any further assistance, I'm happy to provide it."

"Hmm," Tristan mumbled. He was still on the floor. All he wanted to do was hide under his blanket and never come out again. They should never allow a keeper to have a broken bond if stealing other people's dragons is what came of it. The keeper couldn't control their own head. Magic pulled at them to find a dragon that could bond them, even if that dragon was already bonded. Being a keeper was an evil evil curse.

"Blessing," Riven hissed at him. *"It's a blessing with unpleasant side effects."*

"It's a curse that people turned into a blessing to avoid the nasty side effects," Tristan rephrased. *"You won't make me believe otherwise. Being a keeper has always been a curse. It controls people to control dragons. It's an ugly piece of magic designed to trap everyone."*

"You scare me sometimes," Riven trembled. *"Don't try to mess around with that magic. It will be the death of you."*

Pg. 280

Tristan closed his eyes and took a few long breaths. He didn't need to mess around with keeper magic. The only thing he needed to do was the same thing he had always needed to do. Keep Kayla Brixton in sight so he could nudge her should she get out of hand. Despite her claiming Riven, his plan had not changed. He needed Kayla to see him as his friend, so yes, he would take down the curses.

Outside Riven let out a gleeful sound at the announcement. Tristan wiped at his eyes and was surprised when Tia came to sit down beside him and place a hand on his knee.

"You're doing great. It comes as a knocking blow to most people. You'll make it work."

Tristan gave Tia a smile. She was good at encouraging others. He'd thought that everyone had forgotten the reason for why he was on the floor, but perhaps not. He would make this keeper bond work for him, because he sure wasn't going to work for it.

First Sight
Tyler

Tyler plopped down his paperwork on the general's desk and held his breath feeling like he was going to throw up otherwise. He had gotten it all together way faster than he expected, all because Coal had told him King Peyton and Prince Evan were coming to kill him. Tyler hadn't slept. He hadn't eaten anything inside the castle. He was wearing gloves to avoid contact with poison. He had tossed on a charm that he hoped was magical that would protect him. After all of that, he had composed document upon document proving that he should be the king by lineage and wisdom and dragon.

He felt singled out as he searched for help. He couldn't overtake a kingdom all on his own, and he would be slaughtered before he got started if he didn't have the kingdom guards on his side, so he had come to the general to plead his case. Aralot had a Captain of the Guard and Vankerdale had General Reis. Both men performed the same sort of job. They protected the king and kept safe documents and artifacts that were relevant to the kingdom's growth. By showing up today, General Reis could have Tyler killed long before King Peyton ever got around to it.

The general had been reviewing a document that a guard had just handed him, probably information on who was left at the border, but he looked away from it all to cast his brown eyes at the thick stack of papers that Tyler had created. He looked equally weary and his gray hair was slightly sticky with sweat. He skimmed over the first page of Tyler's report, shoved the paper in his hand at the guard with a declaration that he'd look at it later, and looked up at Tyler, who was so tired and so nervous that his hands and legs were visibly shaking. This was not the best way to look when trying to appear confident to handle the role of king of Vankerdale. Tyler kept questioning himself over and over again, but what it came down to was that he didn't trust anyone else to do a better job than himself. He was it.

"Okay," General Reis replied. "I assume you have orders for me then."

Tyler blinked back at the man unsettled. "You didn't look at it all. Do you even know what I'm asking? Are you agreeing to help me?"

"I looked at all of it," General Reis said, flipping through the pile of papers on his desk by ruffling the paper edges. "I've seen it all long before you have. What will you have me do, sire?"

"Just like that? I spent hours —"

"I assume that you have a plan of action that will bring magic back to our borders, create peace with Aralot, and heal the broken minds of our subjects?" General Reis asked.

Tyler nodded, although he wasn't so sure how it would all work out yet.

"Enlighten me on a few of the details, sire."

It was so weird being called that, but Tyler had come with a large speech prepared. He skipped most of it feeling it a waste to have stayed up so late providing the necessary paperwork. Then again, someone would look at it all eventually, so it was needed.

"Kayla Brixton will give us everything we need, but not in the same way that King Peyton demands. I agree that King Peyton was right to give up on Tia helping us any. Switching over to Kayla was the smartest move, but his approach is always horrible. Who wants to help someone that tortures them? That only builds resistance. I've been working on building something else with the princess of Aralot. If you could help me get in to see her, I will prove it to you."

The general handed Tyler's stack of papers to the same guard, told the man to guard it with his life, and then gave Tyler a weak smile.

"I can get you in, but we already have resistance outside again. That bully green dragon is out there squatting, causing SilverWings to hiss and spit. It's only a matter of time before that untamed creature charges. It's more unnerving that he's not done it yet."

Tyler grinned. Tempest was here already! That meant that Conner was here too, and ready for the part of the plan that had Tyler anxious. Tyler was going to get to meet his dragon. Coal, Valiant, and Mr. Grumpy had come in from Aralot to ask Tempest and Conner to set up a distraction. That would keep King Peyton and Prince Evan away from Kayla so that Tyler could reach her. Tempest was sitting there waiting for the signal to charge in. Until he got it, he wasn't going to move, because he was the most tamed dragon out of them all, only no one knew it.

"I asked Tempest to come. He's part of the plan," Tyler told the general. Tyler rushed to the window and stuck his head out trying to see Tempest, or Conner, or better yet, Coal.

"You won't see me that way," Coal provided, *"but I'm excited too."*

Tyler couldn't see Tempest either, but he could make out lazy flying from one of Conner's other dragons. Having spent a few days around Conner's mighty army, Tyler was able to pinpoint which dragons listened to the keeper and linked back into Tempest's thoughts.

"It looks like the right time," Tyler said, catching the ears of the dragon guard. It stopped drifting in an instant to look deeper into the courtyard and chirp out "charge!" Tyler slammed shut the window, because Tempest let out a bellowing roar that was followed by a loud explosive spell SilverWings sent back at him.

Dragon sounds, muffled as they were, rang through the walls of the castle from all over. Conner had a very impressive army. He didn't usually use them all to attack the castle all at once. He had only ever used a select six dragons for the task of irritating King Peyton, but today he had his entire horde of about thirty dragons charging in together.

Most dragons stayed away from any and all of Conner's dragons. Tyler could hear the wild dragons fleeing for their lives to get away from the organized team leaving SilverWings to defend the castle all on his own. So far so good. King Peyton would be out there soon, shooting spells at everyone. Tyler was grateful that Conner was prepared for the chance that he might lose a few dragons to this. It was all up to Tyler on the inside right now. He couldn't lose his perfect moment.

"I need to get down to see Kayla," he told General Reis again.

The general turned away from the sounds of the dragon war with a sharp nod and waved for Tyler to follow him. Tyler hadn't been told where Kayla was kept by anyone in the castle, but Coal had given him a lot of details after he had talked with Valiant. Possessed dragon or not, Tyler couldn't have pulled off this plan without Coal. He reached the correct room where Valiant used to be trapped, and paused at the door that had changed. He couldn't see any way to open it. It was flat metal from the top to the bottom with concealed hinges and no key slot or handles.

"It is sealed with magic. Work your magic, Tyler," General Reis commanded.

Pg. 286

Oh yes. This is where it got harder all right. He had to prove that he could use magic, that he was worthy of being the king, and he had no idea how. Once he had reached for Kayla's keychain, but she had slapped his hand away, and he still had no idea how to make magic move. Lucky for him, the girl on the other side of the door had all the answers. He banged on the door.

"Kayla! Open the door. This thing might be magical. Is it?"

"I suggest everyone else who is stuck in there to get out of the way," General Reis's voice spoke after Tyler's own.

Tyler had envisioned Kayla being alone, but there had to be guards who had no choice but to stand around doing the king's bidding. There was a short tapping from the inside of the room and then the charm in his pocket turned a deep blue and magic flooded toward the door. An excited squeal was the answer to his knocking. The face of Kayla smiling at him was the first thing to greet him. That was followed by a hug. He could have cheered. This was instant proof to General Reis that the girl didn't hate him. She was playing right into his plans.

"You don't have your hood," Tyler noted, returning her hug.

He expected to find her shaking, or hiding, or in the very least crying. She was up and cheerful. It was so strange. Kayla's normally hidden red-brown hair was let down past her shoulders. Her blue eyes were shining even if she had been in prison. She was wearing a light blue dress. The guards behind her looked at the open door just as thrilled to see it ajar as Kayla was.

"I don't have my hood, or the time, or food, or a bond either," Kayla complained. "But I've got you, Tyler, so who needs the rest right?"

Tyler was thrown off by that. She was being just as easy on him as the general, and with a line like that, he very nearly spoiled the end goal of his plan right then to get her to sign a fancy paper. Tyler glanced at the general and wondered if Kayla was saying what she was in order to trick them. She was a Colt after all, even if she wasn't technically labeled as one. He had expected some opposition from her.

"Not from your friends, Tyler. They have the same ideals as you," Coal said. *"But on that note, check your pockets. She probably stole your magic."*

Tyler pulled back from Kayla and reached his hands into his pockets, finding them suddenly empty while Kayla grinned at him. She was in a dress and it didn't look like she had pockets at all! Her hands were empty. She held them both up to prove it to him, but she had indeed stolen everything from his pockets including that magical charm he had just put in there. It was a carving of a fox, unremarkable except for the gems on its eyes that had indeed held magic.

"You little thief." Tyler shook his head at her, but he wasn't about to try to take the magic back from her. She could trap him into something horrible. He had to let her keep the defensive thing.

"I needed that so King Peyton won't kill me. He could, you know. This is the second time I've gone against his wishes to free you from a trap that you couldn't keep out of."

Kayla laughed at him, and Tyler took a step back wondering how much she knew about who exactly had placed her in this current trap to begin with. It was all his idea to have dragons scream her name, separate her from Valiant, and scoop her up when she couldn't move. While Kayla had been running around doing her best to simply stand, Valiant had been going head to head with SilverWings. At least Tyler assumed the dragon was doing that since SilverWings was the creature's largest threat. He was also the largest threat to Kayla. Valiant would be pressed to defend her.

"I met someone," Kayla told Tyler, fidgeting on her feet, "and I swear to you that I wanted to teach him magic because he was so beautiful with it. I can see what you're after, Tyler. If you ask me even once to teach you magic—"

"Not at all," Tyler cut her off, before she could tell him that she would never teach him anything. It had been on the tip of his tongue to ask her to teach him. The stinker. He'd have to read about it instead. He'd figure it out, but this sudden claim that she met a strong spellcaster had him unsettled. Jack was already really good with magic. Who else did he need to worry about down the road, and why would Kayla even tell him this?

"Would that be legal?"

"I didn't do it okay," she suddenly cried, looking rather upset with herself while she understood Tyler's question perfectly, even if she hadn't heard his thoughts. Tyler tried to study her out to decide if she was upset because she hadn't shared her knowledge or upset that she still wanted to.

"Who did you meet?" Tyler asked. Everything with Kayla was important. This was a huge pressing incident on her right now if she was blurting it out without meaning to. It reminded Tyler of the time that she had told him that she was scared of dragons. Sometimes when they were together, he could get Kayla to tell him her darkest secrets. This felt like one of those. He really needed to know what was going on.

"How do you feel about torture?" Kayla asked with a glare.

Yup. This was one of those things she didn't want to reveal. Maybe Conner hadn't gotten everything right. Kayla could be the lead keeper in Aralot, but he was in charge in Vankerdale, and she was going to default to that when on his own soil, assuming he could phrase things just right to get her spilling all those secrets she never shared. Coal had already expressed how hard it was for anyone to get Kayla to talk to them. Tyler was feeling rather lucky that he had extra leeway to make her squeal. He clearly recalled Kayla's exact wording when she had met her Uncle Conner and told him that she never shared secrets.

"I've not got anyone to spill them to apart from Anvil although Ritz tries to get things out of me."

Those were the people Tyler needed to be concerned about next. Anvil, Ritz, and this mystery spellcaster.

"Was the torture bad in there?" Tyler redirected, nodding back to the room that he had helped her break out of.

"I thought King Peyton was going to be bad, but imagine me learning that Valiant's curse that prevented me from connecting with other dragons was taken away. My head's a mess. I think of a dragon and it shows up in my head. I hate it."

She would. She had a hard time accepting Valiant in her head. Kayla was the only keeper Tyler had ever heard about that pushed dragons away from her. There had to be a reason for that, like some instinctual reaction that was different from her broken bond, because Conner didn't do that. He lovingly engaged with his dragons even if it made him feel teary. Maybe it was a result of this nightmare curse no one could solve. Kayla was always fighting the inside of her mind, and to lose part of that struggle made her scared. Tyler made a note to remember this for later. It was rather impressive that she had managed to walk out of the torture chamber smiling instead of screaming at the top of her lungs.

"Even worse, I finally learned why Valiant wouldn't bond me again. Sparkle fanged me! I've been bonded to her for sixteen years, even if my thoughts defaulted to Valiant. King Peyton's torture was nothing compared to that information springing into my head. There's not anybody that's ever had to deal with two living bonded dragons at the same time that I know about, and trust me, if there was something frightening like that to know, I would know about it.

"Valiant and Sparkle are going to fight each other for my bond, even if I think I should be the one who gets to pick what voice I'm stuck with. Why the heck am I telling you this?" Kayla asked him, taking another step away from him and looking down the hallway to spot all the exits.

When she looked back, Tyler noted that her eyes were full of tears again. She was very good at holding in her fears, but some things were hard to contain, like the thought that she might lose the dragon she loved to the nasty nature of ice dragon fighting. They got vicious. They didn't ever back down from a fight once it was started. They went all the way. That was pretty scary, especially considering that Valiant had no training in how to fight anything, and Sparkle had been trained as a war dragon by one of the greatest keepers to have ever lived.

"Stop making me talk to you, Tyler!" Kayla glared at him next, and wiped at her eyes trying to make all her worries go away.

If Tyler was one of the Peyton's he would have used everything she just told him against her, but he wasn't. He felt as though he'd been waiting for this actually. Waiting for Kayla to come to him with her struggles of being a keeper, as if he could make the torture of her head more manageable.

He had always looked up to Aralot's rulers, but they were not without their own share of threats and dark deeds. Jack had been here to threaten to tear Tyler's dragon away, and Tia had let her baby get fanged twice. Double bonding usually killed a person. It took poison to destroy the venom from a dragon. Tia had probably poisoned her baby before she let that second bite happen, all so she could keep Kayla away from Vankerdale and the strange spellbinding dragon who had claimed her.

It didn't make Tyler feel scared. It made him mad. Valiant already had his bond broken and his life chained. He shouldn't have had to live with a destroyed heart all this time too.

"This whole thing keeps getting darker as it goes along," Tyler stated. "Do you want my newest theory? There was a cursed monolith here in Vankerdale that created keepers. Pyro modified the spell to help King Jack be one step closer to being a true king."

That part still bothered Tyler because the closer Jack was to being a king, the closer Kayla was to being a real heir. Pyro might think he was helping Jack solve a mysterious magic they couldn't contain, but it was going to take a toll on Kayla. Tyler didn't mention his fear of her death yet again. He had plans to use her name whether she ended up alive or dead at the end of the day. The result was going to be the same. He was going to start healing Vankerdale from what Aralot had done to it.

It was all new information to General Reis though, who stared at Tyler for knowing all of this and being on such good terms with Aralot. If good was what they even were. He had a theory for that too.

"Aralot and Vankerdale used to be the same kingdom until two brothers split it up at the river. Choladon, the ultra-dragon king that first made the monolith, blocked keepers from existing in Vankerdale and hid inside of Aralot. Now that the spell altered, I think you'll find that you feel a greater respect toward Vankerdale keepers. You guys will open up about your own problems instead of being able to hide them as the spell dictated. Don't blame yourself for sharing your secrets with me. You were meant to all along."

"I don't like your theories," Kayla pouted at him. "I always tell you way too much as if you're actually on my side or something."

"But I am!" Tyler assured her. "The more you tell me, the more I'm able to help you."

"You can't help me!" Kayla continued to wail. "You're too far away. There isn't anything you can do about Aria and Tristan having black souls. I swear Tristan is responsible for cursing keepers, so watch out. There's been someone trying to make me eat keeper poison too, and I can't decide if it's Aria or Tristan. There's nothing you can do to make Valiant beat Sparkle or help me pass my classes that I'm failing because I can't look at dragons. There's nothing you can do about Anvil's Ware being blocked off by Tristan either, and my parents won't because they need Klavian, and he had the counselors sign the order. No one has ever been able to understand how infected keepers didn't want to be evil. They were tormented and broken! There are tons of keepers that vanished from records over the years smashed into the dirt as if they meant nothing, when their hearts cried out for them to be everything. It's all broken!" She concluded.

So that was what had Kayla too busy to look for Coal's missing scale. Her life was being threatened on both sides of the divide. Everywhere she went she encountered people who wanted to hurt her. Then there was the pressure of being Aralot's lead keeper, in charge of keeping all the other keepers safe. She didn't understand that yet. As if that wasn't bad enough, her own curses threatened to kill her off first. There was indeed a race to utilize Kayla's knowledge before they all lost her.

"We're going to fix what we can one step at a time," Tyler told her, trying to make himself sound confident about this. "I have a plan that will start healing both of our kingdoms."

"I haven't the time to trace the path of where the poison may have come from," Kayla kept talking as if she wasn't talking to him at all anymore. It made Tyler wonder who she was talking to, because she wouldn't need to verbalize this if she was talking to her dragon.

"I did manage to create a spell that prevents me from eating keeper poison, although I'll have to put it back on when I get out of here. Tristan gave me a gem for it actually, which was strange because sometimes he can be nice, but other times I want to lob him on the side of his head.

"You have to go see my dad. You'll see what I mean. Pyro and him are being utterly terrifying, changing the rules for how things should be all over the place. Ritz slapped me! But then he was the only one trying to save me from coming back here again, and I just love him for that. Don't you dare tell me that I can't love him. He fights his own tragic life without anyone to share that pain with him. If we could all just try to get along better..."

"Anyone ever tell you before that you're the strangest Brixton there ever was? No one loves Ritz," Conner's voice came from the end of the hallway.

He wasn't supposed to be here! He was supposed to be outside with his battling dragons, but it looked like he had found a way to break in after all these years.

Tyler jumped. General Reis and the observing guards all pulled weapons, but when they turned to look and find him, Conner wasn't to be seen. Where was he? Last Tyler knew, Conner still had that spell on him that kept him out of the castle. Kayla hadn't had enough time to go out and find her uncle. Kayla's face contorted into a fit of rage over the words, only to calm back down when Conner decided to change his mind a little bit.

"But if anyone was going to soften up that old hide, it would be you, Kayla. If he tried to save you, he must love you."

"No one will ever understand!" Kayla wailed again.

Then she ran down the hallway and wrapped her arms around an invisible man. Of course, Kayla would know if there were invisible

Pg. 294

people sneaking about. She appeared to be really good at that sort of thing. Tyler resisted pulling at the sword on his side with how close Conner was to him. Conner had said he would help make Tyler the king, but he was always scheming more than he let on. Tyler had to make sure that Conner was kept away from all the important documents. If he was inside the castle that could only mean one thing. Valiant had let him in, and if Valiant was here, then so was Mr. Grumpy and Coal.

"Where are you?" Tyler whispered, feeling his blood pressure pick back up.

This was it. This was the final moment that would be the beginning of all his mornings. This was the moment where he made Aralot stop hating on Vankerdale. The moment he got his dragon. The release of old curses that only he could crush by bringing back the ultra-dragon king to Vankerdale. The dragon had been born in Aralot, but his breed belonged over here if the things Tyler had been reading were correct. After Gladius, magical dragons stopped showing up anywhere else except inside of Aralot, and if people did manage to keep a magical dragon around, like Wisteria breeding Valiant and King Peyton getting SilverWings to love him, the dragon was always hard to entice out of Aralot if it made it back over there.

"Not hard at all," Coal thought back to him. "What's Aralot compared to you, Tyler?" Coal asked, sounding oddly reminiscent of what Kayla had first said to him. It left Tyler wondering how much of the conversation in the hallway the invisible Conner had heard. How long had he been standing there waiting for a good time to break Kayla out? Tyler questioned if Kayla had been talking to him at all or if she was telling all her problems to her hidden uncle.

"Where?!" Tyler begged, looking around regardless of the fact that three dragons would never fit inside this one hallway unless Valiant had worked magic on them all.

A warm burst of air was shot at the back of his neck, followed by an affectionate hum from a dragon that he had never heard before but recognized instantly. Tyler spun around and at the same time, a blue mist floated over the form of a miniature flying black dragon that turned visible so Tyler could meet him. Tyler hardly paid attention to where Valiant was standing as the spell was cast. His pulse was pounding, excited to see the animal that kept talking to him.

It was love at first sight. Coal was a lot smaller than Tyler had pictured, but he had these brilliant eyes rimmed with green. His scales were hard, solid, and all there. Tyler couldn't spot any of them being lost from what he could see. Coal had a narrow snout, short head spikes that were countered by his longer tail pokes, and perfectly curved claws. Tyler had gotten the sense when he first looked at Pyro that the dragon would be overpowering for him. He didn't get that sense from Coal, even if he was supposed to be mightier. Coal was fierce, but he had a gentleness about him that made Tyler want to cry, knowing about all the horrible things he had been forced to do. If anyone really knew this dragon, they would know that Coal would never flame villages and wares and people out of spite.

Coal hummed at him again, and then flew into Tyler's arms, curling up into Tyler's chest while he hummed his pleasure even louder. Valiant hissed at him to keep quiet but Coal couldn't. Coal started to rub his head into Tyler, who all too happy to hold the dragon while he started to cry. His dragon. He'd wanted a dragon for as long as he could remember and here he was.

"Dwarf dragons roll all over everybody too," Kayla said, sounding annoyed.

Tyler looked back at her. No one ever talked about dwarf dragons. He was jealous all over again that Kayla had this world of dragons that he never got. She wasn't hugging Conner anymore, but she wasn't engaging with her dragon either. It was still sad to see how Valiant had to live life without such affection. Kayla had her arms crossed as she gazed at the ground, determined not to look at Coal. Tyler had to get this girl fixed. This wasn't right.

"No longer want to eat me?" Tyler asked Coal, wishing that he could have a very long moment with his dragon and knowing that he wouldn't get that chance right now.

"*I am still mad at you,*" Coal replied, turning still in his arms. "*But never mad enough to not say hello.*"

"Can I ask a stupid question?" one of the guards who had been watching Kayla ventured to speak. It was a rare thing to happen around King Peyton and Prince Evan for them to speak without being directed to, but Tyler had been talking to the guards ever since he got here, so he looked over and nodded his head.

"Am I correct in understanding that you are a keeper and that's an ultra-dragon king that is mysteriously shrunken?"

"Valiant shrunk him," Tyler laughed, "but yes. Jack and Pyro have created keepers in Vankerdale following the same logic that applies to Aralot. It now runs in the veins of those with the birthright to the kingdom. Kayla is going to fix our bonds right after we stop King Peyton from creating a war with Aralot that they've never wanted and crown me king. General Reis didn't put up much of a protest."

Tyler looked back over at the general now that he had verbally stated his claims, instead of assuming that the man understood them at the first sign of his papers.

"I'm still waiting for the orders," General Reis stated.

"I was hoping that Conner would distract SilverWings so that Coal can advance. The rest of us need to find a way to take down two men that use magic when we can't."

"They will need to be separated," Conner's voice piped up now from a new direction to Tyler's left. Tyler stepped away from him, not liking how the invisible man was moving around. Then again, Conner was going to use that to his advantage. He could sneak around King Peyton like this too.

"Then the general can distract each one with a question or something and I'll sneak behind them and teach them what happens to people who cut apart my family."

"They will have protective spells," Tyler pointed out. "So maybe Kayla should take those down first, and when she's done with that, I'll need her to meet up with me to sign a paper."

"Ah." The general looked at Kayla pulling together the part of Tyler's plan that he had been very careful not to say out loud or think too much about in case Coal spoiled it. "I think that paper should be signed first actually. Did you already hand it to me?"

"I would not betray you…" Coal trailed off, *"…after we're bonded,"* he added.

That sounded suspicious. Tyler knew he was right to leave out this one detail until the last moment. It was the one he really needed to happen or everything else he hoped to accomplish wouldn't matter even if they did kill off the Peyton's.

And no, he hadn't handed the most important paper to the general. He had left it in his pocket so Kayla now had it.

"She took it," Tyler pointed to Kayla. He held his breath as Kayla pulled it out and skimmed over the words that would turn Tyler into the king. Everything was filled out except for one signature at the bottom. Tyler needed to be engaged or married to become the king in Vankerdale.

It wasn't the same way in Aralot, since they had a habit of losing their queens. They could crown a king without needing a woman, but they did have a deadline for when they needed to get married and start trying to produce an heir to the throne.

Tyler didn't have the heir producing deadline. He simply needed a noble to become engaged to him, and he was really hoping that he could get Kayla to take that on. He'd be taking down all the barriers that King Peyton put up, proving that he would make a better king so that he wouldn't have protests across the land. The people would be able to bond dragons. They'd open dragon wares and open the border again between Aralot.

Tyler needed Kayla to make him look good. Then there was that other part where he wanted to keep her away from inheriting anything in Aralot so that she wouldn't die. It was going to be hard to convince her to agree with him without telling her that he thought she was doomed, but if he never tried, he'd hate himself forever.

"I might be able to provide something that could get her to agree," Coal hummed at him.

Kayla wasn't humming. She was staring at the paper as if she wasn't seeing it anymore. There was a dragon cough, and at her feet appeared Valiant with Mr. Grumpy right beside him. Both of them were looking directly up at Kayla's face, waiting to see what she would do. The guards and General Reis gasped at all the rare dragons.

"Seriously?" Kayla asked Tyler looking past Coal in his arms directly at his face. "You want me to take down protective spells so you can kill two people—"

"Conner already volunteered for that," Tyler was quick to put in. He didn't want to kill anyone. He had no idea how. He'd probably mess it all up. He was going to let the man who wanted to get at the Peyton's get at them.

"—which includes destroying a spellbinding dragon, and then you want me to *marry you?*"

Conner, still invisible, snatched the paper from Kayla's hand so that it was floating in the air. He skimmed it, tried to tear it up, and then grunted. Tyler had used one of the magically binding papers on purpose. He couldn't create such a paper himself, but he knew how to use them. The paper couldn't be destroyed by anything less than an ultra-dragon king.

"That would take her out of Aralot. She needs to be there!" Conner challenged him.

"It's an engagement," Tyler said, wishing that Conner was a bit more visible so he could see the guy. "Kayla can still be in Aralot. I'm not asking her to marry me, only to help me become the king over here."

"*I will warn you if Conner gets close. I can smell him,*" Coal offered.

"She's not that stupid," Conner spoke for Kayla. "She knows that it's the same thing in Vankerdale. An engagement is just as binding as being married."

"Actually, engagements can be called off. It's being married to a king that can't."

No one was allowed to divorce a king, but there had been canceled engagements before. He could prove it if Kayla needed to read the evidence. He knew right where to go.

"You did this on purpose," Kayla mumbled, still looking at him.

Tyler looked down at Coal and waited for extra inspiration.

Engagement

Kayla

It wasn't King Peyton or Prince Evan that had captured her into Vankerdale. It had been Tyler the first time, and it was Tyler again the second time. Prince Evan had never learned that looking at dragons and being called on by them would make her collapse. King Peyton shouldn't have learned that either. Tyler was using the king and prince as his instruments to get her over here so he could pull off something like this! She knew that he was after something, although she had thought that it would end with him bagging a dragon. It hadn't.

Why was she letting Tyler get away with it all? She'd even told him her deepest fears, yet again, as if he had some strange magic on him that pulled her to spill her guts. Maybe what it really came down to was that she was missing Uncle Anvil. He would have been the first person she let her frustrations reach, only she couldn't see him anymore, and she was missing the assurance from a person who would tell her that everything was going to work out. She wasn't thinking about how Tyler had "rule the kingdom" in his veins. He was going to do everything he could to get Vankerdale on his side. Oh, he was clever.

He had pulled her in by pretending to care, and tried to help her sort through being a broken keeper. He had turned into a keeper that could offer empathy, and what she was ultimately left with was his real trap.

Kayla stared at him, trying to see behind his eyes to the man she didn't know. Tyler used others to do his dirty work for him, because he didn't want to do it himself. Kayla sighed and tried to flip perspectives.

As a king, that wasn't such a bad move. Tyler couldn't do everything himself all the time, and knowing how to delegate would free him up to do the more important things. He might even have time to spend with his family, unlike Jack who liked to do certain things himself and was usually too busy for Kayla to take her trivial problems to.

It also wasn't an unremarkable move for Tyler to ask her to marry him when their kingdoms were talon on talon. It was peace promoting and could stop the newly bonded dragons of Vankerdale from charging over to the kingdom that had cursed them. This way it looked like the fault rested entirely with the Peytons, instead of with Kayla's mother, who had put that curse on. In that regard, agreeing to this wouldn't be the worst thing she could do to help her kingdom and save her parents from a war. Not that she was agreeing with any of it. She wasn't going to talk herself into this.

"I have to date Tristan right now," she informed Tyler.

"It's only an engagement, Kayla. I swear that it can be changed later. I won't hold it against you if you have to follow the rules of your own land and date Tristan, but signing that paper will save you if he asks you to marry him. I am trying to rescue you from marrying a guy with a black soul that you feel like slapping in the head. That's what any friend would do, provided that he had the chance."

Kayla rolled her eyes at him, keeping her focus off of the small black blob below Tyler's face. Even if she had never expressed her dislike over Tristan today, Coal would have been able to fill Tyler in from all those times he had charged at her and spied on her over the years. There was no way out of it.

"You won't have to put up with Tristan cursing you all the time or saying rude comments. You can forget all about his bug collection."

Kayla groaned. Yup. Here it came. Coal new everything she had verbally expressed that she didn't like about Tristan, and he was going to help Tyler pled for her to marry him. Easy for them to do. She was the one who was going to be getting the backlash for this. They would have easy sailing.

"I'm sure that Vankerdale has plenty of other nobles that you can choose," Kayla deferred.

"Not any that I like," Tyler commented.

That wasn't her problem who he liked. Why did he even like *her?* They'd hardly spent any time together at all. This was all a ruse.

"Not any that are favorable toward Aralot. I need a girl right now, or you can expect that Vankerdale will continue to haunt Aralot forever trying to steal your dragons. Your border spells are down. Your magical ice dragon has left his kingdom. Once King Peyton realizes that, he will cast up so many curses that dragons won't be able to leave this place ever again. If you want me here to bring your kingdom peace, you need to sign this paper. It's peace or war, Kayla, and you get to choose which one."

Grr! She was too young to be thinking about this. She wasn't even in charge of Aralot to decide something like this. This right here was the entire reason why she wanted Aria to help her think like a noble, so that she could get out of things like this! Too bad Aria hadn't been fast enough in her teaching to help with this encounter.

It felt like a trap. It looked like a trap. It even sounded like a trap, and yet Tyler was probably right that if he wasn't put on the throne in Vankerdale someone else who was far worse would take the job. He just had to add in that comment about escaping Tristan. She *did* want to get away from him, but was this the right way to do that?

"Kayla you can save two kingdoms right now. Just scribble on that." Tyler pointed to the floating paper that Conner was holding. He was being super quiet. Kayla knew that the wings and footsteps of Conner and the dragons hadn't been noticed by anyone else except her when they showed up. Despite Conner's usual stealth, that paper was slightly shaking. Was it rage or fear that had Conner's arm unsteady? She closed her eyes, causing Tyler to snort at her.

"I hope that you're not pretending that I'm a dragon you can't look at. Kayla, consider the future here. Would you rather be engaged to me or Tristan Cluster? I promise that I will do my best to be your friend. I will pick you up when you fall, be your eyes when you can't see, your listening ear when you need to scream. I will stand beside you instead of over you as Tristan might do."

He had no idea what he was talking about. Kayla kept her eyes closed and blamed Coal for the information that Tyler was digging up again.

"I will defend you from your enemies, instead of leave you to face them alone. I won't blink an eye when you secretly talk with Ritz."

She snapped her eyes back open. Coal had seen that? What part? Which time?

"He's a very wise friend to have." Tyler smiled at her.

Kayla rubbed at her eyes. Tyler was so weird. No one else would say that to her, so of course, it was the one thing he was going to say to reel her in now that he had her on a hook. Everyone else would tell her that Ritz was a bad friend to keep around. That he was out to trick her, fool her, and use her in some way. He had his moments, but beneath it all, she couldn't help but look up to him.

"We can fix this together," Tyler tried again, "because you already know that you can tell me anything. I will do my best to understand everything you are going through, and I don't have previous judgments in the way that will influence my thoughts about keepers or you."

Tyler was too good at this. She should have kept her mouth shut. She had given him way too much to work with. He was going to tell her pretty little lies until she complied. The worst part was that she wasn't sure how much of a lie his words even were. He did try to understand her thoughts about keepers, because he had never been one before and didn't have any example to follow. He really could believe everything he was saying.

Instead of using the Peytons, Tyler probably saw himself as a hero, rescuing Valiant from imprisonment and reuniting Kayla with the dragon. He was the hero who was putting himself in the way of the Brixtons so that he could end the curse on his land. He was the one stopping a war. He was still asking her to marry him.

Conner was right. Being engaged in Vankerdale was pretty much being married already. Kayla could move in at any minute and start taking charge if she said yes. Was Tyler prepared for that? He trusted her to have that much power over a land she had never lived in? Or did he suspect that she would crawl back across the river and never see him again? Because that's what she was going to do.

Her life wasn't fair. If it was a choice between Tyler and Tristan, Tyler was the sure pick. But what about other guys? She had never dated anybody else. How was she to know if she wouldn't fall in love with some other guy and feel horrible about it because she was already "married." She was only sixteen! She wanted a chance to choose her life. Instead, she was the same political pawn that she had always been.

"What do you think, Valiant?"

"Don't ask me. You already know that I like Tyler and that he and Coal both like you. This is your choice."

"I already regret it," Kayla said as if she had mentally agreed to sign that paper. Most rulers of Aralot didn't get to marry for love, and if things stayed the way they were going right now, she just very well might end up staying with Tristan for the rest of her life. That would be horrible. Tristan killed things for fun and hung them on his walls as hunting trophies. He stuffed them into boxes for his bug collection. She couldn't live like that for the rest of her life.

She would always wonder what evils her "husband" was casting. She would know that Tristan didn't like her. Tristan had come to save her, but his was surely a political motive, because he'd not come after her again when she told him to go away. She might consider running away from home for the freedom it provided if it really started to get thicker inside of Aralot. Her and Tristan. From the moment she was born, she didn't have a choice. Tyler was giving her the only choice she was going to get until she could find some other way to deal with Tristan.

"I sign this and you take the time to find some other girl to marry," Kayla told Tyler, looking him in the eye.

"Sure," Tyler agreed.

He didn't look happy to have said it, but he hadn't said no. Kayla took the paper and signed her name with the pen that she had also conveniently taken out of Tyler's pocket. She had taken everything he had in there because she wasn't sure which of his items could be the magical one without looking at them all. She almost got away with Tyler not noticing.

"I will take that, thank you," General Reis said, reaching for the magically binding document. Kayla watched it go away from her, and

Pg. 306

then looked at the general. Even without a crowning ceremony, she was this man's queen right now. At least she would be once King Peyton was no longer the official king.

"We need to cut off their magical sources first," Kayla said, casting a spell over the three dragons to make them invisible again using the mini fox statue she had taken from Tyler. "Does anybody have a visual on the king?"

"Visual, no? Previous knowledge, yes," Conner spoke. "He will be in the top of the east tower where he can see the entire courtyard and cast out the nastiest spells."

"We need to get our magical dragons out there," Kayla stated, fearing for what Conner was talking about. It was his dragons currently doing all the fighting. Kayla hadn't expected the other three dragons to come inside the castle, but she should have guessed at it because Valiant had told her that he wanted her out, and he would use his own team to free her before he ever turned to a longer battle.

"You need to suck up the Peyton's magic," Kayla told Valiant as she charged down the hallway, not sure where she was going at all. She shouldn't be the one leading everybody because she was the least knowledgeable about how to get around this castle. Give her the castle in Aralot, broken or restored, and she could navigate both of those in her sleep. She had to look behind her and let Tyler pass her when she reached a branch in the hallway. He had no problem taking over as long as it was everyone else that was doing the nasty work for him.

"I'll distract him…" Kayla trailed off in the direction she could hear Conner's light jog.

"And I'll chop his head off for all the torture he put you through," Conner replied.

"And you'll do something relatively cleaner," Kayla amended.

Tyler pulled open a door and screamed as one of his arms was blown clean off with a spell. Prince Evan! They knew where King Peyton was, but Prince Evan had chosen to head off their threat from within, instead of help his dad with the dragons outside. Tyler was in shock. He stood there unable to move as his other arm was torn off next. Coal screamed in fury and started to charge toward Prince Evan, but his dragon sounds were heard and he was shoved, still invisible, into the wall with a loud smack. Unlike Coal, Valiant and Bantin didn't announce themselves when they attacked. Kayla could only tell that they were flying around the back of Prince Evan because she could hear them. She shoved up a shield spell to stop Tyler from completely dying, healed his arms, pushed him to the side of the open doorway, and got ready to take on Prince Evan herself.

She'd never fought a man with the intention to kill him before. It made her nervous, because she was going to have to do this all over again against King Peyton.

"You will not. I'll take the king down while Coal gets SilverWings. You get Prince Evan," Valiant declared. *"Conner will help you."*

With a short chirp, Valiant called the other dragons after him. Coal whimpered before he left Tyler behind, but he did leave him even if Kayla was fairly certain that Tyler hadn't overcome his shock of losing his arms. She couldn't hear him breathing, but he was still standing there now being blocked off by General Reis who was waving his hands before Tyler's eyes to make sure he was still cognizant.

Prince Evan wouldn't be as hard to handle as King Peyton, who had more years of experience reading from the magical library, but he'd still be hard. Kayla felt even warier as Valiant left her. It was a sure sign that they were unbonded when her dragon couldn't face the battle with her. He couldn't stand the thought of letting her down or perhaps seeing her get hurt.

"Perhaps your dragon has faith in your ability to succeed," Valiant thought to her. *"Be brilliant, Kayla. Out think him. It shouldn't be hard. He had Tyler doing his thinking for him earlier."*

"Yeah, so he could focus on learning spells!" Kayla replied as her favorite shield spell obtained a hole in the center a little too close to her heart. She gave one more glance toward the blinking Tyler, and then pushed through the doorway to keep the fight as far away from Tyler as she could. It wasn't much room to work in. They had been inside a narrow hallway, and now she was in a small sitting room that wasn't much larger.

She had no idea what spell Prince Evan had cast, but this was far different than the time she had frozen him before he was ready to react. This time, he was coming at her completely ready. Their next spells clashed in the air, hers designed to chop his head off, who cared about being clean if only she could stay alive, and Evan's designed to knock the wind from her lungs. Kayla watched the spells flip through each other as her lungs started to shove inward. She fixed herself, watched Prince Evan howl briefly as his head started to flip back before he stopped himself from dying too.

The best way to defeat a spellcaster was to get rid of his ability to cast spells. Otherwise, she could be doing this for days on end like her father had done when he first faced off against a spellcaster that wanted him dead. Kayla was not going to do this forever. She grabbed at the energy buzzing around the room, casting it outward into anything that would take the magic out of the castle. It was a rather dangerous act to do, because she had no idea what was suddenly being infused with magic, but right now she didn't really care as long as that magic was far away from Prince Evan. Unfortunately, she couldn't take away any magic that the prince actively had in his hand.

"You'll lose it yourself that way!" Prince Evan screamed at her.

"Then I can knock you over with my impressive battle moves. I've been practicing," Kayla replied. She had been, but all physical maneuvers were easier when she wasn't in a dress. Oh well. She had Conner for that stuff if he would ever move from standing behind her and get behind Prince Evan. He probably thought that it was safer on her end right now. She shifted farther into the room so that she wasn't blocking the doorway and Conner could sneak around her and Prince Evan both.

"Nothing about you is impressive, Kayla."

"You need a better insult than that," Kayla replied, shattering a window to push the shards of glass in his direction. He blocked it and shoved them all back at her. The number one rule with using magic was that she had to be considerate about where she was moving energy from. She couldn't turn the glass shards into bubbles if there were no bubbles in the world. She had to exchange one thing for another, shift around the force, use the power of things that she could understand enough to control. If she tried to use the eruption of a volcano, she'd end up imploding herself because it was too strong for her to hold.

She chose to swap the glass shards for whatever spell it was that King Peyton had just used. She hoped it was a good one because the glass shards now moved toward him while his spell blasted toward Prince Evan. Evan slashed back at the spell only to have it hit him and pass him over.

"Scales? I don't have any scales to incinerate," he taunted, unaware about where she had taken her spell from. She wasn't going to reply back to him. She had just saved a dragon from being injured, and since she didn't have to think up a spell herself, she had plenty of time to attempt to burn Prince Evan up. His hair caught fire first, but he was ready for her too, and the walls of the room caved in around her to squish her flat. Kayla shoved them back while he stopped the flames.

He moved onto weather magic, and Kayla used his work against him, letting the storms tear through the room while she cast a single spell to be invisible to Prince Evan's spells. The room flooded. Doors, windows, and pictures were blown around with such force that Prince Evan had to dodge. The ground shook. The room became blistering hot and then freezing cold all before Prince Evan figured out what her spell was so he could take it down.

Kayla felt like she was doing a great job getting him to use up his available magic, especially since her next spell on him had him repeating every single spell he cast. He tried to break her apart by causing a loud crash that only she could hear to burst her eardrums. Her ears split and she screamed, but she fixed them and deflected his repeated spell since she knew what it was going to be.

Since he had to repeat himself, he couldn't deflect her next spell that attempted to immobilize him, but he must have created a charm to keep that particular spell away after the first time she got him with it. She had to think of something else, so she caused him to move excessively slow instead. It worked for only a few seconds before Prince Evan dragged in the closest dragon to them shattering the wall as it came.

Nasty! She couldn't look at the dragon as it screamed. Prince Evan was getting tired of her, and was trying to drop her down. She couldn't let him do that! Kayla resisted the dragon sounds, having tons of practice if she didn't have to see the animal. She kept her eyes on the spellcaster before her and reversed his spell so that the dragon was flung backward out of her sight. Kayla wasn't sure how much magic she had to work with in this fox statue, but she didn't have time enough to worry about it. The dragon would come back in just a minute, due to the prince still needing to repeat his spells, but that would give her more time to confuse Prince Evan as to what spell she had used. He cast a frantic spell trying to bring the beast back. While he did that, Kayla used the broken objects in the room to tie around Prince Evan's legs and trap him down.

He was just about to free himself when Kayla sent a pointed edge of a picture frame at his chest. At the same time, a knife slashed through the air, and Kayla wasn't sure which of the three things got Evan first. Her pointed frame, Conner's knife, or the dragon that came back roaring flame through the room.

"Conner!" Kayla screamed, as she dispelled the flames and commanded the dragon in his own language to go away. It growled at her and shoved away from the building to return to the outside battle.

"Conner!" Kayla called again, noticing the charred remains of Prince Evan, that included both the knife and frame. Conner's angle indicated that he was personally in the room, but she couldn't hear him breathing, and there was a chance he could be invisibly dead right now. If he was, revealing him wouldn't be pretty.

"Charred a bit," Conner wheezed from right below her knees. Kayla stepped back. He had somehow managed to jump toward her as the dragon came in. She took away his invisible spell so she could see his burns enough to heal them.

"Is he gone?" Valiant asked her. *"We could use some help over here. I can't reach King Peyton when I'm too busy fixing all these dragons! I swear he has a thing with knocking out their tongues. The screams are horrible."*

"Coming," Kayla said out loud, as she resisted looking out of the broken hole in the wall to see the battle for herself. She had been ignoring all the screams, but now that she was listening, they were indeed horrible. Since the sounds in her room had stopped, Tyler decided that it was safe enough for him to look in. He flinched, so she knew that she wasn't the only one hearing about the other distracting battle. At least King Peyton wasn't bonded so he didn't know about Prince Evan's death and get worse with his spells.

"Which way to that eastern tower?" Kayla asked, looking around the hallways that were still intact.

"That way," General Reis pointed, "but I don't think you should stick together. At least one of you needs to survive this."

"I'm going with her. I can't leave Kayla!" Tyler wailed.

"She's not defenseless." The general pointed out. "I've never seen magic like that before. That was horrible!"

"It's malicious when those spells are used, I agree," Kayla said, already running in the direction that the general pointed. She wasn't going to take her time here. Every second was another second where one of Conner's dragons cried out in pain. He had to be inwardly wailing. Kayla was and they weren't even her dragons. She felt the pressure to get out there and heal them all herself, which was probably the same keeper pressure forcing itself over Tyler since he disregarded his general to chase after her.

"Sire!"

"I am not afraid! King Peyton will stop this torture!"

Tyler was very helpful behind her. He directed her to the eastern tower, and while he was doing that, she had tons of time to think up the best spell to shoot at King Peyton. She was going to mess with his mind. It was a complicated spell to get into another person's head and change things around, but he'd used illusion on her before. It was her turn.

"Tyler bring me a picture of King Peyton's wife," Kayla ordered. "Conner when she appears from nowhere—"

"I got it," Conner declared. "Mean of you though."

"Who doesn't want to see the person they love one more time before they die?" Kayla asked, as Tyler ran off down a different hallway with his general behind him.

"Like I said, cruel of you."

"But much faster," Kayla retorted. "Less of a chance that you'll lose a dragon."

"I've lost five," Conner growled.

Five too many. The rage of Conner's voice was filled with his pain and it stabbed at Kayla to know that she was the reason he was in Vankderale in the first place. She had to stop this. All of it. Since Kayla was still visible and the castle crawling with confused soldiers and guards, she had to waste a bunch of magic shoving men out of her way that didn't want to stand down at the sight of her. They screamed, and she had to shut off their voices before she reached them so they wouldn't be able to inform King Peyton that she was coming.

"Got it!" Tyler appeared at her side, bursting out from a side door. She didn't expect it to be him, so Tyler and the general found themselves without voices for a moment while they were stuck to the side of the wall. They gaped like fish at her until she released them and they scanned down the hallway to see all the other men she was talented at trapping.

"It's not like I enjoy this," Kayla remarked. "I'm trying to get it over with. I'd never hurt anything if I didn't have to."

"I'll keep that in mind," General Reis said, to test out getting his voice back, "because you are terrifying." Tyler didn't test his voice. He was holding out the picture to her while he looked ashen toward the wall. Something bad had happened outside.

"*I'm stuck,*" Valiant told her. Yes, that was very bad indeed. "*Coal* is slipping around SilverWings while I try to break free, but he's not an ice dragon so he's not as fast as Bantin. Bantin can't shoot ice anymore. He's very put out about it, but I can't take the time to fix him. He still has his tail and is using it to smack SilverWings on the head when he can reach him. King Peyton keeps shooting things at me so I can't take the time to break my legs and wings out."

"Valiant," Kayla whimpered.

She was taking too long! She grabbed the picture from Tyler's hand and charged toward the tower at a much easier pace now that she had Tyler and the general in view behind her. They waved at the guards to stand down. Her will power was so forceful, so determined, so strong that the image of King Peyton's wife took shape without her wanting it to get started. She had to get the woman inside of King Peyton's thoughts to distract him away from everything else that he was doing. His lovely ash-brown haired wife took on the form of his memories. She went running up ahead of Kayla crying out for her husband.

"The snow is nearly up to the windows again. Come build a snow fort with me! Enjoy life for a moment!" the woman sang. Kayla winced. It would only be a moment of enjoyment alright.

"There will be no snow!" King Peyton screamed back.

"Got one leg out!" Valiant cheered, as he had a moment to free himself from a trap. "You keep that focus up. It's fantastic!"

It was also tiring. Kayla could feel the memories working through the blue glow of her hands. They were not her memories at all or this would have been easier. She stopped on the stairs to pant while she listened to the invisible Conner race up without her.

"I'm going to wear my blue coat. The one with the white fur that you got me for my birthday. You'll be wearing your yellow coat—"

"The gray one," King Peyton's voice responded, as he was stuck in the spell that showed him his own memories. He couldn't help but fill in his part of the details. Kayla heard SilverWings scream in fury from outside about his distracted rider, but the dragon couldn't do anything about it, because she also heard Valiant lob a few spells at him.

"And tea when we get back inside."

"Warm cider," King Peyton laughed. "With those sprinkle cookies that you love."

King Peyton thudded to the floor. Love had been his last word if anyone cared to record it. Despite how mean he had been, Kayla hoped that he got to experience the love of being with his wife again. Kayla waited for the moment that SilverWings cried out the mourning song for losing his rider, only to remember that they were not bonded so SilverWings had no idea that King Peyton was dead yet.

"I'm free!" Valiant cheered.

"Bagaph!" Tyler's words pulled Kayla away from her own thoughts so she could look down the stairs at Tyler, standing with his arms out and stiff. His eyes had turned yellow so that he looked like a demon. General Reis was slowly backing away as if Tyler was cursed. Kayla jumped down the stairs and slapped his face.

"This is not the time to sightshare! Snap out of it, Tyler."

"It's not my fault!" Tyler cried back, rubbing at his stinging face that woke him back up. "Coal got scared and it just sort of happened!"

"Well, you tell him that he's much better at being himself than you are. He does not have to be out of his own head to take down SilverWings. He can do it on his own."

"How did you..." Tyler trailed off as if Kayla had gotten the reason for the sightsharing correct.

Pg. 316

She was only guessing at why he was feeling scared, but Coal shouldn't be feeling scared. He had killed off tons of people and dragons. This shouldn't be hard for him even if he was facing a spellbinding creature that was proving difficult to destroy.

"I've got his spells blocked..." Valiant whispered. There was a rather distinctive strangled dragon sound that filled the air before all the war sounds came to an abrupt end. *"...and done,"* Valiant sighed out. *"So tired! I have to fix Bantin first, and then get more magic from him and fix these dragons, and..."*

"Well it's done," Kayla stated for the rest of everyone who couldn't hear Valiant or Coal's thoughts on the matter. It was time for her to clean up her mess too. She released the guards that had been pinned and silenced to the walls. She turned Conner visible again. He appeared on the other side of her, having somehow gotten past her ears without her noticing. He froze in his tracks when he realized they could see him again.

"And that bonding curse..." Conner trailed off, looking out the window where his dragons awaited him.

Kayla nodded and turned to face Tyler.

"Don't forget to clean your fang wound really well. It will look like a crater for a while and be all green and ugly but it's fine."

With that, she pricked her finger to use blood magic and cast the spell that allowed dragons inside of Vankerdale to bond again. It didn't take them long to notice that their fangs filled up with fluid. Dragons were screaming all over the place, cheering in glee. Kayla rushed to a window conscious of Tyler watching her run off on him. She flung it open, scaled down the building, and rushed outward, avoiding everything with four legs that could fly.

Her direction was that of the portal, and she was scooped up by Valiant and joined by Bantin so they could escape the merry making behind them. It was going to make her sick. So many happy dragons and people that could bond when she couldn't. Valiant was still set on winning out against Sparkle for the right. Sticking around to watch bonding was impossible, but she couldn't leave them to experience the pain any longer. Kayla hoped Tyler was happy. He got his castle and his dragon all on the same day.

Supported

Caleb

Someone had climbed onto his bed. If he was a little kid again living inside his parent's bunkroom with his family that wouldn't have been a cause of alarm. He had a little brother that was very good at being brave around dragons and scared of the rain. It had been some time since anyone had crawled into his space like this, so Caleb jolted, knocking off the intruder gearing up for a brawl.

The fight didn't happen. The person didn't even clunk onto the floor, but regardless, Caleb wasn't the only one that had been woken up by the strange visitor. A candle went on in the back of the room where Malone, the nighttime section leader, usually slept during the day. For him to be here told Caleb the hour instantly. It was just before dawn. Mulligan would be outside, having just swapped places, and Malone would have seen the door open as the intruder snuck inside. With the candle lit, Russel and Notley stirred. Caleb jumped at the person again.

"Kayla!"

He could hardly believe what he was seeing. If this was another illusion, he was going to go crazy. He had spent hours chasing around fake versions of her running at all the ones that were heartbroken and had dragons swooping down to attack them. It had him screaming, and he'd not been much better after King Jack and Pyro had finished pushing the invading force back where they belonged. Charles told them all that Kayla was gone. Caleb might have been the only one that cried, but he wasn't the only one feeling horrible for failing the one person they all needed to protect. Vankerdale's goal had been rather obvious, and they had succeeded. Aralot had lost. That hurt a guy's pride.

But she was back again! Caleb pulled her into a quick hug, wishing he could hold onto her even longer, and did his best to brush away all his personal feelings in favor of being the person she needed him to be. The other section leaders in the bunkroom sat up now that he was being loud, but he couldn't help it.

"Does anyone else know that you're here? What happened? Are you okay?"

"You're my section leader. I have to report to you first," Kayla answered him.

"Your parents don't know?" he questioned, feeling the start of those tears again. She was back! He was so relieved. Kayla could have gone to see anybody and she was choosing to see him first! Turning into a section leader was the best thing that had ever happened in his life.

"I can't run back home to tell my parents. I don't get a vacation for five years."

She gave him a shrug as if he should have expected that, but no one expected that. She was the princess of Aralot. She had to tell people when she came back, because the entire kingdom had been alerted to her going missing.

Kayla had her sweater back on, so she must have stopped by her own room before coming to report, since she had left in a dress. Caleb followed her gaze toward his bed and flipped the blanket over so that she couldn't see what he had been sleeping on top of. He couldn't get to sleep knowing that she was out there in trouble so he had been drawing a lot of pictures. It made it worse that he wasn't allowed to charge after her. Nobody was. Charles said that King Jack had it all under control. While Caleb knew that the man could handle practically anything, Caleb had really wanted to help.

"I used to be scared of your pictures," Kayla said, moving past him and pulling one out that he had been trying to hide.

Caleb's face crimsoned. Why that one, and did they have to have this discussion in front of all the other section leaders? He looked at them, met them in the eyes, but the older men didn't do anything other than lay back down in bed and wait. If this was Anvil's Ware, or even any other person, Kayla would have been kicked out of the room she wasn't allowed inside already. See? She got special privileges.

"Kayla doesn't abuse her status, unlike a few other nobles. I think it makes her more likable," Warner said, proving that Caleb had woken him up by his startled mind. *"I think she came to see what you drew."*

No, it wasn't that. She was in here because she was searching for something else. Caleb wasn't quite sure what, but the room felt thick with waiting.

"It's not real. It would never happen," Caleb said to the picture that Kayla was staring at.

She was looking at his work, and instead of being thrilled, he still felt uneasy. He had been mentally looking for a way to save her even if he couldn't. The picture in her hand reflected that. She was trapped at the top of a tower that was cut off at the bottom and held up by magic. Valiant was strapped down in chains so he couldn't reach her. Kayla had no magic of her own as she looked downward at the far drop. Then there was Caleb on Warner, flying up to rescue her. She was still looking at it.

"Did my pictures scare you before because they had dragons?"

he asked, reaching over to take the image away from her before she turned into a ball of tears. Her eyes were starting to get moist already, and it wasn't even a real dragon. "You thought you'd start crying if you saw them because your bond is still broken."

"I didn't tell you that my bond is still broken," Kayla said, scooting away from him. "Am I really that much of an idiot to think that nobody knew?"

"I had no idea," Mulligan offered.

"I'm your teacher. I figured it out," Caleb said. "I also happened to notice that Valiant is a night dragon. He'll listen to me if the sun is down. I wrote out a new class schedule so he can take a few naps during the day. Maybe he'll start participating."

Kayla had her eyes glued to his wall. At least her hood was not up so he could tell that there was something that was still deeply troubling her. He really wanted to ask her what it was, and maybe his fidgeting clued her into that, because she turned to look at him and asked him the strangest thing she had ever asked him yet.

"Can I pretend that you're Uncle Anvil for a few minutes?"

He nodded, not sure where this was going until Kayla flung herself at his arms and clung on crying. That was probably the release Caleb was waiting for. She needed to release the built-up tension of everything she had just gone through, and she didn't have Uncle Anvil around for that. Caleb felt suddenly honored that she would even consider him a second choice. He had gained her trust somewhere. He wrapped one arm around her shoulders and used his other one to scoop up her legs so she was curled up as tight as she could get. If that's what she needed him to be, Caleb was going to be some other man.

"Anvil was getting some strong arms picking you up like this," Caleb noted. "I think I need to get a few earrings." He smiled at the sight

Pg. 322

of Kayla being in his arms, and couldn't help but deviate away from what Anvil would really say. "Then I'll grow a mustache, a really long one with handlebars. I'll let my hair get super shaggy and make myself one of those uniforms with the image of a sheep on the back."

Kayla sniggered. The only person who had a uniform like that was her mother. It had been a wedding present from Anvil to Tia.

"I might need to make myself more visible though. I'll walk around with bells on my shoes and whistle at all the people who are late to class like I think they're cute."

Kayla slipped from his arms laughing. She went down on the floor letting her head rest up against the side of his bed while she upturned her emotions on the flip of a coin.

"It wasn't all that funny," Caleb said, sitting down to watch her, to make sure that she was okay. She looked back up at him and his chest jumped at the sight of her amused eyes aimed in his direction.

"After what I just went through that is super funny," Kayla noted. "Anvil would never do that! You made a horrible impression. I assumed that you'd be better after all that time you spent getting personally lectured."

He squirmed again. He was hoping that she hadn't known about all of that.

"He threatened to kick me out a lot. Then he finally did." Caleb sighed. He was not on the best of terms with the one person Kayla loved more than anyone, but even admitting his failure to her didn't go over poorly. She was still smiling at him.

"Don't change, Caleb," Kayla suddenly burst, getting off the floor to sit beside him. "You tell me something and I actually believe it. I don't have to guess. I don't have to question your intentions. I don't have to worry about you lying to my face, pretending to be my friend and then trapping me in complicated schemes that will get me in a whole lot of trouble. You say that you'll do something and you actually do it. You're not into torture, or death, or consumed with personal gain. You don't sit around plotting out how to destroy things, or how to make others give you what you want."

Caleb's eyes started to water again. He reached out and pulled her into a real hug, regardless of the other men in the room. He didn't care anymore. She didn't need him to be anyone but himself. What she had come in here to find was a friend, and he had always been her friend.

"They tortured you over there, and you're still in trouble," he interpreted. "Anything I can do to help with that?"

"When Sparkle shows up, stay out of the way," Kayla answered. "I'm probably going to cry…" She trailed off, breathing in and out so fast that Caleb feared she'd make herself dizzy.

"Will Sparkle scream at you? I thought she cooed at your back and called you her baby."

"That's because I was her baby," Kayla wailed, letting her head plop against him.

Caleb had to bite his tongue, because holding Kayla like this broke through everything else that was going on right now. He was going to have to focus really hard to reply back to her as his emotions screamed at him that this was everything he had ever needed to be—there for Kayla. Beside Kayla. Around Kayla. Only he couldn't ever really have her like this. There was no telling when he'd get the chance to hold her in his arms ever again.

He wanted to scream at her to stop dating Tristan and date him instead. Dating could be so easy! They'd sit around together and share personal moments that fortified each other's souls. Was it just him, or could Kayla feel it too that the universe aligned when they were together? Never mind. It was only him. She had just complained about being Sparkle's baby. Nothing in her world felt okay right now. He had to pull back his emotions like always. He could do it.

"The laws of nature don't seem to be working out," Caleb said back to her comment. "Dragon babies are a bit larger." He didn't know why, but that had Kayla laughing at him again. He had to grin at her and shake his head over the emotional wave that she currently was. It made him wonder if this was what it was like when she talked with Anvil after being carried off a field. She was a wreck. Even if she was hurting, Caleb felt envious of all the time Anvil had gotten with her.

"Ice dragons can bond multiple people," Kayla explained. "Sparkle finally told me what happened when I was born as I was being tortured. It was one torture for another over there, and it didn't get much better when I realized I was scammed. Anyway, when Valiant was lost into Vankerdale sixteen years ago, my mom broke my bond to Valiant by cursing Vankerdale. Then Sparkle bonded me." Caleb watched as the other section leaders started to slide out of their beds and reach for their gear. He felt like doing that too. He could tell what was coming. Kayla had two very possessive dragons that wanted her bond. This dragon battle wasn't going to be pretty. Kayla even confirmed it.

"Sparkle's bond broke when Tyler kidnaped me the first time. Valiant and Sparkle are going to fight each other. I don't know what to do. I have two living bonded dragons that want to bash. I don't see how I can stop this. Valiant insists that he has to beat Sparkle or she won't ever respect him. Sparkle refuses to wait any longer, even if Valiant just came back from a war."

There was that name Tyler again. He was a person that her parents knew about, but even though Caleb swore he could name off all of Kayla's cousins and the Colts she most interacted with, he had no idea who Tyler was.

"Who is Tyler?" Caleb asked, not moving off his bed. Warner would tell him if Sparkle showed up. This whole thing sounded like a disaster and he ached down to his bones for Kayla and the confusion she had to live with. "I thought it was King Peyton who kidnapped you."

"No. It was Tyler Valeron both times. He was Prince Evan's servant. The first time he had Prince Evan with him because it was Prince Evan's idea to catch me, but it was Tyler nabbing me. The second time it was all done through Tyler sending King Peyton and Prince Evan to abuse my broken bond so he could get me back in Vankerdale to uncurse everyone. Anyway, Tyler is the new king of Vankerdale, and the dragons over there can bond again. I don't want to tell my mother. Think I have to or can I default to Sparkle telling Mom everything?"

Kayla wrung her hands together. This whole thing was wringing Caleb's heart. She was asking him for help as if she really did need him to defend her when she was so strung out that she couldn't see how to get out of her own problems. A burning resolve to charge at the world for her plowed through his soul. Kayla had been used by the new king of Vankerdale to break curses, and her dragons were going to fight. He couldn't change what had happened in Vankerdale, but he could help her with the other problem.

"Okay. Try to step away from the emotional fear for a moment. I know that sounds hard to do, but you know both of your dragons inside and out. You know their thoughts and their feelings and their souls. You'll know their fighting styles even if you don't watch."

"Are you going to distract her the whole time because Sparkle is here and she is indeed in battle stance against Valiant," Warner provided the information. *"He's curled up into a lump, currently ignoring her. She's hissing at him to get up. The other dragons aren't sure what to do. Charles is looking nervous."*

Pg. 326

"If the problem is not understood, then yes, everyone will be nervous," Caleb answered. "It's terrifying when keepers appear to be fighting each other. Clear the area, Warner. Try to stop anyone else from being hit."

Oh, boy. This was going to hit at them faster than what Caleb expected. He didn't have much time at all to be an emotional coach.

"I know you've never told her what to do, but you might be able to get Sparkle to back down if you talk to her. You were bonded so she'll respect you," Caleb said to Kayla.

The other section leaders, even Malone, all ran out the door, leaving him inside with the broken keeper. This was great. Without them around he scooted father back on the bed crumpling hidden papers, and pulled Kayla in closer to help her get through this.

"I know I was bonded to her, but I can't look at her for more than two seconds without crying. It's as if my body realizes that she stole from me something that should have been with me all along. I can't be mad at her though. All these years she was Valiant's only friend. They could talk to each other so he wasn't alone when he was trapped. Valiant thinks she's beautiful, but she's also controlling."

That was her ice dragon nature. Tia couldn't ride on any dragon that Sparkle might see as a rival or Sparkle would charge after the beast. Caleb had spent hours walking the dragon field as a kid playing a game to decide who was as strong as Sparkle. Lots of kids did it because she was incredible.

"This is great," Caleb spoke, straining his ears for the first sounds of exploding ice. "You understand the struggle from multiple sides. How can you make the friendship side of the dragon's relationship conquer the part of their anger over the lost bond? There has to be something that Sparkle values more than blowing up Valiant. There has to be something that will prevent Valiant from destroying Sparkle with spells for stealing

Pg. 327

you away."

He didn't know what, but he was really hoping that Kayla would think up something. Her father had been fanged by Tia's first ice dragon, and he still managed to find a way to get Misty to back down so he could remain with Pyro. Kayla had to do something similar. She had to find the solution for peace between warring dragon natures. She was a keeper. It should be easy for her to see the solution, if only she wasn't so emotionally exhausted already.

"If you were to step inside their heads, what is it that would ease the tension—" He started to say, only to have Kayla cut him off by grabbing at his arm.

"That's it! You're a genius!" she cried and ran for the door.

Caleb was right behind her. He wasn't prepared for what he saw when the door opened. He had missed the sounds of the first shots because Valiant had put them inside a purple bubble that blocked out sound. Kayla tried to push against the magic to find that it blocked her inside too. Valiant was trying to keep her out of the fight. Kayla couldn't look at them, and if she couldn't hear them, she had no idea what the dragons were doing.

It was bad out there. The field was already covered in fire, ice, and large stab holes where Sparkle's tail had stabbed. The ground smoked and hissed without Caleb being able to hear anything. Other buildings held the purple bubbles too, protecting the structures and people inside from being injured. In that regard, Valiant was a very nice dragon to battle. He kept his fights relatively clean.

Charles and the other section leaders were on top of their dragons above the commotion hovering in a dome formation that was usually used when dragons gathered around to watch dragon racing. Today it was a dome of fear, watching keeper dragons fight. Both Valiant and

Sparkle were giving their whole hearts to the cause of their desires. They were locked in battle in the air with Sparkle's nails stabbed into Valiant's side so he couldn't spin free without ripping the scales off. Sparkle flipped around her tail and stabbed through Valiant's wing, causing him to howl in pain. Her tail continued to stab through his weaker layers as they both crashed onto the ground. This did not look like a bonding battle. It looked like Sparkle was trying to kill Valiant.

Caleb glanced over at Kayla with a gulp, wondering how she was taking this, but she still wasn't looking out at the field. She did respond to his gaze though.

"They won't answer me!"

He didn't answer her either. He went back to looking at the field, scared to say anything to her about what he could see. Sparkle tried to aim for Valiant's face after shredding both his wings. He drew the line right there and shot her with a spell that mimicked dragon-king fire. This was fire so hot and blue that it roasted beneath dragon scales. Sparkle pulled back howling as her entire face turned bloody.

Now free of the talons, Valiant healed his wings, cleaned up some of the flaming field, and healed Sparkle's face before he charged at her again. This time he came at her with a tail that resembled her own. His normally flame-shaped tip was an ice dragon's split dagger ready to break apart Sparkle's body.

Sparkle launched hard ice pellets toward him in a large spray. Valiant charged at her, shutting his eyes and raising his head while a few of his scales were sliced right off. He used his more flexible tail to swipe Sparkle in the face. She bit onto the tail and wrestled him down to the ground. There was another magical explosion that hid them from view and then the two of them were healed again as they rose back to the air and tried to carve out each other's bellies.

"Warner," Caleb meekly thought. He wasn't sure who was going to win and he wanted his dragon's opinion. This whole thing looked like the war that took place inside of Kayla's head all the time. It was harsh. It was brutal, and neither side would give up, because they were both fighting for the same thing—the love of Kayla Brixton. When Kayla loved something, she really loved something.

"Look out!" Warner screamed back.

Caleb glanced away from the battle on the field to look upward just in time. He flinched and pulled two prongs while Kayla remained unaffected and stood still with her eyes shut, voicing her frustration that her dragons wouldn't talk to her. They were too busy to talk to her. They were trying to kill each other off. While they were doing that, Mr. Grumpy had found a way through the dome of hovering dragons overhead, and was charging down toward Kayla with his mouth open. He crashed against the protective purple shield that kept Kayla away from the battle and tried to bite through so he could fang Kayla.

This was madness! The ice dragon didn't even have bonding fangs! They had been cut out when he was a baby, but he was still trying to bond her regardless.

"They noticed," Warner thought to him.

Caleb looked back to the field where Sparkle and Valiant had paused their personal war to growl at Mr. Grumpy. He flipped off the top of the defending sphere while Sparkle screamed at him. Valiant oddly gave him a bow and a pleasant chirp, to which Mr. Grumpy shot a magical ball of ice in his direction. Using the ice dragon tail he still had, Valiant broke open the magic and sucked it all in.

Sparkle screamed at Mr. Grumpy calling him a traitor, and charged toward him while Valiant recharged. Mr. Grumpy adopted the same battle stance that Sparkle usually took, but before she could reach him, he winged himself over her back and shot at her tail. Sparkle was knocked to her face, and didn't have time to get back up. Valiant was there again, holding her head down with his claws and strong arms that now resembled that of an ultra-dragon king. He'd even made the lower half of him black, casting himself as a creature of nightmare.

Kayla stomped her feet. "What are they doing? If I get myself mad enough, I could look."

"They're... fighting," Caleb answered, wanting to hold his hands over her eyes so that she'd never look. This was already hard enough to watch and it wasn't his dragons out there. "I don't think you'd stay mad for long. Don't look, Kayla."

"They are being mean," Kayla pouted. "They're not leaving me with much of a choice but to be as mean as they are."

Caleb took a step away from her not sure how else to react. If Kayla started to add to the fight, it was going to get much much worse. People were small enough to slip around dragon defenses. She could injure both of her dragons, assuming she could keep her eyes shut while she did it.

Mr. Grumpy backed up and then fled as Pyro, carrying both Jack and Tia, showed up. Caleb wished he could hear what they were saying because all three of them had something to say about the fight, and each one was angry about it. Valiant shifted off Sparkle to shoot a spell at the dragon king that trapped him in the air where he raged. With Valiant's back turned, Sparkle jumped on him, trying to rip off his wings. He rolled over and tore off a few of her scales as they both stabbed at each other with their tails. Caleb sighed at the sight of the two dragons bleeding each other. Tia tried to jump off Pyro, only to have her husband trap her against him on Pyro's back, preventing her from running into the way of the death match.

"Blah!" Kayla suddenly screamed beside him. Caleb didn't look over at her because Sparkle was shoving Valiant off. The ice dragon sat down, chirping something to Valiant that had him hiss at her, and then sit as well. Valiant looked in the direction of Kayla sadly, as if he had decided to give up his bond. What had Sparkle said? Had Tia told her to stand down? Valiant couldn't give up! Caleb looked over at Kayla to find that she was staring at him angry.

"Dagra bleff a ga!" Kayla screamed.

What? What was she doing now? Caleb took another step away from Kayla trying to figure out what she was trying to say.

"Translation," Warner provided. *"I am Sparkle trapped inside of Kayla's mortal body and you had better tell her to put me back out there so I can fight. Kayla just told Valiant that she is going to constrain Sparkle's form until Valiant releases Kayla's physical body from his shield and bonds her. If he ever wants Kayla to be herself again, he has to do it. Otherwise, Sparkle is going to be Kayla. I'm glad I won't have to feel Kayla's headache if she stays inside that dragon too long."*

Oh. That's what Kayla meant by she was going to be as mean as her dragons were being. That was indeed very mean. Horrifying really. Sparkle was going to "be" Kayla while Kayla was fanged by Valiant. It was a blow against the dragon's very soul, but it looked like it was going to work. The purple shield that had been preventing Kayla and Caleb from hearing anything lowered. Kayla pulled out a knife, because while Sparkle couldn't control a human tongue, she could still get a human to move, and she was now going to fight off Valiant by being Kayla. Caleb swallowed. That was something he couldn't watch. Kayla loved her dragon. It hurt every rider's heart to see a rider turn against their own dragon. That was the sort of thing infections did.

"Please consider that you and Valiant are good friends," Caleb said, putting away his own prongs so he could turn to his fists and tackle

Kayla. He wasn't sure what moves Sparkle would make Kayla do, but he had spared with Kayla enough to know what she was capable of, and he could prevent her from attacking Valiant. He'd do it even if it did earn him the ire of an ice dragon.

"Friends protect each other even if it hurts them to do so. They take on the pain to shelter the ones they love from being wounded. That's what your bond is. Kayla loves you, only she can't express it until you let her have Valiant back, because you've left her wounded. It's your turn to make it right, Sparkle. Kayla won't leave you if you do this. She'll finally be able to look at you. You'll get her to play with you. The magic that constrains her will be settled, and you won't have to fight for her affection, because it won't be broken."

He talked just long enough that Kayla glared at him, Valiant zipped over, and Tia managed to break away from Jack. Valiant fanged Kayla's shoulder right as Tia reached them. Kayla gasped. Tia screamed at her daughter to release her dragon. Caleb looked into Valiant's brown eyes, watching him pull his venom covered fang back out. For once Valiant gave him a short nod of his head. It wasn't a full bow, but that was the largest sign of respect that Valiant had given Caleb yet. Caleb returned the nod, wondering how to keep this up so that Valiant would give him a full bow.

"You never use sightsharing as a means of control!" Tia screamed, looking at Kayla.

"Very sorry, Mom," Kayla replied, not looking the part, and proving that she had returned to herself as soon as she could. "They were fighting and didn't look like they had any plans on stopping. It would be an endless loop of torture because Valiant can heal them both."

Kayla shrugged. She reached toward her back with her good arm searching for her bag only to realize that she didn't have it on her. Tia pulled out a bandage and handed it to over even if she wasn't done being angry.

"That was the nastiest thing I have ever seen!" Tia screamed again.

"Then it's a good thing it wasn't you with the double broken bond," Kayla replied. "What would you have done? Let them kill each other? Which one was worse, Mom? I saved your dragon's life."

"Tia," Jack dropped to the ground from a rope, tugging at his wife's hand as he regarded his daughter and looked over the field that Valiant was carefully reconstructing now that he had won. Sparkle got in the way of one of his spells and cooed at him until he healed her again. Then while Valiant was distracted, Sparkle started all over again trying to get Kayla to look at her.

Caleb had never felt this way before, but listening to Sparkle was rather nauseating. Kayla had just been bonded to her dragon for the first time that she could remember. She should be with him, not battling it out with her parents while Sparkle blocked her off from Valiant.

"He's patient," Warner reminded. *"Sparkle will leave and he won't have to compete with anything anymore."*

It still wasn't right.

"It's over. Let it go," Jack advised his wife.

"I can't! Kayla can knock my dragon out of her head! She can steal her soul! I am not letting this go!"

"I thought that all keepers protected, not stole, dragon souls." Caleb couldn't help but stand up for Kayla, who hadn't jumped in with her own defense. "I don't think that Sparkle is stolen. She is extra protected. That's very special. Don't feel bad, Tia. Every rider whose dragon ends up inside a keeper bond reacts this way at first. It comes as

Pg. 334

a shock to realize that the control you thought you had is shared with another person, who will give his or her life to protect what you most value."

Tia glared at him for all the times he paid attention to Anvil's lectures. Then she sighed, because he was right. Tia was on the other side of having her dragon inside another keeper's bond. At least she had a lot of good friends that would help her see things in a positive way. She had a great team of riders that stood beside her after she had taken their dragons like this.

"If it was left to me, I never would have done this to you, Mom," Kayla claimed. She resisted saying the rest of her sentence, but Caleb and her parents both knew it was there. Tia had done this to herself. Kayla had put up with her mother's overprotective dragon control long enough. She was old enough to step away from it and go her own way. While Kayla's eyes were dry, her mother's eyes formed tears.

"You both are going to be just fine," Jack soothed again. "I know it has been a long frightening road, not knowing how King Peyton would raise a dragon. Valiant could have very easily held resentment for everything and turned on us all, killing off you or Kayla or everybody for his inner pain. You were using Sparkle as a way to save the dragon from something like that. You were saving Kayla from a beast that was working for the enemy. You won, Tia. You succeeded, Sparkle. You both raised two wonderful beings that would much rather find the path of peace than pain. There have been a lot of bumps in the road, including this one, but every time you're launched into the air you get a great view of where you've been."

"I think the road should have a few forks," Kayla said, glancing to her right.

"I didn't bring you any," Tristan said, appearing in her view from nowhere.

Caleb sighed again. Here was yet another obstacle that stopped Kayla from being with her dragon. Caleb looked out toward Valiant to find him curled back up into a ball again. He wasn't alone though. Mr. Grumpy was beside him with his head touching Valiant's side. It was the friendliest gesture that Caleb had ever seen that ice dragon pull off.

"Field snack," Kayla asked Tristan next. "King Peyton was starving me."

Tristan passed one over and Caleb took a step back, feeling like he wasn't needed anymore. Kayla had Tristan and her parents. It didn't look like they were going to keep riling against each other. Maybe he'd go get Kayla a special breakfast since it looked like she'd not eaten in a while.

Caleb glanced around to spot Warner and found him sneaking over to Valiant. Mr. Grumpy raised his head to watch him, so Warner slowly crawled forward and then hummed when Mr. Grumpy remained silent and went back to protecting Valiant while the tired dragon slept. Warner sat down near them as if he was asking to be part of their herd. He wasn't the only one either. Riven inched over, testing his luck against Mr. Grumpy before the bronze dragon joined the small forces. Then all of them, even Valiant, lifted their heads when the lightest green dragon that Caleb had ever seen charged through the dome of dragon's overhead. They sent flame down after him along with an array of ware dragons trying to stop the wild intruder.

"Don't hurt Reed!" Kayla screamed, before Valiant could rise to his feet in defense of the wild creature. Kayla's words had the other dragons shutting their mouths and leaving the wild dragon alone as the light green dragon landed near the small huddle.

This was Kayla's keeper group, Caleb decided. Even if she wasn't in all of these dragon's heads, they were the ones that wanted to be near her the most. They were the ones that would fight for her life. It was small, but rather strong looking. She had a magical ice dragon, a spellbinding dragon, a wild dragon, his dragon, and Tristan's creature who was probably up to no good but would put himself in the group regardless.

"Reed?" Tia questioned her daughter.

"He's from Vankerdale, and I didn't name him. Lena Sherman named him. She's a spy that came over here and didn't go back home. Reed's been looking for her. He found me Vankerdale and wouldn't stop asking me to search for her when I returned home. Do you think that we have a lot of hiding wild Vankerdale dragons after that attack? They've snuck over." Kayla looked at her dad.

"I'll make some rounds to search, right after you tell me what happened," Jack replied.

He didn't know? Caleb had thought that Jack had been there with his daughter, but it looked like he had left her to fend for herself against an entire kingdom. That was asking a lot from one girl.

"Coal, Bantin, and Valiant killed off SilverWings. I pulled off the Peyton's magical defenses so that Conner could finish them off, and then Tyler became the king. The dragons can bond again. There didn't seem to be a reason left to stop that since Tyler's on our side. Coal bonded him right as I was leaving."

"Everyone is still certain that we can trust this Tyler guy?" Tristan asked.

"Tyler is one of Valiant's best friends," Kayla answered. "He's also Vankerdale's new keeper, and has been researching stuff for Prince Evan for years. He knows what he's doing a little too well."

"That's the part I'm worried about," Tristan agreed.

"He'll do fine." Kayla gave Tristan a shrug and a smile.

Caleb wanted to pry further into her comment when she started to redirect everyone away from it. That was what this girl did when she wanted to hide something. He wanted to find out what she was concealing, because it could end up being rather important later on.

"I'm going to try it," Kayla distracted, spinning around and taking her eyes off the ground to look out toward the dragons.

She started counting. At first, Caleb thought that she was counting the dragons she could see until he realized that she was counting seconds of her time where she didn't feel like falling over. She was better! Her parents were hugging each other. Tristan was being silent for once. Sparkle hooted for Kayla to look at her, and when Kayla looked, the dragon danced on her toes and cheered.

Caleb was very glad that Kayla didn't make him into a liar. She told Sparkle that she would play with her while Valiant was asleep. She started to head that direction, so Caleb told her that he'd save her breakfast.

"I saved something for you too," Kayla said, spinning back around to look at him. She even walked over to him and then rudely stuck her hand into his pocket. Caleb felt a small weight get left behind.

"What is it?" he asked, wanting to pull her over to Valiant so he could watch her take a nap. That would make one adorable picture.

"It's a carving of a fox," Kayla answered. "It reminded me of you."

She left him with a smile and Caleb couldn't help but watch her run off to play with an ice dragon, feeling all over again that he belonged in her world and that she'd never forget about him, even if she had her parents and Tristan. She had given him a present. She had been thinking about him while she had been overthrowing the rulers in Vankerdale and taking on tasks that even her parents hadn't been able to do. Kayla was the most precious person he had ever known.

"Don't stand there speechless. I want to see it!" Warner cried.

Caleb laughed at him and glanced across the field to Warner. He was still a long way off, and the dome of dragons was starting to settle back down, blocking off Warner's view now that the fighting was over. Still, Caleb took out the carving and ran it back and forth in his hands. It was a curled up red fox with a bushy tail and two blue sparkling sapphire eyes.

"Those looks real," Tia noted. She cast a disapproving glance at her daughter before looking at Jack. "Did she just give Caleb magic? She probably stole that from Vankerdale, Jack."

"I should teach that girl not to steal." Jack laughed. He waved his hand through the air as a blue mist trailed after him and then came at the fox. Caleb pulled the object in toward himself but it didn't help. Jack's spell still found it. It cast a few strange images back into the air that Jack shrugged at.

"It's got a few protective spells on it," Jack claimed. "He's teaching a spellbinding dragon. He's got to have something to save him from a dragon like that. Want to get breakfast here? Tristan?" Jack invited his wife and the prince as he gave Valiant a worried glance and sighed at the sight of Kayla playing with Sparkle. "You're coming too," Jack declared, looking at Caleb.

"Yes, sir," Caleb responded, putting the fox back into his pocket with reverence. Kayla had given him magic as if she thought he could be trusted with it. She had plopped it into his pocket without any instruction to not periodically test out bringing the warm blue glow into his hand for the fun of it. If it wasn't for the present in his pocket, and his mission to make sure that Kayla got breakfast, Caleb didn't think he'd get himself off the field. All he wanted to do was be near her.

His first day of class he had taken on the task of getting Kayla to like dragons. He had helped her reach that point, and he wanted to stand around and watch, even if it sort of felt like Kayla had done all the work on her own and he hadn't helped much.

"Then the hero completes the ridiculously hard task and is praised forever. What you never hear being sung about are all those friends who gave that one final ounce of encouragement. Without them, heroes would doubt themselves and might fail the final task, missing that fortification in their soul that they can do this."

For some reason, Kayla's past words slipped through his mind word for word as if she was talking to him right now when she was actually rather distracted dodging an ice dragon tail. It was a little weird how her words had stuck in his mind like that, but he wasn't complaining. Kayla had somehow predicted his future. She might have been the one that solved the bonding issue, and stopped the death match between two special dragons, but she had been a sobbing mess right before that.

It was Caleb that had offered her the kind words she needed to hear. He had made her laugh. The unsung hero today was him, only he didn't go completely unnoticed. Jack was still eying him, as was Tristan and Tia. Maybe they were worried about that magic in his pocket. Kayla had given him the power of a king for helping her get brave again. This was going to make breakfast interesting. He'd better start talking about other things to redirect their attention.

"When's the last time you lost a card game, Jack?" Caleb questioned.

Jack laughed at him because he was the master at winning with cards. He didn't use magic to cheat either. Sure enough, now thinking about playing, Jack invited him to a game. Even if Caleb lost, he wasn't going to feel bad. He had won what he was really after today. He'd helped defeat Kayla's deepest fear and gained Valiant's respect.

Redemption

Kayla

Kayla carefully ran a hand through the hole of her favorite sweater unable to block out the cheerful music that surrounded her inside the castle and yet couldn't touch her mood. Valiant hadn't thought through his location when he fanged her. A hand-sized gap of missing fabric stretched through her shoulder seam and it couldn't be mended without the use of magic. As limited as her magic was right now, Kayla didn't want to waste any of it on mending when she could replace the clothing.

She had three identical sweaters that were fuzzy on the inside and gray on the outside. They were warm, comforting, her lifetime protection against seeing dragons. One happened to be in the bedroom of her house, and the other one happened to be at Anvil's Ware. She had no idea when she would get around to picking up either of those, so she was standing in a corner ignoring everyone else to stare at her misfortune. The easiest way to get what she wanted was to ask her mom to bring it from home, but one look to the castle ballroom floor prevented Kayla from moving.

Joy. Uninterrupted joy filled her parent's faces as they twirled across the smooth wooden floor, excited that their past troubles with Vankerdale were over. This was one of rooms in the castle that kept its original decorations from when Gladius had first built it. The ballroom had alcoves every five feet that featured either a door or rows of blue glass windows. Instead of boring gray walls, the ballroom was white with gold trim and red curtains. The roof was Kayla's favorite part. A flower pattern composed of basil leaves radiated from the center to the edges. Each leaf had a geometric pattern inside, also in blue, red, and gold. Kayla glanced upward at the roof as she gave her sweater a hug. The pattern was beautiful, and the only thing that made her not run away from castle parties within the first ten minutes.

She was yet to attend a party where she felt anything but annoyed that everyone could be so happy. She would have loved to place the blame of her emotions on having a broken bond, but she wasn't broken apart from the stinging wound on her shoulder. Most people talked about how they could not feel the pulse of the venom after a bonding. Kayla could feel it. Her shoulder was killing her, only she refused to use magic on that as well in the unlikely event that a magical healing messed up the bond she had finally gotten. She had waited all her life for this bond to be restored, and it was bothering her that she couldn't feel happy about it.

"You haven't gotten to see me since." Valiant offered a solution to her foul mood. *"You had to put up with Sparkle, give her an ounce of control after she felt so completely defeated. You did the right thing. Come slip outside and see me."*

"Can't," Kayla sighed.

Valiant had been asleep through the ordeal of her rewrapping her wound, heading into the castle, and listening to Jack talk about his impressions of King Tyler's abilities. Her father had good things to say about him, which wasn't surprising since they were both keepers, and keepers defended each other. As far as respecting the neighbors went, they were now in a very good place with Vankerdale. Kayla was happy that she had helped ease her parent's burdens. She still wasn't too thrilled about her own situation, both with Tyler and this room.

Pg. 344

The reason she couldn't leave the party was because Queen Aria was blocking her escape route. She had instructed Kayla to dance as part of her princess lessons. Kayla shook her head and went mute. If she started dancing, she was going to be forced to dance with Tristan. She couldn't dance with Tristan.

He had not glared at her when their eyes met because she was in his dragon's head. He wasn't seeking her out to push nasty comments in her direction. He wasn't paying her any attention at all that she could tell, and it had her unsettled. If he wasn't going to be mean now when he was going to? She could picture him dancing her off to the side, stabbing a knife through her neck, and leaving her there to die so he could get his dragon back all to himself. It made the adrenaline rush through her to feel like she wasn't safe still.

"As for your earlier comment, fear does cancel out joy. You never enjoy parties because you always find something to be scared about. Find a way out of there and come see me!" Valiant wailed.

There *was* more than one exit, but Aria was blocking the most convenient one, and Vermelo was blocking the other. Aria wasn't glaring at her. Vermelo was. Kayla had no idea why because Kayla wasn't doing anything out of her normal character. She always stood in the corner during these parties. People expected to see her here and they did a great job of leaving her alone. Vermelo couldn't know that she was engaged to King Tyler, because she hadn't told anyone. Vermelo's magical spying mirror didn't work inside of Vankerdale, and it was too early for Tyler to have sent a letter to Aralot declaring his ascension which would show Kayla's signature on the bottom. Vermelo had no reason yet to be angry with her.

Kayla glanced around to spot Tristan. He was flirting, of course, surrounded by a group of five girls that were all laughing about something he was saying. All of them were having a great time while

Kayla was left to sulk in a corner. Oh, she hated parties! She hated feeling like she couldn't measure up to anyone around her.

"I think you simply need a friend with you to enjoy a party and you don't have that there. Come see me," Valiant tried again.

Fine. She would risk heading past Vermelo. That way she wouldn't have to worry about the Tristan thing. Kayla slipped around the edges of the room and tried to slip out the door behind him. She didn't even reach Vermelo's side before he was grabbing her arm, still looking at her like he wanted to scream.

"I could use the restroom," Kayla claimed.

"Your lies won't work on me," he hissed into her ear. "Explain Mr. Grumpy, Kayla. He tried to fang you. He doesn't have fangs. Why did you take him? Couldn't you leave him alone? Don't you realize that he might want to be with a person that will actually love him?"

Vermelo's words stopped her cold. He was angry about Bantin. Kayla hadn't done anything to control Bantin's actions during the bonding fight. He knew that he had no fangs. He only charged at her to create a distraction that both Valiant and Sparkle had used. As for Vermelo's accusation, he was concerned about a person that would actually love Bantin. Was that person Vermelo?!

"Bantin," Kayla thought directly to him. *"Do you and Vermelo have a history I don't know about?"*

"I am sworn to secrecy," Bantin answered.

Really? Wow. That was the sort of answer that a dragon gave when they couldn't betray a bond. There was only one way for Bantin to bond, since he had no fangs. In the past, ice dragon fangs and venom were extracted right after they were born and kept locked up in the castle. Kayla didn't know where the venom was located, but it was probably beneath the castle in the tunnels that Merlock guarded.

When Bantin had been released from Herb Felding's torture, he had spent hours on end shooting ice at the castle. That would have bothered Vermelo. It was illegal for anyone to touch the buried venom from a living dragon, but it looked like Vermelo had fallen to sin. All Vermelo had to do to "tame" the monster ice dragon was cut his own arm and dab on some of that ice dragon venom that had been taken from Bantin when he was born. Their thoughts would be shared. The creature calmed. Bantin and Vermelo had been bonded years ago.

They had an illegal Captain of the Guard! Now that Kayla was inside of Bantin's thoughts, she was going to learn of this eventually. Vermelo was glaring at her, worried that she was going to destroy his secret, or perhaps he was simply angry that Kayla couldn't control her own head.

"It's not my fault," Kayla answered. "I didn't try to. Besides, you have nothing to worry about. It looks like he's greatly loved already. Good for him."

"You asked him to go to Vankerdale, Kayla. He went against—"

Vermelo ground his teeth together, but at least he didn't shove his fingers deeper into her arm. She could tell what he wasn't saying anyway. Bantin had left Aralot to enter Vankerdale after Vermelo had told him not to go. The ice dragon had disregarded his rider, who had probably never ridden him, in order to heed the call of the keeper bond. That was the part about keeper bonds that made riders turn against the keeper in the first place. There had been several keepers killed off by the riders in their own group after those riders got tired of their dragons being forced away from them. Vermelo had lost his control, and he was struggling with feelings of his dragon being overrun.

"How was I ever supposed to know?!" Kayla hissed back at him, trying to keep her voice low but failing to keep her own expressions off her face. She did not want Vermelo as her enemy. He knew too well how to kill her. "I'm sorry. I wanted out of Vankerdale. I did what I had to. Without Bantin, everything would have failed. He provided the magic that Valiant needed to get everyone to Vankerdale's castle. I had no idea he had other orders. I will do my best to always leave him an option to refuse me. I promise."

"I am going to hold you to that," Vermelo said, still looking upset with her.

Gee! She had rider wars going on inside her keeper bond! She expected it from Tristan, but she had not seen this coming from Vermelo at all. That had to be why Bantin was still sitting around with Valiant. He was confused, trying to decide whose voice he should listen to.

"*Don't mind me,*" Kayla thought to Bantin. "*I had no idea about you and Vermelo. I appreciate your assistance, but next time if you are needed more here you should stay.*"

"*You needed me more,*" Bantin answered. "*Vermelo is in a bad mood mostly because he missed his date with his wife during all that commotion. He'd already paid for everything and nothing is refundable.*"

"*Come on. He's upset that I told you what to do.*"

"*That's his excuse for his mood. He's jealous that you get what you want and he doesn't.*"

Vermelo had chosen to be the Captain of the Guard. He chose to leave his old life behind to live in the castle. Kayla had never chosen her life path at all. The only choice she got to make was how to respond to what got thrown at her. She didn't make the best choice this time.

"But I never get what I want!" Kayla wailed just a little bit too loud. Several people looked at her, including her parents. She didn't need to see them to know. If she got what she really wanted then she wouldn't be in this room still. She wouldn't be married. She wouldn't have any dragons in her head except for Valiant. She wouldn't ever fight invisible curses that gave her nightmares.

"She can go, Vermelo," Jack's voice cut across the room. "She doesn't need to stay. She's got to be exhausted."

Yes, ever so tired of the drama. Vermelo let go of her arm and he changed his angry look for one of worry again. She didn't like that look on him either. The last time he gave her that look, he had told her not to join Charles's Ware. That look on him was just as restricting. Their views were not lining up, and as long as they stayed different, Kayla was going to be dealing with this rider versus keeper battle. She didn't need another mental fight. She pushed from the ballroom only to find that she hadn't been allowed to leave alone.

"Kayla," Queen Aria, perfectly collected in her satin blue ruffled dress, wasn't about to let Kayla leave without words of her own. Kayla groaned and continued to be uncivilized despite her previous training.

"I won't go in there and dance with anyone. My arm was just fanged. It hurts!"

She could still feel it throbbing and it made a grand excuse to keep away from Tristan. Aria probably wasn't fooled after Kayla had glanced at her son annoyed before she tried to make her escape. Kayla spun around to face off with Aria, unable to keep her ire away. Aria let her expression shift for an instant herself. Her brown eyes turned troubled, a line of sweat formed on the edge of her hairline, and the intake of her breath had Kayla standing stock still yet again. Aria didn't lose her cool over anything. What was this about?

"Did Tyler say anything negative about Aralot?" Aria asked.

Kayla couldn't help but narrow her eyes at the woman. She had answered all these questions already, and Kayla wasn't about to change her answers.

"No. He likes Aralot. In fact, he tried to move here before. He has no intention of picking fights with us."

"He has none right now, but ideals can change. People change. That was Tyler's viewpoint before he bonded a war-ridden dragon. Coal is a monster. How do you see that affecting King Tyler?"

"I thought Coal was very nice when I met him," Valiant provided. *"He did not strike me as war-ridden. I don't think he is going to change Tyler. Isn't it common knowledge that dragons only bond people whose personalities they can match. Tyler wouldn't attack towns for no good reason. I don't think Coal did either."*

Meaning that all those attacks that terrified everyone had a purpose. One perhaps where Coal was trying to find his missing scale. The quest was important to him. So important that he risked his wellbeing, charging in among a full ware of dragons just to talk to her about it before he could reach Tyler.

Aria had an interesting question. By singling Kayla out, Kayla expected that Aria wanted to ask her this to watch her expressions when no one else could influence them. Kayla decided to pick even deeper into Aria's comment. Aria was using the unknown future as a way to get information about Coal who she had called a monster. While lots of people viewed the ultra-dragon king as a devil, most people had looked relieved to get rid of him. Only Aria was coming back around with extra questions regarding the dragon.

"Do you think that Aria is personally invested in hiding that dragon scale?" Kayla asked Valiant. The way her day was going, why not toss in Aria admitting that she had taken a dragon scale from the ultra-dragon

king. Coal had been asking about the scale so Tyler would be aware of the fact. He hadn't asked her about a scale, but had questioned her about possession spells right after he would have heard the dragon's first thoughts.

Kayla was such an idiot! Tyler wasn't being evil. He was trying to save his dragon! This totally fit. Aria's soul was stained black because she was working life magic controlling a dragon's life. She was possessing Coal, making him attack the kingdom to get all the dragon wares mad at the dragon that she didn't want around. It was a clever trick, and it had worked for a long time. So wrong. That spell was going to go.

"You know about those attacks, sometimes all a dragon needs is one friend to understand him in order to help him stop being grumpy and angry. Whatever had Coal upset before is probably resolved now. Tyler is very levelheaded. He won't attack things because his dragon did."

"You're absolutely certain," Aria pressed.

Kayla nodded, assuring Aria that she had nothing to personally worry about, as bad as that felt. Tyler and Coal were not going to be coming into Aralot to kill off Queen Aria for her spell against them, because they were never going to know who had done it. Kayla was going to find that scale and destroy it. Then she would write to Tyler to tell him that it was gone.

"Am I being stupid again?" Kayla asked Valiant.

This was a crime! Everyone around her had committed crimes, and her reaction to solve them was to let them go. She wasn't saying anything about Vermelo and Bantin. She wasn't saying anything about Aria and Coal. She hadn't said anything about Tristan and all those unborn keepers.

"Why am I the keeper of bad news?!" Kayla wailed as she spun around on Aria. That's all she ever got was the worst of everyone's character. She got all the evil terror from Gladius in her nightmares. All the heartbreak. It was a conspiracy! She shouldn't be old enough to handle everyone's crimes.

"Kayla," Aria hesitated behind her.

"You will be fine," Kayla shot back at her without looking. It wasn't fair that she felt compelled to shelter people for their crimes like this.

"Not even if you call it forgiveness?" Valiant asked. *"You see the worst of people, but you also see their potential. Vermelo and Aria both came to you for help tonight. You're the only one who can help them."*

"Thank you," Aria said, as Kayla stomped past a few guards who had been watching. They were always watching. They probably had no idea what the real issue was at play here. Even if they told Vermelo the wording of this conversation he wouldn't know. The most he could do was guess that either Aria or a dragon in Kayla's head had told her bad news.

"I hope you'll understand..." Aria trailed off.

Kayla turned the corner, not wanting to understand why anyone would possess a dragon. Once out of sight from Aria, she cast a spell that would help her start hunting for that possession spell. It was wicked hard to locate an object used for possession, so it was one of those spells that Kayla could pull off without even trying. Naturally. Her father had drilled this spell into her the instant he thought she could handle it. He'd possessed her over and over until she could stop him from making her walk outside and sit in the same tree. Kayla had hunted for and destroyed possessed objects way too many times.

The spell she used created a compass on the palm of her hand that spun in the direction she needed to go to find that lost scale. Kayla took one step in the right direction only to be stopped yet again.

"Mind if I..."

Tristan! Yes, she minded. She couldn't handle any more crimes right now that she needed to cover up. She wasn't looking at him so when his blue glow came at her, she dropped her hand, retracted her finding spell, and jumped into a position to defend herself against a magical attack casting up a shield. His spell didn't land on her at all. It snuggled through her sweater while Tristan laughed at her.

"I was fixing your favorite sweater!" He pointed to what his spell had done, and she could only glare at him for it. When had he paid enough attention to know that the hole bothered her? She wasn't going to fix it herself, so to have him waste his magic on the hole made her oddly grateful and annoyed at the same time.

"You are so predictable. We're having a sporadic party for the safe return of a girl who has vanished from her own party. You lasted longer than I expected you to actually."

"I don't like parties," Kayla stated.

"Don't I know it." Tristan laughed at her. "But you are pretty good at remembering our conversation where I agreed to not cast harmful spells at keepers, and you agreed to let me keep the castle you always try to run away from."

"We did not have that conversation," Kayla replied. She let her protection spell drop.

"Now we have." He grinned at her and gave her a shrug. So he wasn't being unnerving at all. He was the only one that was being his usual annoying self. Fixing her sweater didn't mean that she was going to start liking him.

"I took care of that spell that you'd asked me to help you with. That one and a few others that you hadn't asked me about. Consider your wishes granted for once, because you do in fact get what you want."

Oh no. He was using her words for Vermelo against her. That was so like him that Kayla had to laugh.

"And if I told you that I want you to go away?"

"Not a chance. Not until you agree to trade wants. You wanted those spells gone. They're gone. I want this castle."

"You're asking me for something that I can't give. I don't own this place. Technically no one does. There isn't a real king of Aralot. There's not a real queen. No one has rights to this building. If you're going to be a squatter in this dreadful castle your whole life be my guest."

"That wasn't so hard was it?" Tristan smiled at her like she had given him exactly what he had asked for, when she'd done no such thing. They were all squatters and she'd rather not stay in this cursed building. Too many evil things hid in its walls.

"Now will you leave me alone?" Kayla asked. She frowned when Tristan shook his head and took a step closer.

"I need you to understand."

She was starting to not like that word. She didn't want to understand anything more. All she wanted to do was destroy Coal's missing possessed scale! Then run off to hug Valiant.

"I was seven and scared that I'd lose my dad. I'd only just met him. As you said, Klavian isn't the real king, and when people want fake kings out of the way they kill them. I was only trying to save my dad from upcoming threats not hurt anyone. That's what the spell was about. Can we start over, please?"

"Sure," Kayla gave him a slow smile. "Tomorrow. Starting over requires that I get to take a break from you."

"Sassy when you're tired, aren't you?" Tristan replied. He opened his mouth to say something else but perhaps Riven advised him not to because he closed off his words, gave her a nod of his head, and miraculously headed back to the party without her.

"You talked about forgiveness, Valiant," Kayla thought as she went back to what she was doing, flashing the locating spell, *"but forgiving doesn't overlook crimes. Am I doing the right thing?"*

"Forgiving is about allowing other people to change for the better. Give them that chance, Kayla. I think that everyone is needing your forgiveness today. Sparkle needed it. Tristan needed it. Aria even thanked you for it. Vermelo needs it. We'll keep an eye on them. Don't you worry."

Kayla sighed. That still didn't answer if she was doing the right thing here. It felt constraining to keep silent, especially about the news Tristan had just given her. Rosa and her mom could have kids finally! They'd be thrilled that their current pregnancies wouldn't miscarry. Kayla could get a sibling. That was going to be super strange. She wouldn't even know the kid very well because she had moved out of the house. What if her parents loved the new baby more than her?

"One step at a time. Your parents won't stop loving you. Go find that scale so that you can come see me. I'm still waiting."

Right. Kayla glanced backward at the ballroom, wanting to run back in there just to hug Aunt Rosa and her mom and tell them that another of their heartaches had vanished this week, all because Kayla had managed to break through Tristan's defenses. She was still going to be dealing with Tristan living in the castle, but that wasn't really a game changer. There were many rooms in the castle where she could hide away from him.

Pg. 355

Kayla looked down at her hand again and took off through the castle. She didn't expect Aria to have hidden the scale anywhere but in here. The queen would hide it in a location that dragons couldn't reach. Coal couldn't get the scale away from her, and most people couldn't infiltrate the castle as Kayla was allowed to do. The guards let her go everywhere. She wandered through the servant tunnels, snatching food for the party off the trays on her way past. She wandered herself into King Klavian and Queen Aria's room since the rooms were in the general direction she was going. Nothing there. She peeked into Tristan's room just because, so she could note how much cleaner he kept things than his dad who always had his desk cluttered with books he was reading.

Kayla wandered through the throne room, even if she generally avoided the golden chair, the long red rug leading up to it, and the pillars adorned with fake dragon eggs along the top. No one made any attempt to stop her when she exited the throne room and pulled open the door to the second most dazzling room of this entire castle. Tia was mostly interested in the kitchen and the music room. For Kayla, it was the ballroom and the room of mirrors where she currently was.

The spell on her hand pulsed, meaning that she was getting closer. The missing scale was somewhere around here. Aria would have an easy time entering this room to check on her outfit from all angles. She was always so pristine that it wouldn't be considered odd if she took a while fixing her hair or changing her necklace in a room with mirrors lining the walls. Kayla didn't usually look at herself much when she was in here. She was always looking at the angles of mirrors, noting how some of them cast the viewer into a state of infinity. She skipped over to the correct spot and looked at herself getting smaller and smaller. Then she put on gloves to not smudge the mirrors and started pushing on them. She had never pushed on them before because the room generally inspired awe, but searching for hidden secrets that were not listed on the castle map was something Aria would totally do.

Pg. 356

Even more remarkable, pushing worked. One of the mirrors clicked and started to swing outward, revealing a set of dark stone stairs leading down. Blocking the stairs was a red glowing spell. Death. Aria didn't want others down here. The spell would have been blamed on the past King Gladius if anyone else happened to stumble across it, but Kayla knew the truth of it. She took the spell down and slowly walked down the steps with her heartbeat pounding. She expected to find a single scale shoved in a corner so she was unprepared for what really met her eyes.

There was a heavy wooden table down here, the kind that Gladius used to love with thick legs and rounded ball feet. On top of the table was a list sitting next to the black scale. Beneath the table was a large crate of likewise torn off dragon scales. Kayla inhaled slowly as her skin crawled and her mind screamed. How many dragons had Aria possessed?! She ran at the table and grabbed at the list, skimmed it, and then shoved on her sweater hood so she could scream.

"No! Aria no!"

Was it written somewhere that dragons who had been inside infected keeper minds all went insane too? If it was, Kayla was going to find that information and destroy it so thoroughly that no one would ever read it again. It was wrong. Aria had not been possessing multiple dragons. She had been using Coal for his indestructible hide to kill off the other dragons that had been inside Herb Felding's keeper bond.

Herb was Kayla's grandfather and he had been poisoned worse than Gladius. He'd turned against his kingdom, his dragons, and his own family. Before he died, he had infiltrated dragons in all the wares getting inside their heads. He terrified them because he'd used a few of those dragons to eat their own riders when he took over their form through sightsharing. Tia thought that Kayla was ugly for sightsharing with Sparkle to stop a fight, it was nothing to what Herb had used sightsharing for.

Kayla took in a deep breath and pulled the list back up to her face to see what dragons had been spared Aria's purge. She'd managed to kill off all the wild dragons that had been with Herb. They were all crossed off, although they had no names other than dragon one all the way to forty. She had cleansed through the dragon's that Herb had gotten into at Nile's Ware.

All the dragons that had been at Vincent's Ware were now gone. Charles's infected dragons had been killed off. The only other ones that had not been run down were the dragons at Anvil's Ware. It would be a shame if Aria had managed to reach them, because Anvil's Ware had a lot of dragons that Herb had gotten into, and those dragons were some of Anvil's strongest. Not to mention that they belonged to Anvil's section leaders and most trusted warriors.

Didn't Aria realize that dragons in an infected keeper bond didn't turn crazy when the keeper did? The only dragon that was affected was Herb's bonded dragon and that animal was no longer living according to this list. Aria could have left all the other ones alone. Aralot had a wonderful example of two dragons that had been inside the bond of an infected keeper who had never turned insane. Tempest, Uncle Conner's dragon, had been with Gladius as a young baby. It was the same thing with Indigo, who was now bonded to the ware leader Rogan after he had lost his first dragon to Herb's insanity. Tempest and Indigo had managed to escape the purge against Gladius's dragons. It would have been nice if more of Herb's dragons had escaped this same thing.

Kayla reached for Aria's pencil that she had left on the table and wrote on the back of her page that only the bonded dragon was affected by the keeper poison. There was no reason to harm any of the rest. Kayla didn't think that Aria would believe her. She would probably argue that all the wild dragons that had lost a mental connection had been injured beyond repair. Kayla had never asked Indigo about the struggles she faced when she was lost from a collective hive and had to hide or else die. She'd done well for herself, building up a herd of her own that now protected Kayla's house as well as Rogan's Ware.

"*This is sad,*" Valiant whispered into Kayla's head. "*Ready to come see me yet?*"

"*You're really missing me, aren't you?*" Kayla replied.

She was almost done with this. First, she had to destroy Coal's scale. She cast a spell against it and frowned. Coal sure had some tough scales. It wasn't breaking. She tried a different spell and then shoved the scale into her pocket for Valiant to deal with it. He could cast stronger spells than she could, and his spells were bonding. He still hadn't told her how exactly he got his spells to do that.

"*I would love to help a fellow dragon,*" Valiant told her, as she replaced the death spell behind her to keep other people out of this hidden room and shut the mirror to hide the stairs. She didn't want to understand Aria on this, particularly since it proved that the queen wasn't a novice where dragons were concerned. She could fly them. She could be them. She could make them attack. She had probably asked Tristan a lot of questions while he was learning how to be a dragon rider.

Before Kayla returned to see Valiant, she snuck her way back into Tristan's magic room so she could recreate the spell that protected her from eating keeper poison. The thought of Queen Aria one day hunting down and killing off all the dragons she cared about was too much.

At least this time around Tristan didn't charge into his magic room after her, even if she had to take down his spells to get in. He probably guessed what she was doing. She'd just gotten back from Vankerdale where all her curses and protections had been stripped away. She needed a few of those back right away.

"*Now I'm ready to come see you,*" Kayla told Valiant. He hummed into her head, causing her to smile as she ran from the castle. She was finally out of there! She had spent most of her life only entering dragon wares to reach select people inside, not liking the location at all, but after all the death she had just seen firsthand, she was ready to run to the dragon field and partake in the joy of the rest of the living.

Kayla ran and found herself creeping up slowly when she spotted Valiant. She could make out a voice that was with him, one that was calm, incredibly patient, smart, and funny. The voice was one that she'd fantasized talking to over and over again, only she never had until recently.

"So he thought he was clear of the rest of us and got away with stealing that whole slab of cheese." Caleb was nearly laughing. Valiant hummed at her which caused Caleb to shift and misinterpret the sound. Kayla couldn't see him since she was at Valiant's back, but she assumed that Caleb was sitting down in front of her dragon having a man-to-man talk. It was rather amusing.

"You like cheese? You can't like cheese."

"Don't give me away!" Kayla frantically thought to Valiant. She'd been off taking down evil curses and he had been basking in the easy friendship of Caleb. It so wasn't fair! She wanted a moment to hear him. She heard Caleb every day telling her how to be a better rider, but it wasn't the same as hearing him like this. Valiant snorted.

"I didn't think you'd like cheese. Okay," Caleb continued. "He takes this big ol' bite, stuffs his mouth full, and then hears this snapping sound. Bam! Out of the trees steps this three-year-old wild bronze dragon and she's snarling. Grant doesn't miss a beat. He spits out the cheese and starts mouthing off at the thing."

"Who's Grant?"

"One of Caleb's brothers," Valiant answered. *"Just so you know Grant*

is the youngest. Then there is Mikka, Caleb, and Brandon."

"'You're not getting my cheese either. I stole this fair and square!' Grant goes bragging. As you can imagine Brandon and I had him all figured out and we were sneaking up to nab him and turn him in. Either that or eat all the cheese in front of his face." Caleb laughed. "Except that dragon was there. We both paused and looked at each other. Then we both looked down at our empty waists, devoid of tools as we were wet behind the ears. When our eyes met again there was devotion there. I didn't care what Grant did to steal that cheese. No dragon was taking down my loud brother even if Brandon and I didn't have a dragon ourselves or any real training.

"I start sneaking around to the left and Brandon takes the right. The wild thing snarls again and we both start hissing back the worst dragon sounds we can think of, as if we have any idea what we're really saying. We think we're super clever like we'll confuse the wild dragon and she'll think there's a group of trained warriors coming at her." Caleb laughed again. "I didn't contemplate until later that she could smell us and would know that it was three kids and a block of cheese."

Kayla grinned and ventured sneaking in closer until she was right up against Valiant's back. He hummed at her again and started to lift his head to look at her but then lowered it, remembering that she wanted to hear the story.

"Anyway, what really saved us was the ghost caller. A real dragon sound called out from the near distance. Pardon the oxymoron. The bronze dragon backed away, chirping out a reply to the ghost caller. We chased that dragon, feeling like we were superheroes, and we never saw any other dragon in those trees. I swear. It was the ghost caller. We weren't the only ones to have stories of the ghost caller either. Some people claim that the ghost is magical and likes kids. He saves them from wild dragons."

Kayla climbed up over the top of Valiant and slipped down to his other side, causing the dragon to hum at her all over again. She kept a hand on his side while Caleb sat up. He wasn't facing her dragon at all but had his hands behind his head as he lay on the ground and stared up at the stars while he spoke. Kayla didn't want to ruin his fun, but she was going to.

"I think it was a Colt," she told Caleb. He shook his head at her, but she had her reasons. "I know they pretend to be scared of dragons and such, but my Uncle Conner was a Colt and he got fanged in the woods. My dad was a Colt and was fanged in the woods too. There are more Colts than you know of that have hidden secret dragons. Some of them really like kids. What really happened was that Grant got too close to finding the dragon with her secret rider, so the dragon charged out to defend her Colt, and the Colt snuck off to call away the dragon. Sorry. I'm no fun, huh?" Kayla admitted at Caleb's stunned face.

"Fun? Kayla, you're an absolute genius! How long have you known this?" Caleb asked her with wonder. Then he laughed at his own question. "Your whole life, I guess. Ever since you heard the story of how your dad was bonded. I never connected the lines like that. I'm feeling a little foolish over here. Kids at Anvil's Ware have all sorts of tales about the ghost caller."

Kayla shrugged because she hadn't heard them. It wasn't fun things like this that people in Anvil's Ware talked to her about. A lot of them ignored her, and those who didn't called her mean names. Those who were nice to her greeted her with awkward silences, because not only did she cry around all the dragons, she'd had a curse to not hear anyone talk about the king, queen, or princess. Conversations buzzed through her ears making her rather hard to talk to.

"It's not you that was missing out. I'd love to have a tale about a ghost caller calling a dragon away from me. That would have been the highlight of my year." It would have made being at Anvil's Ware that much easier back when she was cursed.

"And the highlight of *this* year was all messed up," Caleb declared. He rose to his feet and pointed to Valiant. "We're going to do this again the right way. Valiant, the ever-amazing spellbinding dragon, takes friendship and compassion to a whole new level. He just won the victory against an ice dragon after healing his own foe in the face of losing everything he loves most. He extends the kind hand... uh claw... toward the offender, allowing the ice dragon her moment of defeated glory as she gets to play with the rider first. Then the ice dragon leaves and Kayla is all freed up. Wahoo!" Caleb cheered.

Valiant tucked his head down between his arms looking embarrassed. Kayla found herself smiling. This was a fantastic way to end a day, with Caleb cheering for her about the victories he could see. Her parents hadn't and then it was all back to business and curses again. Caleb knew to have fun in the face of adversity.

"Bonded dragon your rider awaits!" Caleb flashed his arms around. "Gaze into each other's eyes. Tell each other jokes. Be as impressive as you like because you've earned this moment."

"He can talk a really looong time," Valiant complained, still with his head tucked down. Kayla laughed at him. She would have loved to trade places. Valiant could have the chore of watching her parents dance, engaging with Tristan, discovering possessed scales and horrible deeds, and she would keep Caleb all night long.

Kayla had to turn her back to Caleb on the thought. She was married. She hadn't told her parents and they hadn't asked. It was too early for Tyler to spread the news, so she was ignoring it as best she could. Right now, she couldn't ignore it. If she moved to Vankerdale, she was never going to see Caleb again. She would never hear his voice pulling her up from the ground. She'd never see his smile. Caleb was her own imaginary friend that she'd had lots of conversations with over the years. He'd ask her questions, and she'd answer him all in her head. Now that she'd looked at him, she was going to lose him. She'd already lost Uncle Anvil. She couldn't imagine losing Caleb too. Her eyes were tearing up when he was trying to give her a very special moment to remember. She was spoiling it and he noticed.

"Crying is allowed. You had some harsh trapped emotions in there. The best thing to do is get those out. Should I go?"

"No!" Kayla spun back around to find him thumbing over his shoulder. He had some wicked fast fists, but he was ever so nice. "I don't want you to leave," Kayla told him.

He shoved both his hands into his pockets, no longer looking excited but a little downcast. Kayla felt horrible for destroying his good mood. He had such captivating moods. He also seemed to be reading her mind.

"I'm not leaving you. No matter what you're made to do, or where you have to go, or what man steals you away from me. I'll always be right here every time you need me." He nervously looked behind him, probably in the direction of his sleeping dragon, and then looked back. "I shouldn't have stated it like that. I will always be your friend, Kayla."

"Translucent sometimes, isn't he?" Valiant asked.

Sort of, but it was what she most wanted to hear. He would still be here for her even if she had to marry King Tyler or Prince Tristan. Caleb wouldn't back away if she made herself look like an idiot. Kayla shut her eyes, wishing she could block the cruel world out so that she could have a chance to take a risk on Caleb. For some reason what Ritz had told her pushed to the front of her mind.

"This feeling of not being loved is designed to push you out into the

world in search of something that could love you, but let me tell you something. You are not to go searching. You have all the love you already need. You just need to open your eyes and see it. Stop hiding. You can change your fate."

Stop hiding. It was all right in front of her. It was behind her too. She had Valiant in the back and Caleb in the front, and both of them had been there for her all along if she would only accept it. She had changed her fate where Valiant was concerned. He was her bonded dragon for real and Caleb was her friend forever. She was going to open her eyes and enjoy their company while she had it. Then she was going to push against fate to get the life she really wanted. One that would make her happy with good friends who didn't shove her about.

"I've always been your friend too," Kayla told Caleb opening her eyes back up. "Only I didn't tell you, and honestly I didn't know what you looked like, but your voice means a lot."

"I drew myself in some of those pictures!" Caleb protested.

So he did. She grinned at him for all the times he had taken the initiative to be her friend and she had let him down. She wasn't going to let him down anymore. She'd give him a reason to be proud.

"And the rider turns to her bonded dragon and declares... Woah," Kayla cut off.

Valiant had told her once that when he was happy with her his wings could shimmer. He was feeling happy with her. He hummed at her and Kayla had to smile, wide, as the dragon emotions in the bond filled her entire heart with his gladness. Valiant's wingtips were lightly glowing silver wherever the wave pattern touched them. He blushed and hummed again, and then trilled out his joy by raising his head into the air.

"We did it, didn't we?" Kayla asked him, reaching out to touch the mesmerizing display.

Valiant was gorgeous. She'd never known a dragon more spectacular. Spellbinding dragons were the greatest. He hooted again and stood up to spread out his wings. Then he rolled over, tucking them down to hide them from view. Kayla heard Caleb ever so slowly shift his bag around to the front and pull out his sketchbook. The result had both Kayla and Valiant blushing to be the object of someone else's fascination so much. But all that went away when Valiant met her eyes again and it was his big brown eyes against her clear blue ones. It felt like the very first time she had been whole in her entire life. That was a feeling that could push away any sadness. She was finally fully connected to her gorgeous dragon, and she had the one friend she had always wanted. No matter what else came, she had her cozy herd.

Ring

Kayla

Snap. The sound broke against Kayla's ears alerting her to the fact that something was horribly wrong. Crunch. That sound was even worse. There was a heavy, dark creeping something really close to her, and she had one guess as to what it could be. A dragon. She had joined The King's Dragon Ware, but last she knew, she was in her bed safely tucked away in her bunkroom with spells around her to keep intruders away and her screams contained. Was this a dream? Her nightmares were getting worse lately, if such a thing was possible.

There was a time that she could easily wake herself up from them. The closer she got to turning sixteen, the harder it got to wake herself up. Now that she had passed her birthday, she'd failed to wake herself up at all. This nightmare spell was the one spell that lingered that even her magical dragon couldn't destroy. It was her last unwanted curse. There was no such thing as rest when this spell was there. There was no peace; nothing but the fear of past dragon keepers that invaded her thoughts, teaching her how to kill dragons, how to fight, how to be brutal.

Thump. Okay, that was it! She was going to wake herself up! That was a real sound. There was something inside her bunkroom coming to get her. The only people who were allowed to use magic inside of Aralot were the royal family and the steward's royal family; although, ware leaders had been given protective charms too, and a few of them actively used magic now that it had been handed to them. With the loudness of this sound, whatever was breaking things beside her had already taken down her magical protective covering. She had to wake up!

Grind. Crunch. Oh, dear. That was the sound of bones. Someone was dying inside her bunkroom! She had to get up so she could fight the person or demon off. Maybe this was the result of Prince Tristan again. Despite his earlier concessions to take down his curses, they were still fighting each other, and they both knew it.

The smell of blood hit her senses next. Kayla tried to scream. Normally she tried not to do that because she didn't want to wake up any of the other girls in her bunkroom with her nightmares. That was why she had so many spells around her when she slept to contain her sounds. The spells had failed! She had never shared a room before because she was an only child and up until now had lived with her parents at the edge of the Northern Farms. Nothing came out of her mouth, although she could feel the struggle holding down her consciousness.

Kayla returned to her old standbys that used to work when she fought herself in her sleep. She bit her tongue, tried kicking, tried reaching for the knife slid into the top of her left boot so she could cut her arm. Anything to jolt through the spells that trapped her so she could return to herself.

It wasn't working, so Kayla moved toward magic. Her nightmares gave her ample fuel for scary spells. She had just had another such dream, one that taught her a bunch of evil spells that her grandfather Herb Felding had used against her dad when they were trying to kill each other. Kayla shoved a river over her entire head. She could feel the rush of the water, feel the fear pulse through her body because she had never learned how to swim. Not being able to enter water that was deeper than her ankle had been one of her curses. She was going to die, and she was going to kill herself if she couldn't get herself to wake up!

The water vanished as if someone else was using magic around her, stopping her from waking up. Kayla heard a dragon growl. The deep throaty tone of it was one she knew well, but it also belonged in her nightmares, so she wasn't sure if she was making up the sound of the dragon or not. This was Coal. He was a special ultra-dragon king that had a hide so thick it was nearly impossible to break through to kill him. He was a jet-black night dragon with moon-shaped claws, gleaming green eyes, and fire that could get so hot it could break through other dragon scales.

Coal wasn't supposed to be scary anymore. He had only been beastly killing off people and dragons because Queen Aria was controlling him in a possession spell. Kayla had just destroyed that spell, so Coal was free to be himself now. He had bonded King Tyler of Vankerdale when Tyler gained his keeper abilities. Unlike Kayla, Tyler liked being a keeper. He enjoyed being able to hold multiple dragon's thoughts inside his head because he loved all dragons.

Being a keeper had drawbacks. Dragons gave keepers special dragon names, and when they called those, keepers felt the magic of their blood constrain against them to answer the call. It was hard to fight against the pressure to help a dragon. Keepers were supposed to be a blessing for the land. They were knowledgeable people that would care for dragons when they were wounded, and play with dragons when they got bored. In that regard, it was keepers that had first created dragon wares. It was keepers leading man and dragon to be best friends instead of worst enemies. It was keepers that were first bonded to dragons, connecting human souls to dragon ones, safeguarding hearts and sharing lives.

The dragon growl came again, along with the question asking her what she was doing. It was still Coal's voice so Kayla was really confused as she tried out a different spell on herself. She started to flatten out her lungs, feeling her body scream with the need for air.

"Fine!" Valiant screamed at her. *"Take over!"*

"Valiant! What's happening?!"

Valiant was her first bonded dragon, her gatekeeper dragon that blocked out all other dragon thoughts from her head so she wouldn't go crazy with the magic her blood gave her. Kayla had spent her entire life having him in her head, but it wasn't until very recently that he had talked to her. He had been trapped in Vankerdale, bait to bring her over to the neighboring kingdom so that Vankerdale could steal Aralot's magic. Tyler and Kayla had saved him from all of that. Now he was safely in the kingdom of Aralot where Kayla lived.

"Coal was looking for you so I brought you over. It's the first day of the week. You're supposed to be sleeping tonight."

Kayla's eyes finally opened, and she instinctively reached for weapons dropping something onto the ground in the process that she had been holding. She was not where she had put herself last. She had gone to bed in her bunkroom, but it wasn't new to her to learn that Valiant woke her up and walked her around in her sleep.

Only bonded dragons could sightshare with their riders. Swapping the essence of their consciousness so that Kayla was the dragon and Valiant the human was usually only done while the dragon and rider team were both awake. Valiant was a spellbinding dragon, a rare breed of dragon that could shoot out magic. He had the unique ability to sightshare whenever he wanted. That usually meant he took over her body and had her draw pictures of dragons in her sleep.

Before Kayla knew that she had a bonded dragon, she thought that she was mentally insane for all the pictures she drew in the middle of the night. She had spent many years double checking to make sure that she wasn't possessed. She had given up on tying herself into her bed to prevent the drawing because she always broke out. Before Valiant told her that it was him drawing through her, she had checked for those pictures every morning and destroyed them. They had scared her. The images were a curse threatening her sanity. At least now Valiant was talking to her so she could explain why she moved in her sleep.

She was out in the woods that rested beside the King's dragon training ware with Coal who was standing in front of her chomping through two dead deer. That was the chomping sound and the smell of blood. Kayla let out a sigh of relief that it wasn't one of her bunkmates dying.

"Is that what woke you up?" Valiant asked her. "I never can quite tell what makes you push against me."

"I heard the sound of bones snapping," Kayla replied. "That would wake up anyone."

"Except that you were being me sleeping in my dragon form out on the field not in the woods. You shouldn't have heard a thing," Valiant complained. "You should pick up that box you dropped. It's for you."

"What was the water for?" Coal's deep voice asked her in dragon speech. Since Kayla had grown up swapping her human and dragon form so much, and hearing dragons talk to her all day long and all night long, she could understand any word in the dragon language. Most people couldn't. They had to resort to the few words they did know, or resort to another dragon translating things for them.

Kayla looked around, noticing how she was still soaking wet. She shook her head and checked on the state of her magical keychain hooked closely on her weapon belt. She had been the one drowning herself and Valiant the one stopping her. It was nothing but herself that had been using magic tonight. Nothing but herself that broke out of the spells in her bunkroom to be wandering around in the woods in the middle of the night. If she didn't love Valiant so much, she'd remind him that having her body move on her like this was utterly terrifying.

"You were asleep!" Valiant complained. "And you can't expect me to *stop being you. You're the other half of me. I can't stop being myself."*

Apparently.

"I'm sorry, Coal," Kayla spoke to the hulking black dragon as she put her weapons back in the weapon belt so she wasn't a threat to him. "The water was me fighting a scary thought. It got a little out of hand. You brought me a box?"

She looked down at the ground to find the object she had dropped that Valiant had her holding before. It was a small wooden box with an intarsia of a wolf face on the lid. Kayla picked it up, opened the box, and let it drop to the ground yet again.

"Shall I tell Tyler of your reaction?" Coal asked her with a short growl.

"No," Kayla replied, taking a step back and a deep breath in. The breath was filled with the smell of dead deer so she frowned. It would have been better if it was Valiant out here tonight getting this from Coal. He wouldn't have made her drop the wedding ring in the dirt. He wouldn't be making faces against the smell of Coal's dinner.

"I simply wasn't expecting..." Kayla trailed off.

"Tyler thinks that you're not coming back unless he reminds you that you agreed to marry him. You ran off on us really fast."

"I didn't forget," Kayla answered. She picked up the box again and pulled out the ring to examine it. It was beautiful for sure. All the gems were inset so she wouldn't have to worry about knocking them out when she engaged in dragon training activities. There was a large diamond in the center and two pink sapphires on each end.

"Why didn't Tyler bring this to me?" Kayla asked. Then she might have stayed asleep because she wouldn't have found herself standing alone in front of Coal who used to be one of her worst enemies.

Asleep or not, her bodily instincts worked just fine, trained and honed by muscle memory and intuition. Coal had tried to bond her before, and if he had gotten away with that, she would have had so many more complications with her gatekeeper dragon Valiant and her mother's ice dragon Sparkle who claimed Kayla as one of her riders too. There was no way she could stay asleep when she was standing before this particular dragon. That's what had pushed her awake tonight.

"Maybe Tyler did come," Tyler's voice said from behind her.

Kayla's shoulders hiked uncomfortably up as she spun around. With glasses, short dark-brown hair, and a beard that framed only his chin and beneath his nose, Tyler was a rather cute person. Kayla gave him a smile so he wouldn't see the real panic that pushed through her nerves.

"It's beautiful! Thank you. I'm sorry about the dropping it part and the water part." Tyler was already privy to her troubling dragon issues, so she had no problem in explaining the one that she was dealing with tonight. "Valiant was being me. I dropped the box because it's a bit scary waking up to find myself out in the middle of the woods without knowing what I'm doing. I just became myself. I was asleep before that."

"You don't need to apologize. You have our sympathy. Coal for one understands a little too well what it is like to wake up without remembering what he had been doing. You told us that you destroyed Coal's possessed scale." Tyler told her this more as a question than a statement. Kayla had no idea that her mouth had told them that. She nodded. Coal had been possessed for quite some time and forced to tear apart dragon wares and towns around Aralot.

Technically Valiant had destroyed the stolen scale, because Kayla couldn't find a way to destroy something so indestructible. Valiant had binding magic so his worked better than hers did against the magic woven through ultra-dragon king scales, even if they both got their magic from the same source. They used magic from Bantin who was the only magic producing dragon between the three kingdoms of Wisteria, Vankerdale, and Aralot. Before Tyler, Vankeredale had been trying to steal Bantin away. Aralot was the only kingdom that could cast spells with a replenishable magic source. The other places cast spells very sparingly because they couldn't risk running out.

"Who was our threat?" Tyler asked.

Kayla shook her head at him, and because he was still standing there, she slipped the wedding ring onto her finger and placed the box in her pocket. She had already told Queen Aria that the woman wouldn't need to worry about the new king of Vankerdale hunting her down for using magic against Coal. Aria had been using Coal to kill off people and dragons that had been inside an infected keeper bond. Kayla had explained to Aria that only the bonded dragon in the bond would have any issues with a poisoned human, and Kayla was hoping that was good enough that the queen would stop killing living creatures that were not infected. Even though Kayla's mother, Tia, had been infected by keeper poison and subsequently cured, there were still too many people that didn't understand exactly how the poison worked. It was common practice to destroy anything that an infected keeper mind had touched.

"I took care of it, Tyler. You don't have anything to worry about anymore. Coal won't be possessed."

"I have plenty to worry about," Tyler refuted. "There's a spellcaster out there that uses magic for evil."

"I took care of it," Kayla stated again, not about to budge on the issue at all. Aria wasn't the only one splashing evil magic around right now. Kayla was aware of quite a few crimes that she was keeping quiet about, simply because she was trying to allow the individuals a chance to repent for their deeds and make things better.

Tyler rolled his eyes when Coal snorted something at him from behind her. She had no idea what Coal thought about, but she was glad that he wasn't thinking his dragon thoughts inside *her* head. She had too much to worry about herself without adding more dragons and their problems to her life.

"I didn't forget that you mentioned that you found a person you want to teach magic," Tyler hinted. "Unknown spellcasters—"

"Tyler, that person will never be a problem," Kayla cut him off.

She hadn't meant to tell Tyler that at all, but her current section leader and teacher at the King's Ware was amazingly talented at using magic. He had cut off her spells once simply by willing the magic away. It took a really strong mind, and respect from Aralot, to make magic work so seamlessly. Caleb Andrade would be an amazing spellcaster. It was for that reason that she had given him a magical trinket that she had stolen from Tyler. She had also placed inside Caleb's trunk one of her early magic books. That was her one crime of the century, because Caleb wasn't allowed to learn magic since he wasn't royal. Even so, she couldn't help but give it to him.

He was beautiful with the stuff, as if it was embedded inside his soul. Her father, King Jack, was the kingdom's spellcaster, so Kayla knew a good magic user when she saw one. Jack hadn't been able to get magic to behave for him so quickly without undergoing an extensive study of the subject. Caleb had the potential to be better than her father, better than her, better than anyone. Magic and Caleb were like watching the sun break over the edge of her horizon. A glorious burst of color, warm, happy, and fathomless. Caleb had a white soul and a caring, loving heart. She had checked with a spell. He was completely brilliant, and would never use magic with an ill intention.

"You're probably smiling about him again," Valiant interrupted her inner monologue.

"No one but you can hear me," Kayla shrugged, and she wasn't

smiling. She was keeping the emotion off her face, because she was talking to her fiancé while thinking about the guy she had a crush on. Not a good combination.

"Why is it that whenever the topic is magic that you go completely mute?" Tyler questioned. "Magic in the wrong hands worries me."

"Which is why I took care of it."

Tyler rolled his eyes at her for not changing her mind. She wouldn't. She wasn't going to tell him how to use magic, even if she had never once seen him try. Maybe Tyler would be good at it too, but she didn't want to find out. Maybe it was a pride issue that held her back, because Aralot had been keeping magic away from Vankerdale for several generations. Tyler was the king. She didn't want to feel responsible for giving him what he was after.

"There's a special luncheon on the seventeenth where you're supposed to meet all the nobles that serve as our councilors," Tyler said next. He put his hands into his pockets as if he could already guess her rejection. "I would love for you to be in attendance."

"I'll do my best to be there," Kayla answered. It was a lie. She wasn't planning on showing up.

"We will be discussing the topic of what to do about the dragons from Vankerdale that have vanished into Aralot after the border spells were taken down. We will also be discussing the start of dragon wares. Your input would be amazing."

Blast! He was trying to make her show up by pushing against her keeper nature that made her want to shelter and care for all dragons. Vankerdale didn't have any functioning wares because they were just barely stepping out of their old curses too. In a way, that made Kayla and Vankerdale remarkably similar. They were both trying to start over.

Tyler would be great at helping Vankerdale do that, but it was a shame that he knew how to push her buttons. Tyler had seen through all her weaknesses before too. In his mind, that wasn't a bad thing, because he had done his best to help her overcome her limitations. However, he had also used that knowledge against her to bring her into Vankerdale twice and get them engaged.

"I will still do my best," Kayla answered, as if the topic of discussion wouldn't change her desire to show up or not. The seventeenth was going to be a rough day. She'd probably spend all of it fretting about ditching Aralot for her responsibilities in Vankerdale.

"Okay. So how are things going with Prince Tristan Cluster?"

Worst topic ever. As the steward's son, Tristan was called the Prince of Aralot. He currently had just as much authority to be the next leader of the kingdom as Kayla did. Neither of their fathers had been crowned with the real crown, because the real crown was a cursed thing that no one wanted to mess with. Legally, King Klavian and King Jack shared the throne. Magically, it was Kayla's father in charge, but that didn't change the way that Prince Tristan saw himself as the inheritor of the kingdom. It didn't change the way that her parents said she had to date him either, or the unspoken words that came along with that telling her that if she married Prince Tristan everyone would be really happy. They'd be joining the two ruling lines into one, getting rid of an age-old rivalry that her parents had mostly done away with already.

"Tristan is in the process of becoming a better man."

Kayla chose her words rather carefully. Tristan had taken down the curses he had put on her and her family, but he would always love sneaking around, stealing, and hunting innocent animals and bugs. He had his own secret stash of magical ice orbs that he kept in the Desert Ware. That alone gave him more magical power than the rightful spellcaster at any given time. Tristan could magically destroy anyone that tried to kill him off, and he had the magical knowledge to do so. Most of the time he rubbed Kayla the wrong way, and she knew that she grated against him even when they tried to be civil with each other.

Tyler pulled his hands out of his pockets to rub at his eyes. "Is it just me or are you being incredibly short with me right now? You normally tell me everything that's on your mind."

Yes, wasn't that unfortunate? It was because Tyler was a keeper like herself. Another part of being a keeper was respecting and protecting all the other keepers. Most people only knew of three keepers total. There was Kayla, her mother Tia, and her Aunt Rosa. People would learn soon that Tyler was a keeper. Kayla knew of five more. Her Uncle Conner had been hiding away in Vankerdale and he had three kids named Sashi, Ruth, and Tova that were going to all be keepers. Her father had just turned himself into a keeper as well. Right before Kayla's mother ascended the throne all keepers kept themselves hidden, because the Clusters had been killing them off. King Klavian had decided to stop killing the keepers because Tia was his strongest supporter in achieving his dreams of being the king. Now everyone was friends, but keepers still felt the need to hide.

"Tyler, it's my one night to sleep. I don't feel like talking. All I want to do is go back to bed with my own body," she added so that Valiant knew she didn't want him to walk her around.

"You can use my body," Valiant whined. *"It's ever so nice to sleep inside."*

"Okay," Tyler gave her a smile and then he stepped forward to pull her into a hug. "Sorry to keep you up. If you didn't have that magic on you, I'd highly consider tying you up to take you home with me where you belong."

Kayla had to laugh at him when Tyler blushed. See! He did it too! It was like whenever they were in the wrong kingdom, they couldn't help but spurt out all the real thoughts going on deep inside.

"I would," Tyler said more resolved this time. "Kayla, I need you there. I know you said that you had a few things you needed to take care of in Aralot first. I respect your time and your commitments, but I need you to come home. Don't be too long?" he asked.

With that, he gave her a short kiss on the cheek and climbed up on the back of Coal, who had finished eating his deer. Coal backed away, and using his powerfully strong wings launched himself into the air to take Tyler back across the river that separated their two kingdoms. Kayla waited only long enough to know that Coal could no longer see her before she ripped the wedding ring off her finger and threw it back in the dirt.

Married! She was only sixteen! ...

Name Bank

Kingdoms:

Aralot	-current location
Vankerdale	-east of Aralot
Wisteria	-north of Aralot across the ocean

Brixtons and Feldings:

Kayla Brixton	-secret princess	Dragon: Valiant
Jack Brixton	-Kayla's father; the king	Dragon: Pyro
Tia (Felding) Brixton	Kayla's mother; the queen	Dragon: Sparkle
Conner Felding	-Kayla's missing uncle	Dragon: Tempest
Esmay Felding	-Conner's Wife	Children: Sashi, Ruth, Tova
Herb Felding	-Kayla's grandfather	
Alice Felding	-Kayla's grandmother	
Gladius Felding	-Kayla's great-grandfather	
Jean (Frizer) Felding	-Gladius's wife	

| Shane Felding | -Kayla's great-great-grandfather | Dragon: Tang |
| Troy Felding | -Kayla's third great-grandfather | Dragon: Bandit |

Mentionable dragons:

Tia's keeper dragons:	Clawson, Pyro, Midnight, Fang, Duchess, Hemp, Darkwing, Lightning, Slasher, and Fern
Nebula	-Conner's water dragon
Luna	-a wild dragon and Pyro's sister

Aralot Castle:

King Klavian Cluster	-steward and son of King Virgil Cluster IV
Queen Aria	-wife of Klavian Cluster
Prince Tristan	-son of Klavian and Aria
King Virgil Cluster IV	-Klavian's crowned father
Vermelo	-Captain of the Guard
Merlock	-a dwarf dragon
Bantin	-also called Mr. Grumpy;

the magical ice dragon

Monastery:

Abbot McLean   -the current abbot

Colts:

Ritz   -ageless leader of the Colts

Fenix, Steve, Bret, and Kyle   - Kayla's uncles on her
                                      father's side

Joss   -Jack's best friend

Vankerdale:

Tyler Valeron   -Castle servant

Narl Valeron   -Tyler's brother

Prince Evan   -Prince of Vankerdale
Peyton

King Peyton   -King of Vankerdale   Dragon:
                                                  SilverWings

General Reis   -the general

Choladon   -the ulta-dragon king
                       that made the keeper

| | monolith | |
| Reed | -a light green dragon | Rider: Lena Sherman |

Anvil's Ware:

Anvil	-ware leader	Dragon: Clawson
Annaliese	-Anvil's wife	
Rosa Cluster	-Kayla's Aunt	Dragon: Pewter
Clark Cluster	-Kayla's Uncle	Dragon: Midnight
Achilles	-a rider in Tia's keeper bond	Dragon: Fang
Caleb Andrade	-a rider and artist	Dragon: Warner
Aiden	-a rider that fights Caleb	
Joal	-a rider that cried at Anvil's Ware	
Tiana	-a rider that helped Joal	
Mentionable dragons:	Galivant	- a pink fire-breathing dragon
	Moondust	-a night dragon in one of Caleb's drawings

The King's Ware:

Charles	-the oldest ware leader	Dragon: Clipshire
Caleb	- section leader	Dragon: Warner
Andrade	over levels 2 and 6	
Mulligan	-section leader over level 8	
Russel	-section leader over level 4 and rider's kids	
Notley	-section leader over levels 3 and 7	
Malone	-night section leader over levels 1 and 5	

Kayla's Teammates

Avery	Dragon: Fisher
Davis	Dragon: Summit
Nick	Dragon: Flint
Norrin	Dragon: Mordred
Sherman	Dragon: Cuprite
Brea	Dragon: Sulphur
Keran	Dragon: Umber
Junia	Dragon: Forge

Mentionable people

Stanford	-a previous section leader who died
Pence	-a rider with blue hair

Sheryl	-a rider with a lost shirt
Maggie	-a rider who wants a picture
RJ	-a past rider friend of Caleb's from Anvil's ware.

Treasure Hunters:

| Ian | -used to be a street urchin in Wisteria |
| August | -used to be a baker in Wisteria |

Other Wares:

Vincent's Ware:	-led by Vincent	
	Shilo	- ice dragon trainer
Vladimir	-past ware leader	Dragon: Giselle
Desert Ware:	-training ware in the desert	
	Dani	-Tristan's past girlfriend
Turid's Ware:	-led by Turid	female ware leader
Rogan's Ware:	-led by Rogan	Dragon: Indigo
Niles's Ware:	-led by Niles	-training ware in the west

Towns and Places:

The Pits	-a stone quarry owned by the Colts
Troni	-the town by the castle
The Castle	
Old Castle	Gladius's destroyed castle in the south

Don't fly off yet!

There is magic lingering in the air encouraging you to leave a **Spoiler Free** review on Amazon or Goodreads. This is an excellent way to spark the flames of another person's fire so they can enjoy the book as you have. I thank you for your time.

For more exciting stories and content please visit my website at:

amandaheit.com

Or my author page at

https://www.amazon.com/author/amanda.heit

Special Thanks

A very large thank-you to my reviewers Amy Fowler and Adam Morse who have gone through a ton of versions of this story and have encouraged me through every flight.

About the Author

Finding meaning in life—feeling like you're contributing to all of humanity in a good way—is a large undertaking. When I write, it's the task I take on. Sometimes, that task is daunting. Sometimes, it's full of laughter, joy, and fear. Reaching the end of a book can put me on top of the world or cause me endless frustration. But I can't stop myself from trying. I can't stop the inner clock that ticks and tells me that writing is something I enjoy the heck out of and there is nothing that will stop me from writing for long. As one of the quiet people in the universe, my best joy and flow in life comes when I'm creating new worlds and exploring characters. For me, each book I create finds new friends that share with me the intimate tangles of their lives. They cheer and I cheer. They succeed and I rejoice. They fall and I'm there hoping for that happy ending right along with them. I hope that you can find something in the stories I create that will bring you the same type of thrill. Thanks for sticking to the end!

Amanda Heit